D1231380

War to the Knife

Book 1 of The Laredo War trilogy

PETER GRANT

Fynbos Press

ISBN: 0692232710
ISBN–13: 978-0692232712

Cover art by Phil Cold:
http://philcold3d.blogspot.com/

Cover image supplied by Dreamstime:
http://www.dreamstime.com

Cover design by Oleg Volk:
http://www.olegvolk.net

This book is dedicated with gratitude to two authors:

LARRY CORREIA, author of the Monster Hunter series;

and **SARAH A. HOYT**, author of the Darkship series.

You've both helped me with advice, encouragement and support.
Thank you very much. I couldn't have done this without you.

Contents

PART ONE

February 27th 2850, Galactic Standard Calendar

CARISTO

The burro whickered a complaint as Jake pulled at the reins, turning it towards the hitching rail in front of the saloon. He applied the brake and dismounted from the wagon, taking a moment to scratch Nellie behind the ears. She whickered again, affectionately this time, and nudged against him with her rough nose, craning her long green neck after him as he turned and walked towards the batwing doors.

He stepped inside, feeling the momentary pressure against his skin of the force field keeping the air-conditioned interior at a tolerable temperature. He took a step to one side and stopped, waiting as his eyes adjusted to the gloom after the glare of the noonday sun outside. The few regulars at the bar nodded greetings to him as they recognized him. He glanced incuriously at four uniformed soldiers sitting around a table in the corner, nursing their beers. They glared at him with the hostility he'd come to expect from the occupiers. A stranger sat at a table to one side of the room, looking at him impassively. Jake looked him over, eyes narrowing as he noticed the orange tint to the tan on the man's smooth face, neck and hands. *That came out of a bottle,* he thought to himself, *and his skin hasn't been outdoors very often, and his clothes are much too clean.* Still, a man's business was his own, and questions were often unwelcome in these troubled times. He started towards the bar.

The stranger examined Jake in his turn. The new arrival looked to be middle-aged or a bit older, tall, lean and wiry, his face lined and care-worn, weather-beaten, tanned to the color and consistency of old leather. His faded hair was unruly, wind-blown, the hat that normally covered it now hanging behind his neck from the long leather thong that served as a chinstrap. He wore a light blue long-sleeved shirt and gray trousers, both made from hard-wearing synthcloth that could handle the dust and dirt, rocks and thorns of this frontier environment. The belt at his waist was thick and broad to support the holster slung at his right hip, the butt of a heavy old-fashioned chemical-propellant handgun protruding from it. A big sheath knife balanced it on his left hip, with a snapped pouch ahead of it. His boots looked roughly made but tough and comfortable, patterned after military-issue jump boots.

"Howdy, Jake." The barkeep picked up a schooner and filled it at the tap. "Your usual?"

"Thanks, Sib." Jake lifted the mug and took a long swallow of the cool beer. *"Aaahhhh! That hit the spot!"* He set it down on the counter. "My son been in yet?"

"Ain't seen him."

"He should be along any time now."

"You heading for the hills again?" Sib gave him a knowing wink, inclining his head the merest fraction towards the soldiers.

Jake nodded infinitesimally, acknowledging the unspoken warning. "Yeah. We shipped most of the last herd to the slaughterhouse last week, so it's time to round up some more cattle."

The bartender shook his head. "Sooner you than me. Hell of a way to make a living, eating dust and drinking your own sweat for weeks at a time, gathering animals that like it fine where they are and don't want to leave."

"Beats not eating at all. Besides, there's only so many ways a man can make an honest living. Can't all be bartenders."

"You got a point, an' it keeps you out of the way."

The batwing doors parted once again and a younger man walked in, looking like Jake must have done a couple of decades earlier. He wore a gray shirt and blue trousers, the reverse of the older man's outfit, and his waist supported a similarly-equipped gunbelt. His face was less lined and wrinkled but seemed older than his years, thin, drawn, eyes hard beneath heavy brows. He carried a thick, heavy rolled fur in his arms. He, too, glanced around the room before coming forward.

"Hi, Dad."

"Hey, son," Jake greeted him, the corners of his mouth quirking in a slight smile. "Beer?"

"You betcha."

Jake nodded to the barkeep as his son unrolled the fur to reveal a brilliantly-patterned orange-and-black pelt. The lips were drawn back in a snarl over sharp pointed saber-teeth, tufts of hair spiking outward above the glass eyes set into the carefully-preserved skull. The body was just over two meters long, with another meter and a half of tail attached. The barkeep let out a long, slow whistle of surprise as the young man laid it out along the bar.

"*Damn*, Dave! That's gotta be the finest ganiba pelt I've ever seen!"

"I've never seen a better one," Jake confirmed as he reached out to stroke it, his hand sinking into the thick luxurious fur. "Quill did a first-rate job of tanning and preparing it."

"He charged me enough, so he'd better have!" Dave said, grinning. "You were right. A fur this good deserved the best preparation, and he delivered."

"Reckon that'll bring five, maybe six thousand bezants in Banka from a visiting spacer," one of the other regulars said, craning his neck from where he sat further down the bar.

"No, it won't." The voice came from a Sergeant, the leader of the four soldiers who had risen from their table and were walking over to the bar. "For a start your capital's been renamed – it's Tapuria now, you hick scum! Second, that fur looks like smuggled goods to me, so we'll just have to confiscate it and send it in for adjudication." He grinned nastily, undoubtedly savoring the bezants he and his men would get for the pelt when they sold it for their own benefit.

There was a sudden stillness in the bar. The regulars turned away or shrank back in their seats.

"I don't think so." Dave's voice was matter-of-fact, but his hand brushed against the butt of his gun as he turned to face the oncoming soldiers, taking a few steps away from the bar to give himself room to move. Behind him Jake eased down the bar away from his son, trying to look as abject and browbeaten as possible.

"Don't get cocky with me, sonny boy!" The sergeant's voice was hard. "You know what we're gonna do to you if you give us any uphill." He glanced at the bartender. "Kill the cameras."

"But I – "

"I said kill the cameras! *Now!*"

"Do it, Sib. No sense you getting into trouble too." Dave's voice was steady. The bartender shrugged helplessly, turned to a console behind the bar, and switched off the security cameras and recorders that, by regulation, monitored everything in and around the saloon.

"Better." The Sergeant halted in front of Dave, thrusting his thumbs into his belt on either side of the tarnished brass buckle. His three men came to a stop on either side of him. "Like I said, boy, we're confiscating that hide. If it's cleared by the court, you'll get it back."

"It'd have to get there for that to happen." Dave kept his voice mild. "We've heard way too many stories of things being confiscated by folks like you, then never turning up in court at all."

"You accusing me of planning to steal it? That could get you into a whole heap of trouble, boy."

"You just ordered the barkeep to switch off the cameras. Without an independent record that you confiscated it, it'll be your word against mine."

The man spat contemptuously on the floor. "Yeah – and the word of four Bactrian soldiers against a frontier hick means the court won't even pause to draw breath before convicting you of whatever charges we feel like bringing against you. Now hand over that pelt!"

"No," Dave said flatly. "Sergeant-Major Garnati down at the garrison issued a certificate that it was legally taken, in accordance with regulations." He winced internally as he remembered the size of the bribe involved. "If you ask him, he'll confirm that."

"That old fart's gotten far too lenient with you rebellious scum. No, we'll leave him out of this and settle it right here, right *NOW!*"

He shouted the last word, clearly intending it as a signal to his companions. The two troopers tugged at short, stubby truncheons in scabbards at their left hips, while the Sergeant and his Corporal reached for the flap-top holsters worn on their right hips. They knocked the flaps upward, grabbing at the butts of the pulsers inside.

Dave's draw wasn't hampered by a flap on his holster; and despite its being cut for a much longer weapon his revolver proved to have a barrel only three centimeters long, without a front sight. His right hand moved almost too quickly for the observers to follow. The gun came level at waist height as his thumb cocked back the hammer. A needle-thin beam of intense green light shone from a projector built into the grip, rising along the Sergeant's body and centering over the bridge of his nose as the young man pulled the trigger. Instead of the thunderous roar typical of such primitive weapons, the revolver emitted only a surprisingly quiet *crack!* The Sergeant's head snapped back as a dozen small holes appeared across his upper nose, lower forehead and the inner halves of his eyes; then he collapsed to the floor like a sack of onions.

Dave began to swing the revolver towards the second pulser-armed soldier, cocking the hammer again as he did so; but from his right another sighting beam appeared, centering on the trooper's face, followed by another *crack!* as his father took a hand. The soldier's face grew a pattern of holes like the Sergeant's, but they were off-center and didn't drop him immediately. Another shot sounded, and the hapless trooper spun around and fell forward onto his face.

Dave didn't waste time watching his father's handiwork. He aimed his gun at the truncheon-armed soldier nearest him, triggering two rounds into the man's head and sending him sprawling. He swung back in the direction of the last soldier on his feet, but the man threw his truncheon to one side as he raised his hands. "Don't shoot! *Don't shoot me!*" His face was suddenly ashen, his voice trembling.

His father's voice came from behind him. "When you meet your friends in hell, tell them it was a bad idea to try to steal from Niven's Regiment."

The soldier's eyes bugged out. "You – you mean – *you're* – ?"

Jake didn't give him time to finish. He fired once more, the pellets from his revolver smacking into the man's face over his right eye. The trooper gave a short, sharp cry and slumped to the floor.

As he fell, Dave swung to cover the stranger seated at one side of the room. He'd slapped both his hands palm-down on the table before him, a clear sign that he didn't intend to get involved in this fight. He glanced down at his chest where the green dot of Dave's sighting beam was centered in the V of his open shirt, just over his sternum, then looked up at the young man, his lean face suddenly pale beneath its artificial tan.

"You're the only other person here we don't know," Dave pointed out, his voice cold. "We've learned the hard way not to trust strangers." As he spoke, his father's sighting beam tracked up the stranger's body and settled on the bridge of his nose.

The man spoke quickly, almost breathlessly. "If you're from Niven's Regiment, I have a message for your commanding officer. It's from Reno."

Jake moved forward. "Reno? If you're for real, there'll be a series of challenges and replies to authenticate you. What's the first?"

The man replied without hesitation, "Castle Pass."

Jake blinked. "Well, well, well... I'd begun to think I'd never hear that particular passphrase. You'd better come with us." He holstered his revolver, motioning for Dave to do likewise.

The man shook his head. "Not yet. What about the first countersign?" Jake leaned forward and whispered into the man's ear, and he nodded. "That's it. The second challenge is – "

"Later. We've got to get out of here." Jake turned to the bartender. "Sib, can you get rid of them" – he gestured at the bodies of the four troopers – "and clean up? If anyone asks, those four took Dave and the fur out the back way. You don't know what happened to any of us after that."

"You got it, Major." As he spoke, the barkeep gestured urgently to the regulars. Most of them started carrying the bodies to a back room, while one collected a bucket and mop from behind the bar and began cleaning the blood off the floor.

The bartender rummaged beneath the bar, took out an unlabeled spray bottle containing a clear fluid and tossed it to the cleaner. "Spray this everywhere the guys walked or carried the bodies. It'll neutralize any DNA left behind. We'll dump the bodies way out in the bush after dark. Scavengers will take care of them by morning."

"What about the interrupted recording?" Dave asked, nodding towards the security console.

Sib shrugged, face breaking into a grin. "What about it? It'll show the Sergeant telling me to switch it off. I obeyed him, of course – I mean, I can't argue with a garrison Sergeant, can I? When he and his men had gone, taking you and the pelt with them, I switched it on again. The others will back me up. No, of course I didn't call the garrison to investigate their own troopers. They'd only have locked me up for wasting their time."

"Fair enough." Dave looked around at the hard-working men. "Thanks, everyone. We owe you."

"No problem, Lieutenant," one of them replied with a grin. "Niven's Regiment takes care of its own. Now get the hell out of town before anyone starts to look for those sods!" He began to roll and tie the pelt on the bar.

Another man came out of the back room. "Here's the Sergeant's wallet, and his Corporal's. They had a few hundred Bactrian bezants between 'em and three military passes apiece." He handed over the last two wallets. "Less money in the troopers' wallets, but still enough to be useful." Finally he produced a communicator and both holstered pulsers.

"Thanks, Brady." Jake took the money from the last two wallets and handed it to Sib. "Beer and a good meal for everyone, courtesy of those scum." He began to strip the charge packs out of the pulsers and communicator. "Got a bag to hold all this stuff? I don't want anyone outside to see what I'm carrying."

"Sure, I'll get you one." Sib turned back towards the bar.

Dave turned back to the stranger. "What's your name?"

"Marvin Ellis."

"Got any gear?"

"Just this holdall." He gestured to a bag next to his chair. "I arrived on the morning train. Hadn't got a room yet."

"OK. Any electronics in there or on you? Anything with a battery or capacitor?"

"Yeah, I've got a – "

"Don't waste time telling me. Take the charge packs out of *everything*, right now. Make sure nothing can emit any signature that might be tracked." He glanced at the bartender as he approached, carrying a bag for Jake. "Sib, help him. Search his holdall, his clothes and his body, then scan them all. Destroy anything you're not sure about and get rid of the remains." He looked back at Marvin. "You'll travel in the back of my wagon until we're well out of town. When Sib's finished, wait just inside the back door. I'll drive past the rear of the saloon in about five minutes. As I pass, slip out the door and climb over the rear gate. Make it fast and smooth, because I won't stop, then lie down and stay out of sight until I tell you different."

"Got it, but won't they – "

"No questions yet – no time. Sib, don't switch on the cameras until we're well clear. That way they won't show Marvin getting into my wagon."

"You got it."

"Take the east road out of town, son," Jake interjected as he loaded three rounds from his belt pouch into the cylinder of his revolver. "I'll go north, then circle round to meet you."

"All right. See you tonight."

Dave half-waved as his father headed for the door, reloaded and holstered his own handgun, then accepted the pelt from the man who'd rolled it. "Thanks, Tom. We need a couple of people who aren't here right now, so they won't show up on the saloon's security vid."

"Todd's around. So is Jaime."

"Ask them to meet us…" – he thought rapidly – "three clicks south of Gamma at sunset. Tell them to look for our wagons. They're to travel separately, keep their eyes peeled and make sure they aren't being watched. If they are they're to lead them away from us, then disappear for a spell."

"Will do. You keep your pecker up and your head down."

Dave laughed. "I'll do my best."

He reached for the beer Sib had drawn for him a few minutes earlier and drank quickly, foam coating his upper lip, spilling a little of the cold fluid onto his shirt. He set down the schooner, wiped his mouth with the back of his left hand, reached into a pocket, peeled a banknote off a thin wad of them and tossed it on the bar.

"Your beer's as good as ever, Sib. Buy a round for everyone on me. We'll be back for more as soon as we can."

"I'll have it chilled and waiting," the bartender promised as he rooted through Marvin's holdall. The stranger looked surprised and – Dave thought – a little resentful at the thoroughness of the inspection, but said nothing.

"Thanks. See you out back, Marvin."

February 27th 2850 GSC, Afternoon

CARISTO AND THE WILDERNESS

Dave drove his wagon slowly past the rear of the saloon. He didn't look round, but felt the load-bed rock as weight was added and shifted position. He called back softly without looking around, "Get under that dark tarpaulin. Pull out enough of it to completely cover you and your holdall. Stay down and stay quiet." There was a rustle of synthetic cloth, the wagon bed rocked again lightly, then all was still behind him. He nodded imperceptibly to himself. At least their unexpected visitor could obey orders and keep his mouth shut. That was a good start.

He reached behind him, pulled out a dusty *serape* of dark brown material, and slipped it over his shoulders before pulling his hat low over his eyes. Surveillance vid had already recorded him driving the wagon into Caristo. He wanted it to show someone with a different appearance driving it out again. He made a left turn, then a right to get back onto the main drag. As the wagon approached the last buildings, where the hardtop petered out into gravel and dirt as it ran into the bush, he saw that the sensor turret above the light pole was scanning slowly in a complete circle. He grinned tightly, slowed his pace until he was sure it would get a good view of the wagon, then drove past it, looking down so his face wasn't visible.

He waited until the wagon had covered three kilometers along the rutted, rough bush road, then reached behind him again and pulled out a canvas bag. He took from it a small black box and switched it on. After a moment a red light began to blink. He watched it and waited patiently for sixty seconds until the box beeped softly and a second, green diode illuminated. Nodding in satisfaction, he dropped it into his shirt pocket.

"You can come out now," he called over his shoulder. "We aren't being watched at the moment."

A rustling came from the bed of the wagon. The stranger climbed carefully over the raised back of the wagon seat and sat down gingerly.

"I want to go through the rest of the challenges and countersigns," Dave began, "to be sure of your *bona fides* before I say any more. Gray curtain."

"Red dawn," the stranger responded at once.

"Blue river."

"Wide ocean."

They ran through four more combinations before Dave said, "All right, you're either legitimate, or the Bactrians have caught the real guy and tortured all that out of him – in which case we're probably finished anyway." He held out his hand. "I'm Lieutenant Dave Carson, commanding Charlie Company of Niven's Regiment. The older man who helped us is my father, Major Jake Carson. He was the Executive Officer of the Regiment under Colonel Niven. When the Colonel was killed during the invasion, Dad took over the Regiment and held it together during the collapse, then took the remnants underground to continue the war as guerrilla fighters. The other regiments did the same, of course. We've been doing that for almost three years now."

"Glad to know you," the visitor said as he shook Dave's hand. "From what your father said in the saloon, I thought he was a cattle dealer."

"It's the perfect cover story for traveling all over the place, stopping off at farms and ranches everywhere and dropping out of sight for days or even weeks, supposedly rounding up cattle that strayed during and after the war and fattening them up for sale. In reality we're keeping track of our people and planning and executing operations. We have a permanent crew of civilians gathering cattle for us. We drive them into town now and then to 'prove' to the Bactrians that we really are cattle dealers."

"Makes sense. I'm just glad you happened to be in Caristo when I arrived. I've come an awful long way to meet you, and it would have been a hell of a let-down if I'd never found you. Why were you so suspicious about my electronics?"

"The Bactrians try hard to smuggle sensors into suspects' gear or homes. Nanobugs and flitterbugs are so small you hardly notice them unless you're looking for them, and tracking devices can be the size of pea gravel." Dave showed him the box in his shirt pocket. "This is the other reason I wanted all your electronics shut down. It'll pick up any active sensors nearby, and radiation from an electrical power source within five kilometers or so. I've left it on to detect any sensors that come within range as we travel. If I tell you to get in the back again, make it fast and hide under that cover until I give you the 'all clear'."

"Will do, but won't the town's surveillance vid show you on this wagon? If they want to find you, all they need to do is look for it on the road. That thing pulling us isn't very fast."

"That 'thing' is a native critter we call a burro, although it's no relation to Earth's donkeys – it's twice the size, for a start. You're right, it's not fast, but it can pull as much as a two-horse team and keep going all day. They won't look for anyone until they miss those four troopers, which should be tonight at the earliest. By tomorrow both wagons will look different and have different drivers. We've done this many times before. They've got decent surveillance in the larger towns, but they simply can't afford to seed the range country with enough sensors to maintain seamless coverage. We usually have time to change our appearance if necessary, or switch to alternative transport."

"And they don't fill in local gaps by using satellites?"

"They can't afford to. Bactria's economy was several times larger than ours before the war, but they paid dear in blood, equipment and budget to take over here. We've continued to bleed them ever since. They took over our existing communications and traffic control satellites, but they haven't been able to afford an orbital surveillance network. That's helped us keep up the fight for the past three years, despite all they could do to stop us."

"I don't think I could endure that non-stop tension for so long. Even a few days of it while getting here have been more than enough!"

Dave shrugged. "They haven't exactly left us much alternative. Now, before I do anything else, let me get rid of this peashooter and put on a gun more suitable for use out here in the sticks."

He pulled a pistol rug from the wagon bed and unzipped it. Inside nestled a revolver whose grips and cylinder were almost identical to the gun he'd used in the saloon, but were mated to a long, heavy octagonal barrel. Dave opened the cylinder to reveal six fat brass cartridges nestling in its chambers. Satisfied, he drew the smaller weapon from his holster and replaced it with the larger one. Next he took a long-barreled lever-action rifle from a leather tube fastened along one side of the wagon, checked that it was loaded, and cycled the action to put a round in the breech. He placed the rifle carefully on the wagon bed behind him, easily available to his hand.

"What *are* those things?" Marvin asked, fascinated. "I've never seen anything like them except in history books."

"That's where we got their designs. It's a long story – too long for right now. Tell me how they came to send you. You're not from this planet."

"No, I'm from New Brisbane. It's part of the Lancastrian Commonwealth."

"How did you get suckered into taking this job?" Dave flicked the reins at the dawdling burro and called, *"Hi-yaaah!* Get on there!"

Marvin grimaced. "I guess I suckered myself. Your Government-in-Exile has been trying to drum up support ever since Bactria invaded Laredo. Trouble is, you're a minor planet in a galactic backwater. You've got nothing that would interest a major power enough to weigh in on your side. Your Vice-President Johns asked the United Planets to investigate what Bactria was doing here, but she has to put down a deposit towards the initial costs – twenty-five million Neue Helvetica francs. It'll be refunded if the investigation proves her allegations were correct. Problem is, she has only two bearer keys to Laredo's planetary account there – the one she brought with her when she left Laredo, and the one held by your Ambassador to the UP. A minimum of three are needed to access it, so she hasn't been able to pay. Until she does, the investigation's going nowhere. She's been trying to persuade friendly governments to bankroll it, but without success. There aren't many of them, and they aren't rich or powerful."

Dave snorted in disgust as the wagon bounced over a pothole, rocking violently. "If they won't put their money where their mouths are, they're no friends of mine. Twenty-five million's not out of reach for any planetary government worth the name, even a poor planet."

"You'd think so, but that's the way things are. She tried approaching a couple of the big private security and investigation firms, asking them to come here, contact the Resistance, and collect your bearer keys to Laredo's accounts and the records of Bactria's atrocities. They either wanted a lot of money up front, which she didn't have, or turned her down flat because of the risk to their operators. I was too small-time for her to ask me – heck, she'd never even heard of me! – but I learned about it through my contacts and approached her. I was the only one with decent references who was willing to take the job on a contingent fee basis with no up-front payment."

"Why? There are lots of less dangerous ways to make a living. If Bactria finds out who and what you are and why you're here, they'll pull out all the stops to kill you rather than let you get away with what you came for."

"True, although they'd have to identify me first. Marvin Ellis isn't my real name – I'm sure you'd already figured that out." Marvin reached into his pocket for a handkerchief and mopped droplets of sweat from his brow. The baking heat of the afternoon sun was taking its toll on him.

Dave glanced at him. "I guessed as much. Don't tell us your real one. What we don't know can't be tortured out of us." He reached down behind the seat again and brought out a canteen. "Water?"

"Thanks." Marvin took several gulps of the lukewarm liquid, then handed it back.

"You don't have a hat?"

"I didn't know I'd need one."

"You do. For now, wet that handkerchief and put it on top of your head. Fortunately there's not much wind, so it should stay put. Keep damping it down." He took a couple of mouthfuls of the water, then held out the bottle again. "How did you persuade the Bactrians to let you onto the planet?"

"I posed as a trader in exotic furs, wanting to buy samples and make arrangements with a local agent for regular orders. One of the Customs officers 'suggested' that I talk to a Colonel Kujula of the Security Service. I did, and he gave me a pass to head into the interior to see what was available. It cost me a hefty bribe in gold, but I came prepared for that."

"Nicely done. It's a good cover, too – you saw that fur I showed at the bar."

"Yes, I did. If you'd only have got five or six thousand bezants for that, you were being robbed blind. I studied the market to prepare my cover story. On New Brisbane an exotic fur of that quality and rarity will bring fifty to sixty thousand Lancastrian Commonwealth credits – that's well over three hundred thousand bezants."

Dave cursed. "I had no idea! I've shot a few ganiba when they hunted the cattle we gather, and sold their pelts to spacers from time to time. I guess they were taking them to other planets and making a fortune out of my hard work."

"They sure were! Have you got other furs, or can you get some? I can show them to that Colonel when I return, to 'prove' to him that I found what I came for."

"Between me and a few others we can see you right. Now, you mentioned decent references. What's your background, that the Veep would trust you with this job?"

"I resigned from New Brisbane's Planetary Bureau of Investigation last year after twenty years' service as a detective. I was pretty good at my job, but they were dead set on promoting me to be an administrator. I didn't want that – I prefer field work – so I set up my own security and investigation firm. Trouble is, it's hard to compete with the big boys in the field unless you've done something to make yourself stand out. I figured if I could bring this off, it ought to go a long way towards making my reputation." He hesitated. "I suppose I should admit it'll also set me up financially. I told Vice-President Johns if I was going to put my life on the line for her on a contingency basis, the fee had to reflect the risk. If I succeed I'll get five per cent of whatever she recovers from Neue Helvetica, right off the top."

Dave's eyebrows rose. "That's a lot, but in view of the danger I guess it's fair. It should be a good payout. We transferred the national treasury to Neue Helvetica just before the invasion. It wasn't much by a wealthy planet's standards, but even so it came to more than half a billion Neue Helvetica francs."

"It'll make this trip well worth it, but I'll also have some pretty hefty expenses to pay. I've lined up a guy I helped some years ago. He owns a couple of tramp space freighters, and his partner was robbing him blind until I caught her. He reckons he owes me, so he'll bring one of his ships through here at the end of March to deliver freight and collect me and anything I can bring back. He's taking a big risk, because if Bactria finds out what he's doing they'll seize his ship at best; so if I succeed he'll get five million credits plus charter fees. I'll also have to pay a few others, plus anyone I hire here, and my own expenses as well."

"All right. We'll have to convene the Council of the Resistance to get their approval to hand over our accumulated evidence to you, and our bearer keys. That'll take a few days, if we – uh-oh, hang on!" Dave reached into his chest pocket and produced the black box. It was buzzing gently, and a blue light was blinking. "In the back again, quick as you can. A drone's approaching."

Marvin hurriedly clambered over the back of the seat and concealed himself beneath the cover once more. Dave pulled a jacket over the rifle to hide it, then adjusted the *serape* and his hat to provide maximum concealment. He allowed the reins to droop loosely in his fingers, knowing the burro would amble along at its own pace as long as he did so, and slumped on the wagon seat, peering out from beneath the brim of his hat to try to spot the approaching drone.

After a few minutes he saw a dark speck over the road in the distance. He lowered his head, feigning sleep as it drew nearer. Its electric motor was almost silent, emitting only a faint whine accompanied by the soft whisper of air churned by its pusher propeller and passing over its wings and fixed undercarriage. It flew overhead, then circled around to the right and made another pass. He knew its sensors would be recording the wagon and its driver from several angles in case of future need, but would not get a clear picture of his face beneath the hat brim.

After its second pass the drone continued down the road. He waited for five minutes, then checked the sensor in his pocket. The flashing blue light had gone out, revealing that the drone was now out of range. He called over his shoulder, "You can sit down again now."

Marvin climbed over the seat back once more as Dave encouraged the burro to make better speed. "What was that thing?"

"It's one of two drones that travel each day for about fifty kilometers up and down each of the roads out of Caristo. They return to the garrison late in the afternoon to download their recordings."

"So they'll know by tonight that you took this road?"

"Unlikely. The security detachment at that garrison is bored stiff, like everyone else there. I doubt they'll review the recordings at all – they'll just file them with all the others, then get drunk as usual. If there's an investigation into the disappearance of those four troopers they may retrieve them, but they won't recognize me on the vid, and the wagon will look different by tomorrow morning anyway."

"Sounds pretty slack to me."

"Yeah. These outlying garrisons are punishment postings. If a trooper screws up in one of the bigger centers they send him out here to the sticks where there's nothing to do. He bakes in the sun and eats dust all summer, then freezes his ass off all winter. They learn fast that if they don't bother us, we won't attack them – live and let live. Their High Command would throw a frothing fit if they found out, but we take care not to do anything in these parts that they're likely to notice. That's how we've hidden in plain sight out here for almost three years, using it as a base to strike at other areas."

"Makes sense when you put it that way."

"It also keeps us from going soft. Living out here hardens you up in ways I'd never have believed when I was a city boy. I – hey, wait a minute! Hel-*loooo*, supper! Don't point or make any sudden movement." He nodded to a rise on the left side of the road, atop which a deer-like creature had suddenly appeared. It was followed by several more, all of which looked at the wagon as it approached, but didn't appear startled.

"What are they?"

"We call them sassabies. They're good eating. That one third from the front is a young female. She won't have bred yet, so there's no danger of leaving an orphaned fawn. They won't spook at the sight of a wagon as long as we don't make any moves that appear threatening, so stay still. Once we're past I'll stand up and shoot over the wagon top. Cover your ears – that rifle's much louder than modern weapons."

"OK."

Dave fumbled in his chest pocket, took out two earplugs and inserted them. He waited until the sassabies disappeared behind the edge of the wagon cover then reached around, picked up the rifle and handed it to Marvin.

"Hold this for a moment while I stop the wagon."

He stepped on the brake and hauled on the reins, and the burro obediently came to a standstill. As soon as the wagon had halted he handed the reins to Marvin, took the rifle from him and stood up, turning in a smooth, fluid motion as he brought it to his shoulder and aimed back over the wagon cover. There was a momentary pause, then a thunderous bellow of sound, making Marvin jump even though his hands were over his ears. The burro whickered and moved restlessly, rocking the wagon. Dave sprang to the ground in an effortless jump, cycling the rifle's action, ready to shoot again from a steadier platform if need be; but he relaxed almost at once.

"She's down. Wait here."

He lowered the hammer to the safety position, slid the rifle into the wagon, then took a refrigeration tub from the rear of the load bed and set out to where the animal now lay motionless on its side. The rest of the herd had vanished.

Marvin stood up to see over the wagon top and watched in fascination, feeling a little sick to his stomach, as Dave took out his knife and cut the sassaby's throat, then neatly removed the best cuts of meat, separating them from the bone and hide before placing them in the tub. He wiped the knife clean and sheathed it, then carried the tub back to the wagon, grunting with the effort. He replaced it in the load bed, switched on its power pack, then washed his hands at the water butt lashed beneath the right side of the wagon.

"That's about thirty kilograms of prime meat," he said with a grin as he slid back onto the seat. "It'll grill real well over coals tonight."

"I'll look forward to it." Marvin grimaced. "I've never before seen an animal killed and cut up like that — it's unsettling. I've only encountered meat as vat-produced protein in ration packs, or ready-cut joints and steaks in the shops."

"Well, this is how meat starts. You're going back to your ancient roots."

~ ~ ~

19

Marvin set down his plate with a sigh of repletion, stretching and grunting in the firelight. "That sassaby lived up to your promises. I've paid good money in restaurants on New Bedford for meat that wasn't half as tasty." He burped gently, covering his mouth with his hand. "Excuse me."

Jake grinned. "First time in a long while I've heard someone apologize for that. We tend to be a bit rough around the edges out here." On the other side of the fire, Todd and Jaime laughed as they nodded in agreement.

Dave said thoughtfully, "Mom used to box my ears if I didn't mind my manners, but for the past three years…" His face twisted with the remembered pain of loss. "Without families around to remind us about that sort of thing, we've let it slide." He reached for the coffeepot and refilled his mug with the bitter black liquid, adding creamer and sweetener capsules.

"Yeah, there's an ancient saying that a man can build a house, but it takes a woman to make it a home," Marvin agreed.

"Those ancients knew what they were talking about," Jaime said as he reached for the coffeepot in his turn. "Rissa's been workin' on me ever since we set up together last year."

"I wondered where the improvement had come from," Dave said with a grin.

"Gee, *thanks!* I wasn't *that* bad, was I?" More laughter.

Dave took a tarpaulin from the back of his wagon, spread it on the ground by the fire, and laid on it his rifle, the short revolver he'd used in town, and a cleaning kit. Jake took out his smaller revolver as well, and they set about cleaning the guns.

"I thought that handgun would make a lot more noise than it did," Marvin commented as he watched.

"The full-sized ones do," Dave confirmed, tapping the butt of the long-barreled revolver that had taken the smaller weapon's place in his holster. "You heard my rifle this afternoon. This fires the same cartridge. You need a heavy bullet, and a big charge of powder to throw it, to deal with some of the larger critters. These smaller guns are different. One of our designers immigrated here from Old Home Earth, where he was a design engineer and military history buff. He told us about a silenced round developed during something called the Vietnam War, at the dawn of the Space Age. It fired a piston that stopped inside the cartridge case, expelling a shot charge but preventing most of the noise from getting out. He duplicated the design for us. They're not completely silent, as you heard, but their sound won't carry too far. They're not very powerful, but if you hit the right spot they'll get the job done."

"I never heard of anything like that. Why not use pulsers?"

"They radiate a power signature, just like carbines or rifles. The occupiers have filled every major town with sensors that sniff out those emissions, so if you carry modern weapons there you'll have them on top of you in no time."

Jake added, "They're illegal for civilian use. When the Bactrians took over they banned civilian ownership of all weapons on pain of instant execution; but farmers and ranchers needed them to control predators that hunted their cattle. Without them the critters ran the herds ragged and scattered them all over the range. Also, rural folks couldn't hunt for meat any longer, so they had to eat more farm animals. Bactrian garrisons soon found they couldn't buy as much meat as they wanted, so they allowed people out here to use chemically-propelled weapons only. Burt duplicated the designs of late-nineteenth-century rifles and revolvers for us, updated the metallurgy, and wrote programs to produce them on the fabbers at most farms and ranches. They're not as efficient as powered weapons and they're harder to learn to use properly – the recoil's a pain, literally! – but within their shorter range they're just as deadly."

"Makes sense," Marvin observed, impressed. He stretched again. *"Damn,* I'm stiff – and my kidneys hurt! I thought I was fitter than this."

"Bouncing around on a wagon will do that to you," Dave observed. "Not to worry. At midnight we'll switch to something a lot faster and more comfortable."

"Oh? What's that?"

"You'll see."

~ ~ ~

The dark shape whined slowly towards the group of men, black against the darkness of night, showing no lights. Dust sprayed out from beneath its lift fans as it settled to the ground. The noise died away, a hatch opened, and a figure looked out.

"Magic Carpet Rides at your service," a contralto female voice called softly.

Dave smiled as he switched off the beacon that had guided the airvan to them. "And the pilot is an unexpected bonus. Hi, Tamsin."

"Dave! I didn't know you were going to be here!" The tall, rangy figure jumped down, ran over and hugged him fiercely. "How's my favorite Lieutenant?"

"Happy to see his favorite Sergeant."

"All right," Jake growled. "We've got a long way to go. Everyone aboard." He turned to Jaime. "Give our regards to Rissa, and our apologies for having to interrupt your home leave. I hope the rest of the sassaby meat will help her to forgive us."

"She'll understand. Todd and I will leave the wagons and burros at Gunter's place, then ride into town with him next day. We'll pass the word to your gather crew that you won't make the rendezvous, so they're to bring in the cattle themselves."

"Thanks. Tell them I said to head for Falfura rather than Caristo. I don't want them running into any trouble that may follow the disappearance of those four troopers."

Jake shook hands with both men then followed the others into the airvan, closing the entrance hatch behind him. The dark interior was lit only by dim red diodes around the cargo compartment. He pulled a fold-out chair from the nearest bulkhead and sat down, fastening its seatbelt.

"Departing," Tamsin warned from the pilot's console, and the craft lurched slightly as the lift fans hauled it into the air. She stabilized it, turned ninety degrees to starboard, and fed power to the motors. "We're going to take the scenic route," she added. "The Bactrians seeded a grid ten kilometers south of the perimeter three nights ago. They dropped a couple of dozen nanobugs and flitterbugs from a hoversat. Looks like their usual technique, searching a randomly selected map reference – they're all staying within two kilometers of their landing point. I left from the north-east quadrant of the base to avoid them, just in case, and we'll re-enter to the north-west."

"Works for me," Jake acknowledged.

Marvin, seated across the narrow cabin, asked, "Why not disable them?"

"That'd be a good way to let the Bactrians know we're nearby," Dave replied before Jake could speak. "If all their newly-dropped sensors went out, it'd be as good as a flashing red light announcing 'The enemy is here!' Instead we'll avoid the area and leave them alone until they run out of power, which takes a week or two. After that we'll pick them up and bring them in, so we can recharge and reprogram them for our own use. We've captured plenty of Bactrian nanobugs and flitterbugs that way, so we know how they work and how to deal with them."

"What are we going to do when we get to your base?" Marvin asked.

Jake replied, "You'll wait there while we round up the members of the Council. That'll take several days, because some of them live in places where we can't travel very easily or safely. As soon as they're assembled, you'll report to them and they'll consider what to do next."

"The General will be real glad to see you and Dave," Tamsin called from her seat at the pilot's console. "There's a problem. You guys might be the solution."

February 28th 2850 GSC

RESISTANCE HEADQUARTERS

Jake walked into the small meeting-room and nodded to the figure at the table. "Morning, Sir."

Brigadier-General Aldred looked up, and his tired, lined face broke into a smile. "Jake! Good to see you again. How are things with Niven's Regiment?"

"What's left of it is doing OK, Sir. I've prepared a brief report summarizing our operations over the past few weeks." He laid a data chip on the table. "All routine, except that we ambushed a bank convoy to Falfura. We walked away with no casualties plus several million bezants. I've kept half to fund our own operations, as usual, and I've just delivered the other half to your Paymaster."

"He'll be pleased to have it. We've found another bribable enemy Quartermaster who'll sell his own mother with no questions asked, provided he gets enough money for her. Sit down, man! Don't tower over me like a tree."

Grinning, Jake did so. "What did you want to see me about, Sir?"

The military commander of the Resistance ran his fingers through his rapidly graying, thinning hair. "Did you hear about the disaster in the Matopo Hills?"

Jake nodded sadly. "Yeah, we picked up their farewell signal. How bad is it, Sir?"

"Drake's Regiment lost most of its surviving people. It's down to no more than fifty now, many of them wounded. They're on their way here."

Jake winced. *"Damn!* I thought Niven's Regiment was in bad shape with only about seventy survivors. That must have been a hell of a fight. How did the Bactrians find them?"

"According to Captain Tredegar, who's their senior surviving officer, one of their patrols ambushed a Bactrian convoy about three weeks ago. They took the weapons and equipment from the enemy dead, as usual, then headed back to base. He says the Lieutenant in charge reported that after a couple of days' travel, he opened the pack containing the enemy transmitter and noticed that its power indicator light was on. He says he switched it off for sure after the ambush. Anyway, he turned it off and watched. Within five minutes it came on again."

"Sounds as if they were activating it remotely, to use it as a tracking device."

"It sure looks that way. He alerted the base, then made a dog-leg to the north to try to make the Bactrians think it was in that direction; but by then he'd laid a trail for two days straight towards it. Captain Tredegar reckons someone on the Bactrian side figured out what had happened, drew a line extending the patrol's original direction of travel, and saw where it crossed the Matopo Hills. With that to guide them, it's likely they used reconnaissance drones to observe for a couple of days and picked up other traffic in and out of the base. They mounted a full-scale assault the following week. Two companies were airlifted in by assault shuttles, followed by a ground element that cut a road to the base through the bush. It brought engineering gear to clear a way through our defenses and destroy the base once they'd finished searching it."

"I don't get it. Drake's Regiment should have been strong enough to handle that many – at the very least to hold them off long enough for most of their people to get clean away."

Aldred shook his head sadly. "I'm afraid someone on the enemy side has been using his head. It was only a matter of time before that happened, of course. We've killed an awful lot of their idiots, so we've cleared the way for smarter leaders to step up to the plate. This time they did something different. Their attack was spearheaded by large quantities of assault nanobugs and flitterbugs. They penetrated our defenses *en masse,* spreading throughout the caves and tunnels, shooting at everything that moved. The base had no defenses against a massed onslaught like that – for that matter, we don't have any here either. If the Bactrians ever figure out where our headquarters are, we're just as vulnerable to that as they were in Matopo. All our underground bases are."

Jake nodded slowly. "I guess we'll have to look for ways to disrupt communications between the bugs and their controllers."

"I've put Mac onto that already. Trouble is, Captain Tredegar reports the bugs he saw were bigger than usual and much more aggressive. He's bringing in a few for Mac to look at. Based on their behavior, he thinks they may be a new, autonomous model that doesn't need to be in constant communication with a controller. They appear to be programmed to hit anything that moves for a certain period, then shut down and signal their location so they can be collected."

'Bastards! If he's right, they're going to be almost impossible to counter. We don't have the tech resources to whomp up a bunch of counter-bugs to intercept them."

"I'm afraid so." The General shook his head sadly. "We've always known there'll only be one ending to this war, Jake. Given the disparity in numbers and resources, sooner or later the Bactrians are going to roll right over what's left of us. They left us no alternative but to fight on, which was very stupid of them, because we've killed three or four of theirs for every one of our casualties and wounded heaven knows how many more; but if they've smartened up to this extent…"

"Yeah. If they're deploying trackable hardware and assault bugs, what else have they got up their sleeves?"

Aldred nodded. "It means the end's in sight for us, Jake. It's only a matter of time now, and not much of it."

They looked at each other in wordless anguish. There was nothing more to be said.

At last the General shook his head, visibly gathering himself. "Enough of that! No sense in getting depressed over something we knew was unavoidable. Your Mr. Ellis couldn't have arrived at a better time. I'd begun to despair that we'd ever find a way to get our evidence off-planet into the Vice-President's hands, or our bearer bank keys for that matter. He's just a messenger, of course, not some sort of secret agent, but he's been able to arrange for a visiting spaceship to collect him and our evidence, which is exactly what we needed. Gloria and I have some ideas about how best to take advantage of this opportunity. We'll put them to the Council of the Resistance for approval before I tell you more about them.

"That brings me back to the Matopo Hills. We scattered our most critical evidence of Bactrian atrocities – original documents, the most sensitive captured material, stuff like that – among several bases, including Matopo. As far as we know – as far as Captain Tredegar was able to recall – it was still there when he left. It was concealed in Lieutenant-Colonel Yardley's office. He was killed early in the assault, so he never had a chance to retrieve it or hand it over to anyone else."

"Let me guess. You want me to go get it?"

"Not you – we'll need your input when the Council meets. This will almost certainly be our one and only chance to get this stuff off-planet, so I want to think of every possible contingency and have plans in place to deal with them. We can't afford to fail. No, I want you to send a patrol there, first rendezvousing with Captain Tredegar so he can brief them about what he experienced and warn them what to look out for. I want them to try to make their way through the wreckage to Lieutenant-Colonel Yardley's office, retrieve the package, and bring it back here."

Jake frowned. "The Bactrians are sure to have demolished the place. How the hell is our patrol supposed to penetrate a destroyed underground cavern system?"

"I don't know. I said 'try', remember? If they can't, they can't – which would be a tragedy, because in that package is some of the most damning evidence against Bactria. It includes the written demand from Major-General Strato to me shortly after the invasion, warning that unless we surrendered at once Banka would be destroyed."

Jake's lips whitened with anguish and fury as he remembered Laredo's obliterated capital city, formerly his home. For a moment he couldn't speak, then he nodded. "I can see why you want it. What if some of those assault bugs are still running around inside the base?"

"I presume the Bactrians collected them before they left, but we can't be sure. Again, I only said the patrol should *try* to get in. I want you to assign your best junior officer to lead it."

"That'll be Dave. Not only is he the best I've got, he's also the only officer I've got here. Trouble is, we didn't bring any of our troops with us. He'll have to borrow some of your security detachment."

"I figured as much. I can give him a couple of them, and I'll have Captain Tredegar ask his people for volunteers to accompany him back to the base." He thought for a moment. "Come to think of it, he's your senior surviving officer, isn't he?"

"Yeah, since Captain Dyson was killed three months ago."

"Then I think it's time he was promoted to Captain. Also, I'm going to amalgamate the remains of Drake's Regiment with Niven's Regiment. I'll promote you to Lieutenant-Colonel as Commanding Officer, and Captain Tredegar can move up to Major as your Executive Officer."

Jake laughed. "No need, Boss. Even with them, I'll have no more than a hundred and twenty combat-effective troops – only three platoons' worth, all told. Even a Major is too senior for that sort of command!"

"It's the principle of the thing. No, as of today you're a Lieutenant-Colonel and your son is a Captain." He rummaged in a drawer and pulled out two sets of rank insignia. "Let's go tell him, and I'll pin these on both of you; then I'll have him prepare to move out tonight with a couple of my people. He'll rendezvous with Captain Tredegar to be briefed and collect more volunteers, then cover the rest of the distance to the Matopo Hills. His partner's among our pilots, isn't she?"

"Yes, Sir – Sergeant Tamsin Gray."

"Then she can fly him there in an airvan, along with another to carry the rest of the patrol when it's assembled. May as well let them spend as much time together as possible."

"Dare I say you're getting sentimental in your old age, Sir?"

"Just as I daresay you are, Jake. We may as well. After all, neither of them is likely to live to anything like our age, are they?"

Jake nodded slowly, grimly. "Not if the Bactrians have anything to say about it."

~ ~ ~

TAPURIA: SECURITY SERVICE HEADQUARTERS

Colonel Kujula looked up as a knock came at his office door. "What is it?"

His aide opened the door. "Sir, Captain Vima requests permission to speak with you."

He frowned. "Didn't you tell him I wasn't to be disturbed except in emergency?"

"I did, Sir. He apologizes, but says this is a matter of the utmost importance that can't wait."

"It had better be! Very well, send him in."

He toggled the holographic display above his desk, reducing it to a mere icon above his lamp. Captain Vima's security clearance wasn't high enough to allow him to catch sight of the report he'd been studying. *Neither is his intelligence,* he thought sourly to himself.

The captain marched to the desk and snapped to attention as the aide closed the door behind him. He was a pudgy, moon-faced, unprepossessing young man wearing an immaculately-tailored uniform, Bactrian Army brown rather than Security Service black like the Colonel's. It was made of a luxurious fabric, far superior to military-issue cloth – and strictly non-regulation, his superior noted with frustration. Unfortunately, the political influence of the Minister of State for Culture was such that his son could not be disciplined over so minor an issue… not without damaging the career of anyone who tried, at any rate.

"What is it, Captain?" Kujula snapped. "Be brief. I'm very busy."

"S – sir, I regret to report that the suspected rebels Monique Edwards, Ronald Welsh and Art Ransom appear to have… ah… vanished, Sir."

"What?" The outraged Colonel surged to his feet, leaning forward, clenched fists resting on his desk, blood suffusing his face.

"T – they've disappeared, Sir."

"How could that happen? I gave you *explicit* orders that they were to be monitored at all times, using every available sensor and technique!"

"Y – yes, Sir, you did, but… Sir, yesterday Welsh went to a restaurant for lunch, Edwards left her place of work during the afternoon, and Ransom attended a reception in the evening. Those following them kept their distance so as not to alarm them – our standard procedure. Each suspect was tracked by means of devices we'd attached to their clothing, accessories and vehicles. When the tracking devices didn't move for a suspiciously long time, our agents investigated. In every case they found the suspects missing. They appear to have abandoned everything to which we had attached trackers. They changed into different clothes, and may have disguised themselves too. They disappeared before our agents noticed their absence."

Kujula sank slowly into his chair, eyes narrowing. "Why didn't our agents report this to you immediately?"

"They did, Sir. Each of them sent me a message to report their failure."

"Then why didn't you inform me at once?"

"Er… Sir, I was at the Military Governor's residence all yesterday afternoon and evening, discussing matters of protocol for our celebrations at the end of next month. His aide invited me to assist her because my father will be among the VIP guests in the delegation from Bactria. I was so busy I didn't have time to check my messages until this morning."

The Colonel bit his lip, closing his eyes to hide the blaze of fury behind them. *How the devil,* he wondered mentally, *am I supposed to guarantee the security of our colony on Laredo when I have to put up with influential idiots like this? Why can't I get more Security Service officers who know what they're doing, instead of having to borrow whatever rejects the Army feels like dumping on me?*

He was silent for a moment, then opened his eyes and waved his hand dismissively. "Wait in the anteroom, Captain. Send in my aide."

"Y – yessir!"

He waited until his aide had closed the door and crossed to stand in front of his desk. He studied her from head to foot as she approached, mentally approving her smartness and poise. She wore Army brown like Captain Vima, but there any similarities ended. She'd graduated from Bactria's Military Academy without any high-ranking officer or politician exercising influence on her behalf, which was unusual, but justified by her very high examination scores. He'd noticed them while scanning the profiles of newly arrived officers, and had asked for her services on temporary assignment to serve as his aide. He'd been pleased to discover that she had a logical, analytical brain and was willing to use it – something he encountered depressingly seldom among junior officers.

"You heard that, Lieutenant Yazata?"

"Yes, Sir. I listened over the intercom, as per your instructions concerning Captain Vima."

"Good. When dealing with a nincompoop who has influence, it's important to have a witness to document his shortcomings. Remember that for future reference in your own career."

She smiled mischievously. "Thank you for implying that I may have a worthwhile career ahead of me, Sir."

He permitted himself a dry chuckle. "So, Lieutenant, what conclusions do you draw from these events?"

Her brow furrowed as she thought. "Sir, three almost simultaneous disappearances would appear to confirm our suspicions about the people involved. The odds are vanishingly small that the incidents are unrelated. Unfortunately, each of them has a wide circle of friends, acquaintances, colleagues and contacts. We haven't yet discovered all of them – perhaps not even most of them – and we don't know which of them may also be involved with the Resistance. There are probably too many to arrest and interrogate them all within a reasonable timeframe."

"I agree. Continue."

She licked her lips thoughtfully. "Sir, have any suspected Resistance leaders in other towns also vanished?"

"That's a very good question. We must make urgent inquiries. We'll also ask our field offices whether any other locals, people we haven't so far suspected, are missing from their usual haunts. If they are, the timing may suggest they're connected to the Resistance as well."

"Yes, Sir. If more are missing, it'll also suggest that Resistance leaders are gathering for some reason. It might be for consultation and planning, or it could be for an operation." She hesitated. "Sir, could they have learned about our upcoming celebration? Might they intend to attack it?"

He felt a chill down his spine. "We've taken every precaution to keep it secret. We haven't even notified most of the units that'll be participating. They'll only be informed two weeks prior, giving them just enough time to prepare their troops and equipment and reach Tapuria in time for the parade. We hoped that such intense secrecy would prevent the Resistance learning about our plans in time to do anything about them. Furthermore, they've taken so many casualties in recent months that we believed they wouldn't have enough able-bodied fighters left to be able to do so. If we were wrong…" He shook his head in dismay. "That could be very bad. Prepare orders for distribution."

She took a slim pen-like object from her chest pocket, pointed it at him and pressed a stud at one end. "Recording, Sir."

"One. Signal every field office to confirm the location of all suspected Resistance leaders immediately. Do not, I say again, *do not* allow them to detect increased surveillance. If any have disappeared or do so in the next few days, or if other prominent Laredans not currently under suspicion should disappear, this office is to be informed at once.

"Two. If any of those who disappear should return, I'm to be informed at once. All necessary preparations should be made to arrest them and send them here at once for interrogation, but no action is to be initiated without my express approval.

He paused, looking at her intently. "Switch off your recorder." She complied. "Lieutenant, are you prepared to put your future on the line in a task of great importance? Success will guarantee you rapid progress in your career. It may even bring an opportunity to transfer into the Security Service, where intelligence and competence will produce more rapid advancement than in the Army. However, failure will doom you to remain a Lieutenant forever – perhaps even be court-martialed for dereliction of duty. What say you?"

She gulped. "I… Yes, Sir, I'm prepared to accept the challenge."

"Well answered. I'm temporarily reassigning you to take over from Captain Vima, and command our counter-espionage agents in Tapuria. It's essential that we detect any preparations for a forthcoming attack in time to neutralize it. You'll have to galvanize your people to renewed efforts and make examples of the least effective among them – you have my permission to shoot one or two if need be." Watching her closely, he was pleased to see that his ruthlessness didn't appear to trouble her. "If our celebrations pass off without incident you'll earn an official commendation. However, if you fail in your mission and an attack takes place, even if it doesn't succeed, it'll be very much the worse for you." He didn't feel it necessary to add that it wouldn't do his career prospects much good, either.

"I understand, Sir. If I'm to take Captain Vima's place, what will he be doing?"

"If he was a Security Service officer I'd break him at once for inefficiency and dereliction of duty. However, he's Army, so I need to motivate a new assignment for him. Because of his family influence it must appear to enhance his career, but in reality I want something where his incompetence will cause him to fail so publicly that we can get rid of him once and for all." He thought for a moment, then called up his display and entered a query. "*Aha!* I thought I remembered seeing this. The commanding officer of the garrison at Caristo was airlifted to Tapuria last week for medical treatment."

"Yes, Sir. If I recall correctly he was injured in an aircar accident. He'll be in hospital for some time."

"That gives me an opportunity to dispose of Captain Vima. The title of 'Garrison Commanding Officer' sounds good, and disguises how bad the place is. Caristo's a punishment posting – it has no redeeming features whatsoever. I've heard some soldiers complain that if there's a Divinity, and if he, she or it wanted to give this planet an enema, that's a likely place to insert it! I've seen surveillance vid of the base – it's dirty, the troops' uniforms are unkempt, much of their equipment is unserviceable, and discipline and morale are very poor. There's no way even a good officer would be able to get them into a fit state to join the parade next month, given so little time to prepare them. I think they should drag Captain Vima down to their level in short order." He began entering a message. "I'll nominate him to take over there, and have him hand over his responsibilities to you at once. I want him out of here by tonight!" He looked sharply at her. "See to it that you don't make the same mistakes. Keep me informed about *everything*, understand? I want no more surprises!"

"Understood, Sir."

"Very well. I – "

His console chimed urgently, interrupting him. He brought up the display to see a flashing purple icon, indicating a top-priority message. "Just a moment." He opened the message and read intently, then thrust himself to his feet, a smile of triumph on his face. "*At last!* The interrogators have been busy with that rebel officer we captured a few weeks ago during the assault on their base in the Matopo Hills. He was too badly hurt to answer questions at first, but he recovered enough for them to start work on him yesterday evening. I thought his resistance would have been greatly reduced by his injuries, but he held out longer than I expected. Still, he's cracked at last, like they always do."

"Has he given us anything worthwhile, Sir?"

"He most certainly has. It turns out he was the commanding officer there. He told us some very interesting news." He consulted his terminal's time display. "I'll see the Captain now to get his transfer under way. While I do that, contact our garrison at Hermonosa and tell them in my name to dispatch combat engineers at once to the Matopo Hills base, complete with heavy equipment to dig through the wreckage they left behind. They're to use the road they cut through the bush for the initial assault, and advise me of their estimated date and time of arrival. I'll signal further details later today, and join them in an assault shuttle once they've started work. There's something hidden in the base that we have to recover."

"Yes, Sir." She hesitated. "May I come too, please, Sir? I haven't been in the field yet."

"Not this time. Your job is to take over Captain Vima's agents and whip them into line as quickly as possible. When you've done that, we'll see what can be arranged."

"Yes, Sir." She bit her lip to hide her disappointment.

He smiled as he watched her walk to the door. It had been a very satisfying week. He'd earned a profitable bribe in untraceable gold from an off-planet fur trader; he'd found a way to get rid of the execrable Captain Vima; and he was on the verge of recovering something the Security Service had been trying to retrieve for years, ever since that idiot Major-General Strato had so stupidly signed it. If he succeeded, it would guarantee him at least a letter of commendation from the Commissioner of the Security Service on Bactria, if not a medal for outstanding achievement. Life was indeed good.

March 1st 2850 GSC

IN THE WILDERNESS

Captain Tredegar held out his hand in greeting. "Good to see you again, Lieutenant – but I understand it's Captain now?"

"Yes, as of yesterday. General Aldred has major's insignia waiting for you at HQ." Dave grinned at his opposite number as he shook hands. The twilight was deepened by the tangled mass of brush, scrub and trees growing well above head height, making it prematurely gloomy on the narrow trail. He sneezed as dust thrown up by the airvans' fans got into his nostrils.

"Looks like both of us are going up in the world. When did you get here?"

"We arrived at that hill just before dawn." He gestured to its bulk low on the horizon. "We laagered up during the daylight hours under camouflage netting, then flew to meet you as soon as the sun set."

"Good – then the Bactrians probably haven't spotted you, or us. We've been moving very slowly and carefully so as not to raise dust or leave clearly visible tracks that would give away our position. How many are with you?"

"Two pilots for the airvans, plus two of the General's security detachment who volunteered to come with me. I understand I'm to get more volunteers from you to make up the rest of my patrol." He gestured to the small convoy of vehicles behind Tredegar, who grimaced.

"That'll be difficult. More than half of us are wounded to a greater or lesser extent. We're relying on our able-bodied personnel to get the rest of us through."

"Were you hurt?" Dave asked with real concern.

"I was too close to an explosion. It blew me into a big rock and broke some ribs. Nothing time won't heal, but it's very painful. Deep breathing's no fun at all."

"I believe it! How about if I take just six of your people? I can offer them an airvan ride back to base instead of having to bump through the bush for another hundred kilometers."

"That should be enough incentive to make *everyone* volunteer! I think we can spare half a dozen."

"Thanks. We brought you as much in the way of medical supplies and rations as we could fit on top of and around our long-range fuel tanks. We need them to reach the Matopo Hills and return, but they take up a lot of space in our cargo compartment, I'm afraid."

"Thanks very much. I'll have my people help you load them into our vehicles, then we'll eat before moving on to make camp for the night. We'll talk later."

They ate a hurried meal from ration packs, building small smokeless fires to boil water for coffee and fill vacuum flasks for later use; then they moved on several kilometers to make a dark, fireless camp in a grove of spindly trees. The vehicles were dispersed beneath camouflage netting while Tamsin took both airvans to a nearby hill and parked them in the shadows cast by several large boulders, also camouflaging them against observation.

Dave joined Tredegar inside his vehicle, a battered six-wheeled transport. "I'm surprised this thing's made it so far through the bush," he observed as he climbed into the rear compartment.

"I am too. We have one captured armored car that we're using to break trail, to ease the load on the other transports. That helps."

"Uh-huh. The General's arranging airvan transport once you reach the Renosa River. He'll have you leave these vehicles there, where the Bactrians aren't likely to stumble across them. That way they won't break a trail all the way to his headquarters. He doesn't want any clues that might lead the enemy there."

"Can't say I blame him. Show me on the map." Dave pointed out the rendezvous, and Tredegar nodded. "We're no more than two days from there. I'll be glad to get back to a decent bed and rest these ribs properly!"

"What can you tell me about the Matopo base? I've never been there."

"It was a deep complex of natural caves in a hillside. Miners found it soon after Laredo was settled. They carved tunnels between the caves and further into the hillside looking for worthwhile minerals, but didn't find much. We expanded it using laser cutters and made it our regional headquarters when we switched to guerrilla warfare. Trouble is, I don't know how you're going to get in. While we were waiting to escape we heard lots of explosions and felt the rock trembling. I think the Bactrians blew up everything."

"Where were you? How did you get away?"

"We used a big cave with a small, well-hidden entrance as our transport pool. It was connected to the main base by a half-kilometer tunnel. We'd rigged the head of that tunnel with explosives to stop any enemy assault coming in from the transport cave. After the Bactrians came in through the front entrance, I took command of the survivors and evacuated them down to the transport pool as a back way out. I waited until the enemy was closing in, then blew the tunnel. I don't think they knew about the transport cave – we never saw a sign of them anywhere near it. We waited there in silence for three days while they did whatever they were doing in the base, then headed out after they'd left."

"That was a damn fine piece of work," Dave congratulated him. "What about rations and medical supplies? You said you had a lot of wounded."

"We made do with what we had. It wasn't enough. We've buried nine people on the way here." A shadow seemed to pass across the Captain's weary face. "We were pretty hungry, too, except for what food we were able to hunt. Your cargo's a Godsend to us! At least we can eat properly now, and regain our strength." He reached for a vacuum flask. "Let me pour us some coffee, then I'll show you on the map the location of the transport cave and the best approach to it. It's well-hidden enough to keep your airvans out of sight while you try to find a way back into the base."

"Sounds good to me."

~ ~ ~

RESISTANCE HEADQUARTERS

Jake rapped on the wood frame around the entrance to the alcove. "You ready to eat?"

Marvin looked up from the camp cot on which he was sitting. "Now that you mention it, I'm pretty hungry. What's for supper?" He rose to his feet, stretching.

"Whatever ration pack you choose, courtesy of the Bactrian Army. We've been feeding ourselves at their expense for a long time now."

"Battlefield captures?" They set off down the connecting tunnel.

"Yes, and convoys we ambush, and corrupt quartermasters who'll take a bribe to look the other way while we ransack their warehouses. All our equipment comes from the invaders now. We used up our own stocks during the initial battles."

They arrived at the mess hall at the same time as General Aldred. "This is my wife Gloria," he introduced the woman at his side to Marvin. "She's the only surviving Minister from Laredo's pre-war Cabinet, and as such she's the *de facto* President of the Council of the Resistance. Gloria, this is Marvin Ellis, the Vice-President's emissary."

"I was only a Deputy Minister, darling," Gloria corrected, "and Vice-President Johns was also a Cabinet member." She was short; Marvin thought she had probably been plump at one time, before the privations of three years of clandestine warfare had taken their toll. Her gray hair and tired, lined face bore witness to the strain. She held out her hand to him, and he took it respectfully.

"Yes," her husband objected, "but she's off-planet as head of our Government-in-Exile, so she can't be a member of the Council."

"Oh, well, if you want to be picky..." They all laughed. "Did Jake tell you the news from Caristo?" she asked Marvin.

"No – what news?"

"Let's get some food before we talk. I'm starving!" She led the way towards a counter where boxes of ration packs were laid out, ready for diners to make their choice. Each of them selected a pack, heated its contents, and filled a cup with water or coffee; then they headed for an empty table. There were few others eating, all looking tired and subdued.

Once they'd settled down on the benches, Jake took up the narrative. "Last night the Bactrians flew in a new Captain to take over the garrison at

38

Caristo. Sergeant-Major Garnati had a drink with Weems – one of my people – over lunch today. He says the new Captain doesn't know his ass from his elbow. He reckons he must have upset someone senior, who sent him to Caristo to punish him; but he thinks he'll be more of a punishment to the garrison, to add to their sorrows at being stuck out there at the ass-end of the planet. Also, there's apparently a big parade scheduled in Banka at the end of the month. It hasn't been officially announced yet and Garnati doesn't know what it's all about, but the new Captain says he does. According to him every garrison will have to send some of its troops to take part. Caristo will send one of its two platoons."

"I'd pay good money to watch that," the General said with a grin. "Like most of their remote garrisons in backwaters like Caristo, its soldiers are among the worst troops the Bactrians have got. It's a punishment posting. If they're going to be in the parade, they're going to drag down everyone else. It's going to be a disaster!"

"You know it," Jake agreed. "What's more, their equipment hasn't been properly maintained in months. They've got to send two of their four assault shuttles to the parade; but two are hangar queens, one's overdue for a major overhaul, and the only one in flying order can't move because all their pilots are overdue for their annual check rides!"

The others laughed. "So I guess they won't be going," Marvin said.

Jake shook his head. "According to Garnati, if they don't show up heads will roll. His new boss is terrified one of them might be his. Garnati says he's got a buddy in the Military Governor's office in Banka. He's begged her to organize a maintenance team for him on the quiet, without anyone knowing. They'll overhaul the shuttles, re-certify his pilots and bring supplies for his birds – they're almost out of fuel cartridges, reaction mass, munitions and other supplies. She's promised to get them there ASAP, along with a couple of drill instructors to pick the best-performing members of his garrison and smarten them up for the parade."

"I wonder if we could steal some of those shuttle supplies?" the General mused.

"Why would you want shuttle supplies?" Marvin asked, puzzled.

"For our shuttles, of course – what else?"

"I didn't know you had any." He tasted his food, and grimaced. "What *is* this stuff? 'Sausage, beans and rice' sounded OK on the label, but it tastes weird!"

Gloria informed him, chuckling, "We call those sausages 'Frankenweiners'. The best I can say about them is that they're not actually poisonous, even though they sometimes taste like it. The Bactrians seem to like them, though, judging by the number we've captured from them."

"They must have cast-iron stomachs. Oh, well, if it doesn't kill them I daresay it won't kill me. About those shuttles?"

Jake nodded. "We got them from the Bactrians too." He took a mouthful of his chili stew, chewed it, and swallowed before continuing. "The day before they invaded, they sent an advance party on a commercial freighter that arrived in orbit claiming it was delivering cargo. The containers they sent to our Orbital Patrol and Customs space station were filled with Bactrian Marines instead of freight. They broke out and took it over as soon as the main landing force appeared, to prevent us using the station's missiles to defend the planet. They were helped by four assault shuttles that launched from the freighter during the attack."

He picked up his cup of water and drank. "Some of the station's crew managed to hide in a cargo compartment near the docking bay. After the fighting died down and the Bactrians had relaxed, they sneaked into the bay and attacked the four Marines guarding the shuttles. When the smoke cleared, a few of our pilots were still alive. Two of them put our survivors aboard two assault shuttles and brought them planetside. Two others took the remaining shuttles at full throttle into head-on collisions with two of the eight Bactrian transports. Each was a tramp merchant freighter carrying a full regiment of troops with all their equipment and supplies."

"Brave people," Marvin observed, even as he mentally winced at the thought of the carnage that must have ensued. Most assault shuttles weighed fifty to eighty tons and could reach one-twentieth to one-tenth of light speed in space. Even lowly tramp merchant ships weighed one-quarter to three-quarters of a million tons and cruised at similar speeds. A head-on collision between two such masses at those velocities would have unleashed kinetic energy far greater than the power of a nuclear warhead. Survival would have been out of the question for anyone aboard.

"Very brave. The Bactrians sent in eight regiments in the first wave, but lost a quarter of their force before it even entered orbit. We bled the rest over the next six weeks until they brought in reinforcements and swamped us by sheer weight of numbers – even fully mobilized, we only had four regiments. We used what we learned from the captured shuttles to eavesdrop on their communications networks and jam their fire control systems and weapons. We also figured out how to disrupt their blind-flying systems, which cost them several dozen shuttles in collisions or crashes on their way to landing sites at night or in bad weather. That disrupted their assaults until they could regroup and bring in reinforcements. While they were disorganized we'd hit them and inflict a lot of casualties before they could fight back effectively. We also captured a lot of their heavy weaponry and turned it against them, as well as enough spares and supplies to keep our two captured shuttles flying until last year. If we could get our hands on more fuel, reaction mass and ammo for them, we might be able to use them for another operation."

"I've never understood why Bactria invaded you in the first place," Marvin confessed.

Gloria snorted. "The last three Satraps of Bactria ran their economy into the ground with grandiose public works projects. Taxes had trebled in half a century, and business and commerce were hurting. To jump-start an economic recovery the new Satrap decided to found a colony, quote, 'for the greater glory of the Bactrian people', unquote – and to get his people's minds off their troubles at home and focused on something outside. It's one of the oldest tricks in the political playbook."

Jake added, "Sergeant-Major Garnati told me once that they wanted a colony planet arable enough to be self-supporting, with good mineral resources. They planned to use convicts as a labor force – they've got a lot, everyone who's classified as a political dissident plus the usual criminals. They couldn't afford the startup costs to colonize a virgin planet, so they decided it'd be cheaper to invade us and take over all the facilities we'd already installed, then use our population as slave labor to supplement their convicts. They figured we were too small and weak to resist."

Marvin grimaced. "You sure proved them wrong! It's terribly sad how many you lost, though. I saw the ruins of your former capital. I never understood how the crew of your dispatch ship could maneuver so recklessly as to cause that."

"They didn't." General Aldred's voice was grim. "We destroyed over half their initial landing force during the first few weeks of fighting. They hadn't expected that sort of resistance, especially from a small reservist army like ours, and they got mad. Their Commanding General gave me an ultimatum: 'Surrender at once, or see your capital and everyone in it destroyed' – that's an exact quote from his message. By then we'd seen what they were doing to those they captured, civilian as well as military, so of course I refused. They'd captured our only dispatch ship the week after the invasion when it came back here, not knowing what was going on. It was a very old, slow ship, and quite small, but it was all they needed. They took it out, turned it around and brought it back on a collision course with the planet, then abandoned ship, leaving its original crew locked in one of its compartments. It entered atmosphere at one-tenth of light speed directly above Banka."

Marvin's eyes were wide with horror. "They claimed the ship's crew accidentally dived into the planet while trying to escape!"

"Yes, they did, and the rest of the settled galaxy bought their story, but we know better. We have their General's hand-signed message, and recorded their signals about it, and interrogated some of their officers we took prisoner. All that's among the evidence we want to get off-planet. They destroyed Banka deliberately."

Jake spoke very quietly, voice dark with remembered pain. "The ship was mostly hollow, of course, not solid like an asteroid, but it still massed fifty thousand tons. It exploded above the city. The blast and energy release flattened Banka and everything around it. A quarter of a million people died, half our planetary population. My wife was among them, along with Timmy and Janet, our two younger children – Dave's brother and sister."

Gloria looked as if she wanted to spit. "After Banka they stopped referring to us as 'the enemy' or 'Laredan forces'. Instead we became 'rebels', because they claimed the Laredo government no longer existed and their Military Governor was therefore the only legitimate authority here. Lately they've taken to calling us 'terrorists' as well. Needless to say, we reject both labels, but there are those in the interplanetary community who'll always buy the 'official' version of events. That's yet another reason

42

why we want so badly to get our evidence to the United Planets, to prove our case that we're still a legitimate national armed force resisting an illegal invasion."

The General added bitterly, "The Bactrians also stopped accepting individual and unit surrenders after Banka. Instead they handed over captured officers and senior NCO's to their Security Service for interrogation under torture, and shot everyone else. The SS did the same to its prisoners when they'd wrung them dry. That's why we no longer allow ourselves to be taken alive if we can help it. We also don't accept Bactrian surrenders any more, although we don't take prisoners for interrogation under torture. We've kept at least some standards of decency."

There was a long silence. Marvin tried to eat more of his meal, but his mouth had gone dry and refused to co-operate. At last he laid down his fork and drank some water.

"I noticed when I landed that a large part of Banka's ruins have been cleared," he observed. "There are prefabricated buildings going up."

Jake nodded. "They're building their new capital on the ruins of our old one. They've rounded up over a hundred thousand of our citizens so far and interned them in labor camps to clear the site. An awful lot of our people have died in the process – they're brutally treated and not fed enough. As each section is cleared the Bactrians lay in new services and put up prefabs to accommodate their own people and administrative functions. They've put up a few permanent structures too. They've just completed a Royal Palace for their Satrap if he ever decides to visit."

"Are the destruction of Banka and the 'no surrender' order what motivated you to go on fighting?"

"That's just the start. The Bactrians have made it clear they regard everyone on Laredo as sub-human. We have no value or dignity in their eyes except as cheap, disposable labor. We refuse to live like that. Emiliano Zapata said before the Space Age, 'Better to die on your feet than live on your knees'. When you know death's inevitable, and your only choice is between being slowly worked and starved to death as a slave or dying quickly and cleanly in battle, it makes resistance the only logical option."

"That's about the size of it," the General agreed. "There's another aspect. More than three out of five of our soldiers became casualties during the period between the invasion and the destruction of Banka. After that,

43

when we knew we couldn't win using conventional tactics and they proved we couldn't surrender by shooting those who did, we went underground to continue the fight as guerrillas. Over the past three years more than half the survivors of our armed forces have been killed. Most of us have lost our families. Less than one in ten of my troops are left now. We've killed for each other; we've killed alongside each other. Far too often we've had to give our comrades the final gift of a quick, pain-free death when there was no other way out. That makes us closer than brothers and sisters, closer even than lovers in some ways. We know that sooner or later we're all going to die too; but we'll kill as many Bactrians as we can before then, and take more with us when we go."

Gloria added, "My father was a retired professor of history. Shortly after the invasion he quoted Winston Churchill: 'You may have to fight when there is no hope of victory, because it is better to perish than to live as slaves'. He was killed in Banka a few days after reminding us of that."

Jake said grimly, "Before the war Dave and Tamsin were planning on getting married. They gave up that idea when they realized that they no longer have a future to plan for. Sooner or later the Bactrians will kill them, together or separately. I wish they'd had the chance for a peaceful life together. I think they'd have made great partners and great parents, and I hold the Bactrians responsible for the grandchildren I'll no longer get from them."

Marvin stared at him for a moment, then shook his head slowly. "I don't think I truly understood until now how... *driven* you all are," he said very quietly. "It... it almost makes me feel ashamed. I'm here as a messenger, just doing a liaison job to establish my reputation as a private investigator and security consultant and earn money to expand my business. I'm much less committed to your cause than you are."

Gloria grinned at him. "I have news for you. While you're on Laredo you're every bit as committed as we are, whether you like it or not. The Bactrians will kill you right along with us if they get half a chance."

"Gee, thanks *so* much for reminding me of that!" They all laughed.

As they left the mess hall, General Aldred signaled to Jake to hang back. He said quietly to him, "That parade the Bactrians are planning – did the Sergeant-Major know anything more?"

"No. He said he hadn't heard anything about it at all until his new boss arrived. He's apparently in a panic over how unready the garrison is to participate."

"If they're going to pull a lot of their troops out of garrisons to attend it, we may be able to take advantage of the situation. It's a good thing we heard about it now, rather than later in the month, or we might not have had enough time to arrange a nasty surprise for them. Let's try to find out more, and see whether it offers us any opportunities."

March 3rd 2850 GSC

MATOPO HILLS

"There's that noise again," Tamsin said, puzzled. They listened to the faint tremor of sound. "It sounds a bit like the high-pitched whine of a stinger flying around a room, but there are none of them in these parts."

"Are we sure all the Bactrians left after they blew up the base?" Dave asked.

"So Captain Tredegar said. He might have been wrong, though."

"I guess – oh, shit! *Freeze!*"

She did as he commanded, both of them sitting dead still on the rocks inside the entrance to the transport cave. Beyond the bushes and loosely draped camouflage nets that hid them, a small flying ball suspended beneath two counter-rotating rotors appeared from behind a rock higher up the hill. It drifted down towards them, the whine from its electric power pack growing louder, and passed over the trees at the base of the hill before turning into the gully that led to the cave. It hovered nearby for a few moments, its sensor turret scanning in all directions, glinting in the mid-morning sunshine, then moved slowly away. There was no increase in speed or any other sign that it might have detected them.

Dave waited, holding his breath, until it was out of sight. He released the pressure in his lungs in an explosion of relief. *'Whew!* I thought we were goners for sure! Good thing it didn't come close enough for its sensors to see us through the camo netting."

"I damn nearly wet my trousers," Tamsin admitted shakily. "Where did that come from?"

"Only one place it could have come from – the enemy," he pointed out grimly. "That's one of their standard small-unit hoversats. It only has an endurance of a couple of hours and it's not very fast, so it must have been launched from somewhere nearby."

"The main entrance to the base, you mean?"

"There was nothing and no-one nearby when we scanned it last night with our sensors during our approach," he reminded her, frowning, "and from what Captain Tredegar said there's no way they could be using the base themselves – they blew it up."

"Then another enemy patrol must have arrived last night after we did. It's the only possible explanation."

"Yeah, and that means we're caught between a rock and a hard place. We can't get in through the tunnel – it's completely blocked by the explosion Captain Tredegar set off – and we can't leave this cave while we might be seen by that thing. We're just going to have to wait out the day in here, then try to sneak out tonight on foot to reconnoiter the area."

She clutched his hand in alarm. "Remember, those things have night sensors too!"

"Sure they do, but we have a few tricks of our own. I'll be careful, I promise. Let's go warn the others."

~ ~ ~

As the sun sank beneath the horizon, Dave finished adjusting his equipment and turned to the two who were coming with him. Swiftly they double-checked one another, making sure that all metal items were covered or secured so they wouldn't clink against each other, and that the thermally neutral battledress, ski masks, gloves and boots covered as much of their bodies as possible.

"Good enough," he said softly when they'd finished. "They shouldn't see us coming, even if one of those hoversats is prowling around. To be even more certain, we're going to climb straight up the hillside for a couple of hundred meters. Every time we saw that hoversat today it was a hundred meters up the hillside or lower. If we get above it, its sensor turret won't be able to look down on us. We'll move around the hill above its patrol altitude and see what we can find."

"Got it, Sir," Sergeant Kane assured him cheerfully as he collapsed the parabolic microphone he was holding and fastened the now tube-like device onto his pack.

"What do we do if we're spotted, Sir?" Corporal Hansen asked.

"We'll split up and make it as hard for them to chase us as possible. Don't come back here under any circumstances – lead them somewhere else. Don't let them take you alive, whatever you do." He transferred his gaze to the others. "If we're not back by zero-four-hundred, you're to leave in the airvans and get as far away as you can before dawn. Laager up under camouflage netting during the day, then head for base to warn the General that we won't be coming back."

Tamsin looked rebellious, but he shook his head in silent warning as he looked firmly at her. She opened her mouth to speak, then sighed as her shoulders slumped. "I guess you're right," she admitted in a desolate tone. "I just hate the thought of having to leave you behind."

"Not half as much as I hate it!" he assured her fervently, drawing shaky laughter from the others. "We'll do our best to make it back; but remember, the General can't afford to lose any more people than he absolutely has to. We've suffered enough casualties in recent months to be really hurting for trained soldiers. Let's not make things worse than they already are!" He picked up his helmet with its attached night vision visor. "All right, people. As soon as it's full dark we'll move out."

~ ~ ~

It took them more than two hours to make their way slowly and carefully around the mountainside, stepping cautiously from cover to cover, watching where they put their feet. Their multi-sensor night vision visors helped them to avoid most of the creatures of the evening, except for those that flew into them blindly. They batted them away as silently as possible.

As they drew nearer to the front part of the mountain where the base's main entrance had been, they noticed a flickering light reflected off the trees and bushes at the foot of the slope. As they eased around a big rock, they saw a group of heavy vehicles laagered up in a circle around a blazing camp fire. A score of soldiers were sitting around, eating, drinking and talking, the low rumble of their voices barely audible at this distance.

Dave shook his head disapprovingly. "Staring into a big fire like that, they've all ruined their night vision," he murmured.

"Good," Corporal Hansen muttered emphatically. "Let's hope they never get it back!"

Chuckling softly, they moved very carefully down the hillside to get closer. Dave called a halt in a group of boulders about a hundred and twenty meters above where the main entrance to the base had been, and about a hundred and forty from the fire. "We'll set up here," he whispered. "Stretch the camo net above us. Set up the parabolic microphone between those two rocks, and don't forget to switch on the recorder. Let's try to find out what they're doing here."

It took several minutes of cautious, agonizingly slow work to silently conceal themselves against observation by passing hoversats and set up the equipment. They linked their earpieces to the parabolic microphone's receiver and settled down to listen.

Underlying all the talking at the fire was a constant low rumble, interspersed with sharper impacts and sounds, coming from inside the mountain. They could feel the vibrations through the rock even as they heard the sounds with their ears. A constant dusty plume was coming out of the old entrance to the base and being carried away by the evening breeze. The soldiers around the fire were talking desultorily about the usual topics – the lousy Army, food, the weather, the damned Army, the opposite sex, their families, and the bloody Army. They hushed as a radio operator stuck his head out of a truck festooned with aerials. He was wearing headphones. "The Colonel's ten minutes out," he called towards the fire. "He wants us to illuminate his landing area."

"Got it," a tall figure called from the entrance to a large tent pitched between two vehicles. "Landing party, let's go!"

He led a group of four soldiers to a clear patch of ground about a hundred meters from the vehicles. They split up, and soon a strobe light began flashing brightly in the darkness. Adjusting their night vision visors, they could see it was at the tip of an infra-red beam shining horizontally along the ground. Seconds later another beam sprang to life at right angles to the first, making a plus sign with their intersection in the center of the clearing.

Far in the distance and high above the ground, a bright white light came on. Within a few moments the growing rumble of reaction thrusters began to make the air tremble. From out of the night sky a black-painted assault shuttle swept over the camp, circled the improvised landing area once, then touched down, rocking gently on its gel-filled tires. As its reaction thrusters stuttered into silence its rear ramp whined down and four black-clad Security Service troops ran down it, spreading out, aiming their weapons with fierce determination at every shadow in the darkness – including the soldiers. Through the parabolic microphone they heard the tall man's softly-voiced exclamation of disgust as he strode towards them. "Bloody SS clowns! When are they going to figure out that combat outfits just laugh at them when they pretend to be heroes?" His voice was attenuated by the greater distance to the landing site, but could still be made out clearly.

Another tall, spare figure walked down the ramp, also in a black uniform, but with an ornate silver crown on his epaulettes. The first man snapped to attention and saluted stiffly. "Captain Amesha reports to Colonel Kujula as ordered, *Sir!*"

"Good evening, Captain." The senior officer's voice was dry, brittle. "Why are your engineers out here around the fire, instead of in the base digging?"

"Sir, half of my contingent *is* in the base digging. There's no room for more of us to fit inside, due to the extent of the destruction and the need for space around our heavy machinery. We'll relieve them at twenty-two, to let them sleep through the night. We'll work until zero-six-hundred, when they'll relieve us again."

The Colonel seemed to relax slightly. "I see. Is the excavation progressing well?"

"Much faster than I expected, Sir. The troops who took this place weren't combat engineers, so they weren't experts at demolition. Their charges brought down a layer of rock from the roof and walls of the stronghold, but didn't completely collapse the caves and tunnels. Our laser cutters and rubble removers are making short work of it. We're already more than fifty meters inside, disposing of the debris in a largely intact side cavern. We should reach the Commanding Officer's tunnel within a few hours if the information your prisoner provided is correct."

"Oh, it's correct, Captain, be in no doubt about that. See for yourself." He gestured back into the interior of his assault shuttle. The other officer looked, and his face contorted in... *is that disgust?* Dave wondered to himself.

The man bit back a muffled exclamation, clearly afraid of saying the wrong thing. He settled for "What did you do to him, Sir? He looks like death warmed up!"

"That's not a bad description. Lieutenant-Colonel Yardley was the rebel Commanding Officer here. He was badly wounded in the initial assault and collapsed. It was thought he was dead, but some of our medics found him still breathing and recognized from his insignia that I'd want him kept that way. They flew him straight to hospital in Tapuria in an assault shuttle, and he was dragged back from the brink of death over the next few weeks. Four days ago he was finally fit enough for my interrogators to take over. Have you ever seen them at work, Captain?"

"Ah... no, Sir." Now Dave was sure of it – that really was thinly veiled disgust on his face. It was the expression of a man with at least some standards when confronted with the unspeakable.

"They start by injecting a special drug in a quantity carefully metered according to the subject's gender and body mass. It has the effect of stimulating every nerve ending, making them exquisitely sensitive. While they're waiting for it to take effect they fit the subject with a head cover containing a neurocranial network, designed to administer direct stimulation to the pain and pleasure centers of the brain. When the drug has taken effect they begin alternately pleasuring and hurting him. His chemically enhanced nervous system magnifies the signals enormously, and they're amplified again by the neurocranial network. They're absolutely unbearable. Nobody can resist for more than twenty-four hours in my experience, and then only the toughest and most determined of men. Most crack within four to six hours. Despite his injuries and weakened condition, he took eleven hours to break and begin to talk – a remarkable performance under the circumstances."

"I see, Sir," the Captain said slowly. "I presume he provided the information that led you to order us here?"

"He did, and I brought him along in case he can provide more while we're here. It seems the rebels have distributed what they laughably call 'evidence' of some of our anti-terrorist actions among several of their bases. He was the custodian of one package of it. We know where he hid it in his office, and I'm here to get it. While we're doing that, the Military Governor is preparing assaults on their other three major bases – Yardley knew them all, and now we know them too. We're conducting reconnaissance to gather more information, and we'll hit them all simultaneously in five days. With any luck, we'll break the back of the Resistance forever."

"That's good news," the other said feelingly. "No matter how the information was obtained, we need to finish this thing. Since we invaded they've cost us over fifteen thousand dead and twice that many injured, many of them maimed for life – and heaven only knows the cost in equipment and military expenditure! The sooner we finish the war, the sooner we can all go home."

"I appreciate your desire to return to Bactria, Captain, but we'll need a sizeable garrison here for the foreseeable future," the Colonel reproved him. "None of us can be sure when our services will no longer be required on Laredo."

"Yes, of course, Sir."

"You brought a senior officer's accommodation van for me?"

"Yes, Sir. If you wish, I'll escort you there now."

"Very well. I'll have my own guards with me during the night, of course. Two will be on watch outside my quarters at all times. My interrogators and the shuttle crew will stay here with the prisoner." As he spoke, he motioned to the armed men who'd preceded him down the ramp. One ran back up it and emerged again holding a suitcase.

"As you wish, Sir."

"There's no sign of any enemies in the vicinity?"

"No, Sir. We've had hoversats out all day sweeping the area, and none of them have picked up a thing. It looks like any of the rebels who survived the destruction of their base have long gone."

"Good. We'll be able to sleep in peace then."

Dave watched them make their way back to the fire, his mind whirling with shock and disbelief. Beside him Sergeant Kane murmured, "What do we do now, Sir?"

"You got all that on the recorder?"

"I sure did."

"Good. Let's head back to the cave very carefully so they don't hear us. We've got to get this news to General Aldred at once, if not sooner! After that, we've got plans to make."

~ ~ ~

Tamsin oriented the satellite dish along the bearing Dave had given her. She adjusted it carefully, and nodded as a tone began to warble in her earphones. "The dish is aligned," she told him as she locked it into position on its tripod.

"Great!" He consulted his watch. "It's almost time. Mac's people are supposed to listen out on the emergency channel from 11:45 until noon and 23:45 until midnight. Let's see if they're awake."

"They'd better be!"

"I trust Mac. He was our satellite comms supervisor before the invasion, after all. He always said the Bactrians were fools to simply leave our own satellites in orbit and use them, rather than replace them with their own, because they'd never be able to figure out all the back doors we'd built into them unless they physically examined them."

"Hey, at a time like this I'll take all the back doors we can get!"

Grinning at her rejoinder, he connected his comm unit to the dish and raised it to his lips. "BOLUS calling TANTO, emergency, over." He waited for a few moments, then repeated the call.

An answering carrier wave crackled in their earpieces. "TANTO to BOLUS, authenticate Papa X-Ray Tango, over."

Dave entered the three characters on his comm unit's virtual keyboard and read off the response. "BOLUS to TANTO, authenticating Golf Zulu Delta, over."

"TANTO to BOLUS, authenticated, go ahead, over."

He began reading from the piece of paper on which he'd carefully composed his message. "BOLUS to TANTO, be advised BILE, EAGLE and RAPID for WELLINGTON, HINDENBURG and WASHINGTON. I say again, BILE, EAGLE and RAPID for WELLINGTON, HINDENBURG and WASHINGTON. This information is verified

CHROME, I say again, this information is verified CHROME. Timeline for RAPID is BASE minus three BAXTER, I say again, timeline for RAPID is BASE minus three BAXTER. Request HAWKEYE on this circuit. Over."

A brief pause. "TANTO to BOLUS, I understand BILE, EAGLE and RAPID for WELLINGTON, HINDENBURG and WASHINGTON, information CHROME, timeline BASE minus three BAXTER. HAWKEYE approved. Over."

"BOLUS to TANTO, thank you. BOLUS out." He folded the paper and shoved it into his pocket, then disconnected his comm unit. "That's it."

As she collapsed the satellite dish, Tamsin shook her head. "All those code words! What were you saying?"

"Bolus is my code name on this mission and Tanto is our communications center. Wellington, Hindenburg and Washington are code words for our remaining three major bases – this one was Bonaparte before it fell to the enemy. Bile means betrayal, Eagle means surveillance, and Rapid means attack. Using those words in reference to anything or anyone makes the meaning obvious. Chrome means that the information is absolutely reliable. Base is a number used as a reference by adding or subtracting a figure from it. For this date base is eight, and Baxter means days, so I just told them that the three bases would be assaulted five days from now. Hawkeye means I can call again anytime on this circuit. They'll mount a permanent listening watch in case I come up with more information."

"Complicated, but useful. Anyone listening in wouldn't know what you were saying unless they knew the code words."

"That's the whole idea. Now, let's get back to the others and make some plans."

"But what can ten of us – eleven including you – do against what must be about sixty of them?"

"Quite a lot, if we play our cards right. Don't forget, half of them will be working deep inside the mountain at any time, so initially we've only got to deal with the other half of them at the camp. Most will be asleep, except for some sentries. We'll see about those inside the tunnel once we've dealt with those outside. Besides, no matter how many of them there are, I'll be damned if I'll leave Lieutenant-Colonel Yardley in their hands! You have stim-tabs in the airvan?"

"Of course, in the med kit."

"We're going to need them to stay awake tonight. We'd better have everybody take one while we talk."

March 4th 2850 GSC

MATOPO HILLS

Dave crouched behind a bush and adjusted his night vision visor. The coals of the fire lent a strange reddish cast to the scene through its sensors, even though the flames had long since died down. He turned his head to Corporal Hansen next to him, touched him on the shoulder and pointed to the nearest armored car, its turret moving slowly from side to side as the person on watch inside scanned the perimeter of the camp. Fortunately, their thermally-neutral battledress could not be picked up by its sensors.

Hansen nodded silently, tapping the grenades in pouches on his chest. No words were necessary – they'd gone through everything before leaving the cave. Dave was about to move away towards his own target when the vehicle's turret stopped moving. Its hatch swung open and clanged against the stop. A drowsy voice called from among the sleeping figures around the embers, "Shut up, dammit!"

The figure emerging through the hatch muttered "Ah, blow it out your butt!" It was a woman's voice, Dave noted. She swung her legs over the side of the turret onto the hull, jumped down to the ground, then headed for the tree behind which Dave and the Corporal were crouching. They edged cautiously backwards, taking cover behind a bush only a few meters away as she came around the tree trunk, undoing her belt. She dropped her trousers and underwear and squatted behind the tree.

Dave made an instant decision, drawing his knife as he crept to his left. The faint sound of his movements was covered by the prolonged splashing of liquid as the woman relieved herself. He came up behind her and struck her head once, hard, with the hilt of the knife. She made a soft grunting sound as she collapsed backwards. Dave took her weight against his body, holding her with one arm around her while he sheathed his knife. The Corporal hurried to help him. Together they lifted her off the ground and carried her further into the bush, silently blessing the bulk of the armored car that helped to hide them from the other enemy soldiers.

About twenty meters from the tree they lowered her to the ground behind a bush. Dave drew his knife again and thrust it upward between her ribs, piercing her heart, holding his other hand over her nose and mouth as he did so. She jerked, but made no sound. He withdrew the knife carefully, wiped it on her uniform shirt and returned it to its sheath, then motioned the Corporal nearer.

"That was an unexpected bit of luck," he breathed into Hansen's ear. "Take her place in the turret, make sure the plasma cannon's loaded, and stand by. Your first target is the other armored car on the far side of the fire. Once you've taken it out, watch the other vehicles to see if anyone's inside. If you see anyone, or if any of them try to move, blast them."

"What about Sergeant Kane, Sir? Won't I hit him if I fire at the armored car?"

"I'll call Kane to take your place, and let you deal with his target. Having a plasma cannon on our side is worth changing the plan. Be prepared to go into action at once if anything goes wrong."

"OK, Sir."

They crept back to the tree, and watched until the slowly scanning turret of the other armored car was turned away from them. As soon as the Corporal was sure its sensors weren't pointed in his direction he moved silently to the nearer vehicle, hoisted himself up to the turret, and lowered his legs through the open hatch, pulling it down over his head as he dropped inside. In a matter of moments the turret resumed the same idly meandering search pattern as before, but Dave noted that the barrel of its plasma cannon now spent more time pointed at the other vehicles than towards the surrounding bush. Its motor made a soft whining sound as it trained from side to side.

He consulted the time display in the lower corner of his visor image. It was almost four in the morning – still just over an hour to go before their planned assault. He moved slowly and carefully back from the camp to where he was sure his voice wouldn't be heard, then activated his transmitter.

"Bolus to Five," he whispered. "Change of plan. Join me."

Instead of an answering voice, he heard a double click over the circuit. He nodded approvingly. He preferred to work with his own Charlie Company soldiers whenever possible, because he knew their ways and they knew his; but these borrowed troops were proving to be every bit as competent, and just as capable of adjusting their plans to fit changing circumstances at the drop of a hat. *Then again, after more than three years of hard fighting and heaven knows how many engagements, they should be,* he thought to himself.

He settled down, waiting for Sergeant Kane to make his way silently around the camp to join him.

~ ~ ~

Captain Amesha coughed, turning his head away from the others as he hawked up a dust-laden gobbet of phlegm, lifted his dust-mask and spat it violently into the rocks beside him. *Why the hell do they never issue us enough filters for these damned masks?,* he wondered resentfully as his nostrils wrinkled with the sudden onslaught of the stench of decaying rebel bodies, left unburied in the cave complex after the earlier assault. He hastily readjusted the mask. Its filter was already so clogged with rock dust that it no longer served much practical purpose, but at least it kept down the stink. Besides, regulations demanded it be worn. If his men had to suffer under such stupidity, he'd suffer with them. That was particularly important because most of his unit consisted of reluctant conscripts. They didn't want to be here, and showed it in the lack of enthusiasm and effort they put into their work. He had to set an example to motivate them to work harder and more effectively alongside his few career NCO's and soldiers.

One of the two men at the front of the rubble remover, guiding its laser cutters as they sliced and diced chunks of rock into pieces small enough to be dumped onto the conveyor and fed back to the discharge point, suddenly grabbed his partner's arm and pointed. The other looked, nodded, and stabbed a finger at the control panel. The rumble of the conveyor died away.

"What is it?" Amesha called.

"You said we were looking for a small metal safe set into the wall, right, Sir?"

"Yes. It was concealed behind a notice-board."

"This may be it, Sir." He pointed into the rubble in front of him. "Looks like it came down with the outer layer of the wall."

"Hold on, I'm coming."

The Captain climbed laboriously over chunks of rock and parts of the machine to reach them. As he approached they scrabbled in the rubble with their gloved hands, tossing aside chunks of rock and pieces of a flat panel that certainly looked as if it might once have been a notice-board. They straightened and turned towards him with a rectangular metal box in their hands. He grinned as he saw the electronic keypad on its door.

"Well done, boys! That looks promising. Let's get it open and see what's inside."

A pair of hydraulic jaws inserted into the door seam made short work of the box. It bent, bulged, then ripped open with a scream of tortured steel. Amesha reached inside and pulled out a stack of papers. On the bottom was a large brown plaspaper envelope, filled with documents from the feel of it. Its flap was glued shut. The front bore a label reading 'FOR VP AND GOVT IN EXILE – EVIDENCE #3'.

"This must be it," he said with great satisfaction, "but only that SS Colonel can say for sure. Stand fast, all of you, while I take it to him. Get some water and relax for a few minutes."

He took all the papers with him to be on the safe side as he turned and headed for the entrance, by now almost a hundred meters behind the diggers down the rock-strewn tunnel.

~ ~ ~

Dave's night vision visor provided enough detail for him to recognize the Captain as he emerged from the entrance to the former base. He stiffened as he saw the papers and envelope clutched in his hand. Had the enemy already found the safe?

The officer headed straight for the van to which he'd led the SS Colonel the previous evening. Dave made a swift decision and keyed his microphone. "This is Bolus," he whispered. "Forget the timetable. Stand by for immediate action." There were no responses, but he knew everyone would have heard him. Adrenaline would be surging through their systems just as it was through his, everyone preparing to fight for their lives. The only way this would work was if they killed most of the enemy before they had a chance to wake up, realize what was going on, and organize an effective defense.

Beside him Sergeant Kane brought up his carbine, settling its shortened stock against the upper panel of his body armor, aiming at the communications vehicle. From their vantage point they could see straight into its open door to where the operator on duty was slouched in a chair, feet up on the counter, reading something on an electronic pad. Dave tapped his arm lightly. "I'm going to get closer to that van," he whispered, indicating the Bactrian officer's destination. Kane nodded without speaking.

Amesha reached the Colonel's vehicle. Two bodyguards leaned against it on either side of the door. They looked at him without expression or greeting. "I've got something for the Colonel to see," he told them. "Wake him up, please."

"He's asleep. No-one disturbs the Colonel when he's asleep," one of them replied indifferently, still slouching against the vehicle.

"Stand to attention when you speak to an officer, damn you!" The man's mouth dropped open in astonishment, but he shambled to a semblance of attention as the Captain went on, "Wake the Colonel. *That's an order!* Give him my respects, and inform him that Captain Amesha has something to show him."

"I – er… OK. I mean yes, *Sir!*" The honorific popped out of his mouth as Amesha glared at him menacingly. He clearly didn't know how to respond to someone who exhibited none of the servility to which SS personnel were accustomed. He vanished into the trailer, closing the door behind him and leaving his colleague outside.

Dave grinned. He could almost bring himself to like this enemy Captain for the way he stood no nonsense, and was clearly disgusted by torture. It was a pity he had to die… but then, no-one on Laredo had invited him or his comrades to invade; and ever since the Bactrian Army had started killing Laredan soldiers who surrendered, the Resistance had stopped taking prisoners too.

After a few moments, during which Amesha tapped his boot impatiently on the ground, the trailer door opened again. The SS Colonel stood framed against the light inside. He'd taken the time to get into his uniform. Clearly the man thought he had to live up to some sort of image.

"What is it, Captain?"

"I think we've found it, Sir." He extended the papers in his hand, the envelope uppermost.

"Let me see!" The Colonel rapidly descended the three steps to ground level, eagerly reaching out to take the documents from the Captain. He read the label on the envelope and laughed aloud. "Splendid! You've done well, Captain. I'll see to it – "

He never completed his sentence. Dave lined his rifle and carefully touched off a single shot that struck the Colonel on the bridge of his nose. His head snapped back and he crumpled to the ground in a lifeless heap. Captain Amesha reacted instantly, dropping as he turned, hand streaking towards the holster on his right hip, but Dave followed his movements with his rifle and slammed two rounds into his upper body as he hit the ground. The Captain shouted aloud in agony, his weapon not yet drawn as Dave raised his sights slightly and fired a third shot into his head, then aimed at the two bodyguards. They were still fumbling with their slung rifles, expressions of panicked shock and utter disbelief on their faces. He couldn't help thinking cynically as he killed them, *I wouldn't trust you incompetent bastards to guard anything, let alone my life!*

The ambush team exploded into violent action at the first shot. Behind Dave the armored car's plasma cannon fired, a ground-shaking eructation that sounded more like a giant's *basso profundo* cough than an explosion. The other armored car on the far side of the embers erupted in a fireball, sending out a spray of fragmented armor plate and other components. The shattered remains of its turret were blown into the air, spinning over and over as they fell into the bush beyond the rest of the vehicles. Meanwhile, the other team members began pouring fire into their assigned targets.

Dave sprinted to the open door of the Colonel's van and fired four times into the figures inside, twice for each of the two remaining bodyguards as they struggled to get up. He found time to marvel at their stupidity for zipping themselves into sleeping-bags in a combat zone where ambush was always a possibility; but even as he did so he was spinning around towards the soldiers jumping to their feet around the fire, shooting as fast as he could aim and pull the trigger. He could hear more shots from the direction of the assault shuttle, and mentally crossed his fingers that Tamsin and her fellow pilot would be able to cope with its crew and the interrogators.

The canvas cover over the load bed of one of the transports was suddenly thrown back, revealing several figures clutching rifles as they began to jump over the tailgate. The turret of the captured armored car whined briefly as it traversed towards the new target, then its plasma cannon fired again, the bolt smashing the vehicle into a tumbling cartwheel across the ground, throwing the figures clear. Dave shifted his aim and silenced the screams of a wounded survivor with a well-placed shot. Out of the corner of his eye he was vaguely aware that first one, then another of the soldiers around the fire had made it into the bushes, seemingly unscathed.

Suddenly there were no more targets. He spun around, checking the camp site as he called, "Bolus to all, report in sequence, over."

One by one the others reported in. By actual count twenty-seven enemy soldiers were down, plus the interrogators and shuttle crew, plus the Colonel, the Captain and the four guards Dave had slain to open the action and the woman sentry further back in the bushes. He nodded in satisfaction. The two he'd seen running into the bushes had not been carrying weapons. They would pose no threat – in fact, they were probably still running.

"Corporal Hansen, can you drive that thing?" he called.

"Yessir!"

"Move it to where you've got a clear shot at the entrance to the base, then use your plasma cannon to demolish it completely. Aim as far inside as you can to bring down the roof, then work back towards the entrance. I want all those inside to stay there forever. They can keep our own dead company!"

"Remind me never to piss you off, Sir. You're too damn vindictive!"

Scattered laughter sounded from those who'd heard the Corporal's quip as he slid down into the driver's seat, engaged the drive unit and started the armored car moving forward. It rolled over some of the bodies around the fire, but he didn't let that stop him.

Dave's radio came to life. "Dave, this is Tamsin. We need you at the shuttle ASAP."

"Dave to Tamsin, on my way. Break. Sergeant Kane, take charge here. Make sure every enemy soldier is dead, then see if we've captured anything interesting in the vehicles."

As he ran towards the shuttle he heard the first cannon shot from the armored car. It was a curiously muffled blast, proving that Hansen had fired deep into the entrance tunnel rather than at the rock surrounding it. Six more shots followed, carefully spaced, showing that the Corporal was aiming each one and not firing blindly. A series of thunderous roars sounded from the entrance, and a choking cloud of rock dust erupted from it and rose into the air.

He skidded to a halt beside Tamsin where she waited at the shuttle's rear ramp. "What's up?"

"It's Lieutenant-Colonel Yardley. He's inside. He keeps asking me to kill him."

He climbed the rear ramp, stepping over the body of a black-clad figure that sprawled halfway down it. Three more of them lay motionless on the floor of the shuttle, leaking blood and other body fluids. "Did you get them all without trouble?" he asked her.

"Sure. They left the rear ramp down, so we had clear shots at them all without even going inside. Only one managed to get to his feet, and as you can see he didn't get far."

Dave sank to one knee next to the stretcher to which Yardley was strapped. The man's head had been shaved bald, presumably to accommodate the head cover the Bactrian Colonel had mentioned. His voice was hoarse, stumbling, his eyes wide and protruding, sweat beading his pale, lined, agonized face. "For God's sake kill me before they come back!" he whispered. "Don't let them take me again!"

"They won't, Sir. I'm Captain Carson, Charlie Company, Niven's Regiment. We didn't expect to find you here, but now that we've got you back we're not letting you go again. We've killed your torturers and that SS Colonel, as well as most every other Bactrian around here. You're safe now, Sir."

Tears sprang into the man's eyes. "Then – then please kill me anyway! I betrayed you all, dammit!"

Dave touched his shoulder gently. "You did better than anyone had a right to expect of you, Sir. Hell, even the Bactrians admitted you'd held out much longer than they expected! None of us have anything but admiration for you. What's more, we heard them talking about what they learned from you. We've already warned General Aldred, and as we speak he's arranging the evacuation of our bases. We'll be long gone by the time the enemy arrives."

"Oh, thank *God!*" The tears redoubled, and Yardley turned his head away as if ashamed of them. "I'm sorry, Captain... I – "

"No need to apologize, Sir. Can you stand?" As he spoke Dave was undoing the straps holding Yardley to his stretcher and helping him to sit up.

"I – I'm not sure. They've been keeping me doped since we left Banka to prevent me getting combative, because I kicked one of the interrogators in the balls as they marched me to the shuttle." Despite his weakness, he couldn't hold back a faint grin.

Tamsin burst into unladylike laughter as she knelt beside Dave. "Good one, Sir! I hope you hurt the bastard. I'm Sergeant Tamsin Gray. I'll help you stand, and if you need anything at all I'll get it for you."

"Did you search the dead Bactrians?" Dave asked her. "I want anything those interrogators had on them, and also their personal kit." He looked back at the Colonel. "Sir, you said they drugged you. Did they bring any of those drugs with them?"

"Yes, both the torture drug and the sedative. They're in that black briefcase." He nodded to where it lay on a folded-down seat against the side of the shuttle.

Dave retrieved it and looked inside. It contained booklets that looked like instruction manuals, several vials of clear liquid, a dozen unused hypodermic syringes with needles, and a cloth cap that was clearly intended to fit over the entire skull. It had straps to tighten it around the head, and was lined with rows of electrodes. Two long leads ran from it, fitted with intricate, complex connectors.

He closed the case and handed it to Tamsin. "Guard this carefully. We've got that SS Colonel on record describing how they use these drugs. Lieutenant-Colonel Yardley can tell us how they affected him, and we've got samples of the drugs themselves and the neurocranial network. General Aldred is sure to want to add everything to the evidence of Bactrian atrocities he's been collecting." He turned back to Yardley. "I'll leave you in Sergeant Gray's capable hands, Sir. I've got to sort out the enemy camp and decide what to do next."

He ran back towards the camp, cursing under his breath at what the SS interrogators had done to an already badly wounded man. Their ruthlessness was notorious, even towards their own Army when it came to alleged breaches of security.

"Look at this, Sir!" Sergeant Kane greeted him enthusiastically, dropping something into his palm. Dave peered closely at it. It was a flitterbug, three small pipes – barrels for the microdarts it fired – emerging below a vid lens in its 'head', its gossamer-thin synthetic wings folded against its plastic body.

"It's bigger than those I've seen before," he observed. "They had only two barrels."

"Yes, Sir. I think this is one of their new assault bugs, the ones that overwhelmed us. There are four cases of them in that transporter, crawling nanobugs as well as flitterbugs, along with consoles to program them. There's also a case of these, Sir." He held out a small box with a belt clip and red and green diodes on its top surface. "From what's written on the inside of the lid, I think they're some sort of identification module. If you're wearing one, those bugs will recognize you as a friend and not attack you."

"Well done, Sergeant! These are just what Mac and his tech specialists need. They can analyze them back at base and come up with countermeasures."

"But will they have base facilities any more, Sir? I mean, won't they be evacuating along with everyone else?"

"I'm sure they will, but Mac will come up with something. He always does. What else have you found?"

"The communications truck has listings of all their current channels, plus callsigns, authentications and crypto key settings for this month, Sir. Also, that SS Colonel you shot had a lot of files in his suitcase plus a couple of high-level military passes in his wallet."

"More fodder for Mac and his boys. We'll take everything like that back with us."

Kane frowned dubiously. "If you want it all, Sir, we're going to be hellish overloaded in those airvans."

"We've got ourselves an assault shuttle now. Tamsin can fly it; she's piloted a captured shuttle before. We'll leave our airvans somewhere the Bactrians are unlikely to find them – we can always come back for them with a couple more pilots – and go back in the shuttle. It has much greater cargo and passenger capacity than an airvan, and it's a hell of a lot faster, too. We'll take only a few hours to get home again."

The Sergeant grinned enthusiastically. "That works for me, Sir. I'll start everyone gathering booty to load up."

"Good. Rip out anything interesting from the comm truck while you're at it, particularly crypto gear. Search all the bodies and their kit, and confiscate weapons, ammunition, currency and so on – all the usual stuff. Lay out the bodies in rows next to the fire, including those from the shuttle and the sentry Corporal Hansen and I dealt with first. He'll take you to her body. I'm going to call base and request further instructions."

He set up the satellite antenna himself this time, since Tamsin was busy with Lieutenant-Colonel Yardley. He lined it up carefully, listened for the warbling tone of the carrier beam, and attached his comm unit.

"BOLUS to TANTO, over."

A brief pause, then, "TANTO to BOLUS, authenticate Echo Lima Alpha, over."

He entered the characters and read off the reply. "BOLUS to TANTO, authenticating Mike Quebec Kilo, over."

"TANTO to BOLUS, authenticated, go ahead, over."

"BOLUS to TANTO. I need to speak with Romeo Six actual, please. Over."

"TANTO to BOLUS, can you wait five to ten? Over."

"BOLUS to TANTO, understand five to ten. Standing by."

He waited impatiently, fuming at the delay while the operators summoned Brigadier-General Aldred to the communications center. At last he heard the familiar voice. "TANTO to BOLUS, this is Romeo Six actual, over."

"BOLUS to TANTO, thank you, Sir." He explained as briefly as possible what they'd done. "Request permission to return in the captured shuttle, Sir. We can move it to a safer place and camouflage it during daylight hours, then fly all the way back tonight. Our airvans can be left in a secure position under camouflage for later collection. Over."

"TANTO to BOLUS, well done! Very well done indeed! Yes, come back in the shuttle, but send one aircar back as well – we need all the transport we can get for evacuations. Conceal the other for collection later. Don't come back to base. We're already in the process of evacuating. Are you recording? Over."

"BOLUS to TANTO, yes, Sir, I'm recording. Over."

"TANTO to BOLUS. Here are a set of co-ordinates, all BASE plus seven. Proceed to that destination and announce yourselves on our usual approach channel as you get close." The General read off a set of figures, then repeated them. "You'll find others already there, and I'll have a medical team standing by for Lieutenant-Colonel Yardley. Over."

"BOLUS to TANTO, understood, over."

"TANTO to BOLUS, very well. Please convey my personal thanks and congratulations to your team. Romeo Six actual out."

As he folded up the satellite dish, Dave suddenly grinned. He'd just thought of another destructive task for Corporal Hansen and his new toy – and, for that matter, for Tamsin and the assault shuttle as well. When they'd finished, Tamsin could blast the armored car into scrap metal using the shuttle's plasma cannon. One way or another the Bactrians weren't going to get anything back from this patrol. It would be a small down payment on what they owed for their destruction of the base inside the mountain and the deaths of so many of its defenders.

March 5th 2850 GSC

LAGUNA PENINSULA

As the assault shuttle settled onto its undercarriage, Tamsin cut the reaction thrusters. Their flickering exhaust died away along with their stuttering roar, allowing the pre-dawn darkness to overwhelm the clearing once more. She retracted them into their housings and switched to the electric motors driving each wheel, following signals from the ground control utility vehicle as it led her out of the graveled clearing down a short road cut through the trees. It led to a roughly square opening in the cliff face ahead of them. Once inside the guide vehicle switched on its headlamps, showing a tunnel leading around a curve. The huge shuttle was a tight fit within its confines, but whoever had cut it had made allowances for such large vehicles and left just enough space for it to pass. The tunnel straightened and led through a double blackout curtain, drawn aside for their passage, into a huge natural cavern, its uneven walls rising out of sight above the glare of lights lining them. Several other vehicles were already inside. Soldiers were unloading boxes, crates and personal kit from them and stacking it along one wall.

Tamsin followed the signals of a man who jumped out of the ground control vehicle and directed her to park close against the opposite wall. As soon as he crossed his lighted wands, she cut the power and lowered the rear ramp. "We're here, people," she announced, turning to look back at the others sitting in pull-down seats along the bulkheads. Lieutenant-Colonel

Yardley lay on his stretcher, head propped up by pillows, while next to him a huge pile of captured equipment secured beneath cargo nets filled the central load area.

Dave released his harness and stood up, looking at Yardley. "Let's get you out first, Sir, then we'll start unloading all this stuff."

As they carried his stretcher down the ramp, four medics hurried to meet them. "Are you Lieutenant-Colonel Yardley, Sir?" the leader asked, looking down at the recumbent man.

"Yes, I am."

His face broke into a broad smile. "Welcome back from the dead, Sir! We thought you'd been killed in the early stages of the Bactrian assault on your base."

"I wish I had been," Yardley said fervently. "It would have saved everyone a whole lot of trouble, and me a whole lot of pain!"

"Now, now, Sir, none of that. Thanks to you holding out long enough to make sure Captain Carson overheard the enemy's plans, we've all been warned in time to get away before they assault our other bases. They'll find only empty caves and tunnels waiting for them."

"That's good to hear." Yardley looked at Dave. "Thanks again for bringing me to safety, Captain."

"All part of the service, Sir."

Dave saluted smartly as they carried him away, then grinned as he saw his father approaching. He hugged him, and they exchanged affectionate backslaps.

"You did real well, Dave. That was one hell of an operation!"

"Thanks, Dad. I couldn't have done it without everyone bringing their part." He gestured to the team behind him.

Jake grinned at them all. "I know that. Thank you, everyone, and well done."

Dave lowered his voice. "I need to talk to you privately. It's very urgent." He raised his voice as he turned to the others. "Please unload everything and stack it over there behind the shuttle – we'll figure out later where it'll be stored. I've got to brief Lieutenant-Colonel Carson about something, then I'll come back and help you."

He ran back up the ramp and emerged with a black suitcase. Jake led him in front of the shuttle where they wouldn't be overheard.

"What is it?"

"This suitcase belonged to that Security Service Colonel I killed. He had a lot of files in it. One of them refers to a big parade that's to be held in Banka on the last day of the month."

"Yes, we've already heard a little about it from Sergeant-Major Garnati in Caristo."

"Did he tell you who's coming and why it's being held?"

Jake frowned. "No, all he knew was that it was planned."

"Brace yourself. The Satrap's coming in person, and bringing the Crown Prince with him. He's going to officially terminate the Military Governorship of Laredo and install his son as the first civilian Governor."

Jake's jaw dropped as he stared at his son. "You're kidding me!"

"No, I'm not. You'll find the file in here, on the top of the pile. Read it for yourself."

Jake accepted the suitcase from him. "I've got to tell General Aldred about this at once! He's not the bastard who gave the order to invade Laredo – that was his father – but he's still the Head of State of our enemy. We've *got* to try to nail him!"

"That's what I figured – but can we? Do we still have enough effectives? Will we be able to reorganize so quickly after evacuating our remaining major bases like this? Oh, yes – while we're talking about bases, where did this one come from? I've never heard of any base on the Laguna Peninsula before."

"It's new. The cave system is natural, of course – it runs through the limestone cliffs along the seafront. It was discovered decades ago, but there were no minerals to be exploited and access was very difficult, so it was ignored. Two years ago General Aldred decided we needed a bolthole, a last-ditch place to retreat and reorganize that the enemy couldn't learn about by torturing those who knew our existing bases. He assigned some of our more seriously wounded people – those who had only one leg or one arm left, that sort of thing – to come here with laser cutters and excavation gear and open up vehicle access to the cave. They worked very slowly and carefully, making sure they concealed every trace of what they were doing. It was finished just a couple of months ago."

"Gotta hand it to him; the General's a fortune-teller or a prophet to have seen this coming."

"I don't know about a prophet, but he's got good instincts. We'll be evacuating our combatants here over the next few days by airvan. Most non-combatants and supplies will travel by ground convoy, but not come directly here – we don't want to leave tracks alerting the enemy to where we are. They'll go to intermediate destinations, where they'll leave their vehicles under cover and be flown here by airvan. We'll all laager up here while we figure out what to do next."

"And Niven's Regiment?"

"Most of us are already dispersed in the Caristo region, so we'll stay put, as will the families of those in other regiments who've found a safe haven in other areas. It'll be for the Council to decide where we all go next, and what we'll do. They're meeting tomorrow to discuss Marvin Ellis' arrival and what to do about it. Your news has given them a lot more to talk about!"

"I thought the General wanted you there for the meeting?"

"He does – I'll be heading back there tonight by airvan – but he sent me here first to help get this place up and running."

"Sounds good." Dave looked at his father soberly. "Without multiple secure bases, can we really go on? Is this the end for us?"

Jake sighed. "I don't know. I sure hope not."

"Me too! I always figured we'd go down fighting, not just fade away like… I don't know, like a rainstorm dying down as it moves off into the distance."

"You'd prefer thunder and lightning?"

"*Hell, yes!* If I've got to die, let it be facing the Bactrians with a heap of their bodies lying around me and a shout of defiance in my throat! Screw 'em all!"

~ ~ ~

TAPURIA: SECURITY SERVICE HEADQUARTERS

"I don't care how busy you were with other things! You were supposed to put your surveillance mission ahead of everything else!"

The agent whined, "But, Lieutenant, you don't understand! Major Moshira *ordered* me to buy the diamonds for him. I couldn't go against his orders – he'd have had me shot!"

Yazata rolled her eyes skyward. She was beginning to understand how the rebels had been able to glean so much information, and steal so many things, from under the very noses of the Security Service. She snapped into the handset, "I'll talk to Major Moshira about this. Meanwhile, submit your excuses to me in writing by not later than fifteen today. You haven't heard the last of this!"

"Yes, Ma'am." The man's voice was sulky, like a child who'd been caught doing something wrong.

As she replaced the handset a knock came at her office door. She looked up to find Major Moshira standing there, his face pale and drawn. She came to her feet, snapping to attention. "Yes, Sir?"

"Have you heard the news?"

"Er... what news, Sir?"

"Colonel Kujula and his team were killed yesterday."

"*What?*" In her shock she forgot to use the normal honorific, but in his agitation he didn't seem to notice.

"He was at the base we destroyed a few weeks ago. The combat engineer patrol he was visiting out there appears to have been wiped out by the rebels."

She recalled with a mental frisson of horror, *I asked to go with him! If he'd said yes, I'd be dead too!*

The Major straightened with a visible effort at self-discipline. "You're about to be summoned to the Military Governor's office. You're to tell him only that the Colonel ordered the engineers to open up the base to retrieve evidence we believed would be there, based on information provided by a prisoner. Don't speculate about anything else. Understood?"

"Er... no, Sir, I don't understand. He's the Military Governor, after all, and we're under his authority. Shouldn't I answer any questions he asks me?"

"*No!* I don't care what the regulations say about who's in charge. We're the Security Service, the *true* guardians of the Satrapy, and you'll do well to remember that!" His voice was snappish, vindictive. "Tell him only what he absolutely *has* to know, nothing else! Be sure I'll know at once if you disobey me, and you won't escape punishment. Understood?"

"Y – yes, Sir."

He turned on his heel and walked away down the corridor.

As she sank back into her seat, her desktop comm unit rang. She picked up the handset. "Lieutenant Yazata speaking."

"Lieutenant, this is Captain Dehghan, aide to Major-General Huvishka, the Military Governor. Your presence is required immediately at the Command Bunker. How soon can you get here?"

"I – ah… It'll take me fifteen to twenty minutes, Sir."

"I'll so advise the General." He hung up without waiting for her reply.

She realized two things as she raced her car towards the Military Governor's compound. First, her agent probably hadn't been joking about what Major Moshira might have done to him had he disobeyed his order to engage in black-market speculation on his behalf. *I wonder if he was using official funds to do that?*, she pondered. The second thing was that the Major must have an informant or some sort of monitoring device in the Military Governor's office – otherwise how could he have known about the imminent summons?

She began marshalling her thoughts. If the Colonel was dead, her temporary assignment to the Security Service was now subject to the whims of whoever took over from him as Commanding Officer of the SS mission on Laredo. That would probably be Major Moshira in the short term… and the Major had a wandering, lustful eye that had mentally undressed her on more than one occasion. If he were now to be in authority over her, she might be faced with a very difficult situation. On the other hand, if she asked the General for a transfer and the Major was listening to the conversation, he'd hear whatever she said to justify her request – which might land her in even worse trouble.

She mulled over the situation as she drove, and by the time she turned into the Military Compound parking area she'd reached a decision. She parked her car, then opened the secure equipment locker bolted to the chassis and took out a small flat black box. She blessed the late Colonel Kujula for trusting her with it as she switched it on, checking to ensure that the red diode indicator was illuminated, and dropped it into her pocket. If Major Moshira was angry with her for carrying it, she'd excuse herself by saying that the Colonel had ordered her to use it when meeting clandestinely with agents, as she had earlier that morning. In her shock at the news he'd brought, she'd forgotten to switch it off or remove it from her pocket.

The security desk at the entrance to the Command Bunker complex was expecting her. A guard escorted her down three levels to a corridor lined with offices, and delivered her to Captain Dehgahn in the anteroom to the Military Governor's suite. He ran his eyes up and down her uniform as he got to his feet, and nodded in approval.

"You'll do. The General likes to see smartness in his officers."

He knocked at an inner door. "Lieutenant Yazata is here, Sir."

"Well, don't just stand there, man – bring her in!" The voice sounded angry.

She followed the Captain into the office. While he closed the door, she crossed the carpet to stand at attention in front of the desk. "Lieutenant Yazata reports to General Huvishka as ordered, Sir!" Even as she spoke, she felt the electronic device in her pocket start to vibrate.

The General was a tall, spare man. He leaned back in his chair and looked at her penetratingly, his cold gray eyes seeming to bore right through her. "What can you tell me about Colonel Kujula, Lieutenant? You worked for him, didn't you?"

"Yes, Sir, I was his aide until a couple of days ago; but before I say more, there's something I must show you." She removed the jamming device from her pocket and laid it on the desk. "Have you seen one of these before, Sir?"

He went very still. "Yes, I have – I used one in a couple of previous assignments back on Bactria. That's a jammer to block eavesdropping devices, isn't it?"

"Yes, Sir."

"And from the way it's vibrating gently against my desk, it's clearly found something to jam here, right?"

"Yes, Sir." She quickly explained about Major Moshira's warning. Turning to Captain Dehgahn, she asked, "Sir, how long was it after the decision to call me in that you actually made the call?"

"Not more than ten minutes."

Major-General Huvishka growled, "Yet Major Moshira knew about it before the call was made. He *must* have been monitoring our conversation in here! What the *hell* is the SS playing at, to treat me as if I were the enemy?"

"Sir, with respect, as far as I can tell they think you *are* an enemy – or at least a rival," she said flatly. "From comments I've overheard, they seem to regard the Army as competing with them for the role of 'Guardians of the Satrapy', as they call it. As an Army officer on assignment there I've often been treated with disdain and distrust, even by their enlisted personnel. If they had enough SS people here to staff their office exclusively with them, I think they'd be a lot happier."

"Thank you for alerting me to this, Lieutenant. That, in itself, has justified bringing you here today. Now, to get back to my question, what can you tell me about Colonel Kujula? He's just got a reinforced platoon of my combat engineers killed – or so we assume – and I want to know why they died. They were sent out on his orders."

"Sir, he told me that a prisoner we'd taken at that base a few weeks before had proved to be a senior rebel officer. He'd been interrogated, and provided information. All the Colonel told me was that there was something hidden in the base that we had to recover. He had me contact our regional garrison in his name, and order a patrol of combat engineers to be sent to the base. They were to dig through the rubble left after its destruction to see whether they could find... whatever it was. He said he was going to fly out there to join them in an assault shuttle. I asked to accompany him, because I've never been in the field before, but he refused. That was when he reassigned me to handle his agents in and around Tapuria, so I don't know any more, Sir."

"It's a good thing he didn't allow you to go with him, or you'd also be dead! You didn't receive any report or signal from him to suggest that they might have found anything?"

"No, Sir. Did they find anything on his body?"

"They haven't found it yet, and they may never do so. The patrol appears to have camped close to the entrance to the base, at the foot of a steep hillside. They made routine calls at twenty, at midnight, and at four yesterday morning – then they never called again. By noon they'd missed two routine calls and the regional garrison was getting worried. They sent a drone to investigate, but all it found was a massive heap of rock at the foot of the hill. They then sent an infantry company out there in assault shuttles. It reported that the mid-section of the hillside, above the entrance to the base, had been undermined by what looked like multiple plasma cannon shots. That brought down hundreds of thousands of tons of rock and soil from the cliffs above. It completely covered the place where the patrol had reported it was camped. The landslide's up to twenty meters deep there."

"And no-one knows what's underneath it, Sir?"

Huvishka made a sour face. "We presume the patrol's vehicles and the Colonel's assault shuttle are in there somewhere, along with all their bodies; but thanks to a panicky sentry yesterday afternoon, we can only guess. He saw two figures emerge from the bushes and fired on them at once without waiting to identify them. They proved to have been members of the combat engineer patrol. They must have escaped whatever happened to it, but since he killed both of them we can't ask them what it was. He'll be court-martialed and executed, of course, but that won't bring them back. The only other evidence is the wreckage of one of our armored cars about a hundred meters from the landslide. It had been destroyed by a plasma cannon bolt."

"Are there no more engineers to dig away the landslide and locate the vehicles and bodies, Sir?"

"Not in that area, and I don't have enough of them to assign another platoon to the job. I only have one battalion of combat engineers, and they're split up into independent platoons and spread all across the continent to support my infantry units. I've asked repeatedly for more engineers from Bactria, but every time I do they turn me down because of cost – infantry are a lot cheaper to train, equip and support in the field. Anyway, never mind that now. Lieutenant, thank you very much for revealing to me the extent of my problems with the SS. To prevent reprisals against you, I'm going to transfer you immediately to my staff. For now you'll assist Captain Dehgahn with his duties as my aide. He has a lot of extra work at present, what with the upcoming parade for the Satrap and our impending handover to a civilian Administration, so he'll be glad of your help."

The Captain grinned. "That's an understatement, Sir! Thank you for thinking of me."

"Thank you, Sir." She hesitated a moment. "May I make a suggestion, please, Sir?"

"Go ahead."

She explained her agent's comments about buying diamonds for Major Moshira. "Sir, if his account can be proved – particularly if he gives you the diamonds, and the money the Major gave him to pay for them can be traced back to SS funds – then that might give you grounds to take action against the local SS office."

"A very good point. Are you prepared to go back to the SS this afternoon? I can send Captain Dehgahn with you if you wish."

"I'll be glad to have him, Sir, in case the Major decides I've been disloyal to him."

"Very well. I want you to get your agent's written report as scheduled. When you've done that, place him under arrest and bring him here for interrogation by my own people, not the SS. We'll see what he has to say."

"Yes, Sir."

"Captain, please escort Lieutenant Yazata back to the SS offices and help her in any way necessary. Take some of my MP's with you to provide assistance as required. If you run into anything you can't handle, call me at once."

"Yes, Sir."

"All right. On your way, both of you."

March 6th 2850 GSC

RESISTANCE HEADQUARTERS

Jake was eating breakfast when the Council's summons reached him. He hastily crammed his mouth full of food, dumped the rest unceremoniously in the trash bin, and hurried down the tunnel to the meeting room.

"Sorry to have kept you, Sir," he apologized to General Aldred as he entered, brushing crumbs from his utility coverall. The General was sitting alone at the roughly-cobbled-together table, drinking coffee.

"No problem. The Council's still assembling." Aldred rubbed his tired eyes. "I was up until the small hours after the aircar brought you back, reading your progress report on the activation of Laguna Base and your son's after-action report on the Matopo Hills affair. That was one hell of a mission!"

"It sure was, Sir." Jake's pride in his son was obvious in his voice.

The other members of the Council trickled in over the next five minutes. As soon as all seven were present, Gloria Aldred called the meeting to order. She looked around, her prematurely gray hair framing a tired, careworn but still determined face.

"We've done everything in our power for over three years to collect evidence of Bactrian atrocities. We're currently assembling it all, including some items that were dispersed to different locations for safekeeping. We almost lost some of the most important evidence at the Matopo Hills, but fortunately that's been recovered, along with intelligence that's going to have a dramatic impact on our future. We should have all the evidence, and our two bearer bank keys, at our new Laguna Peninsula base by tomorrow. There we'll catalog it, assemble it into a package, and duplicate as much as possible for safekeeping in case anything goes wrong.

"Mr. Ellis has arranged for a spaceship to be here at the end of the month to collect him. However, intelligence obtained from a Security Service colonel reveals that at the same time the Satrap of Bactria and his son, the Crown Prince, will be visiting Laredo. During their visit all space traffic will be restricted, and no boarding or disembarking will be allowed. Mr. Ellis will be stuck planetside until the Satrap leaves. If we try to kill the Satrap and his son, even if we fail, the result will be chaos and disorder. The Bactrians will be frantic to find whoever's responsible, and they certainly won't permit any spaceship to leave until they've searched every nook and cranny. Therefore, if we want to attack the Satrap, we have to first find a way to get Mr. Ellis and our evidence aboard his ship, then send it on its way. That's what we'll have to decide over the next couple of days. There's also a major military consideration looming over us. I'll ask my husband to address that. Bill?"

"Thank you, Gloria." The General looked around the table as he spoke. "The single most important reason we've pursued low-intensity operations for as long as we have has been to buy time to get this evidence to the United Planets. If it weren't for that I'd have conducted higher-intensity operations, albeit at the cost of even higher casualties than we've already taken. Let's face it, we can't get off-planet and we can't win militarily. Whether we die sooner by inflicting greater damage, or live longer by inflicting less, still leads to the same outcome for all of us in the end."

Another Councilor shook her head. "I can't help thinking that it may all have been in vain anyway." Her voice was sad, almost despairing. "The United Planets isn't renowned for solving problems – it's more a gathering-place for politicians to see and be seen. The best we could hope for is a peacekeeping mission, and with more than four-fifths of our planetary population already dead that would be pointless. They probably won't bother. As for sanctions against Bactria, even if they're imposed they won't come in time to help us. In the end, who's to say our long fight has been worth anything at all? Haven't we merely delayed the inevitable?"

Gloria Aldred replied, "We haven't surrendered, Maria, and we never will. That counts for a lot in my book. By getting this evidence out we'll at least let people know the truth about what happened here. We owe that to all our soldiers who died for us, and the slaughtered population of Banka, and all who've died as slave laborers. They deserve to be remembered."

"But will Bactria ever be punished?" Maria asked.

General Aldred nodded vigorously. "Ever heard the old saying 'What goes around, comes around'? I'm a student of history. Almost every time one nation has mercilessly crushed another, sooner or later they've been crushed in their turn. We won't be around to see it, but I've no doubt Bactria will pay a heavy price for what it's done to us. It's the 'Golden Rule' applied to nations instead of individuals. What they've done to us, someone else will one day do to them."

He waited for a further response, but none came. He continued, "To get back to our present situation, as you know, our remaining major bases are now known to the enemy. We'll finish evacuating them by tomorrow morning – in fact, this Council will be among the last to leave. We're going to booby-trap them, of course, in order to kill as many Bactrians as possible when they attack them. However, we need to decide whether it's feasible for us to continue to fight when most of our bases are gone. Personally, I don't think it is, particularly because with only one base left to us, it can't be long before it's also discovered by the enemy.

"There's another thing. If we want to attack the Satrap, success will depend on being able to overwhelm local defenses. That'll take every able-bodied soldier we've got. Furthermore, the enemy will throw everything he's got into trying to rescue the Satrap or avenge his death, so our chances of escape will be slim to none. If we attack him, it'll be our swan song – a last stand. I'm not opposed to that if the Council decides it's worth the cost in order to kill him. However, any attempt to send our evidence and Mr. Ellis out of the system will have to precede or coincide with our attack, because afterwards there won't be enough of us left to do anything about it."

There was a long silence as the Councilors digested his words. Eventually Jake raised his hand. "Sir, here's a thought. If we plan to attack the Satrap, wouldn't it be best to make the Bactrians think we're a spent force – that we've shot our bolt and no longer pose a real threat? If so, I suggest we don't booby-trap our bases after evacuating them. Let the Bactrians walk right into them and suffer no casualties. We've booby-trapped things so often before that they'll come in all worried about what's waiting for them, only to encounter a huge anti-climax. I reckon they'll think we either didn't have the stomach for it any longer, or perhaps had run out of the explosives and other things we needed to make the booby-traps. I hope that'll help to make them more complacent about the Satrap's security."

"That's not a bad idea at all," General Aldred said thoughtfully. "I agree that making the enemy complacent will probably work to our advantage."

Maria stirred in her seat. "I agree that it's the Council's decision, but shouldn't our troops also have a say? I'm sure most of them will agree without hesitation – after all, as you've reminded us, General, we've known for some time that there can only be one end to our resistance. However, perhaps one in ten of our soldiers still have wives and children, or parents, or siblings. They shouldn't be asked to abandon them to the whims of fate. In fact, I suggest we offer such people the opportunity to retire from military service, to try to reintegrate into civilian life. Most of them have long since moved their families to quieter regions. The Bactrians have so far left farmers and ranchers alone, because they need the food they produce. We could give each family part of our accumulated funds in Bactrian bezants, and help them establish farms or ranches or take over those left empty by others who've died in the fighting. Let them go with our blessings. Those who explicitly volunteer for what they know will probably be a one-way mission can carry out the attack."

Gloria nodded. "I like that idea. I'll second it."

"Thirded," another council member called.

"Any objections?" Gloria waited, but no-one else spoke. "Passed by unanimous consent. If we approve the attack – which I suspect we will - we'll look into how best to implement that measure as well. Thank you, Maria." She transferred her gaze to her husband. "What else do we need to discuss in order to make a decision on whether to attack the Satrap or not?"

"There are several factors. I'll lay them out for you, and ask you to think about them while we evacuate to our Laguna Peninsula base and I discuss the option in general terms with our soldiers. If we don't get enough volunteers for a one-way mission, there's no point in approving it, is there?" There were murmurs of agreement around the table. "I think it'll take several days to come to a decision, based on all the consultation that has to be done and the simultaneous movement of our people from widely scattered bases to the new one."

He turned to Jake. "While we're doing that, I've got a special mission for your regiment, Lieutenant-Colonel Carson. I need you to reconnoiter the garrison at Caristo. See whether you can steal fuel cartridges for our shuttles' micro-reactors and reaction mass for their thrusters. If we can use them against the Satrap, they'll be invaluable; and even if we don't, having them available in case of need will also be very worthwhile."

"Sure, Sir. I'll need someone who knows shuttles to help us decide what to take."

"All right. Take your son and Sergeant Gray back to Caristo with you. They can enjoy a bit more time together, and she can tell you more about what we need."

"Will do, Sir. I'll have them meet me there. We'll try to be back at the Laguna Peninsula base in four days, to be available by the time you make your decision."

"Fair enough." He held out his hand. "Good luck."

March 7th 2850 GSC

CARISTO GARRISON

"Freeze!"

Dave's whispered warning stopped Tamsin in her tracks. She forced herself to remain motionless, ignoring the tiny midges that crawled over her face and body to drink her perspiration, making her skin itch, getting into the corners of her eyes and making her blink. From behind them she heard the faint whisper of a hoversat's rotors approaching. It passed low overhead, its sensor turret turning lazily as it scanned its surroundings. The hum of its electric motor died away as it moved on down the hillside, disappearing into the gloom of the night.

"OK, you can go on now."

"I don't see how it missed us. It was so close I could almost have touched it!"

He chuckled. "Doesn't matter. Sergeant Dixon's a wizard at electronic warfare. He tapped into the watch console in the guardroom months ago. It controls the perimeter hoversat. When needed, he can disable its sensor turret so that it moves and looks normal, but doesn't pick up anything. He did that tonight, but you never know for sure that it's worked until you run into it and it doesn't react to your presence. Clearly, his patch is working fine. He also replaced its feed with one we recorded earlier, so the guards on duty are seeing it moving over empty terrain with nothing to report. When we finish, he'll restore the circuit."

She chuckled delightedly. *"Damn, he's good if he can do all that!"*

"He's the best I've ever seen – but then, he's had plenty of practice, like all our EW techs. That's one way we've stayed alive so long, by deceiving Bactrian drones big and small." He nudged her elbow and pointed to a bush ahead and to the right. "We've excavated a hollow beneath that bush. There's room for both of us to lie there under cover where we can't be seen."

They wriggled their way beneath the low encroaching branches, and settled down with mutual sighs of relief. She took binoculars from her pouch. As she powered them up and focused them, he extracted an electronic clipboard and prepared to make notes.

"All right," she began, peering intently through the image-stabilized lenses at the brightly-lit hangar inside the perimeter fence, several hundred meters ahead of and below their position. "They're pulling a late shift – must be trying to get the overhaul finished as quickly as possible. Let's see... Looks like three shuttles are already done. They've been washed, which wouldn't have happened if they were still waiting for maintenance. The last one has all its hatches and access panels open. I can see through the rear door that the inside floor panels are raised as well, so they're even servicing the reactor and generator. This isn't just routine maintenance, it's a full-scale overhaul. If they're doing that to all four shuttles, they'll be as good as new by the time they finish."

"I take it we haven't done the same for our two birds?"

"You must be kidding! We don't have qualified mechanics for a start – we learned what we needed for basic maintenance from the on-board documentation, but that's designed for the flight crew, not for technicians. It isn't comprehensive enough for full maintenance. Also, we don't have access to a full toolkit or spare parts. I wish we did!" She sighed. "Ours run rough and they're long overdue for overhaul, but that's not about to happen. At least the SS shuttle we captured in the Matopo Hills is in great shape."

"So it wouldn't help us to steal some tools and spares from the maintenance people?"

"Not really. We'll just take fuel cartridges and reaction mass. It would be great if we could steal some missiles and plasma cannon magazines, too. We have no missiles left at all, and only five magazines."

"Those missiles are big heavy things. There's no way we could carry them out by hand and get them through the perimeter fence."

"You're right. It's a pity we can't just fly in with our shuttles and load them right here," she said wistfully.

Dave laughed aloud, but then suddenly fell silent. After a moment he said, "D'you mean that?"

"No, of course not! I was only joking."

"I'm not. What if we *could* do that?"

She rolled over to look at him, eyes wide. "You can't be serious!"

"Think about it. The platoon from Caristo will take two shuttles to the Satrap's parade, right?"

"I presume so – one platoon's normally divided between two birds."

"OK. Their best soldiers – not that that's saying much! – are being drilled until they drop to get them ready for the parade, while the others do the donkey work of cleaning equipment and getting it into a state fit for inspection. When the good ones head for Banka, what will be left here are the dregs. They'll be exhausted and probably rebellious as hell after all this hard work. As soon as their Captain leaves for the parade most of them are going to get blind stinking drunk. What if we hit them that night and steal everything we can use, including their two newly-serviced shuttles?"

Her jaw dropped as she stared at him. "I... it would... you really *are* serious!"

"I sure am. We know this place backwards. I could walk through that garrison blindfolded and point out everything important. Besides, their new boss will be leading the parade contingent, leaving Sergeant-Major Garnati in command in his absence. We know him, and we know his weaknesses. I think we could take care of the remaining platoon without too much trouble."

"But – but if you could do that now, why haven't you done it long ago?"

"We've been under orders not to make waves out here. This is a secure base area for us. We don't bother them, they don't bother us – it's an unwritten understanding. However, if it helps us nail the Satrap I guess that won't apply any longer."

"Uh-huh." Her mind raced. "One of our shuttles is completely out of fuel for its reactor. The other still has one cartridge. If we steal a fuel cartridge from here before we leave, plus a few hundred liters of reaction mass, that'll be enough to bring our two shuttles here to fill their tanks and load them with weapons. If we steal two newly-overhauled shuttles as well, we'll have four of them – five, with the SS shuttle. That'll make General Aldred *very* happy!"

"Do we have enough pilots to handle that many?"

"Oh, sure. There are half a dozen of us who've flown our captured shuttles in combat. We'll have more trouble finding Weapons System Operators. We cross-trained heavy weapons operators for that job, but there are only a few left out of those with shuttle training. All the rest have been killed on operations."

"OK." Dave thought for a moment. "Let's finish our observations, then go talk to Dad and plan an attack on the garrison, in case the General gives us the go-ahead."

~ ~ ~

They didn't get back to the ranch outside town where they were staying until after midnight. They found Jake waiting for them in the kitchen with a late supper ready for them.

"Rissa slow-roasted two sassaby haunches all day, and we had one for supper," he informed them, rubbing his belly while rolling his eyes ecstatically. "I managed to save two plates for you, although it took some mighty strong threats and a glimpse of my knife to keep off the ravening hordes. I hope you're duly grateful."

Tamsin hugged him. "Thanks, Almost-Dad-in-law!"

He blinked at her. "Say that again?"

"Well, you were going to be my father-in-law until the Bactrians interfered, weren't you?"

He sighed. "I guess so. You two are as good as married anyway – since you met each other, neither of you has looked twice at anyone else – so I may as well make the most of my unofficial status! Anyway, eat up, then tell me what you found."

Pausing occasionally to consult Dave's notes or examine an image taken through Tamsin's electronic binoculars, they provided exhaustive details of the activity around the garrison's shuttles and the cornucopia of spares, supplies and weapons that the visiting maintenance team had brought with them. Dave confirmed that they'd learned enough to be able to mount a quick in-and-out theft mission the following night, then went on to outline his idea about raiding the garrison as soon as one platoon had departed for the Satrap's parade.

Jake rubbed his chin thoughtfully. "That's an almost indecently good idea," he said slowly. "We've always kept a low profile out here, but if we're going to mount a major operation against the Satrap our cover will be blown anyway, so why not make a virtue out of necessity? In fact…"

He fell silent, eyes were far away in thought. When Dave tried to ask him what was on his mind he held up his hand, palm outward. At last he looked at them. "How's this for a plan? There are half a dozen outlying garrisons like Caristo, each with four shuttles. We've used several of them as base areas for our people to lay low between operations. I daresay each garrison will do the same as Caristo – send half their people and half their shuttles to this parade. What if we hit all of them that same night, kill everyone still there, and steal their remaining shuttles and all the weapons we can hang on them?"

Dave and Tamsin looked at him in open-mouthed amazement. "That would be a hell of an achievement, but do we have forces near enough to all of them?" his son asked.

"We have people close to four of them, including Caristo. We might be able to move other troops to deal with the remaining two."

"Do we know them all as well as you know this garrison?" Tamsin asked. "If not, it'll take a lot of hard work in a hurry to gather enough intelligence to be ready in time."

"Good point. We might have to restrict ourselves to those we know well. Even so, if we hit three or four of them that'll get us six to eight more shuttles plus their heavy weapons. If we use them to attack the Satrap's parade, they'll give us a much better chance to kill him and the Crown Prince. It'll still be a one-way mission, but success will be much more likely."

"What about pilots and Weapons Systems Operators?" Dave asked. "Do we have enough to handle that many shuttles?"

Tamsin nodded confidently. "Apart from those already trained, we have a few people who used to fly cargo shuttles and cutters for the old

Orbital Authority. An assault shuttle's not that different. They're all flown by computer, of course; we just tell the computer what to do. I reckon we could bring the cutter and cargo shuttle pilots up to speed in a week of intensive classroom work plus a dozen hours of stick time in our new assault shuttle. As for more WSO's, any qualified heavy weapons specialist can learn to operate the shuttles' systems in about the same length of time."

Jake rose to his feet. "I'm glad to hear it. You get some sleep. I'm going to think about this some more, and call the General first thing in the morning. If he likes the idea as much as I do, there'll be a lot more work for us before the big attack."

March 8th 2850 GSC

TAPURIA: MILITARY GOVERNOR'S COMPOUND

"What the *hell* are they playing at?" Major-General Huvishka's voice was simultaneously angry, incredulous and frustrated as he looked down from the glassed-in viewing gallery at the continental map displayed on the Operations Table. It still showed unit symbols and their directions of movement during that morning's operations. "Not a soul at any of the three bases, and not a single booby-trap set! They've just vanished as if they never existed!"

"This clearly demonstrates that our intelligence evaluations were correct, Sir," Captain Zargham said stiffly. Her black Security Service uniform stood out among the other officers wearing Army brown. "We've been saying for some time that the terrorists' numbers have dwindled to such an extent that they're no longer capable of posing a major threat to us. This proves it. It also shows the Satrap's wisdom in deciding that now is the time to replace the Military Governorship by a civilian administration, since the threat of armed conflict is almost at an end."

The General glared at her. "And what do you suggest killed your late superior, Colonel Kujula, and his SS guards and interrogators, and a reinforced platoon of my combat engineers? Rabid mice, perhaps?"

"No, Sir," she replied resentfully. "That was probably done by survivors of the destruction of the terrorists' Matopo Hills base. It must have taken at least a platoon-sized unit of the enemy to defeat a reinforced platoon of our combat engineers. There's no way a unit of that size could have made its way to the Matopo Hills from another sector without being detected. Our intelligence is too good and our sensor network too tightly woven."

"I seem to recall Major Moshira making a similar claim prior to our assault on the Matopo Hills," Captain Dehgahn pointed out. "However, according to the intelligence he himself certified as correct, we expected to find over three hundred rebels there. When we counted the bodies, there were less than two hundred and fifty. What happened to the others?"

"That's precisely my point, *Captain,*" she said icily. She clearly didn't feel that she had to show respect to Army officers of equal rank to hers. "Those fifty-odd 'missing' rebels are obviously the ones who attacked our combat engineers and Colonel Kujula. We don't know where they may have been hiding. I suggest they probably used another cave in the same area, one that the Army assault force failed to find. If they never left the area, of course our sensor network couldn't have detected their passage, because there *was* no passage. They came out after the raiding force had departed, and were busy salvaging what they could after its inadequate attempts to demolish the base. They may even have been trying to find the same evidence Colonel Kujula went there to collect. As it happens, they were sufficiently strong to overwhelm the engineer unit he sent. His mistake was not in sending them, nor in going there himself, but in trusting the raiding force's demonstrably false claim that all enemy units in the area had been eliminated."

"And where did the rebels go after that?" General Huvishka demanded. "Your sensor network still hasn't shown any indication of fifty-odd people moving out of the area."

"No, Sir; but I doubt that they all survived. Combat engineers are also soldiers. I presume at least half the rebels, if not more, were killed in the fighting. Their bodies must be beneath the heap of rock and soil where the base used to be. The terrorist survivors buried all the evidence of their presence under a landslide, including their own dead, then made their escape in small groups on foot or in single vehicles, both of which are much harder to detect than large groups."

"I suppose that's feasible," he admitted reluctantly. "Unfortunately, it's also speculation – and it doesn't clarify why we've found no rebels in the other three bases you identified."

"No, Sir. We'll have to capture more rebels and interrogate them to find out what happened there."

"And since they show a distinct aversion to being taken prisoner, I daresay that will take some time, eh?"

"Ah… yes, Sir."

"Very well, Captain Zargham. Thank you for giving us the benefit of your insight. You may go."

"Thank you, Sir." She hesitated. "May I ask whether the inquiry into the allegations against Major Moshira has vindicated him yet?"

"They aren't allegations, Captain – they're formal charges. That's why he's still confined to his quarters. I believe there's more than enough evidence to convict him of insubordination, blatant disrespect for the office of the Military Governor, breach of trust, corruption, misuse of official funds and black-marketeering." He held up a hand to forestall her protest. "I'm well aware that an Army court-martial can't try the case of an SS officer. However, I've sent details of the matter to Bactria and requested the empanelment of a fully-fledged inquiry into the conduct and operations of the entire SS operation here on Laredo. We'll see what the Satrap has to say about that. It'll be his decision as to when and where Major Moshira's case is heard, and by whom. Meanwhile, until another senior SS officer can be sent from Bactria to take over the local office, you'll continue as its caretaker Commanding Officer."

"Yes, Sir." She snapped to attention, half-bowed formally, turned and left the gallery.

The General paced back and forth across the viewing gallery, occasionally glancing down at the Operations Table and the staff who bustled around it. At last he turned to his aides. "Three battalions, over a hundred assault shuttles, and an entire morning for us to watch it here – all wasted! We accomplished nothing!"

Captain Dehgahn shrugged. "Sir, we acted on the information available to us, and this time we came up empty-handed. All we know for sure is that the rebels are no longer in the bases we've just seized. They may have left as soon as they learned we'd captured one of their senior officers at their Matopo Hills base. They've done that sort of thing before, after all. However, since we don't know when – or even if – they found out he'd been taken alive, we can't pin down their decision process."

"You don't think they learned anything from Colonel Kujula, or something they might have captured aboard his shuttle?"

Dehgahn frowned. "Sir, he'd have been a complete and utter imbecile if he took classified materials about unrelated operations into the field! I can't believe that an officer of his seniority would have made so elementary a mistake."

"Might they have tortured the information out of him? He was SS, after all, and you know how the rebels hate them."

"Yes, Sir, but they've never used torture. Frankly, I've often wondered why not, since the SS uses it against them. They've limited themselves to killing everyone who fell into their hands, and even that was in response to us doing the same to them first."

"Yes, that was one of my predecessor's most stupid and ill-advised decisions. If he'd offered the rebels honorable terms, perhaps with some concessions to salve their pride, we might have ended this war long ago and saved thousands of lives, ours and theirs. I wish I could have changed it, but when the rebels assassinated Major-General Strato last year, they stated explicitly it was in retaliation for that policy and his reprisals against the civilian population. When the Satrap appointed me to succeed him he told me not to change those policies, because if we did so it might be taken as a sign of weakness or lack of resolution; so we're stuck with them." Huvishka sighed as he turned to his junior aide. "What do you think of this morning's fiasco, Lieutenant Yazata?"

She hesitated, then thought, *Why not be direct? What have I got to lose?*

"Sir, I believe it's possible the SS are underestimating the rebels. Colonel Kujula was a prime example of their mindset. He was an arrogant man, secure in his vision of himself as a puppet-master manipulating everyone around him. He was so busy analyzing other people, judging them, trying to figure out ways to use or block or influence them, that he allowed that perspective to color his official bulletins. He didn't appear to examine his own motives or actions in any detail. That's a subjective impression, of course, but I worked with him for several weeks. I think it's valid. I think the same can be said of Major Moshira, and perhaps of

Captain Zargham as well, although I don't know her personally. I think the rebels may be stronger than any of them would care to admit. Colonel Kujula's death and the destruction of the engineer patrol may be indicators of that.

"However, what we *didn't* find this morning is also an important indicator. There were no records, no weapons or ammunition, no vehicles, no stores or supplies. That might indicate they had sufficient warning to move everything to another place; but we have no intelligence about any rebel base large enough to hold the contents of three others. To build such a big base would have taken a long time, but we've seen no signs of construction or excavation; so if it exists, it must be in a remote area where it was built under conditions of extreme secrecy. Lieutenant-Colonel Yardley didn't tell us of such a base, but if it exists he must surely have been aware of it."

She threw up her hands in frustration. "Then there's the fact that no traffic was detected moving away from the three bases over the days prior to our assault. We were keeping them under drone surveillance all day and night. Admittedly there was cloud cover and some rain, but we should surely have picked up at least *some* indication of an evacuation. Since we didn't, that means either the SS's sensor network and the Army's drones are less effective than we think; or the rebels have some way of misleading or jamming them; or perhaps there wasn't an evacuation at all. Perhaps the bases really were abandoned some time ago. If so, what does that say about the rebels' surviving strength? Are they truly as weak as the SS believes they are?"

"Those are all very good questions," the General rumbled. "How are we to answer them?"

"I don't know, Sir," she replied frankly. "I'm far too junior to be party to all the information the SS has gathered about the rebels. I knew what our agents in and around Tapuria had uncovered, because they used to report to me, but it wasn't much – certainly not enough to suggest that the rebels have any local military capability. I suspect much of the SS's fear of spies verges on paranoia, Sir."

"What's the old joke?" Captain Dehgahn mused. "Just because you're paranoid doesn't mean they aren't out to get you."

She couldn't help laughing. "Yes, Sir, I suppose you're right."

"He is," Huvishka admitted with a smile, "but it doesn't solve my problem." His face sobered. "I have to decide whether to allow the Satrap's big parade to go ahead as planned. If there were any concrete evidence that the rebels had sufficient military strength to threaten it, or any indication that they were planning to attack it, I'd be justified in requesting that it be postponed; but there *isn't* any such evidence. I can't act on hunches or intuitions. I need solid information on which to base my decisions, and justify them after the fact if necessary; but there isn't any – so what am I supposed to do?"

~ ~ ~

CARISTO GARRISON

"He's at it again," Todd whispered, peering through his night vision visor. "Not yet midnight and already he's as tight as a drum."

"Drunken sot!" another member of the squad sniffed.

"Don't complain, Mike," Dave warned. "It makes our job easier, so as far as I'm concerned he can drink all he wants."

"Just as long as he doesn't start singing," another trooper murmured, and they all chuckled softly.

"Think he'll hear us?" Todd asked.

"Not at this distance if we're quiet," Dave decided, "and not with that much rotgut on board."

He clicked his microphone once. Over the secure scrambled network Tamsin sent back two clicks from her overwatch position, confirming that no other sentries were in sight. He knew the two snipers positioned on either side of her would intervene if a Bactrian patrol tried to interfere with the operation. He'd taken every precaution he could think of, so why delay any longer?

"All right, let's go."

Todd lifted the bottom strands of the outer perimeter fence and supported them on forked sticks. They waited a moment, but no alarm came. Sergeant Dixon's patch to the guardhouse watch console had enabled him to disable the motion sensors attached to the wire, and also substitute a pre-recorded loop for the feed from the security cameras covering the entire area.

Slowly, moving as quietly as possible, each man wriggled beneath the wire. Todd led them in a low crawl across the gravel strip of no-mans-land between the fences. It was supposed to be barren of all vegetation; but in this garrison that regulation, like so many others, was honored more in the breach than in the observance. Grass covered much of the surface, providing a welcome cushion against the sharp edges of the gravel, and here and there shrubs grew to knee height. Once safely through the inner wire they hurried across the brightly lit strip along the inside of the fence, running softly and silently on cushioned soles, and took cover in the shadow of the hangar wall.

Tamsin had monitored the area while they were moving. Now she called, "Area still clear. The sentry's sitting against the wall by the side door, head slumped forward, not moving."

Dave clicked twice to acknowledge her message. "Nice of him to pick the one area round here that's just outside the coverage of the security cameras," he whispered to his team as they all pulled on thin gloves to avoid leaving fingerprints and DNA on anything they touched in the warehouse.

"The Bactrians probably teach it during basic training – 'How to stay invisible while drinking'. Very tactical," Todd quipped, and the others grinned.

Dave led them round the back of the warehouse and up the far side, lifting the blackjack clipped to his belt. At the corner he nodded to Todd, who stepped around the edge, took two steps, and gently lifted the cap of the somnolent sentry. Dave whacked him sharply – but not too hard – on the head with his blackjack. He slumped forward, never making a sound. Dave opened the side door to the warehouse office, then Todd put his hands under the armpits of the sentry's limp body and dragged him into the small room. Mike picked up the man's rifle and brought it inside, followed by the rest of the team.

"What next?" Mike asked.

Dave checked the sentry. Apart from being unconscious, he didn't seem to be badly hurt. A trickle of blood ran down his lip from where he'd bitten it as he was struck.

"He'll be all right. Lean him against that wall for now. We'll put him back outside when we're done. Vince, Eric, guard the door." The two drew their blackjacks and moved to either side of the inside of the door through which they'd just entered, flattening themselves against the wall. "Listen for any warning from Tamsin. Todd, Mike, with me."

He led the two men through an inner door into the dimly-lit hangar. Newly-delivered supplies for the assault shuttles were stacked high on racks and shelves running away from them along the nearest wall. The hulking shapes of the four newly-serviced shuttles filled the body of the cavernous warehouse, looming above them in the gloom.

Dave led them down the racks until he came to one that contained boxes of fusion micro-reactor fuel cartridges. "This is the stuff." He couldn't help whispering, even though he knew no-one else was within earshot. "I want to move these boxes, take three cartridges from the rear of the rack, then replace the others so there's no sign anything's missing. With luck it'll be months before they notice some of them are gone." He forbore to tell his men that within a few weeks it was likely no-one would be worrying about the supplies any more. They didn't need to know that; and if they didn't, the Bactrians couldn't torture the information out of them if anything went wrong.

They worked steadily, piling the boxes to one side until they reached the rear of the rack. Dave passed out three fuel cartridges, then they set to work rebuilding the stack. They were only halfway done when their earpieces came to life.

"Someone's coming!" Tamsin hissed as she studied an approaching figure through her electronic binoculars. "It looks like one of those two Sergeants who came out from Banka with the shuttle maintenance team, and stayed on to drill the troops for the Satrap's parade. He's headed straight for the hangar's side door."

Dave nodded to his two men to keep rebuilding the stack of boxes, then sprinted for the office on silent feet. He'd almost reached the inner door when he heard the outer one burst open, slamming back onto Vince where he stood against the wall behind it.

"What the *hell* – ?" a guttural voice demanded.

The intruder abruptly fell silent as Eric bludgeoned him with his blackjack. The Sergeant collapsed forward into Dave's arms as he rushed into the room. He caught him, staggering at the sudden weight, and laid him down beside the still-unconscious sentry.

"Shut that door, quick!" he hissed.

He examined the Sergeant briefly. His eyes had rolled up inside his head, and he was breathing stertorously. "He's out cold," he told the others.

"What are we going to do about him?" Vince asked. "We planned to leave the sentry lying outside, because anyone finding him would simply assume he'd drunk too much. He wouldn't even remember being hit – he'd just have a headache, which he'd put down to the booze. This guy's another matter."

"There's only one thing for it," Dave decided, holding down a gulp of dismay. He turned to the sentry and tightened his fingers and thumbs around the man's throat.

"*Wha* – what are you – ?" Eric gasped.

"*Shut it!*" Dave whispered savagely.

He squeezed grimly as the unconscious man gasped for air, making gruesome choking noises. It took him over a minute to stop moving. Dave held on for another two minutes, making sure that he was dead, then let go. He shook his aching hands to ease the tension in them, then clicked on his microphone.

"Tamsin, all clear out there?"

"Nobody in sight."

"OK. We're coming out."

He turned to Vince. "Go get the other two and bring three fuel cartridges with you. Eric, help me get these two outside."

They dragged the dead sentry and unconscious Sergeant through the door, then Dave fetched the sentry's rifle. He leaned it against the hangar wall next to him, took its bayonet from the scabbard at the soldier's belt and drove it up through the Sergeant's ribs into his heart. The unconscious man gasped, choked, and twitched as he died. While he did so, Dave rearranged the bodies. When he'd finished the sentry was holding his bayonet, its blade still embedded in the Sergeant's chest. The latter's hands were now wrapped around the sentry's neck.

Dave stood back to examine his handiwork, then splashed a little more of the sentry's rotgut over his stained tunic before putting down the bottle next to his rifle. "If you came across those two for the first time, what would you think?" he asked Eric.

97

"I guess the Sergeant caught this guy drinking and got rough with him, which made him lose his temper and stab the Sergeant, whose hands stayed tight around the sentry's neck long enough to kill him. No-one heard the noise of the fight; but out here, this far from the barracks, it's not likely anyone would." He hesitated. "Sorry about my comment in there, Boss. I didn't realize what you were up to. Only problem is, the security cameras won't show the Sergeant approaching."

Dave squeezed Eric's upper arm in a brief gesture of acceptance. "Let's hope they accept the evidence of their eyes and are too lazy to check the recording." He turned to the other three as they came out, each carrying a heavy box. "Back to the fence. I'm going to check inside one last time. They're bound to search the hangar when they find those two, so I want to make sure nothing's out of place."

He ran into the building again and made sure that the hangar looked undisturbed. He shut the inner door, checked the office, closed the outer door behind him, and ran across the open area to join the others at the fence. They made their way beneath the wire, Todd removing the supports from beneath the lower strands after they were all through, then using a brush to erase any scrape or drag marks left in the gravel by their passage. Moving quickly and quietly, they ran up the slope and down the far side, collecting Tamsin and the snipers from their overwatch position as they passed it.

They rendezvoused with Sergeant Dixon at the big farm truck he'd borrowed for the night's work. He used his electronic warfare console to restore the garrison's sensors to normal operation, then shut it down as they all piled aboard. He steered using a night vision visor rather than the lights as the truck moved off slowly down the dirt road leading to town, electric motor whining softly.

"Jeff's waiting for us at the station," he told them. "He stole four small collapsible fuel bladders from the storeroom, washed them out, and filled them with reaction mass. All he had to do was open the non-return valve at the station's filling point. They normally connect tanker cars to it to refill the garrison's tank, but in this case he reversed the flow and drained off eight hundred liters – two hundred in each bladder. It helped that they'd just refilled the garrison tank, of course. He says the bladders are damned heavy, though. It'll take all of us to load them."

"That's us – stevedore soldiers," Eric quipped, and they all laughed. It was as much a gush of release from the tension of the last half-hour as it was amusement.

"We'll have them at the airvans within an hour, then it's all aboard for the Laguna Peninsula," Dave said with satisfaction. "We'll have to laager up somewhere under camouflage during daylight hours, but we should be there by midnight if all goes well."

March 10th 2850 GSC

LAGUNA PENINSULA

Dave and Tamsin stood silently as they watched a work party – cheerful despite the post-midnight hour – move the four heavy bladders of reaction mass and the three fuel cartridges from the two airvans onto a utility truck. The remaining members of Dave's team gathered their kit, waiting for a guide to take them to the side cavern assigned to Niven's Regiment.

"Well, we made it," he said eventually, suppressing a yawn. "Dad'll be along in an hour or so with most of the others. I wonder what the General's going to tell us this morning?"

"I don't know, but he's called an assembly for everyone here, so it's got to be important."

"You bet! Most of the Resistance is here by now. Oh, well, I guess we'll find out in a few hours." He hugged her gently. "Here comes the guide. Let's get some sleep."

"Good idea." She leaned into him. "I'm too tired to do anything frisky, but I'd love to fall asleep with your arms around me, love. We have so little opportunity to be together, I want to make the most of every chance we get."

"It's a deal."

~ ~ ~

Brigadier-General Aldred stepped onto a packing crate, looking out over the assembled soldiers. A technician handed him a microphone, which he clipped to his shirt.

"Good morning, everyone," he began. "I won't say 'Thank you for coming', because we didn't have much choice in the matter!" Laughter greeted his sally. "Nevertheless, it really is good to see you all here, because it means the Bactrians didn't get any of us. Their latest attack turned into a wild swing that hit nothing but empty air. We owe that to a few people in particular. First, Lieutenant-Colonel Yardley held on just long enough under excruciating torture to delay the enemy's discovery that we'd left something of vital importance in his Matopo Hills base." He gestured to where the Colonel sat on a chair next to the members of the Council of the Resistance. There was a rumble of approval from the soldiers, who gave him a round of applause.

The General waited for silence. "That delay meant that Captain Carson and his team arrived there just in time to intercept the engineers the Bactrians sent to retrieve it." He waved a hand in the direction of Dave and his detachment. "Not only did they rescue Colonel Yardley and destroy the engineer detachment, but they also learned about the Bactrians' intention to attack our remaining three regimental bases. They warned us in time to evacuate those bases in good order. That's why we're all safely here this morning, rather than dead in the rubble of our former quarters." The assembled soldiers broke into spontaneous applause, along with a few whistles and shouts of thanks.

"The events of the past week have brought matters to a head for us," he went on once order had been restored. "We've got to face facts. We have relatively little left in the way of armaments and supplies, and we've been reduced to this one last fallback base. Sooner or later the enemy's bound to discover it; and when they do, we all know what's going to happen.

"Before this war we were over seven thousand strong; four regiments, each with a small full-time cadre and many times more part-time reservists. We professionals used to joke that they were 'weekend warriors'. We stopped doing that a long time ago, because when the Bactrians invaded the reservists rapidly became just as professional and as expert as we were, if not more so. Today there are less than four hundred survivors of our Army still on active service. We're all seasoned, hardened warriors, but the Bactrians have eight infantry regiments on Laredo, about fifteen thousand combat troops, plus support units. No matter how individually superior we may be to their mostly conscript soldiers, there are simply too many of them. In the end, the outcome is inevitable."

He looked around the gathering. "We therefore face three possible courses of action. The first is to split up into small groups and continue guerrilla warfare for as long as possible. We'd try to follow the ancient dictum of Chairman Mao; 'The guerrilla must move amongst the people as a fish swims in the sea'. Unfortunately, the sea level is getting lower all the time as the Bactrians conscript more and more of our surviving citizens into their slave labor camps. Almost eighty per cent of our pre-war population is already dead or enslaved. The remainder either lives on farms and ranches where they produce food that the invaders need, or they're waiting to be conscripted themselves. Furthermore, the Bactrians have imposed vicious reprisals in areas where we've mounted guerrilla-style attacks, forcing us to choose targets as far away as possible from our peoples' communities. For that reason, I don't think small-unit guerrilla resistance is a viable long-term option. We'd simply hasten the suffering and death of too many of our people."

He reached for a glass of water offered by an aide, and took a drink before continuing. "The second option is to disband." He held up a hand to stifle immediate calls of dissent. "Hear me out, friends. If we disband, each of us will have to select an area as far away as possible from major Bactrian activity and try to make a living as best we can as civilians. There are many farms and ranches whose owners are dead, or who've fled to avoid conscription or Bactrian reprisals. More than a few belonged to our late colleagues. We can take them over, change our names, and try to live as inconspicuously as possible for as long as possible. The occupiers still need to buy food, so as long as they don't know we were in the Resistance and we're producing something they need, they'll probably leave us in relative peace. It won't be a very happy life and it won't make us rich, but at least we'll be alive. How long that might last, no-one can say."

He drank again, and handed the empty glass back to his aide. "The third option is Armageddon. We mount one last attack against the Bactrians. They've given us one hell of a target if we do. At the end of this month their Satrap is coming here along with his son, the Crown Prince, who's to be the first civilian Governor of Laredo – or, rather, not Laredo; they're going to rename our planet Termaz."

There was a rumble of comment. Aldred held up both hands to still it. "Let me finish, please. I remind you that Bactria's ruling family is a patriarchy, and the Crown Prince is the Satrap's only son. If we kill both of them, there'll be a dynastic struggle between half a dozen rival claimants to the throne. It'll throw Bactria's internal politics into turmoil for years to come, and may even spark a full-blown civil war. Furthermore, if we can destroy the infrastructure they've built up here at the same time that we target the Satrap and Crown Prince, we'll hit them harder and cost them more than we've ever done before. We can literally 'go out with a bang'. It'll be a 'last stand' mission, one from which few of us stand any chance of returning, because we're going to have to penetrate their strongest defensive perimeter to strike, then try to escape through that same perimeter. Our chances of getting away are poor, because after our attack the enemy will be alerted and mad as all hell at us. However, if the end is inevitable anyway, I submit it's better to die on our terms, not the enemy's, and make our deaths worthwhile."

Again he was interrupted, this time by a roar of approval. Dave yelled right along with the others, pumping his fist in the air in agreement. Beside him Tamsin was also shouting, although he couldn't help but notice there were tears in her eyes.

At last the General was able to continue. "I suggest to you that those who still have living wives, children, parents or siblings should not choose the last option. Your families and relatives still need you. I think you should take the second option, trying to live as civilians as best you can. It may be that some others will join you in that."

He waved a hand at a notice-board on the cave wall. "By sixteen today, please put your names on one of two lists over there. One will be headed 'Last Stand'. It's to take part in a final assault, to try to kill the Satrap and Crown Prince and destroy as much as possible of what Bactria's built up here. By choosing that option, you acknowledge that you probably won't be coming back. The other will be headed 'Survival'. Those who have families still dependent on them, or who want to try to make new lives by forming small groups together, should put their names on that list. I emphasize that you've all earned the right to choose for yourselves, and no-one has the right to criticize your choice. You're all brave men and women who've proven yourselves in combat time and time again. If you hadn't, you wouldn't have lived long enough to be here today. Don't try to influence each other's decisions. Don't denigrate what others want to do or put undue pressure on them to change their minds. Choose for yourself, and let others do the same.

"One last thing. There'll be a third list on the noticeboard headed 'Orbital Operations'. *If and only if* you've already put your name down on the 'Last Stand' list, please add your name to 'Orbital Operations' as well if you ever did a course or had experience in the use of spacesuits and freefall maneuvers. Those people will have a special, critical mission as part of our final operation. I know such skills require annual refresher training, but the enemy hasn't allowed us the space, time or facilities to do that for over three years. Therefore, those few who qualified before the war will just have to remember as much as possible and do the best they can.

"We'll reassemble here at seventeen to discuss the options you've chosen."

He jumped down from the crate to a growing rumble of conversation as the soldiers turned to each other, exchanging views and ideas.

Dave put his arm around Tamsin. "You were crying, love. Why?"

"That's a dumb question!" she flashed at him, eyes angry. "I've just learned that I'm about to lose my man. How the hell do you think that makes me feel?"

He opened his mouth to answer, then blinked as the reality of her words hit him. "I... I'm sorry, love," he said with genuine contrition. "I didn't even think about us. I just want to hit the Bactrians so hard that they'll never forget us. I want them to tremble when the name of Laredo is mentioned, even if they rename it to something else. I want their parents to make their kids afraid for generations to come by warning them that unless they behave, the Laredans will come to get them. I want to occupy their nightmares and make them wake up in cold sweats. I... I didn't even think about the fact that we wouldn't be there to see it."

Her shoulders drooped, almost in defeat, it seemed to him. "I know. I guess that's one of the differences between men and women. You know the end's coming, so you're going to face it with a shout of defiance and go out with blood in your eye and the roar of gunfire in your ears and the bodies of your enemies piled before you. Me... I can't help but realize I'm going to lose you regardless, plus any future we might have had together. Oh, I know that could have happened anytime in the past few years, but at least there was always the prospect that you might survive. Now, the end is about as certain as it can get. There's no evading it. Of course, I'm going to die too, so at least we'll be together – but *how* I wish we could have had the chance to *live* together, instead of die together!"

He was silent for a long moment. "We could, you know," he said at last, but she could hear the deep reluctance in his voice. "We could put our names down on the 'Survival' list, if you really want."

She shook her head sadly. "No. You know as well as I do that sooner or later the Bactrians will realize we were part of the Resistance, or one of them will decide he wants whatever we've built together, or they'll run short of slave labor. One way or another they'll come after us, and neither you nor I are the kind of people who'll submit meekly. We'll resist them then if we don't do so now, and the end result will be the same. I'd rather not have to endure the constant knowledge that we're actually living a lie, pretending everything's going to be OK when we know damn well it's not. How could I ever bring kids into a world like that, knowing that sooner or later they were going to die along with us?"

He nodded slowly. "I'm afraid you're right. Still, would you like more time to think about it?"

"No. Delay's not going to change the reality of the situation. Let's put our names down now – and while we're at it, let's add them to the 'Orbital Operations' list too. I was qualified to pilot in orbit as well as planetside, and you did the spacesuit and freefall courses before the war."

"Yes, I did. We'll see what the General has in mind."

~ ~ ~

General Aldred didn't go into detail about forthcoming operations that evening. He climbed back onto the crate, looked around at his assembled soldiers, and said simply, "Thank you for indicating your preferences. More than three-quarters of you have chosen to join me in a 'last stand' assault on the Bactrians. We'll work out the details over the next few days, and start training various teams for their assigned roles. Some of you will leave very soon to prepare the way for the rest of us.

"Just over one-fifth of you have elected to try to survive as families or groups of colleagues. We'll do everything we can to set you up for success, including dividing our remaining Bactrian bezants and non-military supplies among you to give you the best possible start. We'll also discuss farming and ranching options, and make available to you the properties and businesses owned by our colleagues who've been killed on active service without leaving any heirs. I know they'd have wanted you to have the use of them." He was forced to stop as everyone in the cave broke into applause. Those who'd chosen to make a fresh start would clearly do so with the best wishes of their comrades in arms.

Aldred waited for silence once more. "The Council of the Resistance has been discussing options for a final mission for several days now. All that was lacking was certainty as to whether or not we'd have enough volunteers to carry it out. Now that we do, I'll ask them to give their final approval tonight. That's a mere formality, of course, but it's an important one.

"Thank you all very, very much. This will be the last chance I get to speak with all of you together like this, so I want you to know I've never had a greater privilege than to lead you all during these years of conflict. We've made the Bactrians pay in blood and in treasure for their decision to invade us. Now we're going to strike our most powerful blow ever against them." More cheering interrupted him once more.

"That's all for now. Relax and enjoy yourselves this evening. Tomorrow we get down to work."

March 11th 2850 GSC

LAGUNA PENINSULA

Jake led the way into the meeting room. Dave followed him, closing the door as Brigadier-General Aldred and his wife Gloria rose to meet them. After a flurry of handshakes and muttered greetings, they all sat down around the table and helped themselves to glasses of water.

"I've asked the two of you here privately because… well, we need something that I know Captain Carson will find very difficult. Since it affects you as well, Colonel, I thought we owed it to you to broach the subject in private, where you can talk about it freely."

"Thank you, Sir," Jake responded for both of them.

"Captain, you put your name down on the list of those qualified in spacesuits and freefall maneuvers. You're the only officer who did so. That makes you the automatic choice to command that portion of our final mission, but it also means we're going to place a very heavy burden on your shoulders. I'll let my wife explain, in her capacity as President of the Council of the Resistance and *de facto* head of state of our Provisional Government of Occupied Laredo."

Gloria Aldred nodded. "You know that we're going to mount a final mission against the invaders, Captain, one that few of us – including your own father – are likely to survive. That makes what I must ask of you even more difficult. You see… we're going to ask you to escape from Laredo. We want you to survive."

"WHAT?" Dave surged to his feet, incredulous. "You've just told me that you expect to die – that you expect my *father* to die – on this mission. How can you – how *dare* you – expect me to let him die alone?"

The General held up his hand. "It's more complicated than that, Captain. Will you please allow us to explain?"

There was a long silence as Dave stared mutinously at him. Eventually Jake put his hand on Dave's forearm. "Son, please listen to them – because it's me asking, if for no other reason."

"Why *are* you asking? Dammit, Dad, you've got more experience in freefall and spacesuits than I have! Why didn't you put your name on the 'Orbital Operations' list too? Then *you* could lead that mission, and I could be with you!"

Jake looked him in the eye and said slowly, deliberately, "My regiment is about to embark on its final mission. I cannot and will not send my soldiers to their probable deaths without accompanying them."

Dave slowly nodded, then sat down, but obstinate rebellion was still evident in every line of his body.

"Thank you," Gloria acknowledged softly. "Our biggest problem is going to be to get our accumulated evidence off the planet, and make sure it reaches the Vice-President and our Government-in-Exile. For the duration of the Satrap's visit nobody will be allowed to enter or leave orbit except Bactrian personnel. Security will be as tight as possible. That means Mr. Ellis will be trapped here until after our attack on the Satrap. The Bactrians will be in turmoil, and probably won't let anyone go anywhere for weeks, if not months. As for cargo shipments, even personal baggage of passengers boarding spaceships here, they're sure to go through everything with a fine-toothed comb. There's no way Mr. Ellis will be able to smuggle our evidence aboard his ship. That means, if we want to kill the Satrap, we have to plan on getting Mr. Ellis away ourselves, along with all the evidence we've gathered and our two bank bearer keys.

"There's another aspect to that. I'll ask Bill to explain it."

Her husband sat forward. "Please understand that what I'm about to say is no reflection on Mr. Ellis, or whatever his real name is. He's arranged the ship that will take our evidence to the Vice-President. Lack of secure transport is all that's stopped us sending it to her before now, so we're profoundly grateful to him for that. By coming here and putting himself in danger to inform us about it, he's more than earned his fee. Nevertheless, we want to have our evidence and the bearer bank keys escorted and delivered to the Vice-President by our own people.

"There are three reasons for that. One is basic security, of course – we don't know who we can trust off-planet. The second is that… shall we say, a certain firmness may be needed to persuade the ship's captain and crew to take it out of the Laredo system once it's aboard. There'll be all sorts of consternation and monkeyhouse going on, both planetside during and after our attack, and in orbit after the attack you'll have to mount on the defenses there in order to open a window of opportunity for the ship to escape. Its crew may believe they'd run less risk by handing over the evidence and anyone accompanying it to the Bactrians, in the hope that they'll then be allowed to proceed. They won't be accustomed to the Bactrians' methods, after all, nor to their SS torturers. The third aspect is that while our evidence is very comprehensive, essentially it's *things* – objects, data, recordings and what have you. It'll be far more convincing if it's accompanied by eyewitnesses who can recount – if necessary under truth-tester examination – their own experiences of the Bactrian invasion, what they themselves saw and heard and went through. They'll back up the evidence and turn it into something living, something real, for those who read or see it."

"I guess there's a fourth aspect too, Sir," Jake interjected thoughtfully. "If whoever gets the evidence and Mr. Ellis aboard his ship tries to return planetside, that'll no longer be possible. By then most of us will be dead in the ruins of Banka, along with the Satrap and an ungodly number of Bactrians – at least, we hope so. I don't know where the orbital force would go, or how they'd get there. In the turmoil they'd probably be shot out of the sky before they could even land."

"A very good point," the General agreed. "Over to you, Gloria."

"Thank you, Bill." She turned to Dave. "There's another reason for what we're asking of you, Captain, but before I go into it, we need to know where you stand. We can't in good conscience *order* you to do this if you feel it's your duty to die with your father. Therefore, we're asking you to volunteer, and we'll make the same request of everyone else that put down their names for the orbital mission. Only those who accept the burden of survival – and it *will* be a burden, trust me on this – will be accepted for the mission. The rest will be reassigned to join the assault on Banka."

Dave was silent, his mental struggle written plainly on his face. Jake watched him quietly for a while, then said softly, "Son, I'd like you to accept this assignment." He held up a hand to stifle his son's instinctive half-cry of protest. "It's absolutely vital. Unless the orbital defenses are suppressed, the evidence is delivered to the spaceship, and it gets safely away from the system, there'll never be a United Planets inquiry into what Bactria did here, and it'll never face punishment for its invasion of Laredo. Whoever commands this mission will face huge difficulties. Unless it's done right first time, all those who died over the past three years will have wasted their lives, and those of us who are about to die will do so in vain. I can't think of anyone I'd trust more than you to succeed, no matter what the odds.

"As for me…" He shrugged. "I'm sure to be killed in due course, whether in this assault or later. I'd rather not have to watch you die as well. Jeanette, Timmy, Janet and I will live on through you and your kids, on some planet I may never have heard of and will never see. It's not just me, either. All of us will live on through all of you. You'll honor our memories, tell our stories to your children, and explain to others why we fought so hard for so long. I don't know about anyone else, but I'd like to be remembered in that way." Bill and Gloria murmured their agreement.

The lump in Dave's throat was so large and painful he couldn't speak. He looked at his father for a long moment, then gave a slow, reluctant nod.

"Thank you, Captain," General Aldred said formally, his voice husky. "I know you don't want to do this, and I honor your willingness to put your planet's needs ahead of your loyalty to your father." He rose to his feet. "I'll leave you to discuss a related issue with my wife. Your father and I will begin planning a number of the operations that will be integral to this whole affair. When you finish with Gloria, see me and we'll put the question of survival to your team – but we'll swear them to secrecy first, and we won't tell them everything yet. If word should leak to the Bactrians about our plans, they'll make it flat-out impossible for us to succeed."

"I understand. Thank you, Sir."

He stood at attention as the General and his father left the room. As they closed the door behind them, Gloria refilled her glass with water and drained half of it. She brushed back a curl of hair from her forehead, her eyes drawn and weary.

Dave took his glass, walked up the table and sat down nearer her. For a moment her face was outlined against the light from a wall fitting behind her. It looked gaunt, almost skull-like, and he suddenly realized how much she'd changed. At the beginning of the war she'd had a well-rounded, roly-poly figure with a face to match. Now she was almost stick-like, her frame showing the enormous strain of three years and more of watching friends and comrades – not to mention her own son and daughter – die all around her. He'd seen the same thing in his father and the rest of Niven's Regiment, including Tamsin and himself; but since all of them had gone through the process together and they'd all deteriorated at the same rate, it hadn't really struck him until now how much they'd all been ground down by the war.

He broke the awkward silence. "What did you want to discuss, Ma'am?" His voice was still husky with emotion.

"Oh, forget the formalities! We're preparing for our last stand. I hardly think it matters any more who has what rank. Death won't play favorites with us, or go by seniority."

He couldn't help laughing. "True enough. All right, Gloria." He placed subtle emphasis on her name. "What's up?"

"Thank you… Dave. Do you know how I ended up in my present position?"

"No, I can't say I do."

"I was a psychiatrist. I did my basic medical degree here, then went off-planet to specialize. I came back to set up in private practice. In due course I was authorized by Congress to serve as acting, unpaid, voluntary Deputy Minister of Health for mental health issues. When the Bactrians invaded most of the Cabinet was killed in the initial series of strikes. Through a long series of events – not least of which was simply surviving! – I ended up as Minister of Health in President Wexler's underground Cabinet. In due course I found myself its only surviving Minister. As such, the Council of the Resistance co-opted me as its Chairperson after the President died in captivity.

"That may help you to understand why mental health has been my particular focus for years, both before and during this war. I'm very aware of how we've all been mentally and emotionally scarred by this war." She saw his quick frown and hastened to add, "I'm not saying we're mentally *unstable*. We've had to be stable in order to survive, but stability is different in time of war than in time of peace. We've had to abandon anything and everything that got in the way of staying alive. If you think about it, you'll realize that's why you and your comrades have survived this long. You've learned to put aside every distraction and focus on killing the enemy before he killed you. Those who didn't learn that lesson are mostly no longer with us."

Dave said slowly, "I daresay you're partly right, but luck's important too. Sometimes it works in your favor, sometimes it doesn't."

"You're right; but even given good luck, those who didn't adapt very quickly to this new life of war were usually the first to die. Those who've survived this long, despite all the Bactrians could do to them, are those who've adjusted most completely to its demands."

He sipped from his glass of water. "All right, I'll concede that. So?"

"Hasn't it occurred to you how much that's warped and twisted our thought processes? Let me give you an example from just a few moments ago. You've just been offered a chance to live. Instead of jumping at it, you were *upset* by it. You didn't want to leave your father to die alone. You had to be persuaded that living was more important to our cause than dying. I understand where you're coming from, and I truly admire your dedication; but to someone outside this environment, your attitude would be so incomprehensible as to seem deranged. She'd wonder why *anyone* would choose to die when they have a chance to live. Does that illustrate how drastically your outlook on life has been changed by this war? Would you have reacted that way before it broke out?"

"No, I wouldn't; and yes, I suppose it does show how I've changed. I hadn't thought about it from that perspective."

"Thank you." Her shoulders sagged as she relaxed and took a deep breath. "Having said that, I think you'll understand better what I'm about to ask of you. It was because I'm a psychiatrist that I began our 'Witness to War' program almost three years ago. I patterned it after a famous example in history. Did you ever hear of something called the 'Holocaust'?"

"Wasn't that the extermination of a race during the Second Global War on Old Home Earth, the best part of a millennium ago?"

"Not quite their extermination, and it was a religious rather than a racial group, but yes, that's it. Many of those who lived through it never spoke about it. Their memories later died with them. A few decades after the Holocaust some people tried to persuade the remaining survivors to record their memories. It developed into an international project, and its records have long been a treasure-trove for psychologists, psychiatrists, anthropologists and cultural analysts. They're one of the few really in-depth records of genocide from its victims' point of view, even though most were recorded decades after the event, when memories had faded and been modified by later experiences.

"That's exactly what Bactria's tried to do on Laredo – commit genocide, exterminate us. We've suffered proportionately even greater losses than the victims of the Holocaust. About eighty per cent of our original planetary population is dead, missing or enslaved, and frankly I don't hold out much hope for the rest of us in the long term. I realized early on that we were in an almost unique historical position. I wanted to preserve as much of our collective memory of genocide as I could."

"Why?" Dave asked bluntly. "What good will it do?"

"It won't help us survive, either as a people or as individuals, but it'll ensure that we're remembered. That counts for something, I think. Even more important, it'll help psychiatrists – don't forget my professional interest – to understand more about what this experience does to people, and how to help the survivors of anything similar in future."

He considered her words. "I... suppose that makes sense," he said slowly, thoughtfully.

"I'm glad you agree. I started three years ago by sending hand-picked representatives among the survivors of battles, massacres and incidents, asking them to record their experiences. I trained them to ask leading questions, drawing out details that otherwise might have been glossed over. I tried to get them into combat units, but at first you were all too busy. Only after we switched from open conflict to guerrilla warfare did our troops pull back into rear areas and begin setting up secure bases like this one. That gave my people a chance to talk to some of you. Did you ever do so?"

"No. One of them asked me about it, but I was far too busy. Don't forget, I was a part-time reservist Corporal when the war started. I got three promotions in six weeks: first to Sergeant, then a battlefield commission as Second Lieutenant, then three weeks later promotion to First Lieutenant and Commanding Officer of what was left of Charlie Company at the Battle of the Crossing. I had to learn all my new responsibilities 'on the fly', as it were. I was so busy organizing the remnants of my company and helping to establish secure bases that I didn't have time to breathe, let alone reminisce about the fighting. By the time we'd settled down, I didn't want to."

"I can understand that," she acknowledged with a sigh. "Be that as it may, we've accumulated upwards of ten thousand hours of vid and audio recordings of what happened to us, individually and collectively. They're unique in that they were gathered soon after the events in question. They were fresh in the memories of those who spoke to us. We also have sensor recordings of battles, firefights, ambushes; you name it, including the deliberate destruction of Banka and everyone in it. There were numerous security cameras operating in and around the city, and we tried to retrieve as many of their recordings as possible. Some are ghastly to watch, but they're the last monument to those who died there. That gives them a meaning far beyond mere ghoulish voyeurism, I think.

"Taken as a whole, we have an archive of atrocity and genocide and their effects on the human psyche that may rival the records of the Holocaust. Even more important, it's contemporary, not ancient history. I desperately want to get it into the hands of those who can use it to help others like us in future. It'll be part of the records we send off-planet with you. I need you to do your utmost to get it to my alma mater, where I qualified in psychiatry – the Faculty of Medicine at Commonwealth University on Lancaster."

"Why them?"

"Because they helped develop the debriefing program used by the Lancastrian Commonwealth Fleet to help its combat veterans adjust to civilian life. It's widely regarded as the best in the settled galaxy. The people at CU understand combat fatigue and related issues very well. They're probably in a better position to understand and make the best use of these recordings from a psychiatric perspective than almost anyone else."

"But *will* they make the best use of it? Why should they? What's their motivation, apart from publishing a few papers to score academic points off other universities?"

She laughed shakily. "You don't have a very high opinion of academics, do you?"

"Saving your presence, no – but then you're more practical than you are academic."

"Thanks for saying that. No, the right people will understand how vital these recordings are to genuine psychiatric research, not to mention a host of other disciplines. I might add that by getting them to CU, you'll also help yourself and your soldiers."

"Oh? How's that?"

"All of you will have to work through the years of warfare and tension. Remember I said that survival would be a burden? I wasn't joking. The burden will be readjusting to normal life after all you've been through. Throughout history, veterans with the amount of combat experience that you've all accumulated have found it difficult. You'll find it even more so, because everything you knew before the war – and almost everyone – won't be there anymore. You'll have to start afresh in completely new and unfamiliar surroundings."

"I... I guess that makes sense," he said slowly, thoughtfully.

"It does. Something like the Commonwealth Fleet's program for combat veterans will be exactly what you all need. You're not members of the Fleet, so you won't be eligible to participate in it: but the program was developed at CU, so they know it well. I'll ask the Vice-President to make funds available to hire professionals to help you, and the people at CU can put you in touch with the very best. The material we send with you, and your own needs, will effectively form two halves of the same coin. You'll be a treasure trove to CU's psychiatrists. They won't only be able to help you; they'll take what they learn from you, link it to our material, and use it to help others in future.

"There's one last thing. I hope you and your soldiers will add your own memories to our archive; then I want you to use it, and your own experiences, and funds that I'll ask the Vice-President to provide, to tell Laredo's story to a general audience, not just to diplomats and politicians and mental health specialists. I think a very powerful documentary can be produced from the recordings, and probably a book as well – perhaps more than one of each. They'll ensure that we'll be remembered as human beings, not just as abstract academic subjects. You'll be the only people who can

115

give that gift to the rest of us. Too much history is never recorded, and if it is it's never disseminated. I don't want us, or this planet, to be forgotten like that."

He said reluctantly, "I don't want to be a guinea-pig for academics, but you make a strong case. I can't promise anything unless and until we get away from Laredo. If we do, and if the Vice-President agrees to use your material in that way, and if she gives us permission to do as you've asked, and if she makes funds available for it, I'll ask my people to do all they can to help."

She grimaced. "That's an awful lot of conditions. Still, I suppose that's all I can rightfully ask or expect of you right now. Just do your best... please? It's really, *really* important to me. In a way I suppose it's a personal legacy from me to my profession – perhaps the last contribution I'll ever be able to make to it. If I'm going to die soon, I'd like something I've done to outlive me. My children won't, after all. They're already dead."

He studied her for a long moment. "Did your husband know what you were going to ask me to do?"

"Yes. I didn't think it would be fair to place this additional burden on your shoulders without his approval. He said I could ask you to help, but not order you."

"That sounds like something he'd say," Dave agreed as he stood up. "All right, Gloria. It *is* a burden, but I guess it's also a privilege to be asked to do something like this. If I'm spared I'll do my best for you, and I'll ask my people to do the same. You've got my word on it."

~ ~ ~

As the other members of the orbital team followed General Aldred out of the side cavern, Tamsin held back, motioning to Dave to do the same. She looked stunned, confused and conflicted.

"What is it, love?" he asked.

She shook her head mutely and came into his arms, holding him tightly. He could feel her body trembling against his. At last she murmured, "I... I just can't make myself believe this. To be told we might have a chance at life after all, when we'd already made up our minds to die together... it's just too much!"

116

He heaved a long, low sigh. "It shook me pretty badly, too, darling. It was the last thing I expected to hear."

"But can it be real? I just… I don't know how to see light at the end of the tunnel any more. I daren't allow myself to hope! We've known for more than three years that we had no chance of building a life together. That's why we decided not to get married – it would have seemed too much like living a lie. All those others who rushed into marriage when the war began… remember how many of them ended up as widows or widowers?"

He nodded grimly. "Yes – and even worse, those who became mothers and found themselves having to raise a kid who was as likely as not to be killed in an enemy raid. Even those who weren't killed still face the likelihood of being imprisoned in a Bactrian slave camp. That's the best most of them can hope for. I could never understand why anyone would bring kids into a mess like this. I don't see how they could grow up doing anything other than curse their parents for giving them such a sorry excuse for life."

"I saw it the same way. I really wanted to bear your children, but not like that! I gave up hope; but now, to be told that we may have a chance at life after all – and not just at life but at life *together*… it's… I'm sorry, darling. I guess I'm not making very much sense."

"I don't know that I'm doing any better. How about this, love? Let's go on living one day at a time, just as we've done since the invasion. We might still get hurt or killed in operations planetside, and we'll have to fight our way past Bactrian warships to reach safety. One or both of us might not make it. Let's wait until we're sure we're out of their reach before we try to make any plans.

"There's another thing, too." He told her what Gloria had said about needing professional help to work through the years of stress. "If we both need that much help – and I can see her point – we may not be in a fit state to make a long-term commitment until we've worked through everything."

She shook her head vehemently. "Dr. Aldred's right that we'll need help, I can see that: but I made my commitment to you long ago. It's not going to change. As far as I'm concerned, we could get married the day after we leave orbit and it would suit me fine!"

He grinned at her. "And there was I trying to be considerate!"

She slowly began to smile. "Hey, you – how long is it since we last made love? I mean, *really* made love – not just a quickie in the corner because we couldn't find time or privacy for anything more."

"It's probably months."

"It sure is – I've been counting! Tell you what. As soon as we reach safety on another planet, I'm going to keep you in bed for a whole day. At the end of that time you'll be so exhausted you won't be able to resist when I drag you off to whatever they use for a marriage officer!"

He laughed. "It's a deal!"

March 13th 2850 GSC

LAGUNA PENINSULA

Dave leaned back and rubbed his dry itching eyes. He peered at the display once more, then suddenly shook his head in frustration and thrust back his chair.

"Taking a break?" Lieutenant Kubicka asked from the terminal next to his.

"Yeah. My eyes are so tired I can't see straight any more. I'm going to check on the shuttle preparations."

The two shuttles obtained during the first days of conflict, and the new one captured by Dave and his team in the Matopo Hills, were parked in a side cavern. It took Dave ten minutes to reach it, stumbling over the uneven cave floor that no-one had bothered to smooth. He found a crew of technicians hard at work. When the two older shuttles had run out of fuel and supplies the previous year, they'd been flown here and mothballed – powered down, drained of all fluids, sealed against wind and weather. Now they were being restored to flying condition. Two techs were being assisted by half a dozen willing helpers as they pumped reaction mass into a shuttle's tanks from the bladders brought from Caristo. Another two-man team was loading a fuel cartridge into its underfloor fusion micro-reactor. The other shuttle had already been powered up, and a pilot was sitting at its control console running status checks.

As he approached the rear ramp of the all-black Security Service shuttle, Dave recognized Tamsin's close-cropped russet hair, wisps curling over her ears as she bent over the console. Beside her an older man with a mostly bald head and wisps of gray hair over his ears was pointing out something.

She turned to look at Dave as he walked up the ramp, face breaking into a tired smile. "Hey, lover! Come to take me away from all this?"

"I wish I could," he said fervently. "I just couldn't stare at a display any more – my eyes were starting to feel like they'd been bathed in sand." He glanced at the other man. "Hi, Mac. How's it going?"

"Too much work for an old man like me. And you?"

"Too much work for a young man like me!"

Tamsin said, peering at his face. "Your eyes are pretty red. Let me put some drops in them for you."

"Thanks, darling." He sat down in a pull-out chair and tilted his head back.

As she took a squeeze bottle of eye drops from the shuttle's first aid kit and dripped them into his eyes, she said, "Mac's been showing me some of the special features of this assault shuttle. Looks like the Security Service had some toys that aren't found on the normal Army birds."

"Yes," the older man agreed. "They're going to come in very handy in orbit. For example, did you know this thing can generate multiple false transponder codes on traffic control radar?"

Dave sat up with a jerk. "You're joking! Wouldn't that make it a hell of a hazard in a high-traffic environment?"

"Stop jumping around like that!" Tamsin scolded Dave. "Now I've got to put in more drops." She pushed him back down into his seat and suited the action to the word.

"It would indeed," Mac answered Dave, "but when has the SS ever bothered about endangering anyone else? As far as they're concerned, if they need to sneak up on someone that's all the justification they need. That's another capability this bird has – you can set its autopilot to home in on any radio or radar signal automatically. The active stealth features are what interest me most. They'll make it easy for us to sneak up on the space station. They won't know we're coming until we're there."

"Can we operate them without tech training? And surely the station operators will see the docking bay indicators when we arrive?"

"No, we don't need specialized training – they're designed to be used by the typical SS thug, which means a simple interface and lots of artificial intelligence to figure out what the operator wants and deliver it. I'll teach Tamsin and her backup pilot all they need to know. As for the space station; don't forget, that's *our* station. When the Bactrians took it over they left our computer and defense systems intact as an economy measure, rather than replace them with their own." He rubbed his hands together gleefully. "I installed the latest updates to those systems before the invasion. I know them inside-out, back-to-front and upside-down. I can remotely disable docking notifications. Once we're aboard, it'll be up to you and your team to take out the watch on duty in the control room without shooting it up too badly. If you get that right, I'll take care of the rest."

"We'll do our best." He blinked away the last of the eyedrops and the tears they'd produced, wiped his eyes with a gauze swab Tamsin handed him, and looked up at her. "How are the spacesuits? Usable?"

She frowned. "The ten that we captured in the lockers aboard this shuttle are pretty new. They look fine to me. The others we had in storage... not so much. They weren't in airtight containers, and got knocked around a bit during their transfer here. Trouble is, we don't have a proper test facility to check them out. I think a few should be usable after some care and attention. The rest are damaged to the point I don't trust them to be airtight any more. I'm cannibalizing them for parts to repair the others."

"And we need seventeen in all. I guess someone's going to have to go without, although two won't be in spacesuits for the first phase anyway."

She made a *moué* of distaste. "If a hit vents our internal atmosphere to space, anyone not in a suit's going to die a horrible death."

"I know, but there's nothing we can do about it unless we can fix some of the damaged suits. What if we tried wrapping them in good old-fashioned duct tape?"

She looked startled, then broke into a laugh. "Well, duct tape must have been used on anything and everything else in the settled galaxy for at least a millennium, so maybe it'll work on spacesuits too. We've got nothing to lose by trying it. A double layer of tape should slow any leaks enough that the suit will only deflate slowly. If whoever's wearing it stays as still as possible and doesn't move unless he has to, it should be good for ten to fifteen minutes in vacuum. If we aren't safely aboard either the space station or the ship by then, I guess none of us are going to make it at all."

Mac grinned. "That's the spirit! Now, I've been monitoring Bactrian space traffic ever since they invaded, keeping an eye on the ships they deploy to the Laredo system, learning their traffic control schedules and procedures in space and planetside, and analyzing their messages. How much do you know about their warships?"

"Only that they have them," Dave admitted. "Spaceships have never been one of my interests until now."

"All right. Briefly, they have one squadron of eight corvettes – that's about the smallest interstellar warship there is, maybe thirty thousand tons, the same size as a communications frigate. Each carries forty main battery missiles and forty defensive missiles. They don't base them here because they don't have enough of them in service, what with the demands of maintenance, training and so on. Also, warships are very expensive. Even though Bactria's economy is several times the size ours was before the war, she has to spend most of her military budget on the occupation here."

"Are those the small warships that sometimes visit this system?"

"That's right, although they don't stay for long. They use what we call 'armed merchant cruisers' to patrol our system. There are four, all old tramp freighters – some of the same ones they pressed into service as troopships to invade us, as a matter of fact. After the troops had been landed they sent four of them back to Bactria, where they fitted them with fire control systems and installed a few laser cannon and some missile tubes in a couple of their cargo holds. They're slow, the same speed as merchant ships, but there's no real threat to space traffic here so that doesn't matter. All they have to do is stop anyone making contact with us from space, and they've been adequate for that. They carry a lot more supplies than a corvette, so they can stay on station for several months. Of the four one's usually patrolling the Laredo system; one's in Laredo orbit giving local liberty to its crew, doing minor maintenance and preparing for the next patrol; one's back at Bactria for servicing; and one's on the regular monthly cargo and passenger run between here and there. With me so far?"

"Yes."

"OK. Also in orbit will be the Satrap's private yacht – it's a corvette hull that was built without missile cells. They converted the unused space into luxury apartments, and he uses it for official trips off-planet. It's usually escorted by one or two corvettes."

Dave grimaced. "So we'll have to deal with at least one actual warship, maybe two?"

"Yes. The yacht isn't a threat, of course, as she doesn't carry missiles, although I understand she has a couple of laser cannon for self-defense against incoming fire. The corvettes carry enough missiles to reduce any freighter to radioactive molecules."

"What about the cruiser on patrol?" Tamsin asked.

"It'll be no faster than the merchant ship coming to collect Mr. Ellis and our evidence. If she can get outside missile range of the cruiser and stay there, it won't be able to catch up with her."

Dave nodded thoughtfully. "So if she's on one side of the planet, the freighter will head in the opposite direction?"

"That's right, although it's a bit more complicated than that."

"And do we have to destroy the space station as well?"

"Yes, or at least disable it until we've left the Laredo system. If we don't, it can direct other ships to pursue us or broadcast a warning to any ship entering the system that might be able to intercept us. We're looking at ways and means to do that." Mac stretched. "Anyway, enough about my troubles. What about your plans for the attack on the Caristo garrison?"

"They're coming along nicely," Dave assured him. "I'll be taking half the crews of the other two shuttles back to Caristo with me in a few days to set up the assault on the garrison there. We'll be helped by those who plan to settle on farms and ranches in the area. I'll command the assault, but General Aldred's warned me I can't lead it in person. He wants me alive to command the mission to space. Instead I'll have plenty of NCO's to do the dirty work."

Mac grinned. "They won't let me have any fun either until we head up to orbit. Bunch of spoilsports, aren't they?"

Tamsin snorted, "Overgrown schoolboys, both of you! I'm glad I'll be there to help keep Dave under control."

"Oh?" Mac exclaimed in surprise. "You're not going to be flying us down to join him?"

"No, our backup pilot will do that. I've got to be there to supervise the fueling and arming of the garrison's two shuttles, then get them out of the way before our three shuttles arrive so we can fuel and arm them in their turn. We're going to be busier that night than a gang of one-legged people at a multiple ass-kicking contest!"

~ ~ ~

Jake invited Dave and Tamsin to have supper with him that night. He seemed preoccupied, almost distant. They tried to cheer him up, but weren't very successful. At last he pushed back his half-eaten meal.

"I'm sorry. I just can't seem to enjoy my food tonight. Let's get coffee, then take it to my quarters where we can talk privately."

Jake had been allocated a small alcove in the command tunnel as his personal quarters. They were surprised to see that all his gear had been packed and his sleeping-bag rolled tight, almost as if he were about to move out. Dave instantly guessed what that meant.

Jake saw him glancing around, and grimaced. "I see you've noticed. Yes, I'm leaving shortly before midnight. More than half of us will be leaving over the next few days. We learned yesterday that the Bactrians are strengthening their defensive perimeter around Banka in preparation for the parade. The Satrap and his entourage will be right slap bang in the middle of one of their most sensitive zones. We're going to have to infiltrate through multiple layers of security to get to it, so we plan to sneak through before they reinforce them so much as to make them impenetrable."

"What will be your part of the assault?" Tamsin asked.

"I'll be leading the first group to strike. We've got to clear the way for two other groups – yours, going up to orbit, and our shuttles heading for Banka. If we don't get our part right, no-one else can succeed; so we'll take it slowly and carefully to be sure we get through. Once we're inside the perimeter we'll recon possible approaches to our target, then wait for the day. Heaven knows the Bactrians have left enough ruins for us to have no trouble finding holes to hide in!"

Dave reached over and squeezed his father's arm, swallowing hard as he tried to find encouraging words. "I reckon you'll make it. You've done that sort of thing before." He had to take a deep breath before continuing. "I guess what you haven't said yet is that this is goodbye."

"I'm afraid so." There were unshed tears in his father's eyes.

There was a long silence as they looked at each other. Dave eventually broke it with a furiously whispered curse. *"Damn!* Part of me still wishes I could be with you!"

"I don't," Jake assured him. "When my time comes, I want to be able to look up at the sky with my last breath and wave goodbye to you. I don't want to see you die, boy. No parent should have to watch his children die."

Tamsin had tears in her eyes too. "What does one *say* at a time like this? It's… this is just too ghastly for words! How the hell do we say goodbye to you, knowing it's for the last time?"

"I don't know," Jake said simply. "I don't know how to say goodbye to you, either. All I can think of is to tell Dave how proud I am of the man he's become, and you how proud I am of the woman you've become. I wish I could have lived long enough under happier circumstances to see you married, and dandle your kids on my knees while demanding ever more grandchildren in a curmudgeonly tone!" They had to laugh with him.

"Then let's *not* say goodbye," Dave answered firmly. "We may not meet again in this life, but if what the preachers told us before the war is right, there'll come a time. I like the old legend about the dead crossing the river. I reckon you'll have plenty of dead Bactrians to form your honor guard and escort you over the water."

Jake chuckled. "I hope so. If anything goes wrong up there, make sure you provide your own escort when you come to join me, you hear? I'll buy the first beers on the other side."

Tamsin shook her head firmly. "I don't want beer – I want champagne, thank you very much! Not just any old plonk, either; something exotic and expensive."

"I'll see what the bars run to in Valhalla," Jake promised. "However, I hope it'll be a good long while before I see you there."

There was another long silence as they sipped their coffee and looked at each other. Finally Dave said, "I guess that's it, then." His voice was hoarse, a little choked. "There's nothing else to say. It hurts like hell to admit that, but… that's all there is. There *should* be more, dammit!"

"If there is, I don't know what it might be."

"Can we see you off tonight?" Tamsin asked.

"I'd rather not, if you'll forgive me. We're all saying goodbye to our friends and loved ones round about now. If a group of them gather to see us off, there'll be tears and grieving. I don't want that – none of us do. We'd rather just… get on with it. Is that wrong?"

"No. I understand." She reached over and hugged him.

"Thanks, Tamsin. You look after my son for me. I'll leave him in your capable hands."

"I'll keep him safe as long as I'm spared myself. That's a promise."

"You do the same for her, boy, you hear me?"

"You bet." Dave embraced him.

Jake pushed himself to his feet. "All right, you layabouts, we've wasted enough time. You've got your own work to do. Be off with you!"

~ ~ ~

At eleven-thirty that night, by unspoken accord, Dave and Tamsin walked out of the vehicle tunnel and down the road towards the clearing where they'd landed the captured SS shuttle. They stayed to one side among the trees and bushes lining its perimeter. Below the cliffs the waves rolled against the coast in the minimal light of the new moon, occasionally throwing spray high above the rocks, leaving the smell of ozone in the air. It was high tide.

They sat on a fallen log, a remnant of the debris from when the clearing had been cut. She leaned against him, his arm around her. They waited in silence until, shortly before midnight, they heard a low hum from the direction of the cave and the crunch of tires on gravel. As they rose to their feet an airvan moved into the clearing. Its lift fans accelerated, thrusting air downwards and outwards, molding their clothes against their bodies and whipping through their close-cropped hair. Without hesitation it rose, dipped and straightened, then headed out slowly over the sea. Behind it four more airvans followed in rapid succession. They formed up in arrowhead formation low over the waves then turned north and accelerated into the night. Tamsin knew their pilots would be keeping a wary eye on their warning panels, ready to take instant evasive action if radar or lidar transmissions should be detected and activate their masking devices.

126

Tamsin held Dave as she wept silently into his shoulder. She knew he was crying too, because his shoulders were shaking. He reached up now and again to wipe the tears from his eyes.

At last she whispered, "It's hard, isn't it, love?"

"It's harder than I'd ever have imagined possible."

"Do me a favor, darling. Don't ever say goodbye to me the way your father did tonight. Let's just... take what comes our way, in the sure knowledge that we love each other and nothing's ever going to change that, in this life or the next. If I know you're about to die, or you know I'm about to die, let's not burden each other with that. Let's go with a smile on our face and love for each other in our hearts."

"You've got my word."

They turned and walked slowly back down the road towards the cave, arms around each other.

March 14th 2850 GSC

TAPURIA: MILITARY GOVERNOR'S COMPOUND

Lieutenant Yazata blinked weariness from her eyes as she studied the huge wall display. It showed icons of various styles and sizes denoting roadblocks, patrols, radar and lidar stations, plasma cannon and missile batteries, reserve forces to reinforce threatened areas – the entire structure of the security perimeter surrounding Tapuria. It seemed impenetrable, she had to admit. If only it wasn't taking so long for the additional forces Major-General Huvishka had summoned to get here from their garrisons and take up their positions! The perimeter wouldn't be fully secured for at least another week.

She turned to look at the adjacent wall. It supported a similar display of the area inside the security perimeter, including the site of the former Banka that was being rebuilt into a proud, bustling Tapuria. Major installations such as the spaceport, the civil administration center and the military headquarters where she now stood were outlined in red to show the extent of their security perimeters. Within those borders, higher-security zones were highlighted in yellow. She zoomed in on the Command Bunker site, and nodded in satisfaction as she saw that the missile battery on top of the massive reinforced structure was now depicted as having all of the launch units it was supposed to have. Regrettably, some batteries had lost equipment during the years of conflict, destroyed, damaged or even captured by the enemy, but not replaced due to budget constraints. The

General had taken the unprecedented step of disbanding two batteries whose commanders had failed to meet his high standards, and distributing their components to other batteries to make up their deficiencies. His own headquarters had been the first to benefit. She couldn't help but approve, given that the security enhancements added to her own protection too.

As she watched, she saw an assault shuttle icon blink into life at the far corner of the Royal Palace compound. Again she nodded in satisfaction. After two missile batteries had been disbanded there hadn't been enough of them to go around, so the General had removed twenty assault shuttles from those originally assigned to the parade and directed them to arrive at Tapuria a few weeks early, bearing a full warload of missiles in addition to their plasma cannon. They were being placed at points where their weapons would provide additional security to vital installations. Their search radars and battle computers would remain silent, of course, as would those of local batteries. The far more powerful and sophisticated ground- and aerostat-based radar and lidar facilities of the spaceport's Traffic Control could search the entire volume of space over and around the city much more quickly and accurately than any mobile device, and its supercomputers could control missiles and plasma cannon with greater precision.

"What are you doing in the Operations Center this late, Lieutenant?"

The deep voice behind her made her jump. She stiffened to attention as she turned to face Major-General Huvishka, looming above her in the gloom of the glass-enclosed observation gallery. "Good evening, Sir. I thought you'd gone to bed already." She glanced down at the operators on the floor below. None looked up. The soundproof gallery prevented their voices from being overheard.

"I'm on my way there now. I thought I'd stop in here first, to see how things looked. I'm surprised you aren't in bed yourself."

"I was trying to figure out any other ways the rebels might try to penetrate our defenses, Sir."

He regarded her with keen interest. "Has any new intelligence made you suspect that they're going to do that?"

"No, Sir. That's what worries me. At the Military Academy they taught us there were only two ways to force an enemy to fight. One was to attack something she absolutely has to defend. The other is to defend something she absolutely has to attack. If I were the rebels, this parade would be something I'd feel obliged to attack. It concerns me that we've seen no indication they're preparing to do so. They may not have heard about it yet, of course, but enough units are moving to reinforce our security perimeter around Tapuria that the enemy *must* be aware that *something's* going on."

"And what would you do if you were in their shoes?"

"I'd expect them to try to smuggle some of the few heavy weapons remaining to them through our perimeter, but there's been no sign of that as yet. We may have overlooked it, but I don't think that's possible. They can't carry plasma cannon or heavy mortars on their backs through the bush! They can only move them by vehicle, and we've covered the roads and air traffic very effectively. They don't have any long-range artillery left. We know what they had before the war, plus what they captured from us. We've accounted for all of it during previous operations. That means they can't bombard the celebrations from outside the perimeter. The only signs of activity we've seen are a few small parties of rebels who've tried to sneak past various checkpoints. They've all been detected and taken under fire. Unfortunately none survived to be taken prisoner – a pity, because our interrogators might have been able to get useful information out of them."

She swept her finger around the areas of special security. "The interior security zones are all being tightened up, with additional sentries and mobile patrols assigned to critical areas. The most critical sites – the arena, the newly-completed Royal Palace, this complex and Traffic Control – now have triple-layered security, which is inside the city security zone, which in turn is inside our outer perimeter. That's five separate layers of defense attackers would have to penetrate in order to reach them. I don't see how a lightly-armed guerrilla force can hope to accomplish that, Sir."

"I tend to agree with you. Go on."

"Thank you, Sir. I've been concerned about whether the rebels might try to sneak one or both of their captured shuttles into the formation that will overfly the arena, but given the newly revised traffic control precautions I don't think that'll be possible, Sir."

"I haven't seen the latest updates. Refresh my memory about them, Lieutenant."

"Yes, Sir. Due to lack of space and facilities nearby, we've set up a temporary landing field here for the assault shuttles flying in from our garrisons for the parade." She indicated an icon twenty kilometers south of the security perimeter. "All of them are scheduled to arrive by not later than sunset on the thirtieth. Their troops will be taken to temporary barracks near the arena, from where they'll be bussed to the parade early the following morning. The crews will spend the night with their shuttles, then launch in sequence from zero-eight-hundred on the thirty-first. They'll form up in five groups over the field, then depart at zero-nine-forty-five to slowly overfly the arena from south to north at ten hundred precisely."

"How will Traffic Control prevent any marauding rebel shuttles from interfering?" General Huvishka asked.

"Each shuttle – in fact, everything in the air – will be assigned a new secure transponder beacon ID by TrafCon for the duration of the Satrap's visit, Sir. That'll protect it from being targeted while overflying our secure areas. All air defenses will be centrally controlled and activated through TrafCon. Anything not using one of the new transponder codes will be shot down at once, without prior warning."

"That should take care of that problem. Very well, go on."

"The shuttles will overfly the arena in formation before peeling off to land in the parking area outside. The Satrap and Crown Prince will then inspect the troops and equipment paraded inside, after which their motorcade will exit the arena and drive through the assembled shuttles to take the salute of their crews. When the parade is over the shuttles will return to their temporary field to collect their troops before departing for their garrisons later that afternoon."

"What anti-aircraft precautions are in place at the arena itself?"

"We have eight shuttles stationed there, Sir, two at each corner of the grounds. They're each equipped with eight missiles plus their plasma cannon."

"That should suffice, given the multiple defense layers an enemy would have to penetrate before getting anywhere near the arena in the first place."

"I hope so, Sir."

"Only 'hope', Lieutenant? Are you still not sure about the Satrap's safety and security?"

She shrugged helplessly. "Sir, I'm out of my depth here. I've never commanded a unit in the field – at least, not yet." She saw a flash of approval in his eyes at her qualification of that statement. "All I can say is, judging from the amount of damage the rebels have done to us over the years, I daren't underestimate them, even if it currently appears that they're no longer capable of interfering. I think it might be as dangerous to be overconfident as it would to be paranoid about them."

"I approve of your mindset, Lieutenant." The General stretched wearily. "If there's one law that applies to situations like this, it's Murphy's Law. Did you ever hear about it?"

"Isn't that the Old Home Earth saying, 'If anything can go wrong it will', Sir?"

"That's it. There's also a variation that warns us, 'Nature always sides with the hidden flaw'. I'm fully expecting both Murphy and an unsympathetic Nature to show up when we least expect them. We'll just have to be ready to deal with them when they do."

March 15th 2850 GSC

LAGUNA PENINSULA

"How are your preparations coming along?" General Aldred asked as he shook Dave's hand.

"As well as can be expected at this stage, Sir. This afternoon we'll be put through our paces in the spacesuits. It's hot, sweaty and uncomfortable wearing them planetside, but that's the way it has to be, I'm afraid."

"Yes, we've no other option."

"How are you going to get the garrison attack party back to Caristo tonight, Sir? We'll need a lot of airvans – nothing else can cover the distance fast enough."

"Yes, so we'll do it over two nights to make the best use of our limited number of vehicles. They're stretched to the limit right now ferrying more than half our strike force to within walking distance of Banka, to make their way through the fortified perimeter. The remainder will hit the four garrisons we've targeted, then board the assault shuttles we capture there and use them to join us. Your orbital team will meet you in Caristo in the SS shuttle, of course."

Gloria sighed. "All we'll be able to do for you at that point is to cross our fingers and pray hard. It'll all be up to you." She gestured at the large hard-sided suitcase on the table. "We hope this will help you to accomplish all the tasks we've laid on your shoulders."

The General opened the lid and took out four trays, laying them next to each other on the table. "We had our techs modify the suitcase and make up these trays on a fabber. Let's start at the beginning." He pointed to the lowermost tray, which was divided into compartments holding data chips and optical storage units. "We've duplicated every one of our records from the last three and a half years, including Gloria's 'Witness To War' material, and consolidated them all onto these media. You've got magnetic and optical storage versions as backups for each other."

"Each chip is in a protective case," Gloria pointed out as she opened one to demonstrate. "They should keep the data intact against anything short of a close-range electromagnetic pulse. The optical media aren't vulnerable to that, of course. The suitcase itself has been lined with a Faraday cage to provide another layer of protection."

"The next tray up is the physical evidence," the General continued as he touched it. It was a deeper unit containing several packages and envelopes, lying flat next to each other in specially constructed compartments lined with shock-absorbing material. "There's a detailed inventory in this envelope. These are all originals, of course."

"This is the critical stuff, then," Dave observed.

"Yes. We can produce copies until we're blue in the face, but Bactria would simply insist that they were forgeries. These are actual original enemy documents, including their signed threat to destroy Banka. There are also electronic storage units from captured hardware and other things that can be analyzed forensically, such as the torture materials you captured in the Matopo Hills, your recording of that SS Colonel speaking about them, and Lieutenant-Colonel Yardley's report on his experience of them. Any UP inquiry will need this evidence to verify our claims."

"And the Bactrians won't be able to dispute it?"

Gloria laughed scornfully. "Oh, they'll dispute it all, you can be sure of that! They'll fight tooth and nail to neuter any inquiry. They'll almost certainly try to exclude physical evidence altogether. It'll be up to Vice-President Johns and our Ambassador to the United Planets to get an inquiry resolution with teeth, one that'll admit physical evidence and allow for its verification. That'll give us a much better chance of proving that Bactria has been guilty of crimes against humanity, including genocide. If we do, interplanetary sanctions against them will be almost guaranteed."

"The UP won't send a peacekeeping force to kick them out of Laredo?"

"Only if member nations are willing to pay for it and contribute forces. I'm not sure they will. Frankly, we're a tiny polity in a galactic backwater. We liked it that way, of course; we could do our own thing and ignore the rest of the settled galaxy. Unfortunately, our independent natures bit us in the butt when Bactria invaded. We simply weren't, and still aren't, important enough for the major powers to overly concern themselves about us." Her voice was bitter. "That may be unpalatable, but it's the reality of interplanetary politics. Still, we've already resisted militarily, and made Bactria pay a far higher price in blood and money for Laredo than they ever foresaw. We'll do that again at the end of this month. This," and she patted the suitcase, "is a continuation of our resistance by other means. Who knows? In the long run it may cost Bactria even more than we've already made them pay."

Dave scowled. "Let's hope so."

"Indeed!" The General turned to the next tray. "Now we come to a more interesting tray. You're going to incur all sorts of costs in getting to Vice-President Johns. There'll be space travel, the cost of clothing, meals and other essentials, possibly some bribes to pay if you pass through less civilized planets… we simply can't predict all your expenses. That being the case, we're going to give you almost all that's left of our hard currency and assets. You'll draw on them for your needs, and deposit the balance into our Treasury account on Neue Helvetica."

He indicated several overstuffed banknote-sized envelopes, each in its own compartment. "Those contain cash: Laredo pesos, Bactrian bezants, Earth neodollars, Lancastrian Commonwealth credits, Neue Helvetica francs and New Bavarian marks. They add up to the equivalent of about half a million of our pesos in all. They'll be useful to pay a quick bribe, or something like that.

"The real value is in this next section." He lifted a box from the tray and opened the lid. It was sub-divided into padded compartments, each containing a stone. "These are alluvial diamonds from the Renosa River, uncut and unpolished. Locals used to sieve the gravel at the bottom of the river for them. They'd occasionally find a good stone, but mostly they got only small stuff – a carat or two at best. The Bactrians brought in dredgers soon after they arrived, and ripped up the entire riverbed for fifty kilometers above the delta. They made the mistake of using our people as slave labor on the project, so all the best diamonds they recovered came to us instead of being sent back to Bactria. The finest of them, twenty in all, are in this little case. They all score very high for clarity and color according to our local experts. Ten are between fifty and one hundred carats, five are one to two hundred, one's two to three hundred, two are three to four hundred and one's four hundred twenty carats in weight. We've been told by those who know the trade that their combined value is probably over three hundred million Neue Helvetica francs, even in their uncut state. That's almost half as much as we've got in our Treasury account."

Dave stared at them, fascinated. "I'd never have thought that nondescript-looking stones like that could be worth so much."

"They are, believe me! The Vice-President will have to select an honest diamond broker to sell them on her behalf. There are apparently lots of sharks in that profession, but with a little research she should be able to find someone trustworthy. We've buried the others that were smuggled to us in five separate locations." He showed Dave a fat envelope at the bottom of the box, beneath the stone-filled compartments. "That contains images of the sites, plus their planetary co-ordinates and bearing and distance from local landmarks, in case you're ever able to retrieve them. They're smaller stones, but there are a lot more of them. In total they're probably worth almost as much as the stones in this box. The envelope also contains initial expert assessments of each of these stones, plus a provisional valuation."

He replaced the box in the tray, removed a cloth bag from the next compartment, untied its drawstrings and poured its contents onto the table. They were small metal shapes, cubes or oval rounds made of solid gold. "These are gold *taels*. It's an ancient measure of weight for precious metals, about thirty-seven and a half grams. They're very common in commerce on planets with Oriental populations, particularly Chinese, where they're regarded as equal to cash or even better." He picked one up and showed Dave the seal of the mint where it had been cast, and the fineness grading stamped on it. "There are seventy-nine of them in this bag. Use them for expenses during your journey, or for a quick bribe if necessary." He scooped them back into the bag and returned it to its place in the tray.

"Finally, there are these." He took an envelope from the last compartment and extracted several check-sized documents made of heavy plaspaper, impervious to the elements, each with an embedded and chipped seal. "These are Neue Helvetica bearer bank drafts."

"I've never heard of them before, Sir," Dave confessed.

"Think of them in the same way as cashier's checks. They're issued by major banks on Neue Helvetica, like the Handelsbank where we keep our Treasury account. The issuing bank guarantees that it holds funds to the value of the draft. It'll pay them on presentation, or transfer them to a bank of the bearer's choosing on any planet. They're widely used and trusted in interplanetary commerce – the next best thing to a gold bar, I suppose. Local businesses had some that hadn't been cashed when the war began. They come to a total of over twenty-five million Neue Helvetica francs." He replaced them in the envelope. "Use them as necessary to cover your expenses. You'll find branches or agents of the bigger Helvetica banks on most major planets. They'll validate the drafts and cash them in hard currency at a five per cent discount to face value. That means you'll get ninety-five per cent of the funds. The balance is the bank's profit, and also covers the cost of redeeming them at Neue Helvetica."

"I get it." Dave grinned suddenly. "You're being very trusting, giving me all this money."

"If you're not trustworthy, we've wasted our time on you all these years! Besides, if we don't give it to you, the Bactrians will get it all eventually."

"Anything but that!" Gloria said emphatically.

"Agreed." He turned to the fourth, uppermost tray. "This contains a number of items. First, there are diplomatic passports for all the members of your team, valid for ten years, accredited to our Government-in-Exile." He displayed a sheaf of chips, each with a diplomatic seal. "Vice-President Johns will have to register them with the United Planets, but that's just a formality – they're valid as issued. We've also included several dozen blank passports, both diplomatic and regular, plus the authentication program to encode them with the bearer's details and activate them. We have no further need for them, but she may find them useful."

"Yes, Sir."

"Next, these chips contain master files that should be readable by most fabric extruders, autotailors and fabbers. They contain detailed instructions to produce Laredo Army uniforms and medals. I've included a certified list of the awards all of you have earned over the years, even though we've usually notified you of them through your commanders and issued certificates rather than held formal investiture parades."

Dave frowned. "Sir, medals seem pretty meaningless after all the fighting we've seen. Besides, most of us lost what originals we had when we abandoned bases in a hurry during enemy raids. I can't say I've missed mine. Why bother with them now?"

"Because you'll be dealing with diplomats and politicians who'll be impressed by them, and most particularly because other military men will recognize that you earned them the hard way. They'll speak volumes about your experience, and hopefully earn you the respect of those who may be able to help you. A fabric extruder can duplicate the ribbons, and I want you to have a fabber produce copies of the medals. A jeweler can polish and enamel them as necessary. All of you should wear them with your uniforms on formal occasions. Do I have to make it an order?"

"No, Sir. We'll do it, but only because it's you asking."

Aldred sighed. "I suppose I should be flattered." They all chuckled. "Very well. In this next compartment are two pulsers, each with a holster, spare power pack and ammunition. They're in scan-proof boxes. Unless someone searches the suitcase by hand they won't be detected – and a hand search is unlikely, thanks to these." He indicated a transparent envelope containing a stack of seals. "These are diplomatic seals to be applied to this suitcase. Coupled with your diplomatic passports, they should be sufficient to get this stuff through Customs without it being inspected – at least, they will on the larger, more law-abiding planets. If you end up on some backwater planet where civilized standards aren't the norm, they probably won't help you."

"I'll try to avoid places like that, Sir."

"Good. Remember that you can't carry weapons on most planets, even with diplomatic passports, unless you qualify to do so under local laws and regulations. Once you're aboard the ship you're going to have to dump all your military weapons before landing anywhere else. In fact, the skipper will probably insist that you put them all into your assault shuttle, then he'll

drop it into the star of some uninhabited system before going on to his –
your – destination."

Dave shook his head. "It'll feel like being naked to be unarmed after
so many years with a weapon always on or near me, Sir."

"I know. That's why I included these pulsers in the suitcase. They
won't be as easily accessible as a weapon on your person, but at least you
know they're there. If you get any warning of imminent danger, you'll
hopefully be able to get to them before anything blows up."

"Thank you, Sir."

"Then there are these." He took two small envelopes from the
penultimate compartment. "They're our two bearer bank keys for Laredo's
Handelsbank account. One was in the custody of the Secretary of the
Treasury and the other of the Secretary of State for Foreign Affairs. Before
the war our account contained something over six hundred million Neue
Helvetica francs – not much by the standards of major planets, but a
fortune by ours. It's all still there. Guard them with your life until you
deliver them to the Vice-President. They're as important as the evidence,
because without them she can't access the funds needed to initiate a UP
investigation."

"Will do, Sir." Dave hesitated. "If she hasn't had access to our
account, how has she been able to pay for her needs over the past few
years?"

"We sent funds and hard assets off-planet with her – all we could
scrape together on such short notice. She's had to operate on a tight
budget, but she's coped, or so I'm told."

"Yes, Sir. I understood she has a key, and our Ambassador to the UP
has the fourth. Who has the fifth, please, Sir?"

"The fifth was held by President Wexler. When the Bactrians captured
him, they got his key too. They tortured him until he signed a letter
authorizing them to use it, then tried to withdraw our funds from the
Handelsbank; but of course the bank refused, because any transaction
requires the physical presence of three of our five bank keys. The Bactrians
were furious, and even tried to get the United Planets to exert pressure on
their behalf; but it has no jurisdiction over private banks, so they got
nowhere. By then President Wexler was dead – of disease according to
them, but we believe he died as the result of torture – so they couldn't use

him to pressure the Vice-President or our Ambassador to the UP to hand over their keys."

"I see, Sir. What happens if I can't get to the Vice-President at first? Say I meet up with our Ambassador to the UP. Should I give him the bank keys and the rest of this stuff?"

"Not under any circumstances! We're not entirely sure of the Ambassador's loyalty – he's made noises in the past about 'the need for a negotiated settlement with Bactria'. Your orders state specifically and unequivocally that the *only* person off-planet who's entitled to give you orders or take custody of these articles is Vice-President Johns. No-one else is in your chain of command once you leave here, unless and until she tells you differently. Until you reach her, you alone are in charge of the keys and everything else in this suitcase. Your orders make that clear. Understood?"

"Understood, Sir... but that's a hell of a responsibility for a junior officer, if you don't mind my saying so."

"It is, but you're a hell of a responsible officer, if you don't mind *my* saying so."

"It's good to be appreciated, Sir. Can I have a raise, please?" More laughter.

"When were you last paid, anyway?" Gloria asked

Dave shrugged. "A couple of years ago, I think. I must have built up a pretty good sum in back pay by now!"

"Take it out of the suitcase for all of you once you figure it out," she suggested. "It should be enough for a heck of a party somewhere."

"I don't see why not," her husband agreed. "Last but not least, here are your orders." He took another envelope from the last compartment in the tray. "They're in electronic format, but I've included a printout." He handed it to Dave. "They're in accordance with our discussions over the past couple of days. Read them carefully, and if there's anything that isn't clear see me before you leave."

"Will do, Sir."

"I've tried to cover all the bases, because once you leave here we'll no longer be able to advise you. I want to highlight a few points. First, you've been appointed Commanding Officer of all external – that is, off-planet – armed forces of the Republic of Laredo. Since we can't really have an officer at junior level occupying such a post, you'll be promoted to the rank of Major with effect from the day you leave this planet. You've been given the authority to recruit, enlist and commission personnel as required, and promote them – including yourself – and assign them to combat and non-combat missions and responsibilities. That authority will remain in force and effect unless and until terminated under the authority of the Great Seal of the Republic of Laredo. Our Declaration of Emergency when the Bactrians looked certain to invade assigned the Seal to Vice-President Johns in her capacity as President *pro tempore* of our Government-in-Exile. We registered the Declaration with the United Planets to ensure that other planets recognize that authority. She may surrender it only to her freely chosen successor in that office, or on demand to a President of Laredo legitimately elected under our pre-invasion Constitution. Only the authorized bearer of the Seal has final authority over Laredo's external assets, personnel, policies and actions.

"Second, your primary mission is to get this evidence to Vice-President Johns. Thereafter you'll make yourself and your detachment available to her. In the event that you're unable to reach or receive orders from her, I've given you sole discretion as to your future conduct. You're free to continue hostilities with Bactria as best you can; or you can disband your unit and discharge its members from the armed forces of Laredo, giving them an opportunity to make a new life elsewhere. If you can't arrange for a United Planets inquiry, you're requested to publicize what Bactria did to Laredo, using this evidence as effectively as possible under the circumstances confronting you. To accomplish all these things you're authorized to use as you see fit the contents of this suitcase and any other external resources of Laredo that may be available to you."

Dave swallowed. "That's a pretty heavy load to put on my shoulders, Sir."

"It is, but I see no alternative. Do you?"

"I guess not. I'll do my best, Sir."

"Good." He began to replace the trays in the suitcase. "I'm sure I don't have to remind you – but I will anyway – to instruct the other members of your orbital team what to do with this suitcase in the event that you're incapacitated or killed."

"Yes, Sir."

"All right, then." He closed the suitcase and fastened its latches. "I'll put this aboard your shuttle, to join you after you take the garrison at Caristo."

Dave shook his head. "Sir, with your permission I'd rather take it with me. It'll be no less safe in our hideout near Caristo than it will be here, and that way I won't be worrying about it all the time. I can have some of our attack team mount guard over it if you wish."

Aldred frowned, then reluctantly nodded. "I daresay you're right." He handed over the suitcase. "Two last things. First, we're entrusting you with two of our nuclear demolition charges."

Dave's eyes widened with surprise. "I thought the Bactrians got them when they took the space station, Sir."

"They were kept there for use against asteroids or space hazards, but when the survivors escaped planetside they brought the five charges with them. We've kept that quiet and hidden them ever since. We're in the process of burying three of them in a remote spot. I'll give you the location for future reference in case you're ever able to retrieve them. The last two will be put aboard your shuttle, along with instructions in their use and the necessary codes and keys to activate them. Use one or both to destroy the space station. If you have one left, shove it out of the freighter with a half-hour time setting when you reach the system boundary, then hyper-jump away before it goes off."

"Will do, Sir."

"Good. Second, here's a satellite back-door channel." He handed him a folded slip of paper. "In the event that you get away, and you need to communicate with any of us who survive on this planet by sending a ship the way Marvin has, tell whoever you send to try a tight-beam link to our comm satellite network at midnight every night, Banka time. Use that channel and our standard codebook. If we're able to, someone will answer. If we don't, it'll probably mean the Resistance has collapsed and we're all dead."

"Understood, Sir."

"In that case, all that remains is for us to wish you success. We'll see you and the garrison attack team for the last time tonight, to bid you farewell and Godspeed."

PART TWO

March 30th 2850 GSC

TAPURIA

Jake pulled down the corner of one of the blinds and glanced through the cracked, dirty glass at the street below. An armored car rumbled past, tires crunching over scattered dirt and debris. Its power pack whined and its badly adjusted turret made a grinding noise as it turned slightly from side to side. Its commander looked over the barrel of the vehicle's plasma cannon as he scanned the street ahead, not bothering to turn his head to examine the half-ruined warehouses lining it. He looked bored in the rays of the setting sun. Jake knew that here at the outer edge of TrafCon's security zone, nothing ever happened – not with missile batteries, plasma and laser cannon, and security forces within arm's reach, ready to open fire at the drop of a hat and drop it themselves if they felt like it. No-one in his right mind would start anything here.

Jake let the blind fall as he grinned to himself, thinking, *No-one ever said the Resistance was in its right mind – and the Bactrians have gotten careless about checking just outside the zone. They only worry about what's inside it. That's going to hurt them. In just a few hours we're going to demonstrate that a security zone's only as good as the people who run it... and sometimes they're not very good at all.*

He turned back to the others. "It's just another street patrol. Nothing to worry about."

"Supper, Sir?" Lieutenant Kubicka asked.

"I may as well eat," he grunted, scanning the selection of ration packs lined up on the table. He reached for one labeled 'Meat Stew'. "This is easy to digest, even if it isn't very tasty."

"It won't give you gas like the beans and sausage, either, Sir."

"Yes. It'd be just too much to go into action farting. I bet the Bactrians would complain we'd used poison gas on them!"

Those standing nearby chortled, but their laughter was brittle, strained. Jake knew their minds were on the morning, and what would almost certainly be the last day of life for many of them. He was having the same difficulty himself. The tension was a red-hot wire threaded through his guts, tugging, pulling, burning. Their target was right slap bang in the middle of Banka's security zone. Getting away after the attack would be very difficult. *What will death be like?*, he found himself wondering for the umpteenth time. *Will it hurt? Will I be able to control myself and die like a man? Or will I scream helplessly, like I've seen too many good people do when they were driven beyond self-control by roaring red agony?*

He thrust the memories from his mind by turning his thoughts to his son. He knew Dave would be preparing to brief the force about to assault the Caristo garrison, just as he was about to speak to the rest of Niven's Regiment. Would the boy live through the night's assault and tomorrow morning's desperate fight in orbit? Would he escape to start a new life somewhere else? *I'll probably never know*, Jake thought sadly to himself; then cursed softly and again tried to drive the dark shadows out of his mind. There was too much still to be done.

He sipped coffee as he walked to the store-room against the rear wall and checked his combat gear yet again. His last clean uniform was laid out, complete with underwear and a brand-new pair of socks – a rare treat. His electromagnetic rifle was cleaned and ready, along with a dozen hundred-round chargers of ammunition and two spare power packs. He grinned wryly. The Bactrians actually made a decent infantry weapon, accurate and reliable, with which the entire Resistance was now equipped thanks to plentiful captures and a shortage of ammunition for their original carbines. As for heavy weapons, they hadn't been able to smuggle them through the security perimeter around Banka, but their shuttle-borne comrades would bring some with them and they'd capture more from the defenders if they needed them. They'd done so often enough in the past, after all.

He checked for the umpteenth time that his earpiece and microphone were securely clipped to his helmet and the encrypted radio on his battle belt was set to the right frequency. His visor displayed all its six modes correctly as he ran through them. The power pack on his belt was fully charged, to provide a day and night of power to his battle tools. Finally he took a miniature Bible from his pack and tucked it into his shirt pocket.

He swallowed the last of his coffee and walked to the door of the storeroom. In the half-wrecked upper-level office space outside, part of its roof missing since the explosion that had destroyed nearby Banka, the troops were also checking their gear.

"All right, everyone, gather round!"

Jake waited as his forty soldiers filed to the front of the room, sitting down on boxes and crates in a rough semi-circle before him. He switched on a portable projection unit and checked its display against the wall, then asked one of the men to hang a white sheet against the partition so it could be seen more clearly. He'd finished by the time the last person sat down.

"I know all of you have been curious during the past couple of weeks," he began. "You've trained to attack targets with a specific layout and configuration, but without knowing what or where they were. You were told that this is a volunteer mission with little chance of survival, but not why it was so important as to be worth your lives. I can only thank you all for accepting the challenge. Tonight I'm going to tell you more about our part in this mission. Strike teams from our other three regiments are waiting in the ruins of Banka just as we are, standing by to attack as soon as we open the way for them. Four more teams of our comrades are preparing to assault distant garrisons tonight. They'll kill every Bactrian there and take control of their assault shuttles. They'll arm them, then bring the shuttles here to help us tomorrow."

The soldiers grinned their approval, exchanging comments in quiet tones so as not to alert any passing Bactrians. Jake waited for silence, then pointed out, "We in this room are the key to this entire operation. We have to succeed if our comrades are to succeed. If we fail, they can't achieve their objectives – but we won't fail. In fact, through their laziness and stupidity, the Bactrians have made our job possible. You see, two years before the invasion Laredo invested a lot of money in new traffic control systems. We bought a supercomputer and ground- and aerostat-based planetary radars, and upgraded our space station equipment too. When the Bactrians took over they didn't see any point in replacing perfectly good equipment; so they kept it, merely adding their own interface to bring it into conformity with their standard operating procedures."

He grinned ferally. "They made two crucial mistakes. The first was combining spaceborne and airborne traffic control in a single new facility down here, instead of keeping them separate. That's great for centralized control, but it's a lot easier for an enemy to disrupt things, because he only has to take out the central node for the entire network to disintegrate. Second, our radar and comm feeds all went to the basement of the old traffic control center. The above-ground portion was severely damaged during the destruction of Banka, but the basement levels, including the computer center, were left intact. When the Bactrians built their new TrafCon they saved a lot of time and money by making it simply an operations center. They left the computer and the radar and comm feeds in the basement at the old center and laid new connections to them, instead of moving them all to the new building.

"They included both buildings in their high-security zone, but their contractors decided to take a short-cut to save time and make a bit of extra profit. Instead of cutting a new secure cable tunnel between the two buildings, they dug a short connecting tunnel to the main service tunnel beneath the street. They then ran their conduit along the roof of that tunnel until it passed the new center, where they dug another connecting tunnel into its basement. Unfortunately for their security – but luckily from our perspective – that service tunnel passes through a four-way intersection with another tunnel halfway between the buildings. The cross-tunnel passes out of the high-security zone with only a heavy gate to bar access to it, and runs beneath the road outside. It even connects to this warehouse to allow tie-ins to city utilities.

"We're going to use those tunnels to sneak beneath the enemy's defenses and take over the old traffic control center tomorrow morning. We'll hold off the Bactrians while our technicians," and he nodded to several people at the rear of the group, "use emergency consoles in the basement to make some creative adjustments. Some of them worked on this system before the war, so they know exactly what to do. They'll clear the way for our shuttles to move in on the Satrap's parade, to kill him and as many enemy troops as they can. While they're doing that, we'll cut the links to the new TrafCon to cause as much confusion as possible, then rig the supercomputer for demolition.

"The attack on the arena will trigger a massive knee-jerk response from other Bactrian forces in the city. They'll rush to rescue their Satrap, but to do that they'll have to pull defenders from other important targets. That'll be the cue for our raiding parties to come out of hiding and attack the civil and military headquarters compounds and the central stores depot. They'll wreck the planetary administration from end to end. Furthermore, while all that's going down, another team under the command of my son Dave will be taking out the space station and dealing with the warships in orbit before putting all our evidence aboard a waiting freighter whose visit was set up by our Government-in-Exile. It'll take it to our Vice-President, who'll use it to demand action against Bactria by the United Planets for its crimes against humanity."

There was a moment's awed, shocked silence, then suddenly everyone was on their feet. They didn't forget the need for relative quiet, but even so, hardened troopers fist-bumped and hugged each other in excitement, their eyes sparkling. Jake let the muted hubbub go on for a few moments before he called for order. "Come on, people! We've still got a lot to do. Settle down!"

He waited for the celebrations to subside, then said solemnly, "General Aldred has assigned to Niven's Regiment the most important task in this entire operation – taking over the traffic control network. If the network is operational the Bactrians will detect our shuttles coming in and shoot them down, and be able to co-ordinate the response of their own assault shuttles to our attacks in the city. They'll also warn their forces in orbit about our attack here, putting them on alert. If we take over the network they can't do any of those things. More to the point, they've slaved all their defenses against airborne attack to the TrafCon supercomputer. If we control it, we can do all sorts of interesting things with their defenses – and we will!

"As soon as all our attacks are under way across the city, we'll destroy the computer center and set up booby-traps for enemy responders. We'll then try to make our way out of the city in small groups, using captured vehicles and if necessary hiding in the wreckage of Banka that the Bactrians haven't cleared yet. That's going to be difficult, because we're right in the heart of their defenses and they'll be sending in troops from their outer perimeter to assist those under fire inside the city. Frankly, I don't think most of us will make it out, but we'll sell our lives dearly and take as many Bactrians with us as we can. Even if we die, we'll hurt the enemy worse than he's ever been hurt before – and he'll still have to answer to the United Planets. Killing us will be a Pyrrhic victory."

He paused for a moment as he looked around the gathering, gathering his thoughts. "This is probably our last stand as an organized Resistance. We stand foursquare in the tradition of Horatius and his companions at the Sublicius Bridge; of Leonidas and his three hundred Spartans at Thermopylae; of Roland and his companions at Roncevaux Pass; of Travis, Bowie, Crockett and the volunteers at the Alamo; of the Jewish resisters in the Warsaw Ghetto who freely chose to fight, even knowing they had no chance of survival, rather than meekly submit to genocide. We stand with the thousands upon thousands of others throughout history who've followed the example of such heroes. There must have been far, far more of them than the few whose names are known – and they're all here in spirit with us tonight.

"I couldn't ask for better friends and comrades than you. That's what we all are to each other – friends and comrades, not just fellow soldiers. We've lived together as best we can while so many of our comrades died around us. Now it's time for us to honor their memory in our last fight.

"I'm going to run through our briefing for the last time in one hour from now. Until then you're free to prepare yourselves in your own way for what lies ahead." He took the Bible from his pocket and held it up. "I'm going to be doing that according to my Christian tradition. Those of you who share it are welcome to join me, as well as any others who are interested." He indicated the store-room he was using as his office and bedroom.

"No matter what your faith or philosophy, remember the ancient words of Judas Maccabeus: 'Arm yourselves, and be ye men of valor, and be in readiness for the conflict; for it is better for us to perish in battle than to look upon the outrage of our nation and our altar.' That's the way I see it, too."

~ ~ ~

152

CARISTO

Dave laid down the pointer he'd been using to indicate important features of the garrison layout. "Sergeant Dixon will jigger their security systems for us one last time, so there should be no alarm as we penetrate. The critical thing is that we've got to assault every building simultaneously and take out everybody at once, before anyone has a chance to sound the alarm or radio their headquarters. If any warning gets out this entire operation will be over before it's begun, and we'll all be screwed. That's why it's even more important than usual to make sure that none of the enemy survives. Put them down fast, hard and permanently. Make sure they're dead, so we don't have to worry about what they're doing when our backs are turned."

He looked around the room. "As soon as you call your area clear, summon the corpsman to treat any friendly casualties, then double-check the enemy to make sure they're all dead. Your senior NCO's and myself will verify that there's no further threat, then we'll tell you to move to your assigned positions to prepare the assault shuttles. The pilots and Weapons System Operators are in charge of that. They're the experts, so don't try to anticipate or second-guess them! We've got to get the garrison's two birds ready as quickly as possible, but they should already be fully fueled, so that'll help. Our other three shuttles will be flying in. We need to get these shuttles out of the hangar by the time they arrive, so we can take the new arrivals inside to refuel, rearm and prepare them in their turn. We've got to finish that job for all the shuttles by not later than zero-three-thirty. At that point the support team will return to their homes and prepare for whatever may follow our attack – including a disappearing act with their families if necessary – and the shuttles will depart for Banka. After they've gone I'll give the final briefing to the orbital team. Any questions?"

A soldier raised his hand. "Sir, what about the people in town? Won't some of them call in an alarm when they hear the shooting?"

"Perhaps, but they'll have to call it in through the garrison. All the comm lines and circuits go there – they were re-routed that way when the Bactrians built it. Sergeant Dixon will shut down all external circuits so they can't call through to any other center. He'll tell them everything's under control, it's just an exercise, and they can go back to sleep."

"But, Sir, what about when assault shuttles start flying low over their heads?"

"All part of the exercise, of course."

"Oh. OK… I guess, Sir."

"If they complain, we can always invite them to come down to the garrison and do so in person. That should shut them up." The troops laughed. They all knew that complaining about such frivolities to a Bactrian garrison was likely to land the complainant in very hot water.

"Any further questions?" No-one raised a hand. "All right, people. You're free for the next hour. We'll reassemble here at ten to kit up and check each other. We hit the garrison just after midnight."

Dave looked at each soldier as he spoke slowly and carefully. "We know this is probably our last mission as an organized Resistance. I advise you to prepare yourselves for that in whatever way suits you. As Shakespeare put it, 'Stiffen the sinews, summon up the blood'. I've already warned the other half of the team, those coming in on the shuttles, to do the same before leaving base.

"I want to leave you with a thought from Marek Edelman, the last commander of the Jewish resistance fighters against the Nazis in the Warsaw Ghetto during Old Home Earth's Second Global War. You know we've taken inspiration from their fight because we face a similar enemy in the Bactrians, who are determined to exterminate us or reduce us to the status of slaves. Edelman said many years after the war that it was easier to die fighting than in a gas chamber. It's going to be easier for us to die fighting the Bactrians than it will for our fellow Laredans, the men, women and children being worked to death right now in Bactrian slave labor camps. We mustn't feel that we're heroes and they're just poor saps who wouldn't fight or couldn't get out of the way in time. Their deaths will take longer and be harder than ours. We're fighting, and a lot of us have died and will die, so that *their* sacrifice, *their* suffering, will be known and remembered. Let's not fail them."

As the troops filed out, some silent, others talking among themselves in low voices, Sergeant-Major Deacon came over to Dave with two soldiers. "Can I have a word, please, Sir?"

"Sure, Sergeant-Major, what is it?"

"Sir, General Aldred spoke with me and a couple of others before we left the base. He told us that above all else, we're to ensure your safety during the assault on the garrison. He asked me to make sure you didn't join in the fighting yourself, but stayed back until the danger was past. I know in space we'll all take our chances, Sir, but we can't afford to lose you up front. Will you please stay out of the line of fire until then?"

"He said something similar to me, Sergeant-Major. It just goes against the grain to ask my soldiers to expose themselves to risks when I don't."

"That's why they give you that exalted title and pay you so much, Sir." The other two sniggered, although Dave was in no mood to be amused. "Seriously, Sir... please? I don't want to have to tell Sergeant Hein and Corporal Bujold to sit on your chest and hold you down while the rest of us take care of business."

"Don't worry, Sergeant-Major, I'll be good. You're a bunch of spoilsports, you know that?"

"That's a senior NCO's job, Sir. Didn't I teach you that during basic training?"

He heard a soft laugh from behind him. Tamsin said, "You certainly taught me! I don't think I forgave you for years!"

The Sergeant-Major tried without much success to look hurt. "After all I've done for you, this is the thanks I get?"

"What do you expect, a kiss? Those I save for my Captain."

"Huh! Well, they do say rank has its privileges."

"You bet it does – and right now I'm going to spend our last hour of peace and quiet with him, so the three of you can run along and leave us alone."

The three broke into broad smiles. "Have fun, Sir," Hein said as he turned away with the others.

Tamsin put her arm around Dave. "That was well done, lover," she murmured. "You said what needed to be said."

"Thanks."

"And having said everything, there's one thing more. If this is going to be our last hurrah, I want us to go out with a bang – in more ways than one."

"Is this one of those privileges of rank the Sergeant-Major was talking about?"

"Rank, hell! It's a privilege of lovers!"

He laughed. "Well, whatever it is, you don't hear me complaining."

March 31st 2850 GSC, 00:00

CARISTO: ON THE HILLSIDE ABOVE THE GARRISON

Dave pulled the command headset over his eyes, and blinked at the sudden visual overload. A schematic of the garrison buildings was laid out before him, transmitted from the sensors of the hoversat they'd launched to fly directly overhead. Icons showed the position of each member of the attacking unit, and each building was labeled with its purpose, size, and the number of people it was supposed to contain.

"Damn, this is a useful little toy!" he whispered to Sergeant Hein beside him. "I wish I'd had it available for some previous operations. Now I understand why some of our ambushes failed, if the Bactrians were using this sort of thing against us."

"Is everyone safely tucked up in bed, Sir?" Hein asked. The NCO and Corporal Bujold had stuck to him like glue during the approach, and accompanied him to the overwatch position without bothering to ask for permission or approval. Dave knew they were quite prepared to 'sit on his chest', as the Sergeant-Major had put it, and make him behave if they had to.

"Everyone except those in the guardroom and whoever's in the Captain's office – its light is on, but with the blinds closed I can't see who's inside. Let me check the outlying areas." Dave expanded the area of surveillance. The hoversat's sensors scanned the entire area within the fence surrounding the base, but showed no sources of body heat or movement. "Looks like nobody's out and about," he confirmed.

Hein observed, "Now that their Captain's gone, taking the best troops with him – not that that's saying much, mind you – most of the others are probably drunk."

"Let's hope so," Corporal Bujold whispered from Dave's far side. "In a way I guess they're lucky. Hangovers usually make me feel as if I want to die. They're going to experience the reality before the feeling can set in!" Dave and Hein snorted in subdued amusement.

As the time display in the headset ticked down the minutes, Dave watched the icons representing his assault team. They'd spread out to their assigned positions smoothly and silently. He knew that Sergeant-Major Deacon would initiate the attack on schedule, and all he had to do was sit back and watch; but he couldn't help feeling – irrationally, he knew – as if he were somehow letting his people down by not being there with them.

~ ~ ~

TAPURIA: COMMAND BUNKER

Lieutenant Yazata replaced the comm handset with a grimace of distaste as she turned to the Major in command of the evening watch. "Caristo has nothing to report, Sir."

"Very well. You seem unhappy about something?"

"I think the Sergeant-Major to whom I spoke had been drinking, Sir."

He shrugged. "Hardly surprising in a punishment posting like that. Caristo was the last one, right?"

"Yes, Sir. None of our outlying garrisons have seen any sign of increased rebel activity."

"Good." The man's voice was brusque. She knew he resented her running the Military Governor's errands, thereby denying him the opportunity to report directly to his boss and be noticed, but he had the good sense to keep his feelings under control. "Does the General want us to obtain further updates during the night?"

"No, Sir. This was just a precautionary check. The General wanted to be sure there was no rebel activity that might indicate an attack. He still thinks they might try something to take attention away from tomorrow morning's parade."

The Watch Commander shrugged as he glanced around the Operations Center. "They can't have more than a couple of hundred people left, scattered all over the continent. We've captured or destroyed most of their heavy weapons. What sort of credible attack could they possibly mount?"

"I don't know, Sir," she said neutrally. "I'll tell the General all's well."

She found her boss rising from his desk as he switched off his terminal display. "All's quiet, Sir. No sign of rebel activity."

"Thank you for checking." He stretched, a bone-creaking release of the day's tension. "I'll be glad when this is all over. I wonder how the Satrap is enjoying his new palace?"

She smiled. They'd both watched the feed from the sensors installed throughout the building to guard against rebel infiltrators. They had shown the Satrap and the Crown Prince enjoying an opulent meal.

"I wonder if we could conscript the Satrap's cooks for duty with your Headquarters, Sir?" she asked mischievously.

He snorted with amusement. "Do please make sure you don't repeat that where the Satrap can hear it. I'd hate to lose the services of so efficient an officer due to a charge of *lèse-majesté.*" He winked at her.

She solemnly returned it. "Does the General require any further assistance?"

"No, I think I'll try to get a few hours' sleep before the big day. I suggest you do the same."

"Yes, Sir."

~ ~ ~

CARISTO: GARRISON

Sergeant-Major Garnati scratched at his stubbly jowls as he replaced the handset. *Damn that interfering busybody Lieutenant!* he thought resentfully as he rose from the heavily cushioned chair. *Who the hell does she think she is, taking senior NCO's away from a well-earned bottle at the end of the busiest month they've ever experienced, just to find out that nothing's going on as usual? Paranoid bitch!*

159

He lurched towards the door opening onto the walkway in front of the administration building, already unsteady on his feet from the half-bottle of moonshine he'd consumed before being summoned urgently to the Captain's office to take the call from Tapuria. His glance fell on the glass-fronted liquor cabinet, and his eyes suddenly gleamed. His new boss might be an asshole, but his family was rich enough that he could afford to indulge in the finest food and drink. He'd brought a lot from Tapuria, along with his own private chef, waiter and valet – all of whom he'd taken back to the city with him for the parade.

Garnati bent, opened the doors and pawed through the serried ranks, muttering to himself as he read the labels. He straightened with an ornately fluted crystal bottle in his hand. "Huh! 'Satrap's Private Reserve, matured in the cask for 20 years'. Well, I'll be damned! This ought to give me the most expensive hangover I've ever had!"

He stripped the foil from the neck and used the Captain's silver corkscrew to roughly, impatiently yank out the stopper, hands shaking with sudden need. He put the bottle to his lips and upended it. A trickle of brown liquid flowed from the corner of his mouth and ran over his chin and down his neck as he swallowed, head tilted back, eyes closed in ecstasy.

"Damn, that's good stuff! Beats the local firewater all to hell!" He lifted the bottle mockingly to the empty chair behind the Captain's desk. "I'll be sure to drink a toast to you with the last mouthful, you pompous pimp! I reckon you'd have been pissed if you'd seen my non-commissioned ass sitting in your princely chair just now. Better be careful – it might give you boils!"

Chuckling semi-drunkenly to himself, he fumbled at the door of the office, swung it open, and stepped onto the walkway outside. He frowned as he saw four dark figures crouched around the door of the guardroom, further down the building.

"Hey, you! What – "

~ ~ ~

CARISTO: ON THE HILLSIDE ABOVE THE GARRISON

Dave's heart lurched in his chest as the door to the Captain's office swung open and the familiar figure of Sergeant-Major Garnati stepped down onto the walkway. He swung towards the guardroom where four members of the assault party crouched, ready to burst through its door. Dave couldn't hear any words from this far away, but he saw one of the assault team spin around. The whip-like crack of a shot echoed across the garrison compound and up the hillside. Garnati's head snapped back and his body crumpled bonelessly to the walkway.

Over the radio Dave heard Sergeant-Major Deacon's voice. *"Go-go-go!"* His well-trained, experienced assault teams didn't turn a hair at the unexpectedly early signal. They burst through the doors at which they'd been stationed, turning their weapons on the bleary-eyed, fumbling, sleep-dulled members of the garrison. Several more alert individuals scrabbled for their weapons, but only a few were able to reach them and only one managed to fire a shot before they were all cut down.

Dave ignored the barracks, all his attention on the guardroom. The duty watch was supposed to remain awake and alert, but he knew that after a month of unexpectedly rigorous drill and inspections they were more likely than not to be as drunk as their comrades on liberty. He fervently prayed, *Please, God, don't let them get to the alarm button!* It was on a direct circuit to the Bactrian operations center in Banka, and was the only means of communication Sergeant Dixon could not suppress. His heart leapt into his mouth as the four-member assault team burst through the guardroom door, and pounded unmercifully as shots sounded from within.

Almost immediately a voice came over the circuit. "Guardroom secure, no alarm sounded, no casualties." It was followed by the other teams in sequence, as they'd trained.

"Barrack One secure, no casualties."

"Barrack Two secure, no casualties."

"Barrack Three secure, one casualty, need corpsman ASAP."

"Barrack Four secure, no casualties."

"Gatehouse secure, no casualties."

Sergeant-Major Deacon replied, "All teams check enemy dead. Corpsman to Barrack Three. Come on in, Captain."

"On my way," Dave replied, then ripped off the headset, blinking as his eyes were suddenly deprived of the light sources to which they'd become accustomed. He hurriedly put on his helmet, activating its visor's night vision mode that gave him a hundred-and-forty-degree field of view almost as clear as daylight, and seized his rifle. "Come on, Sergeant, Corporal, let's *go!*"

~ ~ ~

CARISTO: GARRISON

"Who is it?" Dave asked as he burst through the door of Barrack Three.

"It's Todd," Jaime said, his voice filled with worry. "One of those bastards must have been awake in his bed. He bounced up, grabbed his carbine and got off a wild shot before we could nail him. It ricocheted off that bunk stanchion there," he pointed with the barrel of his weapon, "and hit Todd's inner thigh below his protective gear. He's bleeding real bad."

Dave looked down at the medic kneeling in a pool of gore on the floor, struggling to save Todd's life. He knew better than to disturb him with pointless questions at a time like this. Judging from the amount of blood and its rich red color, the round had punctured Todd's femoral artery. His eyes were closed, his face a ghastly pallor, his breathing rapid and shallow.

"Keep me posted. I've got to check the rest of the base."

"Will do."

Dave turned on his heel and left, whispering a a soft but heartfelt curse. Todd had been in his basic training class as a fellow recruit. He'd moved up steadily through the NCO ranks, even as Dave had progressed to a commission and ultimately command of a rump company. It hurt to see a comrade-in-arms of such long standing fighting for his life... but it was hardly the first time he'd experienced that.

He quickly checked the other barracks, finding all in order, and ended up outside the guardroom. He was puzzled to see a bottle lying on the Bactrian Sergeant-Major's chest. Its contents had gurgled out all over his torso. "Guess you were the first to die in this operation, Sergeant-Major," he said in a conversational tone as he picked up the bottle and sniffed at its neck. His eyes widened at the tantalizing aroma of top-quality liquor as he read the label. "Where did you find this? I've only known you to drink rotgut before." He looked through the open door of the office, and immediately spotted the still-open liquor cabinet. "Stole it from your new boss, did you? Well, if he survives tomorrow he'll just have to find something else in which to drown his sorrows. I hope he'll have plenty to drown!"

"Talking to the dead, Sir? They say that's a bad sign," Sergeant-Major Deacon called from the guardroom, chuckling.

"It probably is," Dave agreed as he set the lock and closed the office door. *No sense in leaving an open liquor cabinet in plain sight,* he thought to himself. *I want my people sober!*

"Is everything OK on your end, Sergeant-Major?" he asked as he entered the guardroom.

"Yes, Sir. I've just called the airvans to move in. They'll be landing next to the hangar in five minutes."

"Then we'd better get over there and have the doors open ready for them. We're going to be busier than all get-out for the next few hours."

They were pushing back the last leaf of the second door when two airvans whispered out of the night and touched down on the hardstand. Their doors opened and the pilots and WSO's emerged. Three of them began unloading the strike team's field packs and other gear, while Tamsin came over to Dave.

"All OK?" she asked with a smile.

"Yes, but Todd took a bad hit. The medic's working on him now."

"Damn!" Her face fell for a moment until she visibly collected herself, bracing her shoulders back. "Let's check out the armory."

He accompanied her into the armory that opened off the rear of the hangar. The Sergeant-Major had already unlocked it using the master key fob from the guardroom. She walked rapidly up and down the rows of weapons, pointing while Dave made mental notes.

"I want eight of those four-missile racks for the shuttles going to Banka. Each of them can handle one under each stub wing – they're in the hangar ready for installation. They've got multi-mode sensors and a decent-size warhead."

"All right. How many people do you need to prepare them?"

"I trained two teams to insert the missiles' batteries, run system checks and get them ready for mounting. I'll need half a dozen more for the grunt work." She indicated two powered carts with extended arms. "Those things will pick up two missiles at a time and carry them to the tech area over there. We'll spend a few minutes preparing them, then load them onto the rack. As soon as a rack is filled it'll be moved out to a shuttle and mounted. Working on two missiles at a time, we can probably mount three to four racks every hour if we move fast. While we're doing that, other teams will refuel our old shuttles and restock them with any battle stores they need."

"OK. I'll leave all that in your hands. Anything else?"

She pointed to a stack of flat rectangular ordnance pods. "I'll have another team filling four of those with a mix of sensor-fused munitions and anti-personnel fragmentation bombs. The pods don't have to be mounted – the shuttles will pick them up from the ground using their tractor beams, and lock them in place beneath their bellies once they're airborne and their wheels have retracted. There's also the plasma cannon, of course." She counted rapidly. "They've got twenty loaded ten-round magazines in stock. I'd have liked more, but beggars can't be choosers. We have five for our two old shuttles, so that'll give each shuttle going to Banka six mags, with one left over. I'll snaffle that for our SS shuttle to replace the one we used in the Matopo Hills to bring down the hillside. We can't use these missiles in space – they depend on aerodynamic forces for control, and there aren't any in vacuum – so I'll have to rely on the cannon if we need a weapon."

"Won't we burn out the barrel if we fire too many rounds?"

She snorted disdainfully. "We probably will. These single-barrel cannon are a lot less efficient than the tri-barrel units we had before the war. Unfortunately, all ours got burned out or destroyed long ago. We'll just have to use a lower rate of fire unless things go critical, in which case to hell with the barrel!"

"All right."

"First things first. I must check that these two birds are fully fueled and ready to go. I've got to get them out of here as soon as they're armed so we can bring out the refueling gear for the other two. You get on with something else, love. I'm going to be too busy to talk to you for a while."

He squeezed her arm wordlessly, then turned and walked out of the hangar. Already the others in the team were readying hoses to transfer reaction mass, opening boxes of ration packs to fill the shuttles' lockers, and making sure everything they'd need was to hand.

Jaime walked towards him, shoulders slumped, head down. His body language told Dave what he was going to say even before he spoke.

"Todd... didn't make it, Boss."

Dave hugged him gently. "I'm sorry, Jaime. I know how close you were."

There were tears in the man's eyes. "All the way from basic training through three and a half years of war, and just about to retire and go into ranching together... and now *this!*"

"Look at it this way. He's the first of a whole lot of our people who'll die today. He'll be in very good company up there. Know what you can do to honor his memory? You and Rissa name your first boy for him, and raise him to be proud of the godfather he never knew."

Jaime raised his head and braced back his shoulders. "I... we'll do that. Thanks, Boss. I almost lost it there for a moment."

"Just make sure you don't lose it when little Todd poops all over you while you're changing his diapers."

"Y'know, Boss, it'd be *just* like big Todd to inspire little Todd to do that!" He looked up at the night sky and shook his fist at the stars, the ghost of a smile on his face.

March 31st 2850 GSC, 03:00

TAPURIA: SERVICE TUNNEL

Jake watched as Corporal Harper delicately inserted the narrow tip of a glass funnel into the hole he'd drilled at the top of the lock. He turned it until he was sure it rested on the parts he wanted to access, then reached for a bottle in the small container at his side. He carefully began pouring the liquid inside it into the funnel, a few drops at a time.

"I suspect you've done this a time or two before," Jake said in a soft whisper.

"Yes, Sir. I used to be a thief before the Bactrians came. The authorities let me out of jail on my promise to fight. I've been stealing from the enemy ever since, every chance I got."

Jake bit back a laugh. "You've atoned for all your past crimes tonight, Harper. You're going to help us damage the enemy like he's never been damaged before."

"Glad to hear it, Sir – but I wish there were also a bit of gold at the end of this rainbow, if you know what I mean. It's a professional weakness, I'm afraid." White vapor began to rise from the lock, and Harper warned, "We need to step back now, Sir. You really, *really* don't want that stuff in your lungs in high concentrations."

Jake backed down the narrow tunnel, glancing over his shoulder to where the rest of the raiding party waited ten meters back from the grating. As he approached, the first in line whispered, "Looks like it's on fire up there, Sir." The haze from the acid biting into the electronics had formed a mist that was slowly rising to a vent in the ceiling as air currents caught it.

"Not a bad comparison, soldier, but it's the enemy we want to get burned."

There came a faint *snap!* from the lock, audible even several meters away. Harper smiled. "That's it, Sir."

"Just like that? No fuss, no bother?"

"Sure, Sir." He shook his head in professional disapproval. "Lockmakers usually set their products to default to fail-open mode, so that if the electronics stop functioning for any reason the lock opens. Thieves love that. It makes our job much easier. Instead of having to defeat multiple barriers or cut through hardened steel alloys, all we have to do is shut down the electrical side. You can change the setting to fail-locked, of course, but only security-conscious folks do that. They don't mind paying for a locksmith, just as long as their stuff stays safe. Most people would rather not be locked out of their homes or whatever they're securing. Those who installed the lock in this grating probably didn't even think about it. They just fitted it as it came from the factory, coded it for secure access, then went on to the next job."

"And it won't sound an alarm?"

"Not from the lock, Sir – its electronics don't exist anymore except as slag. I've bridged the wiring to the three sensors attached to the grate itself. When we open it, they won't know about it." As he spoke, he led the way back up the tunnel.

Jake sneezed unexpectedly as the acrid aroma of the acid bit into his nostrils. "I see what you mean about that stuff. If it smells this bad after the ventilation system has sucked in most of it, I hate to think what it'd be like at full strength."

Harper smiled. "You wouldn't smell it for long before your sniffer melted down, Sir."

"What a charming thought!"

Grinning, the Corporal inserted a pry-bar and tugged hard. With nothing to resist its forcible withdrawal, the bolt slid back into the lock. He pushed the hinged grate, swinging it open into a recess in the tunnel wall. The long loops of bridging wire between its sensors and their cables on the ceiling of the tunnel pulled up and out as it moved, but didn't reach full extension. The Corporal tied orange warning tape around them, cinching them to a pipe on the wall to pull them out of the way as far as possible, then waved a hand invitingly up the passage. "We're in, Sir."

"That was very well done, Corporal! Thank you very much."

Jake turned and signaled to the others. They began to move forward as he stepped through the grate opening and walked down the tunnel, moving carefully to avoid knocking into the multiple conduits and pipes that festooned the sides and ceiling of the tunnel. They increased in size and quantity as they penetrated further into the security zone, crowding inward, producing a claustrophobic effect through the artificial perspective provided by their night-vision visors. Jake eventually paused, took off his web gear and unslung his weapon, and held them before him as he slid between the obstacles so that they didn't catch against anything. Behind him his team followed his example without having to be told.

At the cross-tunnel he stepped into the branch leading to the old traffic control center, then waved each of his soldiers through to other arms of the tunnels until the techs came up.

"You take point from here on, Quincy. Are your toys ready to play?"

"You bet they are, and so are we!" Grinning, the lead technician waited for Jake to move into another arm of the tunnel, out of the way; then he and his two assistants eased their way past and headed for their target. Each carried several containers strapped to their web gear, and a complex electronic console on their chests.

Seventy meters down the tunnel they came to a side branch, much narrower than the main one. Quincy turned down it, followed by the other two. Jake signaled his soldiers to hold in place, then followed them. He caught up to them as they squatted at the end of the short branch. The tech nearest the partition at the end, into which the broad, heavy conduit above their heads disappeared, took a set of tools from a pouch and began to unscrew a ventilation grating. The other two opened containers and began extracting tiny mechanical figures with wings, laying them out in a long row on the floor of the tunnel. Peering through his visor, magnifying the image, Jake could see that the 'head' of each insect-like device bore a tiny lens set above two miniaturized tubes which vanished into its body.

"How many of these do you have?" he whispered.

"Lots!" Quincy assured him. He scowled. "The Bactrians modified their standard bugs, though. Across the settled galaxy security flitterbugs and nanobugs like these use a paralyzing neurotoxin for which there's an antidote. They disable temporarily rather than kill. The Bactrians use a deadly poison on their microdarts for which there's no antidote."

"If they're so dangerous, how did we get our hands on so many of them?"

"At first we went back to the ruins of the bases they'd infiltrated with them. They have so many of these things that they didn't bother to recover those that ended up in hard-to-reach places. We waited until we knew their batteries would have run down, then we looked for them, brought them back to our main base, and analyzed them. Once we knew what we were dealing with we deliberately targeted their operators, trying to capture their bugs before they could launch them – also their control consoles. We also stole several shipments of them from resupply convoys, and your son brought us a very useful number of their latest assault bugs from the Matopo Hills. Most of those we've recovered are here now, ready to give the Bactrians an unpleasant surprise."

"It couldn't happen to nicer people," Jake grinned, savoring what he knew the bugs would do to help the attackers – including his own team – in just a few hours' time.

"I won't argue with you about that!" He glanced at his subordinate, who was lowering the grating to the floor. "All clear?"

"Sure, Quincy."

"OK, let's make certain it's safe to go in."

Jake watched, fascinated, as the techs used their consoles to activate the flitterbugs. Tiny synthetic wings unfurled and flapped furiously, lifting their miniaturized 'bodies' off the floor in almost complete silence. They flew through the aperture left by the grating and fanned out, each sending back vid from the lens set into its 'head'. Quincy and his assistants hastily poked antennas through the aperture to make sure the weak signals from the flitterbugs' tiny transmitters would reach them. They plugged their visors into the console, using them as displays to monitor the feedback from the flitterbugs.

"As far as we know they don't have any staff in the basement levels," Quincy explained. "They control everything from their new TrafCon three blocks away. The only people here are off-shift guards getting some sleep in the security building on the surface, plus a two-man duty watch in the guardroom and two more on the gate."

"So we can work down here without them knowing anything about it?"

"As long as we're quiet. Of course, as soon as we cut the links to TrafCon it's going to scream blue murder at the guards to get down into the tunnels and investigate."

"At which time your little friends here will be ready to meet them, right?"

"Oh, yes. Our little friends have one last harvest to reap – this time on our side!"

As the flitterbugs moved through the different floors and rooms in the basement levels, some of them attached themselves to walls and doorframes to act as communications relays for those going ahead. The operators were able to keep track of their progress and see everything they saw. As soon as the bugs confirmed that no-one was present on any of the lower levels, the assault unit opened the partition blocking the tunnel and made their way into the old control center. Jake dispersed them among several rooms and advised them to get what sleep they could. "Things will get real interesting in a few hours," he reminded them, "so I want you rested and ready."

He didn't take his own advice. He stooped over the terminal where Quincy sat, tapping at its keyboard, brow creased in concentration.

"What are you doing?"

"I've just entered the special transponder ID's and instructed the computer to completely ignore them. It's not to issue any warning of them to any other traffic, nor display their whereabouts either here on the planet or in orbit at the space station. As far as TrafCon is concerned, they'll just be invisible little black holes in its coverage."

"Thanks." Jake squeezed his shoulder gratefully.

"Just you wait. What was it they used to say in the old days? 'You ain't seen nothin' yet!' I'm now setting up the feed for the shuttles and copying the Bactrians' sensor feed, directing both to a special channel. I'll activate it once the attack begins, and aim one of the backup satellite dishes on this building towards the space station as an ultra-broad-band relay. Dave and his people can record it on their shuttle until the space station or our dish is destroyed, then they can take it with them as evidence of our last stand. After that, I'll upload our targeting programs and queue them to execute on command."

He frowned in professional disapproval. "The Bactrians really should have changed the tech support codes on our traffic control computer. I suppose they assumed since we'd never be able to gain access to it again, that wasn't necessary. Besides, they don't have many tech-savvy people to begin with, so they probably decided to employ them on what appeared to be more important tasks. Well, their carelessness is about to bite them in the ass."

~ ~ ~

CARISTO: GARRISON

Dave looked around at the orbital team as he continued, "When we lift off in a few minutes, the traffic control system planetside and in space will recognize our transponder ID and completely ignore us. We won't be plotted on the Bactrians' displays as we leave here and climb to orbit. They won't know we're coming."

One of the soldiers raised his hand. "But, Sir, that's only TrafCon's radars. What about the warships? Won't they plot us on their own radars as we get closer?"

"No, they won't, because it's standard operating procedure for them to switch off their radars upon entering a parking orbit. The Bactrians found it caused too much interference if all their ships had radars broadcasting in close proximity to one another on common frequencies. Instead they all take a radar feed from the space station, showing every ship in orbit around or near the planet – but it won't show us, of course."

"What about our drive emissions, Sir? Won't they detect them?"

"Not if we come in carefully. We'll climb to orbit on the far side of the planet from them, then cut back our power as we close on them slowly from behind. We'll drop it to no more than five per cent for our final approach. Don't forget, an assault shuttle's gravitic drive unit is minuscule compared to that of any spaceship, with emissions to match. What's more,

171

this SS shuttle has electronics that mask even that. They shouldn't see us coming at all, not even when we dock with the space station."

"And if they do, Sir?" the soldier asked stubbornly.

"Then we'll just have to die as bravely as possible, won't we?"

There was a roar of laughter from the others as the man sat down, flushing scarlet.

Dave clicked on to the next image. The portable projector threw a diagram onto the wall. "Here you see the spaceships currently in orbit. This is the space station in the center of the group. The Satrap's yacht is on its port side, with two corvettes of the Bactrian Navy. The yacht is unarmed except for laser cannon for point defense, so given our limited number of weapons we're going to leave her alone but take out her escorts. There's a converted armed freighter on the other side of the station, which we'll also target, plus one of her sister ships patrolling the system. We expect her to be far enough away from the planet to allow us to escape in this ship, here." He indicated an icon beyond the warships. "She's the *Benbecula*, a freighter from New Brisbane, a planet of the Lancastrian Commonwealth. As I explained earlier, we'll be boarding her with our evidence and Mr. Ellis as soon as we've dealt with the space station and the warships.

"We've had a lucky break. The crews of the Bactrian ships and the space station are at half strength, because they've sent the other half planetside to take part in the parade this morning. That means they'll all be operating what I'm told is called an 'anchor watch'. Mac, would you take over at this point, please?"

"Thanks, boss." The tech specialist rose to his feet. "At minimum staffing levels, they won't have weapons or battle systems manned. They're fools to do that, but they've grown complacent because there's never been any armed opposition in space since they took over Laredo. It's made them sloppy and negligent. We're going to take full advantage of that."

Another soldier put up his hand. "But, Sir, when we open up on the warships, won't they fire back at us?"

"They'll try, but they'll find it difficult. Let me explain how this is going to go down…"

172

March 31st 2850 GSC, 06:00

TAPURIA: MILITARY GOVERNOR'S COMPOUND

The sentries at the rooftop transport pad snapped to attention and presented arms as they approached. General Huvishka raised his hand to the gold-inlaid peak of his cap as he passed between them. Following in his wake, Captain Dehgahn and Lieutenant Yazata merely nodded at them.

The General's personal pilot and bodyguard came to attention next to his aircar. Both were in formal parade uniform, but the bodyguard wore in addition a white cross-shoulder belt supporting a pulser in its holster. His rifle was visible in the vertical weapon clamps in the middle of the console.

"Good morning, Sir," the pilot greeted her boss. She was a Captain – wearing, Yazata noticed, no less than three medals for valor in action. The bodyguard, a Staff Sergeant, wore a similar number. Clearly the General believed in entrusting his safety to those who'd demonstrated more than once that they could and would do whatever it took to ensure it.

"Good morning, Captain. Are we ready?"

"All except for our new transponder code, Sir. I'll have to get that from Trafcon just before we exit the security zone around the Command Bunker."

"Very well. Let's go."

He and his aides arranged themselves in the rear, the General alone in the back seat and Dehgahn and Yazata in facing pull-down seats, while the pilot and bodyguard got into the front compartment. They all strapped themselves into four-point harnesses. The pilot ran through the pre-flight checks and lifted to a low hover over the pad as she activated her microphone.

"Laredo Six Alpha to Trafcon, departing Command for arena, request transponder ID, over."

"Trafcon to Laredo Six Alpha, authenticate Papa Alpha Golf, over."

She tapped three keys on her console and peered at the code it threw up in response. "Six Alpha to Trafcon, authenticating Bravo X-ray November, over."

"Trafcon to Six Alpha, confirmed. Transponder ID now being transmitted to your console. Acknowledge receipt. Over."

After a brief pause the flight computer beeped, displaying a four-digit code. The pilot entered it into another panel.

"Six Alpha to Trafcon, entered zero-niner-three-one, squawking, over."

"Trafcon to Six Alpha, ID is correct and your transponder has now been registered. You are cleared to proceed direct to the arena from your present position. Over."

"Six Alpha to TrafCon, understood, thank you. Laredo Six Alpha out."

Looking out of her window, Yazata could see the laser cannon nearest to the transport pad on top of the bunker. It had trained around to aim at them as soon as the aircar had lifted into a hover. Now it turned lazily back onto its normal bearing, aiming out over the ruins of what had once been Banka as the aircar pulled away from the bunker, climbing steeply. She relaxed inwardly. Battle systems were supposed to be fail-safe, but what human ingenuity had devised, human ingenuity could also screw up. The Bactrian armed forces had learned that the hard way during their years of hard fighting on Laredo. Technology was all very well as long as it worked. When it didn't…

Her thoughts were interrupted as the General gestured towards the newly-built Royal Palace. They were passing it well to starboard. "I wonder if the Satrap and Crown Prince slept any better than we did?"

"Considering the huge meal they ate last night, Sir, I venture to doubt it."

He grinned. "As long as they don't burp on parade. That's so terribly un-military!"

Yazata had to stifle a sudden giggle, even as she noticed that Dehgahn, the pilot and the bodyguard coughed and spluttered, the latter putting his hand hastily over his mouth. Clearly they were no strangers to their boss's sometimes irreverent sense of humor.

Huvishka looked slowly and carefully around the city, as far as he could stretch his neck and twist his body. "Everything looks peaceful. No sign of enemy action during the night?"

"No, Sir," she responded. "I checked with the operations room just before we left. Everything's quiet."

He glanced across at her. "You don't sound very happy about that."

"I'm not, Sir. I still think this is an event the rebels have no choice but to attack if they're to retain any credibility. It's too quiet for my peace of mind."

"That's a nasty suspicious attitude, but I entirely approve of it. Oh, well, we've at least done all we can to be ready for any attack."

"Yes, Sir."

The pilot changed the channel on the aircar's radio. "Laredo Six Alpha to Arena, over."

"Arena to Laredo Six Alpha, go ahead, over."

"Six Alpha to Arena, approaching VIP parking area bearing from me zero-one-fiver degrees, range from me two point zero clicks, squawking transponder ID zero-niner-three-one, over."

"Arena to Six Alpha, we have you on our plot. Come ahead. Over."

"Six Alpha to Arena, thank you, out."

Yazata couldn't help but compare the crisp professionalism of the career soldiers surrounding General Huvishka with the slackness of those she'd encountered in many conscript units – even among the black-uniformed minions of the Security Service. She shook her head in dismay. *If I ever get to command a unit,* she thought to herself, *no matter what it may be, I've got a new standard for which to strive and against which to compare it.*

The pilot brought the aircar slowly down towards the huge paved parking area outside the arena. It was mostly bare of vehicles this morning, but there were a hundred painted symbols evenly spaced across the plascrete where the shuttles would land after the flypast. The VIP entrance to the arena had been roped off, as had a special parking area beside it. A company of heavily armed troops provided security. Several of them doubled towards the spot where the aircar would land, forming a hasty honor guard.

The aircar touched down, rocking gently on its undercarriage, and the pilot cut the fans. As their hum died away the General, Captain Dehgahn and Lieutenant Yazata released their harnesses and climbed out. The bodyguard did likewise, but the General shook his head as he looked at him.

"Sorry, Staff Sergeant. The Satrap's Head of Security has ordered that no personnel with loaded weapons may be present inside the arena, except his own bodyguards. You'll have to wait with the pilot for us."

The man frowned with professional disapproval, but said only "Yes, Sir," as he got back into the car.

General Huvishka returned the salute of the officer in command of the hastily-formed honor guard. "Good morning, Lieutenant. Is everything as it should be out here?"

"Yes, Sir. Nothing to report. If you'd care for breakfast, Sir, we've set up a field kitchen adjacent to the parade control center in the commentary box. There's still ten minutes before the first parade units arrive." As he spoke, the pilot drove the aircar away towards the secure parking area next to the entrance.

"Oh, really? Enterprising of someone to think of ferrying a field kitchen all the way up there. It surely didn't fit into the elevator or up the stairs, though."

"They flew it up slung beneath an assault shuttle by tractor beams, Sir."

"Ah. Yes. Logical, really, when you think about it. They couldn't have done it any other way." He glanced at the others. "I find myself suddenly hungry. Care to join me?" Their smiles were sufficient answer. "Come along, then. We'll have something sent down to my pilot and bodyguard."

~ ~ ~

LAREDO ORBITALS

Tamsin glanced at her console. "We're at orbital altitude – thirty thousand kilometers."

"Thank you," Dave acknowledged. "Isn't that a bit high for geostationary orbit?"

"It is for a ballistic orbit, but we're in a powered orbit. So are the spaceships out there, and the space station too, for that matter. If you're using a gravitic drive to maintain your orbital trajectory, it can be at almost any altitude and any velocity."

"Makes sense. Are we in line-of-sight with *Benbecula* yet?"

"Yes. We can set up a tight-beam anytime."

"All right." He twisted around in his seat. "Marvin, would you come up here and take the spare seat at the WSO's console, please?"

"Will do." Marvin unbuckled his harness, rose from his place among the troops in the cargo area, and walked forward, holding his spacesuit's helmet under one arm. "I was expecting to have to float there, but I see you've still got your artificial gravity field operating."

"Oh, yes," Tamsin assured him, grinning. "There's no point in free-fall unless you have to for some reason."

He slid into the seat next to the WSO. "What now?"

"I'm about to lock a tight-beam onto *Benbecula*. I want you to tell her captain we're coming."

"Can do. I'd better tell him it's me, then transfer him to Dave for further instructions."

Tamsin raised a tight-beam turret from the roof of the shuttle and trained it on the distant icon that was *Benbecula* in their small plot display. She took extreme care over its alignment to ensure that no spillover from the transmission would be heard by the Bactrian warships nearby. At last she glanced at Dave. "We're ready."

"Go for it."

She pressed a key on her console. A red light flashed, indicating that the tight-beam transmitter was sending a signal to *Benbecula*. Dave knew that broadband receivers on the ship would note its presence and identify it as a tight-beam transmission. The ship's communications computer would automatically slew a tight-beam dish onto the bearing to receive further input and transmit replies.

In less than a minute the red flashing light changed to a steady green, indicating that the circuit had been established. "Go ahead, Marvin," Tamsin advised.

"Thank you." He keyed the handset he'd picked up from the console. As he did so Tamsin pressed a button to relay the conversation through the console speaker.

"This is Fur Trader calling *Benbecula* on tight-beam transmission, over."

A moment's pause, then, "This is *Benbecula*, Officer of the Watch speaking. Say again your name, please. Over."

"*Benbecula*, this is Fur Trader. Please advise Captain Grassby that I'm calling. He's expecting to hear from me. Over."

"*Benbecula* to Fur Trader, stand by."

They waited almost five minutes before they heard, "*Benbecula* to Fur Trader, Grassby here. Go ahead. Over."

"Hi, Tom, this is Manuel. How are things with you? Over."

"Not so hot. We've been stuck here in orbit for three days, and they tell us it'll be three days more before we can leave. They won't even let you board us until then, so we're stuck twiddling our thumbs. What are you up to? Over."

"I'll be coming aboard a lot sooner than that. In fact, you might want to bring all your systems to readiness for departure real soon now. I'm going to put someone on the circuit to explain more. Stand by." He looked across at Dave. "Take it."

"Got it, thanks." Dave toggled his own microphone. "Captain Grassby, this is Captain David Carson of the Laredo Army. We're on our way to rendezvous with you, but there's going to be a lot of shouting and tumult before we reach you. We've got to take care of those Bactrian warships, to ensure you can make your getaway without any problems. Remain in your present position relative to the space station. Do not, I say again, *do not* depart from it until we've boarded you. That applies even if you're ordered to do so. Don't move without my clearance. Any deviation might get you a missile right up your butt, and we wouldn't want that. Over."

"B – but this is *preposterous!* Where are you? You're not on our plot! Over."

"No, we're not, and we won't be until this thing goes down. Don't bring up your radar to look for us and don't ask any more questions – I don't want to risk the Bactrians picking up any leakage from this tight-beam circuit. Just come to readiness for departure, then wait. Nothing's going to happen for a few hours. You'll know when we arrive – you won't be able to miss it. We'll board you shortly after that, and take it from there. Acknowledge. Over."

"I... Grassby to Carson, acknowledged. I hope you know what the hell you're doing! Over."

"Carson to Grassby, so do I. I'm going to take down this tight-beam circuit now. Carson out."

He released the microphone switch. "Did that sound like your friend, Marvin – or should I say Manuel?"

Marvin/Manuel smiled. "Yes, that was him. I told you Marvin Ellis wasn't my real name. I suppose you may as well know who I am now. I'm Manuel Espada."

"And I'm just the same old lovable Dave I've always been." Tamsin snorted disdainfully, grinning, but made no comment as he looked around at the others. "All right, let's relax and get some food. Everyone take another stim-tab while you're at it. It's been a long night, and the main attraction's still a few hours away."

March 31st 2850 GSC, 08:00

DEL MAR PASS

The pilot turned her head and called over her shoulder, "The Pass is right ahead, Sir, and it looks like some of the others are here already."

Brigadier-General Aldred gently shook his wife. "I've got to get up, Gloria." She stirred drowsily from where she leaned against him and lifted her head from his shoulder, blinking for a moment before she nodded and straightened in her seat.

He unfastened his four-point harness, stood and walked to behind the pilot's console, bending to peer through the viewscreen. The bright morning light showed the towering peaks of the Sierra Madre mountain range looming up ahead, gashed by the sheer walls of the Del Mar Pass as it twisted and turned its way between them. A big white radome gleamed atop the highest summit in the range, and he indicated it with his hand. "Has that thing picked us up?"

"It must have, Sir, but no alarm's been sounded that we can detect. Our transponder codes are being acknowledged without any fuss."

Aldred exhaled, feeling some of the tension leave his body. "Looks like Lieutenant-Colonel Carson and his people have done their job – the first part of it, anyway. Where are the others?"

"Look at the base of the pass, Sir. There are four shuttles down already, with two more circling to join them."

The General peered ahead. "They're just tiny specks to me – I'm not wearing a helmet, so I don't have distance vision capability."

"We'll be there soon enough, Sir."

Within ten minutes the shuttle seemed to jump slightly in mid-air as the pilot hovered low over a cleared area at the foot of the pass and released the underslung ordnance pod. She left it lying on the ground as she moved the vehicle slightly to one side and lowered its undercarriage. The gel-filled wheels bounced lightly as they settled onto the ground. A crowd of uniformed onlookers turned their backs to protect themselves from flying dust, twigs and gravel, then turned back and advanced towards the new arrivals, grinning. Aldred walked down the rear ramp of his shuttle to greet them, followed by the fifteen troops aboard.

"Welcome to sunny Del Mar Pass, Sir," Lieutenant-Colonel Yardley said cheerfully, saluting. "We've got the fire going to boil water for coffee."

"But our shuttles can provide hot water internally," the General pointed out as he returned the salute.

"Well, Sir, if this is to be our swan song, I'd like to smell burning sangar wood for the last time."

"I can't argue with you. It's a lovely smell, and it seems to make coffee taste better too. How are you feeling?"

"I'm glad I'm flying to my last battle rather than having to walk. The Bactrians took all the starch out of my legs – I wouldn't make it more than a couple of kilometers on foot."

"Make sure you get back to the shuttle to make your escape, or borrow another vehicle from the enemy." He looked around at the eight hulking shuttles now settled on the ground. "Just two more to come."

"Yes. The four shuttles from Caristo – two newly captured plus our two old ones that they refueled and rearmed – got here first. We arrived from Benito a little while later, a few minutes ahead of you. There's just the two from Ligarda still to come; and if that rumble in the distance is anything to go by, they aren't far out."

"Reaction thrusters are noisy things, aren't they?"

Yardley shrugged. "Atmosphere's too thick low down to use gravitic drives, so we don't have much choice. I pity those poor bastards on parade in the arena this morning. Having eighty shuttles flying low and slow overhead – ninety including us – will be enough to deafen them."

"We'll just have to make sure they don't suffer for long." They grinned at each other.

They were drinking fire-percolated coffee and eating breakfast by the time the last two shuttles touched down. Bantered greetings flew between the shuttle crews as the new arrivals hastened to fill their cups. The tension in the air was something palpable, but different to what he'd felt before other operations, the General realized. It was still the same pre-combat nerves, but now overlaid with a sense of resignation, an awareness of mortality, a determination to make this one count. As he walked to where an NCO was taping a chart to the side of his shuttle, soldiers on all sides called greetings, offered gentle jibes, raised their mugs of coffee in informal salutes. His heart swelled, aching with pride in these men and women who had served so long and so faithfully.

The troops gathered around as he turned to face them. "The late garrison at Calinda was kind enough to leave this chart on the wall of their briefing room. It confirms all we learned from the Security Service Colonel that Captain Carson shot in the Matopo Hills, and provides some useful last-minute updates. For example, the altitude of the fly-past has been increased from two to three hundred meters, presumably because of the immense noise made by so many shuttles traveling so close together and so slowly. That couldn't be better as far as we're concerned. It makes the enemy's shuttles better targets for the missiles we're going to launch at them.

"We've been monitoring Bactrian frequencies ever since we took off. No-one's raised the alarm and there's no sign that the enemy knows anything's wrong. Niven's Regiment has clearly succeeded in penetrating the old Traffic Control building and inserting our transponder codes into the computer system. It won't show us on any TrafCon displays – we're effectively imitating holes in the air as far as they're concerned. Even better, the special transponder codes Trafcon is issuing to Bactrian forces for the Satrap's visit all begin with zero-eight or zero-nine. Pilots and Weapons Systems Operators, update your targeting systems accordingly. When the balloon goes up, if you identify any airborne vehicle using those transponder codes, kill it!" His audience grinned, making rude remarks about the fate of any enemy personnel aboard.

"I remind you that the Bactrians have placed all missiles and plasma cannon in the security zone under the control of TrafCon for this parade. Therefore, we're going to hang back and let Lieutenant-Colonel Carson's people do their thing. After they've thoroughly disrupted proceedings, we'll overfly the arena and the grounds in our prearranged formation. It's spaced so as to cover everything with a mix of fragmentation bombs, to kill as many as possible of the five thousand troops on parade, plus sensor fused munitions to destroy as many vehicles as possible, including any surviving shuttles, weapons systems and ground transport." There were more approving noises from the assembled troops.

Aldred waited for silence. "Once we've overflown the arena, we'll split up. Assault Force Arena will follow me down, using our plasma cannon to clear our path, then we'll dismount and go after the Satrap if he's managed to escape the initial strike. We want to make absolutely sure he and his son are dead. Assault Force Banka's shuttles will drop their troops at the prearranged rendezvous points, then assist them with their missiles and plasma cannon. Watch for Bactrian forces to begin leaving your targets for the arena, trying to rescue the Satrap. Delay them as long as you can."

He looked around. "Getting away afterwards will be very tricky. Those of us who can board shuttles will make our escape in them, but we don't know how many will be available. Some will be able to commandeer vehicles and make a run for it. Others will have to hide from enemy reinforcements as they rush to the sites we attack, then try to get away once they've passed. We know many of us won't make it. I can only say to you that the greatest privilege of my life has been to command men and women like you over the past three and a half years. You've done your planet and your people proud. If this is the last day of my life, I couldn't ask for better company with whom to cross the river."

A ramrod-straight, iron-haired Sergeant-Major called, "General, Sir, there's one unexpected advantage to this possibly being our last mission."

"Oh? What's that, Sergeant-Major O'Connor?"

"I won't have to eat any more of these bloody Bactrian ration packs!" There was a roar of laughter and a spatter of applause.

Shoulders shaking, Aldred looked at his watch. "All right, people. Mount up, strap in and get ready. We lift at nine for the last leg."

~ ~ ~

183

TAPURIA: OLD TRAFFIC CONTROL CENTER

Jake eased his way into the crowded branch tunnel leading to the main service tunnel. Two technicians and four of his troops were completing their tasks. He watched from behind them as two soldiers ran a ring-main between the multiple loops of detonating cord wrapped around the bundle of cables running from the computer center out towards the service tunnel. As soon as they'd finished they moved back towards Jake, running out a wire from the detonators behind them. He backed into the basement to make room for them. They eased past him, then waited for two more soldiers to join them. They'd passed multiple loops of det-cord around every conduit, pipe and cable run in the main service tunnel, whether or not they knew their purpose. When the loops blew they'd take two-meter bites out of everything. Anything dependent on those wires and cables for data or power would shut down at once.

The other two made their way along the branch tunnel to the basement, unreeling their own wire behind them. They bent over the wires from both sets of detonators, splicing the ends together before connecting them to the terminals of a firing handle. Straightening, they double-checked that the safety lock was engaged, then set the handle on a table. The senior among them turned to Jake. "The cord's got enough slack to carry it out into the corridor behind, us, Sir," he said. "Just close the door behind you, get clear of the dividing wall, disengage the lock and press the plunger. You'll cut every circuit in the tunnel."

"That's exactly what I'll do in a little while," he promised. "Well done, all of you."

As they worked, the two techs had been busy with their own tasks in the service tunnel. Now they too came down the branch tunnel and into the basement. Both wore electronic consoles strapped to their chest. They straightened as they entered the room, and came to attention as they saw Jake waiting.

"Everything's ready, Sir," one reported. "We've placed ten of the new assault nanobugs on either side of the explosion zone in five sets of two, each pair set five meters further down the service tunnel from the next. They'll interdict this branch tunnel from either side. Anyone trying to get in here through the tunnels will find thirty poison darts waiting to meet him no matter which side he comes from. The bugs are on timers. They'll activate five minutes after the bang."

"And they're far enough away from the explosions that they won't be damaged by them?"

The tech adopted an expression of injured innocence. "Would I make an elementary mistake like that, Sir?"

Jake had to smile. "Sorry if I hurt your feelings. It's my job to check and double-check these things."

"I guess it is, Sir. Don't worry. I haven't screwed up that badly since the last time."

"And when, precisely, was the last time?"

"Last week, I think, Sir," he retorted with a cheeky grin.

"Oh, *great!* I feel *so* much more confident now!" Everyone in the basement chuckled softly.

The other tech said thoughtfully, "I suppose it's too late to point out that once those bugs activate, not only will no-one be able to get in here through the tunnels, but we won't be able to get out through them either?"

Jake heaved a sigh. "I'm afraid that's unavoidable. The enemy also has identification modules, so if we programmed the bugs to let people through if they're wearing one, we'd leave ourselves vulnerable to being taken from behind. The only way to guard against that is to disable the bugs' identification program so they'll shoot at anything moving, no matter who or what it may be."

The man shrugged. "Oh, well. It's not like I had anyplace else to go." Another quiet rustle of amusement ran around the room.

"Don't worry," Jake assured him. "Those of us who try to escape through other tunnels won't be close enough to the bugs to activate them."

"Can we tell whether the shuttles are on time, Sir?" another asked.

"I'm afraid not. We could have the traffic control computer display their transponder codes instead of ignoring them; but anything we display on the backup console here will also show up in TrafCon, where the Bactrians can see it. We have to take it on trust that our comrades captured the eight shuttles they were after, and refueled and rearmed our two existing birds at Caristo. All being well…" – he consulted his watch – "they'll be leaving Del Mar pass shortly."

"And your son in orbit, Sir?"

"They'll be setting up to dock with the space station in about an hour from now. With any luck the station won't see them coming until they're aboard. They're scheduled to hit Orbital Control at precisely the same moment that our attack begins at the arena and we blow the connection to TrafCon. After that they'll have to deal with the ships nearby."

"There's no way we can know whether they're doing OK up there, is there?"

"No. The same objection applies. Any information we call up down here will also be visible to the enemy. We have to run this operation according to a strict time schedule, and trust that everyone's adhered to it. If anyone's late or out of position, it's going to be their problem."

March 31st 2850 GSC, 09:40

SPACE STATION

Dave felt as if his heart would hammer its way right up his throat and out of his mouth. He watched dry-mouthed as Tamsin cut the gravitic drive so as not to cause interference with the space station's much larger drive. She switched to reaction thrusters and eased the shuttle closer to the gaping maw of the station's docking bay. Her eyes scanned her console, trying to spot any indication that the Bactrians had detected her.

"It seems to be working," she said in a half-whisper. "Stealth technology doesn't make us invisible to radar – only harder to spot – and we've been close enough for the past half-hour that they can't possibly have missed us with the honking great radar on this station. That means the program Jake put in planetside must have kept our transponder beacon from showing on OrbCon's displays. Even though their radar must have picked us up, they still don't know we're here."

"Let's keep it that way as long as we can, OK?"

"You can say that again!" she assured him as she conned the all-black craft out of the glare of sunlight, unimpeded by atmosphere, into the shadows of the docking bay. Twenty airlock stations confronted them, most empty. Three were filled by cutters and two by cargo shuttles, standard space station commuter craft. Fifteen bays were empty.

Tamsin half-turned towards Mac, who was sitting at the WSO station. "Which airlock, Mac?"

"That one." He pointed. "It's farthest away from the Docking Bay vestibule reception desk. If anyone's on duty there, they're least likely to notice us arriving at that gate."

"We'll take them out first thing if they're there," Dave promised. "Have you deactivated the alarm that announces something's engaging the docking mechanism?"

"It's already done. We should arrive silently, unless Tamsin has a rush of blood to the head and rams the damn thing." Soft, tense laughter came from the soldiers seated on either side of the cargo area behind them.

"I'm leaving it up to the automatic docking program," she assured him. "I haven't docked in space in over three years. After that long out of practice, if I tried to do it by eye I'm sure I'd hit something."

"Let's not," he suggested with a grin.

"If we do, blame the flight computer on this bird or the docking software, not me!"

As the shuttle edged closer to the airlock, the tractor and pressor beams of the space station's docking system engaged it and turned it one hundred and eighty degrees, facing outward into space, then pulled it backwards to meet the docking arms that slid out to receive it. They mated to receptacles in the sides of the shuttle, then tugged it gently towards a trunk that extended from the station towards it. The edges of the trunk slotted over flanges on the outer frame of the shuttle's rear ramp, then inflated to seal it tightly. A red light above the ramp came on, changed to orange as the air pressure in the trunk equalized with that on the station, then flickered to green.

"We're in," Tamsin whispered.

"Why are you whispering?"

"*Idiot!* It's because I'm tense!" More soft laughter came from the others.

"Fine thing, telling your Commanding Officer he's an idiot," Dave protested, trying – but failing – to keep a straight face. He turned to the two soldiers at the rear of the shuttle, nearest the ramp. Both were wearing black Security Service uniforms removed from the dead guards at the Matopo Hills. They'd been laundered to remove the bloodstains, and the holes had been patched as well as possible. From a distance they'd look normal. "All right, you know what to do." As he spoke Tamsin lowered the rear ramp, letting in a noisy *whuff* of different-smelling air from the space station. As she did so Mac activated the shuttle's recording module, tuning it to the channel prearranged with Jake some weeks before, ready to accept whatever material his team was able to send them showing the attack on the Satrap and Banka.

"Yes, Sir!"

The two walked carefully down the flexible trunk to the airlock, entered it and closed the outer door behind them. The others heard the clunk as the interlocks engaged. They waited in silence for two minutes, clutching their rifles, hardly daring to breathe, the tension rocketing upward until the interlocks clunked again and the outer door opened once more. One of the two came back into the shuttle.

"All's well, Sir. There was one Spacer on duty. We put her down with our silenced pulsers, then checked the security cameras. We've locked out all of them except one on the far side of the docking bay, so if someone in OrbCon checks the security system that's the only feed they'll see from here."

"Well done! Right, everyone out, and let's get one of these charges positioned."

They hurried through the airlock in small groups while Dave and Mac carefully loosened the shock webbing holding one of the nuclear demolition charges in place. They activated its power-assisted cart and steered it into the airlock once everyone else had passed through. They emerged into a brightly lit vestibule, big enough to accommodate several score spacers at once or a mound of cargo for transshipment.

"Where d'you want it, Mac?" Dave asked.

"A five-megaton thermonuclear warhead will reduce this station to its component parts no matter where it blows. Let's shove it in that cargo locker. It'll be out of sight there."

They pushed the demolition charge over to the locker. Mac lifted the cover from the bomb's operating panel and looked up. "I suggest three-quarters of an hour, no more. If we're not off the station by then we won't be leaving anyway. There's no sense in waiting for a boarding party to disarm the bomb, then capture what's left of us and take us to the torturers."

"Works for me." Dave's heart was pounding like a jackhammer again. He'd never been so close to an active weapon of mass destruction before today.

Mac carefully set the timer, then inserted a key in a lock. Dave took his own key from around his neck and inserted it in a second lock on the other end of the device, far enough away from the first that no single person could operate both at once.

"Ready?" he asked.

"Ready. On three: one, two, *three!*"

They turned their keys simultaneously. The mechanism gave a loud *beep!*, then the timer began counting down. Dave activated another timer on the chest panel of his spacesuit, then watched the bomb's console as if mesmerized. *44:53… 44:52… 44:51…*

"All right," Mac prompted. They removed their keys, then pushed the charge into the locker. Mac closed the door on it, slid the padlock through its hasp and clicked it shut, removing the key. He dropped it into his pocket along with his arming console key.

"What about the other one?"

Dave shook his head. "That's for emergency use. If we get away from here, we may need to blow up something else – or ourselves, for that matter, to avoid being captured."

"Fair enough. If I go down, don't forget to take my key."

"Or you mine."

"OK."

As they spoke the two soldiers who'd exited first took the rifles handed to them by other members of the party. They slung them over their left shoulders, muzzles down, then tucked their silenced pulsers inside their waistbands behind their backs with their right hands.

"All right, lead the way," Dave instructed them as he picked up his own rifle. "Walk as if you owned the place – you know how SS goons behave." They nodded. "One of you keep slightly behind the other. As you turn each corner, keep going if it's clear. If not, the rear person must give a hand signal. We'll wait until you've dealt with whoever's there."

"Yes, Sir."

The others fell into line, everyone in a predetermined position based on their duties. Dave led the spacesuited file out of the vestibule in the wake of the two fake SS troopers.

The three-minute walk to OrbCon passed in excruciating tension, but without incident. As they passed two side corridors, one leading to the crew quarters and one to the Administration and Engineering sections, three groups of four peeled off from the main body and headed for their targets.

Dave glanced at his watch as they approached the final corner. Glancing up, he saw the two leading soldiers looking back at him. He gave them a thumbs-up. It was 09:59 precisely.

They turned the final corner. As they did so, the second soldier flipped his hand outward, then down next to his left side. There were sentries on the doors leading to OrbCon, as Mac had predicted.

"Who are you? What are you doing here?" they heard a puzzled voice call from further down the passage.

"We've just arrived," Dave heard one of his soldiers reply as they kept walking, closing the distance between them and the sentries.

"Wait a minute! We weren't warned to expect any SS traffic! What — *unphf!*"

The speaker's voice died away in a grunt of agony as the two soldiers drew their silenced pulsers from behind their backs and put two rounds apiece into both sentries, their weapons making popping noises that, even suppressed, sounded like thunder in Dave's apprehensive ears. *They must have heard something inside Orbcon, even if they didn't know what it was!,* he thought desperately as he rounded the last corner and broke into a run. Even now the operators would be getting to their feet, looking at each other, wondering... His pace was made shambling and awkward by his spacesuit, its helmet bouncing behind his back. Furiously he redoubled his efforts as he unslung his rifle.

"Come *on*, people! Let's *go!*"

March 31st 2850 GSC, 10:00 – Tapuria

LAREDO ARMY SHUTTLES, APPROACHING THE ARENA

Brigadier-General Aldred sat in the second pilot's chair. Behind him his shuttle's crew was tense, ready for action, weapons braced on the floor and held upright in their hands. Gloria clutched her medical kit, ready to establish an aid station as soon as she could find a suitable place.

The General peered up through the viewscreen. They were hugging the ground, lined up directly behind the Bactrian shuttle formation three kilometers ahead. It was straightening out of its final turn, perfectly positioned to overfly the stadium in precisely one minute. A group of twenty shuttles led the formation, followed by ten more, then twenty, then ten, then a final group of twenty.

"Are all our shuttles in the right formation?" he asked his pilot.

She glanced at her console display. "Everyone's spread out at the correct intervals, Sir. We're set to drop as soon as Lieutenant-Colonel Carson clears those buggers out of the way for us."

"Then stand by, because in a few seconds all hell's going to break loose!"

~ ~ ~

OLD TRAFCON

Jake crouched against the corridor wall, looking up, counting tiles in the suspended ceiling. *Seven, eight, nine — yes, that puts me clear of the wall between the basement and this passage. If the bang blows down the wall, it won't land on top of me.* He focused on his helmet visor as he flicked off the safety lock on the plunger, then grasped the firing handle, eyes glued to the time display. *9:59:57… 9:59:58… 9:59:59… 10:00:00.*

As the final second vanished into history Jake rammed the plunger down. Instantly a thunderous roar erupted from the connecting tunnel. The door to the basement room blew open, a cloud of smoke and dust billowed through it, and dozens of ceiling tiles collapsed onto everything in sight, including him, bouncing off his helmet and shoulders. He ducked and covered until they stopped falling, then rose, coughing, and sprinted round the corner to the secondary control room. He burst through the door to find that no tiles had fallen inside.

"What's happening?" he called urgently.

"We're live, Sir!" Quincy answered, not looking around as his fingers flew over the console. "I've activated the feed to orbit and initiated Phase One of the attack. Every airborne vehicle squawking a transponder code beginning with 08 or 09 has just been designated an enemy target."

Jake gave an evil grin. "Then let's see how many of their own the Bactrians can shoot down for us, shall we?"

"You're on, Sir!" He pressed a key. "Phase Two activated!"

~ ~ ~

TAPURIA

Six missile batteries, each with four launcher vehicles carrying eight missiles each, plus twenty grounded assault shuttles, each with four missiles under each of their two stub wings, protected the airspace over and around Tapuria. Their three hundred and fifty-two missiles were backed up by a dozen laser cannon plus the plasma cannon on each shuttle. According to the carefully-crafted Operations Order for the Satrap's visit, in order to prevent confusion or error all anti-aircraft units had switched off their local sensors and been placed under the control of TrafCon's systems. The huge domed radar antennae atop three hills around the capital city all fed their data to the central supercomputer. It could scan, detect and classify hundreds of targets at a time, and target them much more efficiently than local control if necessary. However, it hadn't had to deal with a real enemy target since the antennae were installed almost three years before, after the previous ones had been destroyed along with the city of Banka.

Suddenly, as the Phase One computer program was activated, every one of the eighty assault shuttles over the arena was squawking a transponder code that identified it, no longer as a friend, but as a foe. Even as the computer digested this unprecedented situation, the Phase Two program was activated by TrafCon – actually from the secondary console in the basement of the old TrafCon building, but that was irrelevant at this stage. *Engage the enemy! Weapons free!*

The artificial intelligence system digested its new instructions and acted on them faster than thought. With so many hostiles, all terrifyingly close to the person designated as its primary defensive priority, there was no time to lose. All across Tapuria missile launchers began to vomit their warload. Every shuttle's fire control system was instantly activated, receiving its targets' details from the central computer via datalink and passing them to the missiles beneath its stub wings. A split-second after the missile batteries began firing, the shuttles joined them.

Within fifteen seconds one hundred and seventy-six missiles, fully half of those available, had been activated. Nineteen malfunctioned in one way or another – their launch containers failed to eject them properly, or their rocket motors failed to ignite, or their aerodynamic moving surfaces malfunctioned, or their guidance systems froze. The remaining one hundred and fifty-seven missiles streaked towards the eighty shuttles just beginning their low, slow pass over the arena.

~ ~ ~

OLD TRAFCON

"Holy *shit!*" Jake exclaimed in feral glee as he bent over the display in the basement. Now that there was no need to conceal anything from TrafCon – all of whose displays had just died – it showed all airborne traffic in and around the city. As they watched a horde of missile traces began to spread across the display, all heading directly for the enemy shuttle formation. "There must be two missiles for every shuttle!"

"That was the idea," Quincy assured him as he tapped rapidly at his console. "I loaded a pre-written program telling the system to allocate multiple missiles to every high-priority target – and that close to the Satrap, any target designated as hostile is automatically classified as a top-priority threat." He pressed a key triumphantly. "Phase Three program is loading!"

~ ~ ~

ABOVE THE ARENA

"Holy *shit!*" General Aldred unconsciously echoed Jake's exclamation as he stared in awe through the viewscreen of his shuttle, now two kilometers behind the main enemy formation.

Without warning the white smoke of missile traces popped into sight, seeming to come from all points of the compass, some passing directly over the low-flying Laredo assault shuttles but ignoring them. The Bactrian shuttles' slow-moving formation couldn't possibly have presented a better target. The missiles streaked into it and began to explode. Shuttle after shuttle tumbled from the formation, trailing flame and smoke, shedding clouds of shattered and twisted pieces of metal. Many smashed into the arena, causing massive casualties among the five thousand troops and more than ten thousand carefully selected spectators below. The surviving shuttles began to dodge and jink wildly, diving and weaving in a desperate attempt to evade the incoming missiles – but they kept coming in a seemingly endless stream, exploding against shuttle after shuttle, sending them careering earthwards.

Thirteen shuttles out of the eighty made it to ground level. Five couldn't pull out of their flat-out evasive dives in time and smashed into the soil, breaking up in clouds of smoke and dust, wreckage bouncing in all directions. Another scored a direct hit on the arena's commentary box, wiping out the entire parade control staff and their radio links to every unit involved. The troops on the field, already running in all directions to escape the chunks of metal large and small plummeting among them, were now cut off from contact with the Command Bunker in Tapuria, and therefore bereft of central control and organization.

Almost everywhere the troops' flight was blocked by the two-meter plascrete walls below the viewing stands surrounding the sports field on which they'd paraded. The only way in or out was through eight tunnels beneath the stands, spaced equidistant from each other around the arena. Unfortunately for the soldiers, all but two were partly obscured or blocked by the military vehicles and weapons systems arrayed for inspection around the arena perimeter. The main tunnel was concealed beneath the reviewing stand, out of sight of the soldiers – and at a time like this, out of sight was definitely out of mind. Its twin was at the other side of the stadium, offering a means of escape towards which nearby soldiers ran – just in time to be smashed into red ruin by a crashing assault shuttle that fell right in the mouth of the tunnel, sealing it completely.

Seven shuttles managed to pull out of their dives, scorching along a few meters above the ground, so low as to brush against the tops of the trees in their path. They scattered in all directions, pilots ramming their throttles through the gate. The last missiles pursued them, felling another three before the incoming barrage ran out. The four surviving vehicles raced on, heading away from the city. No orders came for them, so their pilots independently but unanimously decided not to wait for anyone to issue them. The further away they could get from that maelstrom of hell, the better. The panic-stricken profanities of the others on board merely solidified their decisions.

General Aldred's pilot slid her throttle smoothly forward as he activated his microphone. "All Laredo shuttles, go, *go*, GO!"

~ ~ ~

ARENA

Lieutenant Yazata's jaw dropped and her eyes bulged in astonishment as the first missile slammed into its target overhead. She saw the shuttle reel out of formation, all the reaction thrusters on its starboard side blown clean off, twisting and tumbling in mid-air as it fell towards the arena. Before she could take in what was happening she was bowled off her feet by a hurtling human body. "GET THE SATRAP OUT OF HERE!" she heard Major-General Huvishka bellow as he felled her.

196

Most of the officers and dignitaries on the reviewing stand were frozen, gaping in shock and horror. Beside her Captain Dehgahn grabbed her belt and hauled her unceremoniously to her feet, even as more shuttles plummeted towards them. "MOVE!" he roared at her, then leapt to follow the General. Numb with shock, she instinctively followed him.

The General plowed through the ranks of the Satrap's bodyguards as if they were so many bowling pins. Most of them were staring skyward in dumbfounded astonishment. Ignoring them, he seized the stunned Satrap in a bear hug and swung him bodily towards the stairs at the rear of the reviewing stand, yelling at the Crown Prince, "COME ON!" Before the younger man could respond Captain Dehgahn reached him and grabbed his arm, dragging him bodily in the wake of the General as he pushed his way through more of the bodyguards, some of whom were coming to their senses and trying to form a screen around them.

Lieutenant Yazata followed in their wake, bending to seize two rifles dropped by fallen members of the bodyguard as they struggled to get to their feet. As she reached the stairs she looked up to see pieces of a destroyed shuttle falling towards the reviewing stand. "LOOK OUT!" she screamed, and the others heard her. The General glanced up, then threw the Satrap bodily over the edge of the stair railing and dived after him. Without hesitation the Captain did likewise, tossing the Crown Prince over the rail then jumping himself, and Yazata followed him without giving herself time to think. A few of the Satrap's bodyguards followed their example, but too many were bunched up, getting in each other's way, some hesitating at the sight of the five-meter drop.

She couldn't keep her feet as she hit the ground. Releasing the rifles as she fell, she rolled to one side, then grabbed them again as she struggled to her knees. The Satrap was screaming, clutching his left leg as the General reached for him, foot bent at an impossible angle. *That's a broken ankle,* she thought to herself as she came to her feet and glanced over to the Crown Prince. He didn't seem to be injured, but was wheezing and gasping for breath as Captain Dehgahn hauled him upright.

"INTO THE TUNNEL!" the General yelled, pointing at the access tunnel behind the reviewing stand as he pulled the Satrap over his shoulders in a fireman's lift. Under normal circumstances sports teams would make their entrance through this portal, but now it offered their only means of escape.

Even as they dashed towards it, joined by several bodyguards who'd made the jump, the stand behind them shook as something big and heavy smashed into its left side, pulverizing it and bringing down half the platform. There were agonized screams and shouts from above as splintered timbers and scaffold steel rained down. Miraculously they avoided the falling debris as the General and Captain Dehgahn carried and dragged the Satrap and Crown Prince into the tunnel. Yazata followed numbly, feeling inexpressible relief as the roof of the tunnel closed over her head. Surely with so much reinforced plascrete above them they would be safe now?

~ ~ ~

ABOVE THE ARENA

Brigadier-General Aldred couldn't help exclaiming with glee as he watched the destruction unfold ahead of the formation of Laredo shuttles. Even as the pilot gunned the thrusters to gain height to their bombing altitude of a hundred and fifty meters, he exclaimed, "That's incredible! They've lost almost every single shuttle, and the few survivors are fleeing as fast as they can travel!"

"Look at the arena," the Weapons System Operator advised grimly. "It's like a disturbed ant heap in there with all the wreckage falling on their heads like that – and they can't get out. They're trapped by the interior walls."

"Just where we want them," the pilot agreed. "Take it, Wizzo."

The WSO keyed his microphone. "All Laredo shuttles, this is Shuttle One. On my mark... stand by... three, two, one, *MARK!*"

The ten shuttles had spread out into a carefully calculated formation, each vehicle positioned so as to cover overlapping swaths of ground with their weapons. As the WSO called the mark, the battle computers began to release fragmentation bombs and sensor fused munitions in a precisely timed sequence from the ordnance pods suspended beneath the belly of each shuttle.

The sensor fused munitions ejected multiple small homing explosive bomblets, their sensors seeking any large objects like missile batteries, assault shuttles or other vehicles, particularly anything moving. As each found a suitable objective within range it oriented itself towards it and fired a charge to produce an explosively formed projectile, devastating the target below. The pattern of bomblets covered the vehicles in the VIP parking area outside the arena walls and all the armored cars, artillery pieces and other hardware arrayed around the walls inside the arena, ready for inspection. Almost all were hit. Many were destroyed outright, while the rest were damaged so badly as to be unusable. Only a few light vehicles furthest away from the arena escaped unscathed.

The fragmentation bombs dropped in a carefully calculated evenly-spaced pattern over and around the arena. Every one ejected forty fifteen-centimeter shrapnel balls in mid-air. Each comprised a central explosive core with a short-delay impact fuse, surrounded by a double deeply-scored steel shell sandwiching a springy rubber-like compound between its inner and outer layers. As each ball struck the ground the compound compressed, then released, bouncing the bomblet two to four meters high before it detonated, spraying shards of its double casing with lethal velocity over a fifteen-meter radius.

Almost five thousand surviving soldiers in parade dress milled in terrified confusion across the arena. Almost ten thousand surviving administrators, bureaucrats and clerks struggled panic-stricken among the steeply banked spectators' seats above them.

One thousand six hundred shrapnel balls rolled over them all from one side of the arena to the other. The targeting grid had divided the area into three-by-three-meter squares. The shuttles dropped at least one ball into each, blasting at least two shell fragments into every square meter.

The carnage was indescribable.

~ ~ ~

SATRAP'S PARTY

Four bodyguards sprinted ahead of the royal group as they headed towards the far end of the tunnel, and six others followed behind. They held their rifles ready as they neared its exit, which opened onto the VIP parking area – then slammed to a halt as explosions began to rock the vehicles outside. A black ball-like object hit the ground, bounced upward and struck the roof of the tunnel at its entrance, then bounced further inside before it blew up with a thunderous blast. Shrapnel shrieked down the tunnel, ricocheting off the walls. Two bodyguards collapsed. One clutched his almost-severed left leg, screaming as the blood fountained, while the other was ominously silent.

Beside Lieutenant Yazata Captain Dehgahn grunted, doubling over, holding his stomach, releasing the arm of the Crown Prince. As he fell to the ground she dropped to her knees beside him, seeing the red blood staining his fingers. He looked up at her, face drawn in an agonized grimace, and she saw the wordless pleading in his eyes. Outside at both ends of the tunnel the crackle of explosions grew to a thunderous cacophony, deafening everyone within. The blasts seemed to merge into a single gigantic roar of fury and destruction that pounded their ears and tore at their bodies like a wind, buffeting them as the floor and walls shook. She tried to say something, but couldn't even hear herself think in the tumult. As it slowly receded it left desperate screams, shouts and cries for help echoing in their battered ears as if from a great distance.

She thrust the two rifles in her hands at a bodyguard behind her. "Here! You! Carry these!" The rasp of authority was in her voice, and the startled man instinctively took the weapons from her even though she wasn't in his chain of command. She turned to the Crown Prince. "You! Take his other arm! MOVE!"

"That's right, Lieutenant!" Major-General Huvishka said approvingly as they pulled the Captain's arms over their shoulders and lifted him to his feet. Their CO was holding the Satrap over his shoulders as effortlessly as if his ruler had been a baby. "We can't go out into that." Continued scattered explosions confirmed his words. "Into the changing-rooms, quick!"

They turned around and stumbled back up the tunnel to where double doors were set into both walls, one for the home side, one for a visiting team. Yazata tried the handle of the nearest door, but it was locked. She looked at the bodyguard carrying her rifles. "Shoot that lock off!"

The man obeyed, holding her two weapons by their slings in his left hand as he brought up his own with his right. He fired a long burst, the echoes deafening all of them anew as they reverberated off the plascrete walls. The lock area disintegrated and the double doors sagged inwards. Yazata kicked them wider open and dragged Captain Dehgahn through.

"Stop!" he gasped. "Wait! They'll be... coming!"

"What do you mean?" she demanded through the ringing in her ears, breath sobbing in her throat under the exertion of half-carrying him.

"This is too... well planned! They've got too many... shuttles and too many weapons!" He panted for breath. "They're bound to land troops as well... to make sure they get the Satrap. They'll know... the only way he could have got clear... of the reviewing stand is through this tunnel... and they'll come looking for him. I... can't run anymore. Leave me here with a rifle. I'll delay them... while you go through the changing-rooms... and coaches' offices. There... should be vehicles on the far side of them... further away from the arena. Some... may still be usable."

Huvishka wasted no time. "He's right. Give him a rifle."

The bodyguard carrying the rifles Yazata had picked up handed one to the Captain. She took the other from him and checked to make sure it was loaded as the General took one arm from around the Satrap's legs and gently squeezed Dehgahn's shoulder. "Thank you. Die well, lad."

"I'll do my best... Sir. Live well."

"If the bastards let us!"

Hurrying down the corridor, they could hear the Captain's gasping, pain-filled breathing behind them as he braced himself against the wall behind a vending machine filled with sports drinks, aiming his rifle back towards the doors.

They tore through the changing-rooms at a dead run. Two bodyguards raced ahead to shoot open the door to a suite of offices set aside for visiting coaches and team officials, then did the same to the door on the far side that exited into the parking area. They ran outside ahead of the rest of the group, rifles at the ready, slamming to a halt and standing back-to-back as they scanned for threats – then they disintegrated in a cloud of dust and dirt as a plasma bolt came in, seemingly from out of nowhere, digging a smoking crater in the parking lot where they had been standing.

The General managed to skid to a halt just before he reached the door. "No good! Back the way we came!"

As they turned to retrace their steps they heard the sound of rifle fire from the direction of the tunnel, followed by a loud explosion and an agonized scream.

~ ~ ~

ABOVE THE ARENA

Brigadier-General Aldred didn't waste time admiring the results of the air strike. He keyed his microphone. "Laredo Six to all shuttles. Well done, everybody! Split up and proceed to your assigned targets. God be with you all. Laredo Six out."

All the shuttles released their now-empty ordnance pods. The four shuttles of Task Force Arena, including the General's, banked steeply, their pilots hauling the craft around almost by main force, reaction thrusters screaming. While turning, each of the four took final advantage of its temporary immunity from the Bactrian central fire control system by targeting one of the pairs of assault shuttles parked at the corners of the arena grounds, firing two missiles at each shuttle. Sixteen missiles blazed short-range paths of destruction through the air, blasting the vehicles before their stunned crews could pull themselves together, switch to local guidance systems and return fire.

Two of the Laredo shuttles turned towards the VIP parking area outside the arena, where the waiting vehicles had been shredded by exploding sensor fused munitions. The WSO in the lead shuttle spotted two rifle-bearing Bactrians rushing out of a door into the parking lot, and vaporized them with a well-aimed snap shot from his plasma cannon. The other two shuttles made for the reviewing stand inside the arena. Their plasma cannon began to fire as they cleared a landing area for themselves. In the process they pulverized the remains of the reviewing stand, reducing it to shattered fragments, revealing the tunnel through which the Satrap had been carried to temporary safety. The troops carried by all four shuttles readied themselves for action as they touched down, sprinting down their rear ramps and fanning out into combat formation.

The six shuttles of Task Force Banka split into three groups of two, their courses diverging as they headed into the city. Two made for the huge supply depot next to the spaceport, two for the civil administration center, and two for the Military Governor's compound. As they flew, their transponder ID's protected them from the defensive systems deployed throughout the city. Any Bactrian weapon that could harm them was still under the control of the central computer, which adamantly refused to allow any of them to fire at the intruders.

On their way to their target areas, the shuttle crews witnessed the next acts in the last stand of Laredo's Army. Their cameras and sensors recorded everything they saw, as they had since the attack began, and transmitted it to waiting antennae on top of the old Traffic Control building. There the traffic control computer sucked up everything and rebroadcast it via tight-beam to another dish on the space station in geostationary orbit far above.

~ ~ ~

NEW TRAFCON BUILDING

The Bactrian traffic control operators gazed in horror out of the windows at the top of the hundred-meter TrafCon Tower. Within a matter of seconds, it seemed, their world had fallen apart. All their consoles had gone blank; missile batteries and shuttles all over Tapuria had begun firing without orders; and the parade of eighty shuttles flying over the arena had been devastated. Huge columns of smoke were rising from all around the stadium.

The Watch Commander, a Major, was the first to pull himself together. He snatched up his microphone. "Give me an open circuit – all channels!" he snarled at the communications operator. As soon as the shaken man had made the connections, he keyed his mike. "All stations, this is Trafcon. *Emergency! Emergency!* The Satrap is under attack at the arena! All stations are to send every available soldier and vehicle to the arena! Flash priority! *Emergency! Emer–*"

~ ~ ~

TAPURIA

The traffic control supercomputer accepted Quincy's Phase Three program. Its artificial intelligence system considered its newly-assigned targets, then reallocated its resources.

Thirty per cent of the remaining multi-sensor missiles were targeted on the Trafcon Tower and its critical central communications hub, spread from top to bottom of the structure. Another twenty per cent were aimed at the Military Governor's compound, instructed to seek out and destroy every missile battery and vehicle on the grounds. The last fifty per cent were programmed to take out almost every major radio signal target in the city, from the three TrafCon radomes, to the Command Bunker's antenna farm, to the surviving assault shuttles in key areas, to most buildings supporting a tower sprouting aerials and dishes. Each missile was pre-programmed with the location of its objective. As it approached, its sensors would detect the transmissions from its target and use them to guide its final suicidal dive.

As soon as its electronic brain was satisfied that all missiles had received their instructions, the artificial intelligence system released the weapons. The thunderblast of launching missiles and detonating warheads once again filled the air over the city.

The operators at the new TrafCon building had time for only the briefest glimpse of their doom speeding towards them. Fifty-two missiles were targeted at the building. A few malfunctioned, but forty-four struck home, four smashing through the angled windows of the control room itself to explode in their midst. The Watch Commander was blown into red rags before he could complete his transmission. Other missiles wrecked the tower from top to bottom, taking great bites out of its plascrete core, destroying the integrity of its structural steel framework. The building staggered, leaned drunkenly, and collapsed into a pile of rubble and a choking cloud of smoke and dust.

As its radar domes on the hilltops were destroyed, the central computer found that it could no longer detect or monitor airborne traffic. It automatically released all remaining weapon systems in the city to local control. There weren't many of them left. Those still able to do so activated their own radars and lidars and began frantically looking for targets – just what the approaching Laredo shuttles had been waiting for. As each transmission was detected, a WSO aimed a missile towards it or slewed the vehicle's plasma cannon onto the bearing and let fly. Defenders rapidly learned that to give away one's own position by the use of active sensors was fraught with peril. They switched to passive thermal and optical sensors and open sights.

All over Tapuria military vehicles jerked into motion, abandoning their assigned positions and heading towards the arena in response to the Watch Commander's emergency call. Their crews didn't look up, but focused on the roads immediately ahead of them as they sped around corners and through obstructions. That proved to be the undoing of many. Those within range of the airborne Laredo shuttles were greeted with carefully-aimed single shots from their plasma cannon, blocking the roads with their burning wrecks.

The assault shuttles at the Military Governor's compound tried to lift off just as the second wave of incoming missiles arrived, smashing them back to the ground, destroying the now-empty missile batteries and their associated laser cannon, blasting away every aerial and antenna, cutting off radio communication between the Command Bunker and the forces remaining in the city. The Laredo shuttles began to search for the few heavy weapons that had escaped damage so far, turning their missiles and plasma cannon on them. It didn't take long for the inexperienced, poorly-trained Bactrian conscripts to realize that remaining in the vicinity of such weapons had suddenly become nothing more than an unusually spectacular and explosive way to commit suicide. They abandoned their posts in droves and scattered in all directions, leaving their professional colleagues raging in frustration, yelling curses after them.

After dropping their troops at the arena, the four Laredo shuttles there rose into the air once more. Their pilots and WSO's prepared to use their missiles and plasma cannon against relieving forces, to buy time for their comrades on the ground to complete their mission. They also listened for any calls for help, ready to turn their weapons against pockets of resistance in or around the arena.

The three groups of Laredo resistance fighters who'd assembled in underground hideouts after sneaking through the security cordon around Banka had been waiting for this moment. As chaos spread throughout the city above them, they emerged from their basements, sewers and tunnels. The three pairs of shuttles in Task Force Banka landed briefly at prearranged rendezvous points, dropping their contingents of soldiers and the heavier weapons they'd brought with them, then lifted off again to provide airborne cover for as long as possible. Their teams joined forces with those who'd previously infiltrated the city and made for their assigned objectives.

The three reinforced groups struck hard. Within minutes one assault force had fought their way into the civil administration complex. They began destroying critical records, files and computer systems and wiring the buildings with explosives and incendiary devices. Another group attacked the Military Governor's compound, calling in the location of enemy heavy weapons and strongpoints so that their comrades in the shuttles could blast them out of the way. The fighting there was less one-sided as the Bactrian forces began to recover from the shock of the attack and reorganize themselves. Focal points of resistance began to emerge. A Laredo shuttle took a direct hit from an optically-aimed plasma cannon. It staggered in mid-air, turned over onto its back and plummeted onto the guardhouse at the entrance to the Military Governor's compound, killing a dozen Bactrian servicemen, even in its death throes clearing a path for its comrades on the ground.

The third Laredo assault force penetrated the perimeter of the immense supply depot, blasting its way through the confused defenders – mostly freight handlers and clerks, some hastily issued with rifles, some completely unarmed – while suffering minimal casualties of its own. The depot was home to a regiment of forty-eight armored cars, each equipped with a plasma cannon, tasked with escorting supply convoys to and from garrisons and bases across the continent. The regiment's personnel were all on parade at the arena, so none of its vehicles were manned and ready – a shortcoming the attackers rapidly rectified.

The shuttle contingent used the heavier weapons and explosives they'd brought with them to blast their way into the armory. They seized every nearby transport and filled them with plasma cannon magazines, more rifles and ammunition, and all the explosives and incendiaries they could find. Meanwhile the other raiders checked the armored cars and started the first row of them. The shuttle party drove up, tossing loaded magazines to the car crews, who filled their turret racks. As soon as the first vehicles were fully armed they headed for preselected points and began to shoot at everything in sight. The massive energy impact of the plasma cannon bolts hurled vehicles and stacks of supplies flaming into the air, and collapsed building after building as their supporting structures were blown away.

Thick, choking clouds of smoke and flame began to obscure the entire depot and everything in and around it. Meanwhile, the shuttle party loaded all the remaining armored cars with ammunition for their plasma cannon.

As they destroyed scores of billions of bezants worth of weapons, equipment and supplies, the armored cars protected their occupants from the desultory light weapons fire of the few defenders who had not yet fled or been killed. As each vehicle's plasma cannon barrel burned out, its crew drove it back to the regiment's motor pool. They took any remaining ammunition with them to another vehicle, used its cannon to blast the armored car they'd just used, then got back to work.

Meanwhile the shuttle party commandeered several armored cars to add firepower to their transports, then fought their way out of a side gate. Five blocks ahead of them, the Security Service headquarters building stood so far unscathed amid the chaos spreading across the city.

~ ~ ~

OLD TRAFCON

Jake whirled on his heel. "I'm going to make sure we get our hands on as many vehicles as we can find!"

Quincy called after him. "I've instructed the computer to continue relaying the progress of our attack to orbit until the space station can't forward it to your son any longer. While you're busy up there we'll lay demolition charges down here, then stand by for further orders."

Jake paused in the doorway. "Good man! While you're doing that, we'll prepare a warm reception for Bactrian relief forces fighting their way into the city from the outer perimeter."

The rest of Niven's Regiment hadn't waited for their boss. An assault team burst into the guards' rest area as soon as the tunnel explosions went off, pouring bursts of fire into everyone present. All died without having time to fight back. The two on duty in the guardroom and the two in the gatehouse fared little better, but had time to seize their weapons and fire at least a few rounds in their own defense. Two of the attackers went down, one killed outright, the other grievously wounded with two rounds in his abdominal cavity. His friend knelt beside him.

"How – how does it look, Mike?"

Mike shook his head. "Sorry, ol' buddy. It's real bad. Let me give you something for the pain." He fumbled for his preloaded injector of painkiller.

"Mike... if it's that bad... please?"

His friend's face contorted in anguish. "I – I can't, Paul! I just *can't* – not like this!"

"Then take my... pulser out of my holster... and put it... in my hand." The man's words were punctuated by gasps of agony.

Weeping, Mike did as he asked, then bent awkwardly and embraced him.

"Go on! Get out of here!" Paul commanded, forcing himself to hold back another groan of pain. "The others... need you!"

As Mike ran towards the gate he heard a single shot from behind him. Wiping tears from his eyes, he didn't look back.

The others spread out, reconnoitering the area. Whenever they came across a usable vehicle or heavy weapons system they did whatever they had to do to kill the crew and take it over. They incurred several more casualties in the process, but within fifteen minutes their booty included two armored cars, three heavy transports, four light utility vehicles, five plasma cannon on tripod mounts, and six portable multi-sensor short-range missile tubes. The intruders loaded the weapons and their associated mounts, power supplies and ammunition onto the Bactrian vehicles and carried them back to the old TrafCon building.

As some hurriedly installed the plasma cannon on the captured heavy transports, bolting and spot-welding their mounts to the load beds using tools at a nearby maintenance center, others planted explosive charges at key points in buildings, beneath elevated roads and pedestrian walkways, and anywhere an enemy vehicle was likely to pass. Some they detonated at once, forming mounds of rubble and debris that blocked major roads, using plasma cannon fire to increase the destruction. Other devices were concealed in garbage cans or piles of rubble or behind windows close to the street, sensors waiting for a vehicle to get close enough to be devastated by the explosively formed projectiles they would generate. The two techs who'd planted bugs in the tunnels beneath the complex did the same to several intact buildings in the security zone, emplacing nanobugs and flitterbugs, preparing to unleash upon the Bactrians the same nightmarish weapons they'd so often deployed against the Resistance.

March 31st 2850 GSC, 10:00 – In Orbit

SPACE STATION

The two fake Security Service guards crouched over the sentries they'd just killed, one on either side of the double doors leading to the Orbital Control Center. They watched Dave as he ran down the passage towards them. He shook his head and raised his voice. "Don't just stand there! *Get inside and stop them warning anyone else!*"

They sprang to the doors, opened them and dashed through, renewed popping sounds coming from their silenced pulsers. Dave reached the doors a second later, the butt of his rifle braced against his spacesuit as he entered OrbCon, trying to remember the layout Mac had drawn for them. It looked as if the Bactrians had kept everything as it had been before they invaded. A man was reeling back behind the Watch Commander's elevated station, hands to his face, blood spurting from his mouth. As he collapsed out of sight behind the console, Dave turned to his right and began firing at three panic-stricken operators trying to reach a side door. Within seconds he was joined in the room by other members of his team.

There were only six operators on duty, and none stayed on their feet long enough to transmit a warning message to the nearby warships or the planet below. As the last of them collapsed Dave yelled, "CEASE FIRE! *Cease fire!* Don't hit the equipment! We need it!" He shook his head to clear his ears of the ringing caused by the concussion of repeated shots in so confined a space. Even though an electromagnetic firing mechanism accelerated the projectiles rather than chemical explosives, the *crack!* as they broke the sound barrier was very loud. From further down the passage he could hear more gunfire and a couple of explosions – caused, he knew, by the other groups taking care of off-duty personnel and anyone working in Administration or Engineering.

"Mac!" he called.

"Here." The technical specialist ran into the OpCen, grimacing at the blood on the floor. "Get that body out from behind the Watch Commander's console so I can use it."

Two of Dave's team dragged the Bactrian officer unceremoniously off the raised platform on which his console stood and dumped his body in the corner of the room. Others piled the bodies of the watch crew beside his as Mac seated himself, scanned the displays, and grinned. "I don't even need to hack my way into the system. He's logged in with full command authority – must have been a senior guy. I can do everything from here."

"I'm glad to hear it," Dave informed him waspishly. "How about getting on with it? There's a live nuke ticking away down that corridor. I want to be long gone by the time it blows!"

"Where's your sense of adventure?" the other mock-protested, grinning.

"I left it planetside!"

As the others laughed, Mac entered a rapid sequence of commands. "There. I've cut off the news feed from planetside to the ships, and put up a message saying it's only temporary and will be back in a few minutes. That should prevent any alarm from the parade reaching them, unless they tune in to planetside news transmissions. For a brief delay like this, let's hope they don't."

Mac glanced at the huge Plot display on the wall and nodded, satisfied. The Satrap's yacht was a thousand kilometers to port, with two corvettes respectively five hundred kilometers ahead of and behind her – no more than point-blank range for the space station's defensive missiles. An armed merchant cruiser was a thousand kilometers to starboard, with LMV *Benbecula* another thousand kilometers out and two thousand behind, emphasizing her lowliness in the hierarchy of orbiting vessels. He trained a tight-beam dish on the latter vessel. "The circuit's on the way. Take it there. Wait for the green light." He pointed to the communications console.

"Thanks." Dave walked over to the console, put on a headset, and waited for a green light to illuminate. When it did, he pressed the switch below it.

"This is Captain Carson of the Laredo Army calling Captain Grassby of *Benbecula*, over."

A brief pause, then, "Grassby here, go ahead, over."

"Carson to Grassby. I'm only going to say this once, so listen very carefully. If you're not at immediate readiness for departure, come to that state at once and stand by. All hell's about to break loose. Do not, I say again, *do not* attempt to leave your assigned orbit under any circumstances, even if someone orders you to do so. Ignore all such instructions. Any deviation risks attracting a missile or two, and there's no future in that. As long as you stay where you are, you'll be safe. Do you understand me? Over."

"Grassby to Carson, I get it, but what the hell are you up to? Over."

"Carson to Grassby. I've no time to answer questions at present. We'll be coming aboard within an hour. Wait for our arrival. As soon as we've docked, head for the system boundary at full blast, in the opposite direction to that Bactrian armed merchant cruiser patrolling the system. She's a full light hour from us at present and heading further away, so she shouldn't pose any threat provided you keep her at a safe distance. Got it? Over."

"Grassby to Carson, understood. Where's Manuel?"

"Carson to Grassby, he'll be coming aboard with us. Over."

"Grassby to Carson, can I speak with him, please? Over."

"Carson to Grassby, wait one." Jake turned to Manuel, who'd entered the OpCen with Mac and was now standing against the wall, looking nauseated as he stared at the dead bodies and blood on the floor. "Manuel, he wants to talk to you." He flipped on the console speaker as the visitor came over, and offered him a hand-held microphone as he said, "Carson to Grassby, here he is."

"Manuel, this is Tom. What the hell's happening? Why all the mystery? Over."

"Manuel to Tom, I don't know, but I'm not a military man. I suspect Captain Carson doesn't want the Bactrians to overhear his plans. That way they can't do anything to stop him. Over."

"Hmpf!" The merchant skipper's voice was disgruntled. "I suspect he doesn't want us to do anything to interfere either! I can't say I'm wildly impressed with the lack of information. Are these guys really OK, Manuel? I'm being given instructions that make no sense – in fact, they seem to me to threaten the safety of my ship and crew. Over."

"All I can say is that he's kept me alive and safe since I got here. He's killed enemies in my presence, so he's not exactly your soft cuddly type, but he's for sure on my side. That puts him on your side too. You can trust him. Over."

"Tom to Manuel. I'll take your word for it, but if one of those missiles hits us, I'll sue you when we get to hell!"

Dave had to grin as Manuel retorted, "At least there'll be plenty of lawyers there!"

He cut in. "Carson to Grassby, no time for more now. One last thing. Stand by for a nuclear explosion and its associated electromagnetic pulses. Shut down your communications, withdraw your aerials, and activate all your protective systems for your electronics. Your hull provides Faraday cage protection, right? Over."

"Wha – I – *are you crazy?*" The other's voice sounded shocked and outraged.

"Carson to Grassby. No, I'm not crazy. You're far enough away to be safe from the blast and radiation, but your electronics will be affected if you don't take precautions. I say again, is your hull equipped with Faraday cage protection? Over."

"I… Grassby to Carson, yes, it is, like all well-found spaceships. Over."

"Carson to Grassby, very good. Stand by for action, and remember; stay where you are and don't move until we get aboard! Over." He didn't add that it wasn't so much the ship's safety as their escape that he was worried about.

"Grassby to Carson, understood – but I don't like it!"

Dave removed his headset and looked across at the Watch Commander's console. "How's it going, Mac?"

"I'm just locking in the last targeting instructions." He was tapping at a keyboard as he spoke. "I told you I knew this system backwards. We'll be ready in under two minutes."

"Sounds good." Dave turned to the doors as a dozen of his people trooped through them. "Any problems?"

"No, Sir," Sergeant-Major Deacon answered for them all. "Twelve off-watch personnel, three on duty in Engineering, two in Administration. All down, Sir."

"Excellent! We put down six in here, and we know the rest are planetside taking part in the Satrap's parade. By the time our shuttles have finished with them, I doubt any will need a ride back up to orbit."

~ ~ ~

The Watch Commander was dragged back to consciousness by throbbing, burning pain in his face, caused by the pulser shot that had shattered his jaw and front teeth. He tried to open what was left of his mouth to gasp for breath, but stiffened as a surge of unbearable agony speared through him. He gurgled aloud through the blood in his mouth, but the noise was covered by a sudden burst of laughter. *Laughter?*, he wondered dizzily to himself. *Who's laughing? What —*

He suddenly recalled the two Security Service men bursting through the doors and firing at him with handguns. He froze, careful to make no movement that might alert anyone looking, and opened his eyes the barest crack. Through his eyelashes he could see a spacesuited man talking to a group of similarly clad people. They were laughing at something he'd just said. He strained his eyes to look sideways at his command console. An older man was seated there, entering instructions.

He felt something sticky on the floor. All the others in the room seemed to be looking at something else, so he risked turning his head slightly, wincing at the renewed pain. He was sickened to see the bodies of his watch crew tossed carelessly into a pile, bleeding on each other, dripping onto the floor. A rivulet of blood had run across the tiles and had just reached his hand.

Fury exploded through him, overriding his pain. *Whoever you bastards are, you're not going to take over my space station without a fight, damn you!* Stealthily, excruciatingly slowly, he began to slide his hand towards the holstered pulser at his waist — then stiffened in horror as the man at the console entered a last command, nodding in satisfaction as the computer accepted it. He looked up at another space-suited intruder and said, "Ready to proceed, Sir."

"Weapons free, Mac."

214

"Weapons free, Sir!"

The Watch Commander instantly realized what was happening. *I've got to stop them!* he thought desperately as he grabbed at the butt of his pulser, dragging it from his holster, aiming at the back of the man sitting in his chair.

~ ~ ~

Everyone was looking at the Plot screen, waiting for the appearance of missile traces heading for the ships nearby, anticipating the destruction to come, when the blast of a pulser echoed through OrbCon. Mac was thrown forward across the Watch Commander's console, a cry of agony wrenched from his lips.

Dave spun around, shouldering his rifle as another shot sounded. One of the two men dressed as Security Service guards arched his back and collapsed in a heap. Before the shooter – the fallen Watch Commander, Dave suddenly realized – could fire again, he was torn apart by slugs from several rifles. He collapsed inert against the bulkhead, pulser falling from his fingers.

Dave sprang to the console. *"Mac!* Are you OK?"

The older man sagged, sliding down the console limply, trying to say something; but he couldn't form the words. Dave caught him and eased him back into the chair. "CORPSMAN! Tamsin, where are you?"

"Here!" She ran towards him.

"How the hell do we fire these missiles?"

"I don't know!" she said frantically, eyes scanning the multiplicity of dials, panels, indicators, switches and buttons on the console. "The display says 'READY TO EXECUTE' so… there!" She pointed to a red button protected beneath a flip-up clear cover. The label over it read, 'FIRE'.

"That must be it!" Dave flipped up the cover and jammed his finger down on the button. There was a brief, agonizing pause. His brain screamed at him, *It's not going to work! You've failed!* – then he gasped in relief as he felt a shudder reverberate through the space station.

~ ~ ~

The computer absorbed Mac's instructions, passing target information through its datalinks to the station's forty missiles. Ten were aimed at each of the two corvettes, their impacts programmed to cover the length of the ships' relatively tiny thirty-thousand-ton hulls. The remaining twenty missiles were aimed at the armed merchant cruiser. Her half-million-ton bulk dwarfed the corvettes, but was full of a lot of empty space in the middle and lower hull in the form of cargo holds and storage compartments. Most of her critical systems were sheltered beneath her reinforced spine, so the missiles were aimed to penetrate her hull plating from the side, just below it.

As soon as the computer was satisfied that the missiles knew their targets, it released the weapons. The hundred-thousand-ton bulk of the space station began to shake as missile after missile was ejected from its tube by powerful mass drivers. Each was, in effect, a miniaturized spaceship equipped with its own gravitic drive, imparting enormous acceleration. As it cleared the field generated by the station's drive unit it engaged its own, turned towards its target and streaked away into the blackness of space.

~ ~ ~

Dave ignored the continued vibration of missile launches as he looked down at the only medic in his team. He was kneeling beside Mac, who'd slid out of the chair onto the deck. "How is he?"

The corpsman shook his head. "Sorry, Sir. His backbone's shot through and the round shredded his lung on the way out of his chest. He won't make it."

Sergeant-Major Deacon called from the floor, "James is dead, Sir." He looked around. "Who shot that guy? Why wasn't he shot again to make certain he was dead?" His voice was angry.

"It – it was me," the other black-clad man mumbled, trembling, tears in his eyes as he looked at his dead partner. "I was *sure* he was dead! You could see blood all over his face!"

"Blood doesn't mean dead," the Sergeant-Major said bluntly. "You *know* that, dammit! You've been fighting since this bloody war started!"

The other nodded dumbly, then suddenly reached for the pulser at his waist and tried to insert the muzzle in his mouth. Two others sprang to restrain him. He fought to overcome their grasp. *"Let me go, damn you!"*

"Take that pulser away from him!" Dave commanded. Another obeyed, ripping it from the man's grasp then stepping back.

Dave walked over to the black-clad man. "You're going to have to live with it, Tony," he said quietly, as compassionately as possible even though he shared the Sergeant-Major's outrage at so amateurish a mistake. *I should have thought to double-check, too,* he reminded himself bitterly. *It's not all Tony's fault. I took too much for granted.* "I can't afford to let you kill yourself. You're our backup shuttle pilot. Even if we reach safety, I've only got fifteen people in my team now. I need every one if we're to succeed in our mission."

Tony writhed in the grasp of the others. "James was... I... for God's sake, *let me die with him!*"

"Instead of dying with him, I need you to make up for your mistake by living for him, and helping to do his share of our work in future. Will you do that – for me and all of us, not just for James?"

Tony sagged helplessly. After a moment he nodded. "I – I'll try, Sir," he said hoarsely.

Dave squeezed his shoulder. "Thank you. Now, pull yourself together. Our work's not finished yet, and we need you."

He turned back to the medic, who was lowering Mac to the floor. As he watched, the man reached up and closed Mac's eyes. "Sorry, Sir. He's gone."

Dave blinked sudden tears from his eyes. So near to final success, and then... *this!*

Sergeant-Major Deacon called, "The missiles are almost there, Sir!" Everyone looked back up at the Plot display.

~ ~ ~

The three Bactrian warships were operating only a reduced 'anchor watch', two NCO's and an Officer of the Deck in their Operations Centers plus a couple of people in their engineering spaces. The rest of their reduced crews were either sleeping during their off-watch periods or busy with routine activities. There wasn't much they could do with half of their complements planetside to take part in the Satrap's parade, so everyone was feeling lazy.

The signatures of missile launches from the space station came as a complete surprise, freezing those on watch in shocked disbelief for a few dumbfounded moments before they could come to their senses. Klaxons blared their atonal *aaa-OOO-gah!* warning throughout the ships as the alarm sounded for General Quarters. Their diminished crews began to race towards their action stations, but few reached them and even fewer had time to put on their spacesuits. The watchstanders tried to bring the ship's defensive weapons to the action state, but with so few people available to do work normally requiring three to four times their number, they ran out of time.

The armed merchant cruiser was closest to the space station, so the twenty missiles targeted along her length arrived first. From bow to stern a rapid-fire sequence of explosions tore plating from her hull and devastated internal compartments, the kinetic energy unleashed by each ultra-high-speed missile's impact vastly amplifying the damage inflicted by its explosive warhead. The incoming fire missed her bridge, sparing those on watch. The others struggling to reach their action stations weren't so lucky. Her main fore-and-aft passage was blasted open to space in at least five locations, venting her internal atmosphere. Many of those aboard were sucked out with the air, to die silently screaming in vacuum as their body fluids boiled away. More missiles struck in or near the gravitic drive, reactor and capacitor ring compartments, sending the reactor into emergency shutdown and cutting the ship's wiring harness in several critical places.

As the last missile hit the merchant cruiser's docking bay and destroyed her cutters and cargo shuttle, the first of the weapons aimed at the corvettes reached their targets. Their much smaller hulls were tightly packed, every cubic meter crammed with systems, equipment, weapons and supplies; so every hit did far greater damage than had been inflicted on the more open, less cramped construction of the converted freighter. Ten explosions ripped each corvette from bow to stern, tearing great holes in their hulls, venting internal compartments to space, killing every non-space-suited member of their crews, cutting off power, rendering their communications, sensors and weapons systems unusable without major dockyard repairs.

The Satrap's yacht had also been operating an anchor watch, most of its crew idling or asleep. They, too, were summoned to their emergency stations by blaring klaxons, and watched in disbelief as missiles hammered their escorts. Their Captain was planetside with the Satrap, so the Executive Officer was in charge. He didn't know why his vessel had been spared from attack – at least, so far – but he wasn't about to hang around to find out. He kicked his vessel's gravitic drive to maximum power and headed away from the planet as fast as he could, steering towards the protection of the only surviving warship in the system – the patrolling armed merchant cruiser, now on the far side of Laredo and a full light-hour distant.

~ ~ ~

The watchers in OrbCon were disappointed not to see any dramatic explosions or destruction depicted on the Plot display. At such distances, the only visual change was that the icons depicting the corvettes and armed merchant cruiser showed that they were no longer broadcasting transponder beacons.

"They're dead in space," Dave observed as they watched the Satrap's yacht scorch away from orbit, turning to head towards the distant patrol vessel. "All right, people. They won't be able to interfere with *Benbecula*'s departure. We can board her now."

"What about Mac and James, Sir?" Sergeant-Major Deacon asked.

Dave hesitated, then said, "Leave them here. It'll slow us down too much to carry them back to the shuttle. We've got to get as far away from here as possible before that nuclear demolition charge goes off, and it'll give them as good a cremation as we could anywhere else."

"Yes, Sir." Deacon looked around, silencing the murmurs of protest from some of the others with a sharp, "The Captain's right! Don't argue! There's no time!"

Dave ejected a data chip from the console. Mac had inserted it at the start of proceedings, to record the attack on the warships. All its information about the strike and its results would be added to their data archive for Vice-President Johns, as would the recording being made in the shuttle right now of the feed relayed from Banka, showing everything the shuttles were seeing in their assault on the city.

He knelt, rummaged through Mac's pockets for the two keys he'd put there after arming the demolition charge, then stood again. "All right, let's go. Back to the shuttle, quick as you can!"

He maneuvered himself next to Tamsin as they ran down the passage. "D'you think Tony will be all right?" he asked quietly.

"I don't know. He and James were like us – lovers as well as partners in combat. I'm not sure if he'll get over this. You did the right thing to remind him that all of us need him. That might help him to hold on, by forcing him to think of others besides himself."

"I hope so. Can you handle the shuttle on your own for the last leg?"

"I sure can!"

As they exited the corridor into the docking bay vestibule and turned towards the shuttle, Dave glanced at the locked cargo compartment door. It was just as they'd left it. He checked the timer on his chest panel, and swore as he read '15:41'. He raised his voice. "People, we've got fifteen minutes to get a safe distance away from a cosmic catastrophe! Let's *move!*"

Tamsin made sure she was among the first group through the airlock. As the others took their seats and waited for the next group, she started up the shuttle's systems and brought the reaction thrusters online. "Tell the rest to *hurry!*" she urged as she pulled her four-point harness over her shoulders. "The sooner we're out of this docking bay, the more distance I can put between us and the explosion!"

She didn't even wait for the last group to take their seats before raising the rear ramp. As it sealed itself against the shuttle's body she disengaged the trunk, feeding power to the thrusters before it had fully released the rear of the shuttle. Those still on their feet staggered as the vehicle strained, then abruptly jerked forward. Their comrades steadied them and helped them to sit down.

"Hey, wait a minute, Tamsin!" one of them protested. "Let me strap in first!"

"Like hell!" she retorted. "We've got no more than ten minutes to get clear. We need to be at least a hundred clicks from this thing to avoid it frying all our systems. I'm about to go to full blast. Hold on tight!"

As soon as the shuttle was far enough away to be clear of any interference between its own gravitic drive field and the larger, more powerful drive of the station, she cut the reaction thrusters. Even as they began retracting into the hull, she gunned the gravitic drive to full power. The inertial compensator beneath the floor whined shrilly, louder than any of them could recall hearing one before, as it absorbed the crushing burden of acceleration. It dumped most of it into the gravity well of space's dark matter, but even with that assistance everyone aboard grunted, groaned and sweated under the sudden impact of several times their normal body weight. The shuttle sprang forward towards LMV *Benbecula,* almost three thousand kilometers distant.

Tamsin watched her console instruments like a hawk, fighting the stress of acceleration, sweat beading her forehead. As their velocity increased by leaps and bounds she withdrew all communications antennae, shut down the electronically-scanned phased array radar panels and invoked every EMP resistance measure built into the shuttle's systems. As she finished, she glanced at the range display and let out an exultant shout. "We're clear!"

Seven seconds later the space station disappeared in a five-kilometer-wide fireball. At first it was so bright that anyone looking directly at it from that distance would have been temporarily blinded. It seemed as if a gigantic photographic flash unit had exploded. The light rapidly faded from bright white through pale yellow into orange before dissipating into deeper and deeper reds and blacks. Every electromagnetic frequency in the vicinity instantly fuzzed and sputtered with impenetrable static.

As the shockwave hit the shuttle everyone aboard was jolted in their seats, but they were far enough away to avoid any damage. Dave knew the shock would hit *Benbecula* within seconds. He called to Tamsin, "Bring up a tight-beam circuit to the ship!"

"I can't," she said over her shoulder. "That explosion will disrupt the entire orbital radio spectrum for a while. We should be able to call them in fifteen to twenty minutes, but by then I hope to be preparing to dock with her – assuming she hangs around long enough for us to reach her, that is!"

"She'd better, or we're screwed! If you can't use radar or lidar, how will you find her?"

"Our passive sensors still work, so we'll pick up her gravitic drive emissions as we close in; and I aimed straight for her as we left the space station, so if neither of us changes course we'll end up within a few clicks of her. We should be able to see her lights at close range, or climb a bit to silhouette her against the planet below."

"You're the expert. Do whatever you have to do to get us aboard."

"No, Mac was the expert on this sort of thing." Her voice was sad as she remembered the man who'd become a friend and mentor to her, as well as a colleague.

Her forecast was proved correct. They saw *Benbecula*'s running lights as they approached, and Tamsin spotted the open door of her docking bay near her stern. She braked hard using the shuttle's gravitic drive, then switched to reaction thrusters as they entered the larger ship's own drive field. As she turned the shuttle to enter the relatively small docking bay backwards, she activated her radio on the orbital frequency.

"Laredo Army shuttle to *Benbecula*, over."

"*Benbecula* to shuttle." Captain Grassby's voice sounded rattled. "Did you set off the explosion that destroyed the space station? Over."

"Shuttle to *Benbecula*. I'll let Captain Carson explain once we're aboard. I'm about to enter your docking bay. Please activate your docking systems to receive us."

"*Benbecula* to shuttle, before you dock, listen carefully. This is an order from me as skipper of this ship. You are to leave all your weapons aboard your shuttle. You may not, I say again, you may *not* bring any weapons aboard this vessel. Is that clear? Over."

"Shuttle to *Benbecula*, wait one." Tamsin twisted in her seat to look back at Dave. "Is that OK with you?"

Dave thought rapidly. "It's his ship and his rules. We're just passengers while we're on board. Tell him I said OK, we'll do it."

She keyed her microphone. "Shuttle to *Benbecula*, Captain Carson says we will comply with your instruction. Over."

Captain Grassby's voice sounded slightly mollified. "*Benbecula* to shuttle, thank you. I must admit, I'm surprised. I expected him to argue, in which case I wouldn't have let you aboard at all! There's only one open airlock, so approach it and let our docking systems bring you in. Over."

"Shuttle to *Benbecula*, understood, out."

Dave looked around the shuttle as Tamsin brought it closer to the ship. "You heard. All weapons stay here, including any personal weapons, backup handguns, anything at all. Take them off now and dump them in the cargo area before we go through the airlock." He mentally decided to leave the two pulsers in the case of evidence. They were scan-proof, so if the case wasn't searched – which he wasn't about to allow – they'd be safe enough there.

"What about knives, Sir?" Sergeant-Major Deacon asked. "I've got my father's knife with me. It's important to me – sentimental value, you know?"

"I'll ask the skipper about that when we're aboard. Make sure everyone brings their personal gear aboard with them. Don't leave anything aboard the shuttle that you're not prepared to lose. Bring those two cases of bugs, too, and their consoles. I'm not leaving them behind."

"Yes, Sir."

Dave turned back to Tamsin. "Dump the shuttle's memory module to a data chip and bring the copy with you. It'll have our mission details on it, plus all the vid and sensor records transmitted from the planetside attack until the station blew up. I'll add it to our evidence archive."

"Will do."

Captain Grassby was waiting for them in the vestibule of the ship's docking bay, accompanied by four burly-looking Spacers. They glowered aggressively at Dave and the first group through the airlock, but their expressions grew more and more concerned as others joined them. They clearly felt outnumbered.

Manuel introduced Dave to the Captain. As they shook hands, Dave asked Grassby about the Sergeant-Major's knife and similar items. The Captain thought for a moment, then nodded. "Anything like that can be checked into the ship's safe. You'll get them back when you disembark. No electromagnetic or beam weapons, though."

"Fair enough, Sir. Thank you for understanding."

"Thank you for being reasonable. I must admit, I wasn't at all sure about having a group of armed men aboard this ship, particularly when we don't have either the weapons or the training to stop you if you tried to take over. Frankly, it's only because Manuel vouched for you that I was willing to take the risk. I hope this turns out to have been worth all the trouble my crew and I have been through."

"I think it will, Sir. I know you're being well paid for this, but even apart from that, we're all personally grateful to you for giving us a chance to get our evidence to the United Planets. It's our only hope of getting some sort of justice for all those who've died on Laredo."

"I hope you succeed. Now, I'm going to get us the hell out of here! The Bosun," waving a hand to one of the four with him, "will show you to an empty berthing compartment. It has only eight cabins and there are sixteen of you, so you'll have to pair up and hot-bunk for the duration of our journey to New Brisbane – or sleep on the floor, because I see you have bedrolls with you. The eight cabins share a common fresher. Please come to the bridge once you've stowed your gear. I want to hear more about what's been going on." He turned to his crewmen. "Bosun, leave a Spacer with them to escort Captain Carson to the bridge. Collect any knives and personal items they want to put in the ship's safe."

"Aye aye, Sir."

"May I bring Manuel and one of our shuttle pilots to the bridge with me, please, Sir?" Dave asked, thinking to himself, *It might help Tony if I can keep him busy.*

"Yes, that'll be OK."

"Thank you, Sir."

As they gathered up their personal gear to follow the Bosun, Tamsin asked, "Help me with this, please, Dave?"

"Sure." He picked up the thick, heavy bundle she handed him, then stopped short as he recognized the way it felt in his arms. "This is my ganiba pelt! It's heavier than I remember, though."

"It sure is, honey. I put it in the shuttle when you weren't looking. I figured you deserved at least one decent souvenir of Laredo." She leaned closer and whispered, "Your civilian rifle and gunbelt are inside it. I don't think they're classified as weapons on many planets nowadays, because hardly anyone uses such old technology. I figured you'd like to keep them."

He laughed aloud as he hugged her. "What would I do without you?"

Smiling, they followed the others.

March 31st 2850 GSC, 10:30

ARENA

Lieutenant Yazata ducked as the burst ricocheted off the wall above, flattening herself even harder against the floor behind the water cooler, nestling her eyes into the crook of her arm to protect them from the spray of plascrete chips and dust. As soon as the patter of debris had stopped she peered around the base of the cooler, trying to locate the source of the incoming fire. It was hard to see anything clearly through the haze of smoke and pulverized plascrete dust that hung in the air throughout the sports team facility.

In the changing-room behind her General Huvishka was finishing work on the Satrap's ankle. As she glanced over her shoulder at them, she inwardly gave thanks to whatever Gods there were that the stadium was equipped to stabilize broken limbs and other injuries prior to transporting players to hospital. The Satrap had been in agony until the General had administered a nerve-block anesthetic. He hadn't been able to hold back a whimper of relief as the block had taken effect, even as the General studied the instructions on the inflatable cast and muttered, "Damn these new-fangled models! What was wrong with the old ones that we all understood?" She hadn't been able to suppress a chuckle, and he'd grinned wryly at her before going to work. Even with the anesthetic, the Satrap had bitten his lip as his broken ankle was straightened as gently as possible, placed in the cast, then swaddled in bandages to protect both ankle and cast from debris.

She ducked again as another burst of enemy fire screamed down the passage. This time she thought she saw a flicker of movement behind a bench set against a wall thirty meters away, near the exit door. She lined her rifle, held her breath to steady her aim, and spaced three rapid rounds across it, shooting through the imitation wood. A cry of pain rewarded her efforts.

"Nice shooting!" the General praised from behind her as he straightened. He looked across to an open door from which came hammering, crunching noises and called softly, "Is it open yet?"

"Still trying, Sir!" a guard replied from the other room, desperation in his voice.

"Well, *try harder,* dammit!" Huvishka glanced at the Crown Prince, who was backed into a corner with two members of the Satrap's Guard planted firmly in front of him. "You all right, Your Highness?"

"I suppose so," came the shaky reply. Fear was a ragged edge underlying the young man's tone, but she could hardly blame him for that. He wasn't a military man, after all. He'd held up better than she expected after initially freezing in shock, as anyone might have done under the circumstances – *including me, until the General bowled me over,* she silently admitted to herself.

"We'll get out of here as soon as we can break through that internal partition. Damn the builders for doing such a good job! Couldn't they have been sloppy for once, and not put in so much bracing and reinforcement and sound-proofing?"

The Prince's guards grinned. One called, "At least it's not plascrete, Sir."

"Yes, we should be thankful for that, I suppose." The General picked up his rifle, one he'd taken from a fallen guard a few minutes earlier.

Yazata tensed as a hand appeared around the corner of the passage up ahead and rolled a small round object towards her. *"Grenade!"* she shouted, and thrust her rifle into the passage like a baton to stop the rolling object then flick it back up the corridor. It hadn't returned more than a few meters towards where it had appeared before it exploded with a deafening roar, scattering fragments of its casing in all directions. She cursed as one sliced through the skin of her forearm, making a nasty gash that instantly began to well with blood. Another cut across her calf, producing more gore.

One of the Prince's guards saw her plight and dashed forward to tap her ankle. "I've got it, Lieutenant. Get those wounds dressed, quick!"

She wriggled backwards, letting him take her place. As soon as she was out of the line of fire she stood, leaning her rifle against a chair. The General was ready with a pair of scissors to cut off the sleeve of her shirt and the lower leg of her uniform trousers. He cleaned the wound areas with disinfectant wipes, then sprinkled a powder into them that contained clotting agent, a painkiller and nanobiotics.

"You missed your calling, Sir," she said shakily. "You make a really good medic."

"I'll take that as a compliment under the circumstances," he retorted with a grin. "I prefer being a General, though!" He placed absorbent pads over the wounds, then wrapped her arm and leg in bandages and clipped them in place. "That'll have to do until we can get you to a doctor. Can you still walk and fight?"

She flexed her arm experimentally and put weight on her leg. "Yes, Sir. These are just flesh wounds."

The Satrap had watched from his chair. "You were on the reviewing stand with us," he recalled, his voice still a little hoarse from the pain. "Who are you?"

"This is Lieutenant Yazata of my staff," General Huvishka introduced her. "She's done yeoman work for Your Majesty this morning. It was her warning about falling debris that allowed us to get off the stand so fast. Those who moved more slowly... well, they're still out there."

The Satrap winced. "So she's why you threw me off the stairs and broke my ankle?" There was a ghost of a smile on his face as he glanced at the General. "I suppose I shouldn't complain, considering the alternative." He turned back to her. "You're certainly fighting like a tigress for me now."

He looked around the room. "All of you are to bear witness if necessary. I award to General Huvishka, that Captain who held the corridor for us earlier..."

"That was Captain Dehgahn," Huvishka interrupted.

"Thank you, General. To you, to Captain Dehgahn, to Lieutenant Yazata, and to all my guards who made it off the reviewing stand and helped to protect us in here, I award the Star of Bactria for utmost heroism in defense of your Satrap and Crown Prince. If I don't survive, those of you who do are ordered to report these awards to the appropriate authorities for action."

"Thank you, Sir," the General replied formally. "I hope you'll be able to act on it yourself."

"As a matter of fact, so do I!" His sally was greeted with shaky laughter from the guards. "Apart from rewards, there's also going to be punishment for some. I now see what you meant about wanting a full inquiry into the Security Service's activities here. If they provided no warning whatsoever about an attack this big, there's clearly something very wrong indeed. Heads will roll, I promise you!"

A ripping, rending crash came from the other room, followed by a triumphant cry. "I'm through, Sir!"

"Good man!" The General slung his rifle across his back, then turned to the Crown Prince. "Help me carry your father. These others will cover us, then fall back to join us."

The younger man came forward, linking his hands and forearms with the General's to make a seat for his father, who supported himself with his arms around their necks. They carried him through to the next room, where she heard them muttering and cursing as they negotiated the newly-broken-down partition between it and the administrative suite on the far side of the wall. After a few seconds she heard the General call. "We're through! You're next!"

"You go first," she told the guard behind her. He didn't argue, but disappeared through the door as she tapped the ankle of the man lying on the floor. He looked up. "I'm going to take up a standing position in that doorway," and she nodded to it. "While I cover the corridor, you crawl through low down so you don't get in my line of fire. Go through the hole in the wall, then take up a high cover position while I come through low in my turn. Got it?"

"Yes, Ma'am!"

She thought she saw a flicker of movement as the guard crawled past her knees, and fired six rapid shots, spacing them across the corridor, to discourage any attempt to close with them. Another scream of pain proved she was on target. As soon as the guard called "Ready, Ma'am!" she scuttled

228

across the inner room, bending low, and eased through the splintered hole, cursing as sharp edges scratched her skin through what was left of her shirt and trousers. The General and Crown Prince had already carried the Satrap out of the room. She followed them as another guard took station next to the one who'd preceded her through the hole. She quailed inwardly as she suddenly realized there were only three guards left.

The General glanced at her as she entered the foyer of the office suite. Its door to the parking lot outside was still closed and locked, but through its glass panes they could see craters across the black surface, debris scattered around, and smoke rising from damaged vehicles. A few uniformed soldiers were alertly scanning the area. Their uniforms were faded and well-worn, but their weapons were clean and ready for use.

"Rebels," the General said succinctly, jerking his head at them. "Thank heaven whoever designed this suite specified one-way glass for the external doors and windows!"

The Satrap nodded. "I nearly had a heart attack when you carried me through here. One of them was looking right at us through that big cracked window. It was only when he turned away that I realized he couldn't see us."

"Why haven't they tried to get in?" Yazata wondered.

"They don't suspect anyone's in these offices," Huvishka said. "They must – "

He was interrupted by a flash of light outside, almost as if a photographer had taken a picture with the aid of a lighting unit. They all blinked.

"What was that?" the Crown Prince asked.

Yazata hurried over to the window. All the soldiers in the parking lot were looking upward, pointing, exclaiming, high-fiving each other. She followed their gaze and saw a small bright ball of light very high above, fading from white into yellow and orange as she watched. She described it to the others, frowning in puzzlement.

Huvishka snapped, "That's the space station! It has to be. The rebels have destroyed it!"

They all goggled at him. The Satrap found his voice first. "But – but *how?* How could they get up there? They don't have spacecraft! And how could they destroy something so big?"

"I don't know how they did it, Sir, but look at the reaction of those rebels out there. They're excited, congratulating each other. This wasn't a surprise to them – they were expecting it. What's more, if the light came from a fireball it was probably a nuclear weapon exploding far outside atmosphere. We know the Laredans had a few nuclear demolition charges to deal with asteroids or other space threats. My predecessor reported they'd all been disposed of by the enemy to prevent us capturing them. Having seen that flash, I now suspect he was… optimistic in his report. I think we've just seen one of them being used – and if they've used one, how many more do they have?"

Yazata said carefully, "Sir… if the rebels can cause carnage like what we saw in the arena this morning, and do that *without* nuclear weapons… what might they achieve *with* them?"

"I wish you hadn't asked that question, Lieutenant," her boss said with a sigh. "They're certainly motivated enough to use them. The attack here is bound to be a one-way mission for many of them, and they must know that. Forces from the security perimeter outside Tapuria are undoubtedly already on their way to relieve the city. The rebels must be hoping to kill as many of us as possible and destroy as much as they can before they get here. They'll then try to make their getaway in the confusion, accepting heavy losses in return for inflicting massive damage on us. That shows a level of fanaticism and commitment that goes beyond anything I've seen so far on this planet. If they have more fanatics out there, and they still have a few nuclear warheads, there's no telling what they may do next."

"But I thought we'd crushed them!" the Satrap objected.

Huvishka sighed. "Does Your Majesty remember what I said to you when you appointed me Military Governor of Laredo?" he asked.

"Yes. You said I'd been given poor counsel thus far, and that we'd treated the population here far too harshly. You asked permission to try to reconcile them to our rule."

"Yes, Your Majesty; but you wouldn't permit me to do that."

"I put it to my Council, but they were irrevocably opposed to what they considered a sign of weakness. Some even wanted me to revoke your appointment on the grounds of what they called 'deficiency of character' for even daring to make the suggestion." He sighed. "I suppose that's partly the fault of my father and grandfather. They chose advisers who shared their vision of Bactria as superior to all other nations. They encouraged my father to invade Laredo on the principle that 'might makes right'. I didn't share that opinion, but he didn't consult me. I came to the throne two years after the invasion, when it was too late to alter our position."

The General nodded towards the door. "There, Your Majesty, you see the fruit of such counsel. Even if their forces here today are all killed, the rebels have scored a major victory. They must have wiped out almost everything we've built in Tapuria, judging by the smoke covering the horizon as far as we can see. They've certainly killed most of those in the arena this morning, including a third of our combat forces on this planet and many of our colonial administration personnel. We just saw them destroy our space station. They've demonstrated that when you oppress and grind down a people, those who continue to resist become stronger, not weaker. We've already killed all the weak ones. In the process we've distilled and refined the rebels until those that are left are harder, stronger and more dedicated than all those who've died. We've created our own worst enemy."

The Satrap gazed at him for a long moment. "So you wouldn't advise reprisals against the remaining Laredans for this morning's affair?"

"We've already killed or enslaved four-fifths of the planet's population, Your Majesty. This" – he waved his hand towards the devastation outside – "is what that's brought us. No, far better to halt the most repressive actions at once, then try to find leaders among the surviving locals with whom we can slowly improve relations. The hard-liners among your advisers won't want that, but you've seen for yourself what their counsel has wrought. It won't be easy, and it'll take time; but if I were you I'd appoint wiser counselors, ease up on the local population, and try to find a better way forward."

"Do you know, after this morning I'm more than half inclined to agree with you," the Satrap said slowly. He glanced at his son. "What say you?"

"What the General says makes sense to me," the Crown Prince declared.

"Then you're showing more understanding than I did at your age. However, we've got to survive before we can do anything about our policies. How are we going to do that, General?"

They were interrupted by a fusillade of shots from the room behind them. Yazata hurried to the door, flattening herself against the wall before looking cautiously through. "One of the guards is down," she reported.

"The other two are still on their feet." She turned to face the General. "Sir, we've got to split up before they join forces and overrun us."

"What do you mean?" the Satrap demanded.

Huvishka stared at her intently, then nodded slowly. "What she means, Your Majesty, is that there are too few of us and too many of them. Within a few minutes they'll have informed their forces outside that we've broken through to these offices. They'll then attack from out there while those inside try to get through the wall, just as we did. We'll be pinned between both forces. Our only escape is up those stairs, to try to lose ourselves in one of the levels above and hold out until relief forces get here."

"What about the elevator?" the Crown Prince interrupted. "Won't that be easier for my father?"

"You can't see what's waiting for you, Your Highness," Yazata explained. "If the enemy is already on the floor you're going to, they'll gun you down as the doors open. You won't stand a chance."

The young man winced. "Forget I asked!" he said hastily.

Huvishka continued, "If we stay together and they catch us, we'll all die – we don't have enough people to defend ourselves, and no heavy weapons. If we split up, two smaller groups might be able to find hiding-places that won't be so easily discovered. One or both groups might survive until help reaches us. Lieutenant Yazata is right, Your Majesty. Our best chance for one of you to make it is for us to split up."

The Satrap nodded decisively. "Let's do it. You take charge, General."

"Thank you, Your Majesty. Lieutenant, take the Crown Prince. I can't spare a guard to go with you, because there are only two still uninjured. Two of us will have to help the Satrap while the third covers us. Head up the stairs. Pick one of the top three floors, then get as far away to the right as you can. We'll give you a minute's start, then go to the left on a lower floor to increase the separation between us."

"Yes, Sir." She turned towards the stairs. "Come on, Your Highness."

"Just a moment." The young man hugged the Satrap. "God be with you, Father."

"And with you, my son." He hesitated, then said softly, "If you survive this day, remember what you've heard and seen and learned this morning. Now go!"

~ ~ ~

OLD TRAFCON

Jake was watching the fitting of a captured plasma cannon to a heavy transport's load bed when the flash erupted. They all looked up to see the fireball form and swell high above their heads.

One of the soldiers grinned, holding out his hand. "Congratulations, Sir! Looks like your son did his work well."

"It certainly looks that way." Jake shook his hand. "Let's hope they got away in time. Now they've got to take all our evidence to the ship that's waiting for it, and get it out of the system."

The other man shook his head, grimacing. "Sooner them than me. At least here I've got my feet on the ground and fresh air in my lungs. I'd hate to have to fight with nothing but vacuum all around me and the nearest solid ground thirty thousand clicks below!" The others laughed, even as they nodded in vigorous agreement.

Jake left them to carry on with their work as he turned away, clambering over rubble tossed randomly about by the demolition of buildings at crossroads. When he reached a clear area he paused for a moment, looking up at the last of the fireball as it died away.

"Go with God, son," he murmured softly. "I hope and pray you and Tamsin make it out of the system OK. Have lots of kids, and remember me kindly to them, will you? I wish I could live long enough to see them… but that's not likely to happen. God bless you, my boy."

Wiping a tear surreptitiously from his eye, he hurried back to the old Trafcon building and clattered down the stairs to the first basement level. Quincy and the other communications techs were gathered there, waiting.

"Dave blew up the space station," he told them. "We saw the fireball."

"We figured as much," Quincy agreed. "The feed to the station just cut off dead."

"Right. Are you all set to blow the charges down here?"

"We're rigged and ready."

"Then let's go."

They hurried up the stairs, one of the techs unreeling a long cable behind them, and ran down the entrance drive, past the gatehouse and up the road in front of the building. They didn't stop until they were fifty meters away. Another tech cut the insulation from the cable and connected it to a plunger. He offered it to Jake.

"Would you like to do the honors, Sir?"

"I did the tunnel. Quincy, I think this one's for you."

"Why, thank you, Sir! I didn't know you cared."

As the others chuckled, the senior tech took the plunger and pushed it down. The ground trembled beneath their feet as a thunderous roar rose from the old TrafCon building. The single-story guard accommodation above ground collapsed into the triple basement levels as the station, the supercomputer, and all the communications gear was shattered by demolition charges. Smoke and dust billowed upward.

"Between bringing down their new TrafCon Tower and blowing up their computer and other equipment, I reckon we just cost Bactria close to half a billion bezants," Quincy mused as they watched the destruction.

"That's just the start of it," Jake assured him. "Bactria has to import a lot of its high tech. Its bezants are too weak to be easily convertible on the interplanetary market, so it has to buy hard currency at extortionate exchange rates, or pay in hard assets like gold. If the arena strike went as well as I think it did, and the space station, warships, assault shuttles, stores depot, and civil and military administration complexes have been destroyed as planned, we're talking up to a trillion bezants in losses, maybe more. That's half Bactria's annual gross planetary product. It'll cripple their economy if they try to replace all they've lost in less than five to ten years, on top of their other expenditures. By resisting from the beginning, we made Laredo a constant drain on their Treasury instead of the economic bonanza they expected. With today's work, we've turned our planet into a financial millstone around their necks."

"The day's still young, Sir. Let's see if we can't give their collective wallets something more to complain about!"

"We'll probably find some worthwhile things to shoot at as we fight our way out of the city. All right, everyone, get aboard." He indicated the captured transports ahead, with armored cars at the head and tail of the convoy. "Let's get the hell out of this maze of streets before relief forces arrive."

~ ~ ~

SECURITY SERVICE HEADQUARTERS

The assault force wasted no time. As they drew nearer to the hated building, the armored cars took the lead and used their plasma cannon to flatten the entire perimeter wall and every guard post and tower along it. The sentries carried only light personal weapons, the SS having relied on the defensive perimeter around the city to protect their headquarters from any major onslaught. They died at their posts or fled in panic as the building was laid bare.

The armored cars took up position in the parking area, spread along the façade of the black building. They blasted the main entrance into rubble, allowing their comrades to charge in, weapons blazing. As they spread throughout the ground level, they passed word back to the cars whenever they encountered a pocket of resistance. By counting windows along the façade, the vehicles could aim their plasma cannon precisely at the trouble-spot. If a single shot didn't solve the problem, a second usually did. Before long the entire ground floor was secured.

Demolition specialists followed the assault force down to the cells in the basement levels. They killed every jailer, interrogator and torturer they found, then opened every cell, growling in anger as they saw the condition of some of those inside. The leader of the assault team ordered his soldiers to assemble all the former prisoners in the entrance foyer among the rubble, and laid things out for them.

"The city's surrounded by forces that are even now on their way here to crush us. We expected that. Before they arrive we'll have killed the Satrap and thousands, perhaps tens of thousands of their fellow soldiers and colonial administrators. We're destroying the entire military and civilian infrastructure they've built up here. When we've finished, those of you who are too badly hurt to walk will join our wounded aboard our surviving assault shuttles and be flown out. The rest of you have three choices. You can stay here and wait for the SS to return. I don't recommend that." There was a growl of agreement from those who'd recently had to endure their hospitality. "Besides, the building won't be here much longer." Laughter and applause.

"The second choice is to find a hole to hide in. We'll give you a couple of ration packs and a weapon. You can wait until the fighting dies down, then try to sneak out of the city on foot. I don't think you have much of a chance, but if worst comes to worst you can at least try to take some of the bastards with you. The third option is to join us. We'll give you a rifle and ammunition and teach you how to use them if you don't already know. We're going to split up into four or five convoys of transports and armored cars and try to escape. We'll launch hoversats that we've captured from the enemy to identify their approach roads, and try to dodge around and between their columns. It'll be very risky, and we know a lot of us won't make it, but that's the best option we've got. What do you want to do?"

The overwhelming majority of the able-bodied former prisoners chose to join the convoys. The few who elected to hide and try to escape later were armed, given some captured ration packs, and allowed to go their own way. Meanwhile the demolition experts laid charges in the basement against every pillar and reinforced wall they could find. They didn't have time to set them very efficiently, but compensated by using more than four tons of explosives, enlisting the eager help of former prisoners to unload it from the trucks and carry it down the stairs. Any attempt by those on the upper floors to shoot at them was met with plasma cannon fire from the armored cars. The defenders rapidly learned to lay low, keep quiet and do nothing if they wished to survive even a little while longer.

As soon as the charges were wired into a ring-main, the leader of the team put everyone aboard the vehicles and sent them several blocks away for safety while he connected a plunger to the wire.

"Ready?" he asked his deputy, crouching beside him behind the cover of the smashed perimeter wall.

"Ready. Blow it!"

He shoved the plunger down. A massive shockwave rolled over them as the ground bounced and shook. The ten-story building heaved, shuddered, and collapsed straight down into its own basement, taking with it hundreds of screaming SS personnel trapped on the upper nine floors. A huge choking cloud of smoke and dust rose high above the ruins.

The two kept their heads well down until fragments stopped falling on and around them. The leader glanced at his deputy, shaking his head in a vain attempt to clear the ringing from his ears. "D'you think we might have used a tad too much explosive there?"

"Perhaps just a skosh."

"Oh, well. They were SS, after all."

"True. If anyone deserved overkill, they did."

"My feelings exactly. Come on, let's go!"

Grinning, they raced for the transports through the fog of smoke and dust.

~ ~ ~

MILITARY GOVERNOR'S COMPOUND

The Bactrian Army offered more resistance at the Command Bunker than at any other site in Tapuria. The assault force managed to cut their way into the Military Governor's administrative building without too much difficulty, but that was because the forces guarding it chose not to die at their posts. Instead they made a fighting withdrawal into the adjacent underground bunker, covering each other's retreat, carrying their wounded. Soon the bunker was filled with over a hundred defenders. A similar number prepared defensive positions around its perimeter, hurriedly digging foxholes and scrapes, and beat back all attempts by the attackers to penetrate it.

The leader of the assault force consulted her subordinates, then made a decision. Technical specialists filtered their way to the front line, each carrying cases and boxes, consoles strapped to their chests. As they opened the containers and set up their gear, she contacted the surviving shuttle still supporting her group.

"I need you to open a way for the bugs," she told its pilot. "Can you use your plasma cannon to shoot a hole in the earth over the bunker, all the way down to the roof, and then through it?"

"Might be tricky – that's hardened plascrete under there. I don't want to burn out my cannon by firing too many shots too quickly. Let me call one or two of the others to help."

"OK, thanks. Quick as you can, please. We're taking casualties."

Two more Laredo shuttles swiftly joined their colleague. They formed a circle overhead, following the lead of the first shuttle. As each passed over a landmark building near the perimeter they fired a single shot from their plasma cannon, aimed at an angle into the mound of earth above the bunker. The first five plasma bolts did no more than dig out massive quantities of soil, raising a cloud of dust and depositing layers of grit and grime on attackers and defenders alike. They momentarily forgot their differences in a barrage of lurid curses directed at their airborne tormentors. The sixth shot exposed the plascrete roof. It took four more bolts to cave it in and open a huge hole to the sky.

"You got it," the lead shuttle radioed the assault team leader. "I'll – "

Whatever the pilot was going to say was lost in the bellow of an explosion as a shoulder-fired missile slammed into the shuttle. It wiped out half the reaction thrusters on the port side. The shuttle shuddered in mid-air, then flipped over on its back before the pilot could reduce power to the starboard thrusters. Once inverted, with the thick lower atmosphere making it impossible to use its powerful gravitic drive, there could be no recovery. It plummeted to earth and smashed onto the perimeter fence before exploding in flames.

The leader crossed herself. "Jesus, Mary and Joseph, receive their souls," she prayed. "While you're at it, watch out for mine, please, just in case." She keyed her microphone. "Tech teams, the roof is open. I say again, the roof is open. Start the attack."

The technicians heard, and reached for their consoles. The assault bugs that Dave and his team had captured in the Matopo Hills had been reprogrammed in time for this assault. A swarm of over a hundred flitterbugs rose from the ground and flew towards the hole in the mound of earth over the bunker, while a similar number of crawling nanobugs advanced across the uneven ground towards the perimeter. Defenders who saw them coming tried to shoot at them, but had to expose themselves to incoming fire to do so. Many were hit, and the others were forced to hunker down in their foxholes and scrapes. Some reached for identification modules and switched them on, only to learn the hard way that these bugs didn't respond to their signals. All around the perimeter defenders began to scream, struggle and die as the nanobugs crept up on them and fired toxin-laden needles from point-blank range.

The flitterbugs ignored the outer defenses. They flew down into the hole blasted into the upper level of the Command Bunker, spreading out along corridors and down stairwells, operating in autonomous mode, penetrating to every floor in their search for targets. Any movement invited a poison needle fired into exposed skin – face, neck, hands, wrists, whatever was available.

Some of the bunker's defenders, warned by the death throes of their colleagues, shut themselves in offices, toilets or other rooms, hoping that the doors would keep out the intruders. The flitterbugs dealt with all the targets that were immediately available, then those with needles still in their firing tubes settled along the ceiling of each corridor, folded their mechanical wings, and waited. Their battery packs held enough power to keep them in standby mode for a week to ten days. If anything moved during that time, they would swoop down and fire on it. Any rescuers trying to penetrate the Command Bunker to extricate their colleagues would also be targeted.

As the nanobugs eliminated the last defenders outside and the firing died away along the entire perimeter, the assault force leader called in her troops and counted heads. Fewer than half her soldiers were still alive. She divided them into three groups of approximately equal size.

"Let's put our most severely wounded aboard a shuttle, then get the hell out of here," she told them. "The enemy's bound to be bringing in reinforcements from the outer perimeter. We've got an hour at most before they get here. Find any usable vehicles nearby and load them with any portable heavy weapons that are left in the bunker defenses, then take to the side roads. Avoid major transport arteries at all costs, because they'll be using them. If you run into them, sell your lives dearly. After all we've done today, particularly – we hope – killing the Satrap, you know prisoners won't be given a quick or easy death."

The others nodded, shook hands, embraced and said their farewells to friends in the other groups, then scattered to search for vehicles in the surrounding streets and buildings.

~ ~ ~

ARENA

Gloria looked up as two soldiers helped a third into the aid station she'd established in one of the dressing-rooms. She peered through the smoky haze, then jumped to her feet as she recognized her husband.

239

"He's not too badly hurt, Ma'am," one of the soldiers hastily assured her. "It's his arm." They helped him sit down on a bench next to the table where she'd laid out her instruments, medications and bandages.

"All right, thanks, boys. You can run along now."

"Thanks, Ma'am."

As they hurried out she was already cutting away her husband's sleeve. She sucked in her breath at the ruin of flesh, muscle, blood and bone that was his forearm. "What the hell hit you?"

"That was courtesy of Major-General Huvishka," he said, wincing as she used forceps to gently pull a piece of grit out of the mangled flesh. *"Ow! Easy there!"*

"I'll inject a nerve-blocker before I fix you up. You mean you were fighting your opposite number in person?"

"Yes. He was leading the Satrap and some others along a corridor. The reflective glass in the windows had been blown out in places, and our people in the parking lot saw them. They fired at them, but missed, and they ran down the passage into a set of offices at the end. I was with a nearby patrol, and we hurried over there and bottled them up. We tried to mount an assault before they had a chance to set up defenses, but they were too quick for us. Huvishka's a damn good shot, I'll give him that. He had only a split-second to see me crossing a doorway, but he still hit me with a snap shot. The rest of my boys put down covering fire to make him pull back while a couple of them dragged me out and brought me here." He sighed as the nerve blocker began to take effect. "Oh, that feels better!"

"It won't last," she warned. "I can't do a proper job on this with first aid alone. It needs a hospital."

"Well, we don't have one handy, do we?"

They looked into each other's eyes for a long moment before she shook her head. "No."

"Then fix it up so I can fight. I'll use a pulser in my other hand."

"Was the Crown Prince with the Satrap?" she asked as she took up forceps and swab.

"There were four people. We identified the General and the Satrap, but didn't get a clear look at the other two. I think he's probably there — after all, they escaped from the arena together. We've killed several of their guards, which accounts for their reduced numbers."

"So what are you going to do next?"

"I've called in fire support from a shuttle. There's no point in risking our lives in a frontal assault – we didn't have enough troops to begin with, and they've whittled us down just as we have them." The stadium trembled to a monstrous impact. "That'll be the shuttle now. I told the pilot to give my people time to get clear, then take out that entire section of offices." Another mighty blow shook the building, then another, accompanied by the blast of a plasma cannon from high outside.

As she was winding a bandage around the dressing covering his entire forearm, a soldier came running in. "We got them, General, Sir! The shuttle blew the whole suite to rubble and ruin. We went in and picked our way through the wreckage. The Satrap's head is rolling around the floor – we don't know where his body is, probably underneath the wreckage. There are a couple of body parts sticking out from beneath the rubble. One's wearing Bactrian Major-General's insignia on the only shoulder we can see. The head's been crushed by rubble. It's unrecognizable."

Aldred sighed. "I'd have liked to have seen them all dead in person, but I'll take what I can get." He waited while Gloria fitted a sling around his neck and tucked his arm into it, then rose to his feet. Bending, he kissed her gently. "It's time for us to get the hell out of here. We've got two shuttles still in the air. I'll have them land outside, then I'll bring a few able-bodied soldiers to carry our wounded aboard. Go with them. I'll follow with the surface convoy. We've found three utility vehicles, a truck and an armored car that are still usable. They'll be enough for our survivors."

"All right, darling. The nerve block will last a couple of hours. After that, use your injector."

"I'll do that. I love you."

"Love you too."

He kissed her again, turned, and was gone.

March 31st 2850 GSC, 12:30

LMV *BENBECULA,* IN SPACE

The Spacer escorting Dave, Manuel and Tony knocked on the frame of the doorway. "Permission for three visitors to enter the Bridge, please, Sir?"

Captain Grassby looked up from his command console. "Yes, send them in. Thank you, Spacer." He glanced approvingly at the visitors' fresh clothing and still-damp hair. "I see you all took the opportunity to clean up."

"Yes, thank you, Sir," Dave acknowledged. "After hours in a spacesuit I was a bit whiffy, to put it mildly."

"I'm afraid that's an occupational hazard. I'm glad you're here. We may have a problem." He stood up. "Come to the Communications console with me. I want you to hear something."

As they walked across the spacious bridge, he told them, "Bear in mind that the speed of light is something we have to take into account when it comes to communication and what we see in the Plot display." He indicated a three-dimensional holographic projection at the next console. "That's currently showing the space for two light-hours around Laredo. Note the patrolling Bactrian merchant cruiser – that red icon – and the Satrap's yacht that fled the space station – that's the blue icon."

"They're almost touching," Manuel observed.

"Yes. What you're about to hear is a string of voice messages between the two ships, with delays due to light speed removed to make them sound like a continuous conversation." He turned to the woman at the Communications console. "Play that sequence of messages, please, Judy."

"Sure, Skipper." She pressed a button, and they listened as the console speakers played back what she'd recorded.

"*Satrap Dadarsi* calling *Oxyartes*. Emergency! Emergency! Missiles have been fired from the space station at our two escorts and at your sister ship! They've all been hit – I don't know how badly. My Captain and half our crew are planetside, so in the absence of orders I'm heading in your direction to come under the protection of your missiles. Over."

"*Oxyartes* to *Dadarsi*, I'm altering course to close the planet. There's no sign of any hostile forces in the system, so I can't fathom why the station fired on the other ships. Have you any idea what's going on? Over."

"*Dadarsi* to *Oxyartes*. We've just begun to pick up messages from ground stations indicating that something's wrong in Tapuria. There seems to be some sort of widespread attack going on down there. Over."

"*Oxyartes* to *Dadarsi*. That means the rebels are involved in this somehow. I don't know what we can do about it yet – we're going to have to wait for more information and orders from planetside. Join me and proceed in formation until we know more. Over."

"*Dadarsi* to *Oxyartes*, understood and will comply. *Dadarsi* out."

There was a brief pause, punctuated by a burst of static. "That's when the space station blew up," the Communications operator explained.

"*Dadarsi* to *Oxyartes*. The space station's just blown up! It's a damn great fireball over the planet! Over."

"*Oxyartes* to *Dadarsi*. We see it. That makes this rebel action for sure. What's that foreign freighter doing? From here it looks like she's just sitting in orbit. That's suspicious in itself. If she had any sense she'd be getting the hell away from the missiles, like you did – not to mention that bloody great explosion! Over."

"*Dadarsi* to *Oxyartes*. Could she be waiting for something or someone? Over."

"*Oxyartes* to *Dadarsi*. I think you've put your finger on it. I'm going to head straight for her. We'll send over a boarding party to see if they're up to anything. Start to turn now, so you can pull up alongside me in formation as I pass you. Over."

"*Dadarsi* to *Oxyartes*, understood, out."

Another brief pause, then, "*Oxyartes* to *Dadarsi*, that freighter's leaving orbit. She's turned towards the system boundary and is accelerating at what looks like her maximum drive power. Did you pick up any indication of any other vessel joining her? Over.

"*Dadarsi* to *Oxyartes*, negative, but of course a cutter or gig wouldn't have a drive signature big enough for us to detect at anything but close range. Over."

"*Oxyartes* to *Dadarsi*, you're right. I'm going to pursue, and order her to await my boarding party. Stand by."

There was a brief pause, then, "Patrol vessel *Oxyartes* to Lancastrian merchant vessel *Benbecula*. You have not been authorized to leave orbit. Return to orbit at once and await my boarding party. Over."

A few seconds of silence.

"Patrol vessel *Oxyartes* to Lancastrian merchant vessel *Benbecula*. I say again, you have not requested or received clearance to depart Laredo orbit. Return to orbit at once and await my boarding party. Over."

Another pause.

"Patrol vessel *Oxyartes* to Lancastrian merchant vessel *Benbecula*. I am placing your vessel under arrest for non-compliance with system traffic regulations. Brake to a standstill relative to the planet and await my boarding party, or I will fire on you! Over."

"That's where it ends so far," Captain Grassby informed them, frowning. "I don't think their threat to fire was serious – they only have short-range patrol-craft-type missiles, not a warship's fully-fledged main battery missiles. At a range of over one light-hour from us they can't possibly control or guide them, let alone reach us. Even so, they've arrested us. That could be difficult to deal with if they make a formal complaint to the Interplanetary Transportation Union that we ignored system traffic regulations and evaded arrest. The fines can be pretty steep, even if they don't accuse us of somehow being involved in the destruction of their space station."

"We'll publicly take responsibility for destroying the space station," Dave assured him. "That'll happen as soon as we get to Neue Helvetica and report to the President Pro Tem of our Government-in-Exile. We'll make sure to add that no other ships were involved."

"Thank you. That'll probably be sufficient to avoid us being arrested on that charge, but we may still have to pay a hefty fine."

"How much is it likely to be?"

"It can run as high as a million credits – that's Lancastrian Commonwealth credits."

"We'll pay it if it comes to that. My word on it."

The Captain's eyebrows rose. "You're very free with your money. I suppose this means that Manuel's mission was successful?"

Manuel nodded. "Yes, they've got the bank keys with them. The Vice-President will be able to pay me, and that means I'll be able to pay you."

The Captain grinned, and everyone on the bridge broke into broad smiles. "That's excellent news! It's going to make this a very profitable year indeed for the ship and my entire crew. They're all on profit share, with a special bonus for this trip, so they'll all benefit."

The crackle of the speaker on the Communications console interrupted him. *"Oxyartes* to *Dadarsi,* it's no good. That freighter's maximum speed is at least as fast as mine – she may even be a little faster. What's your maximum speed? Over."

"Dadarsi to *Oxyartes,* we can do the same as the corvettes – after all, we have the same drive unit. That would be one-quarter of light speed at max power. Over."

"Oxyartes to *Dadarsi.* Do you have a corvette's full sensor suite as well? Over."

"Dadarsi to *Oxyartes,* yes, we do, over."

"Oxyartes to *Dadarsi.* Excellent! That means you can follow another ship by her emissions, even if she switches off her transponder beacon. Stand by to receive my cutter. I'm coming aboard, then we'll use your greater speed to intercept *Benbecula.* Over."

"Dadarsi to *Oxyartes,* I don't understand. We have no missiles. Over."

"Oxyartes to *Dadarsi,* you have three laser cannon, right? Over."

"Dadarsi to *Oxyartes,* yes, but those are defensive weapons to intercept incoming missiles. Over."

"Oxyartes to *Dadarsi,* they've got a range of half a million kilometers. If you know what you're doing with them and you get close enough, you can

take out specific compartments of another ship with pinpoint accuracy – her drive unit, for example – or slice her up like a trussed turkey. Your ship has the speed, the sensors and the cannon, and I have the training and experience to make use of all of them. I'll bring an armed boarding party with me. Between us we'll make these interfering bastards wish they'd never come to our system! Now stand by for my cutter. *Oxyartes* out."

"Oh, *shit!*" Captain Grassby's face and voice were suddenly deeply apprehensive. "We're in trouble. If she can do point two five Cee, that's two and a half times faster than this ship at maximum power."

"How long before we can hyper-jump out of the system?" Manuel asked.

"The system boundary here's nine hundred eighty-eight million kilometers from the star. That means..." and he glanced at the Plot, "we're about seven and a quarter hours from it right now. Trouble is, that yacht can move much faster. Plot, assume a velocity of one-quarter Cee for that yacht. How long until she catches us? Assume we stay on course at our present speed."

"Just a moment, Sir." The Plot operator tapped instructions into his console. In the display a yellow line appeared, extending from the present location of the Bactrian ships to an interception point on *Benbecula*'s course line. It was some distance short of the system boundary. "She still has to accelerate from her present velocity, Sir, and she's got a long way to catch up, but it looks like she can reach us in about six and a half hours."

"That'll give her more than enough time to use those laser cannon to disable us before we can hyper-jump out of here," Grassby said gloomily, his shoulders slumping.

"I'm not sure I understand," Dave said, puzzled. "I thought a gravitic drive could accelerate a spaceship continually, reaching almost light speed, with its only limiting factor being mass gain at higher percentages of Cee. Am I wrong?"

"That's fine in theory, but there's another issue. We generate a gravitic shield ahead of the ship to deflect small debris – tiny bits knocked off asteroids, garbage dumped by careless spaceships, that sort of thing. The faster we go, the more powerful that shield has to be. It won't protect the ship against large objects, but they're usually mapped, and we can pick them up on radar in time to avoid them. As for smaller ones, the kinetic energy released by a collision at cruising speed with even a pea-sized piece of gravel would badly damage us. Therefore, the faster we go, the more of our drive power has to be diverted to the gravitic shield. Right now we're at max cruise of one-tenth Cee. At that velocity almost all our drive power's going to the shield, not to propulsion. That's what limits our speed."

"Oh. I get it."

Manuel asked, "You can't shut off your drive, change direction slightly, and coast without any emissions those ships can track? I'm no spacer, but doesn't a spaceship retain its velocity until it's actively braked by some means?"

"Yes, it does, but you heard them say that yacht's got a corvette's sensor suite. That means she'll have much better active and passive sensors than a merchant vessel. She'll detect our radar or radio transmissions at long range, and it's a big risk to shut off the radar. If there's anything in our path, like a wandering asteroid or an unmapped big piece of debris, without radar we wouldn't know it was there until it was too late to avoid it. If we accepted that risk we might evade her, but if her skipper – or, rather, the skipper of that patrol vessel – uses her radar to search for us, he might find us even if we shut down all emissions. This is just a regular merchant freighter, after all; she's not stealthy like a warship. I'd hate to depend on luck when our lives are at stake!"

"Do you have to decide what to do at once?" Dave asked.

"We'll see what happens. They can't touch us this far away, but if they get too close, I may have to surrender rather than see my ship destroyed and my crew killed."

"You *don't* want to surrender. You've no idea what Security Service torturers will do to you in an effort to extract information."

Grassby frowned. "They'd better not! We're all citizens of the Lancastrian Commonwealth. They can arrest us, sure, but if they do anything illegal the Commonwealth Fleet will be all over them like white on rice. That's one of the reasons I agreed to take this job. Our citizenship, and the ship's registration in the Commonwealth, both give us a measure of protection."

Dave couldn't help rolling his eyes in frustration at the man's naiveté. "Not as far as the SS are concerned. They're thugs. They don't care about any law but their own regulations. For the past three years Bactria's refused to allow us to surrender. They either shoot captured Resistance fighters on the spot, or if they're officers or senior NCO's they hand them over to the SS for what they euphemistically call 'interrogation'. When they've sucked them dry, they shoot them too. I doubt they'll have any compunction about doing the same to you. After all, the Commonwealth has to learn what happened to you before it can retaliate. If you just 'disappear' or your ship is 'destroyed while attempting to evade arrest', what are they going to do about it? Go to war with Bactria without any clear evidence that it's done anything wrong?"

Manuel said quietly, "Tom, he's not joking. I've seen and heard things on Laredo that I wouldn't have believed possible in a civilized society. Believe him when he says it would be a really bad idea to surrender."

Grassby threw up his hands in frustration. "So we're trapped between the devil and the deep blue sea!" He paced back and forth, frowning. "I guess we'll have to see what the next few hours show us. If it looks like they're going to catch us, we may not have many options left."

~ ~ ~

Three hours later it was clear that the Satrap's yacht was closing even faster than they'd expected. "She must have cut her gravitic shield," Captain Grassby guessed gloomily. "She's up to one-third Cee already. Her skipper's taking a hell of a chance, but if it works he'll have that much more time to shoot at us at his leisure. He'll start braking soon, so that he won't overshoot us and give us time to duck out of his way." He looked at Dave. "I'm sorry, Captain, but I'm not prepared to risk the lives of my crew for this mission. Despite your warning, I'm going to have to surrender."

Dave thought fast. "Sir, if I can pull those bastards off your back, will you undertake to deliver Manuel and our evidence to Vice-President Johns?"

"I... I don't understand."

"Just answer my question, please, Sir."

"Well, of course I will – but how can you possibly stop them?"

"I'm going to call for volunteers among my people. We arrived here in a Security Service shuttle. It's got lots of electronic warfare goodies on board – I don't understand most of them, that's a pilot's or WSO's job. If we launch, we can move off to one side over the next hour or so, then start broadcasting the drive signature of another ship – perhaps a warship of some kind, something that'll be a threat to them. They'll have to either investigate it or take avoiding action, which means you'll have more time to reach the system boundary and make your escape."

"But that's suicide! Even if they don't blow you out of space with their laser cannon, an assault shuttle doesn't have enough range to return to the planet from this far out!"

"That's my problem, Captain, not yours. Will you let me do that, and see Manuel and our evidence safely to Neue Helvetica?"

There was a long silence. Eventually Grassby said slowly, "I'll do that, Captain. If I can't take him there myself, I'll make sure he and the evidence are put aboard a trustworthy ship headed that way. I've got to say, this is just about the bravest thing I've ever heard of. You have my respect, Sir." He drew himself up and saluted formally.

Dave returned his salute. "Thank you, Sir. I'll go and ask my team for volunteers. Manuel, would you mind waiting here, please? This will be a private moment."

"Sure," the investigator agreed. "I understand."

Tony followed Dave as he hurried down the main passageway to the accommodation unit that had been allocated to his team. He burst into the common room to find the others assembled there. Everyone had showered and changed. Some were watching a program on the holovid projector, while others talked quietly among themselves.

Tamsin looked up with an eager smile as he came in. "How long until we hyper-jump out of the system?" she asked.

"There's a problem." Her face turned to stone as he explained what had been going on. "The ship won't have a chance unless we distract the Satrap's yacht, make it turn away to investigate the shuttle instead of trying to intercept this vessel. I need a few volunteers to come with me aboard the shuttle, including at least one person who knows how to work the electronics on that thing so it'll broadcast the gravitic drive signature of another ship. I'm sorry, but it'll be a one-way trip. The ship can't come back to pick us up later, and the shuttle won't have enough range to get back to Laredo."

"Count me in," Tamsin said as she stood up. "Mac taught all of us pilots how to use the EW systems on that bird. We can make it look like a destroyer or frigate, complete with the right drive signature and radar emissions to suggest that its fire control radar is locking up a target."

Dave looked at her helplessly. "I want you to survive, darling," he said softly.

She shook her head. "No. I *will* live with you, but I *won't* live without you. If this is the way it has to be, and you have to go, we'll do it together, one last time."

Sergeant-Major Deacon said, "She's right, Sir. I reckon we all feel the same way. We came on this mission together, so let's finish it together."

Dave struggled to find words. His shoulders slumped. "I really, really wanted to give most of you a chance to start again somewhere else," he said softly. "If anyone ever earned that right, you all have. I... I don't know what to say."

"You don't have to, darling," Tamsin said gently. "It's already been said."

He heaved a sigh. "All right. Let me tell Captain Grassby."

He picked up an intercom handset and pressed the button marked 'Bridge'. After a short pause, he heard, "Bridge, Communications console."

"This is Captain Carson. Let me speak to Captain Grassby, please."

"Captain Carson? But you just left!"

"I... I don't understand."

"Your pilot, Tony, just left the ship in your shuttle. He said you were aboard."

Dave's jaw dropped in astonishment. After a moment he said, "No, I'm in our accommodation unit. Tell the Captain I'll be there as quickly as possible."

He slammed down the handset as he turned to the others. "Tony just launched in the shuttle! He was with me coming down the passage. I thought he came in right behind me."

"No, Sir, he didn't," Deacon assured him.

"I don't know what the hell's going on, then! I'm going back to the bridge." He turned and ran for the door, followed by everyone in the room.

They reached the bridge in a body. Grassby's eyebrows rose as they all trooped in. "What's going on?" he demanded. "I thought you were with your pilot – at least, that's what he told me."

"I've no idea, Sir. Has he communicated with you since he left?"

As if to answer Dave's question, the Communications operator said, "Tight-beam link from the shuttle, Sir!" Without waiting for orders she put it over the speaker.

"Laredo shuttle to Captain Grassby, over."

The Captain seized a microphone. "This is Grassby. Go ahead. Over."

"Sir, I misled you, I'm afraid. I launched on my own while Captain Carson was asking for volunteers to accompany him. He's going to be mad at me when he finds out. Over."

"He's just come to the bridge, along with the rest of his party. What the devil d'you think you're playing at? Over."

"I'm not playing, Sir. Please put Captain Carson on. Over."

Grassby handed him the microphone. Dave said, "It's me, Tony. Over."

"Hi, Sir. Sorry about that, but you're too good a man to die like this. I killed James and Mac through my stupidity earlier today. I need to atone for that, and I can't think of a better way to do it than this. There's one problem with your idea to decoy that Bactrian ship. What if it isn't decoyed? It might realize your signals were fake, and ignore you and go after the ship anyway. You need a more certain way to stop it. I can do that for you, Sir. Over."

"What do you mean? Over."

"Remember how our pilots stopped two Bactrian troop transports when they first invaded Laredo, Sir? Over."

"I – *oh!*" Dave was dumbstruck.

"That's right, Sir. They steered their captured assault shuttles into head-on collisions with them, killing themselves and everyone aboard the enemy ships. I can do the same with this shuttle, Sir. It's got that useful homing feature, where if I tune its systems to an enemy transmission – like the radar frequency being used by that Bactrian yacht – it'll head straight for it. They won't pick up a small craft like this until it's too close for them to avoid, particularly if I use all its stealth features and minimum power on the drive. Over."

Dave opened his mouth, but no sound came out. He was completely at a loss for words.

Tamsin took the microphone gently from his hand and keyed it. "Tony, this is Tamsin. I think I speak for everyone when I say that we owe you our lives, buddy. If you hadn't done this, we were all going to join Captain Dave on his last mission. All I can say is 'Thank you'. Yes, you screwed up earlier today, but you're making up for that and a whole lot more by what you're doing now. Over."

"I bet you say that to all the good-looking guys," Tony quipped, drawing a short, sharp burst of brittle laughter from the others.

Dave took back the microphone. "Tony, Tamsin said it for me. Thanks, buddy. Is there anything more we can do to help you?"

"Let me speak to the ship's captain, please. You take care of your lady, Captain, and have lots of kids together, you hear me? Oh – one more thing. If you get someplace that has a Hindu temple, burn some incense for James and I in front of a statue or icon of Yama, will you, please? Over."

"We'll do that. Stand by."

He handed the microphone to the ship's captain, who said, "Captain Grassby here. Go ahead, Tony. Over."

"Captain, please give me the frequency of that Bactrian yacht's search radar, and a course to steer to intercept her from this position assuming minimum acceleration on my part. Over."

"Wait one." He turned to the Plot. "Calculate that course, quick as you can. Comms, what's the frequency?"

He waited impatiently for the information he needed, then passed it to Tony. "Remember you're already moving at our speed towards the system boundary. When you reverse course, particularly at minimum power settings, you'll decelerate very slowly from the velocity you're already carrying. Your speed won't be very high when you meet the Bactrian ship. Over."

"Yeah, I know, but if she's still moving fast that'll make up for it. The kinetic energy release should be pretty spectacular. Over."

"It certainly will. We'll record it for the newsreels. Over."

"All right, there's no sense in talking any longer. I'm outta here. This is Tony, signing off for the last time."

~ ~ ~

No-one left the bridge. Captain Grassby invited them to share the few visitors' seats behind his command console, but nobody wanted to sit down. They stood against the walls, talking softly, desultorily among themselves, all eyes on the Plot display where the icon representing the Bactrian ship drew ever closer to their own position. At last, seemingly an infinity later, the Plot operator announced, "The shuttle should reach the yacht in the next three to five minutes." Everyone gathered around the three-dimensional display, staring at it as if they could help Tony by willing him on.

Captain Grassby ordered, "Train the external cameras on that bearing and show the feed on the bridge display." Within moments the large rectangular screen mounted on one wall flickered to life, showing the small bright ball of Laredo's sun far behind them and a few dots that Dave knew were the planet itself and much more distant stars. He felt a shiver pass through him as he realized this might be the last time in his life that he would see Laredo.

They watched and waited in silence until suddenly a pinprick of light appeared in the display. It swelled from a point to a tiny globe, then faded out over the course of a minute or so. At the same time the icon representing the Satrap's yacht vanished from the Plot display, replaced by a starburst icon. The operator announced urgently, "Nuclear explosion from the vicinity of the yacht, Sir! Her reactor must have let go!"

Grassby nodded slowly, sadly. "There won't be any survivors from that. The nuclear explosion is actually insignificant compared to the kinetic energy released by a collision at that closing velocity between two bodies massing that much." He drew a deep breath, then looked around. "He's cleared the way for us. There are no other ships on the Plot except the Bactrian patrol vessel." He indicated *Oxyartes'* icon, still about one light-hour behind them "She can't catch us. We'll be at the system boundary in just over an hour, and no ship can follow another once they've hyper-jumped. We'll reach New Brisbane ten days from today."

Tamsin crossed to where Dave still stared at the fading spot of light in the display, and slipped her arm around his waist. "A Hindu temple, he said?"

"Yes."

"I reckon we'll find one somewhere on New Brisbane."

"We'll do that. While we're at it, let's burn incense for everyone who died on Laredo today. There are bound to have been some other Hindus among them, and I daresay the others won't object, whatever their faith may have been."

"We'll do that – and you and I have business with the first marriage officer we find."

He hugged her. "It's a date."

April 2nd 2850 GSC

TAPURIA

The morning was gray and cool. Rain fell in a soft, gentle mist from the lowering skies, trickling over the ground, forming muddy pools in the craters left all across Tapuria. Several fires still smoldered, their smoke sagging unhappily along the ground, unable to gain altitude in the heavy moist air. All over the city, Bactrian units attempted to gather the dead and make some sort of order out of the chaos that surrounded them.

A Colonel wearing combat field gear stood at the rear of his command shuttle, drinking a cup of coffee brought to him from a field kitchen set up nearby. He stared at the destruction all around him, drooping with weariness after the hard fighting that had finally died down only the evening before. He was about to take another sip of his coffee when he saw a utility vehicle approaching. A red-and-gold flag was flying from its front bumper. His eyes widened and he called, "Adjutant, an honor guard, quickly! The Crown Prince is coming!"

By the time the vehicle halted at the command shuttle half a dozen servicemen had been hastily drawn up in a line, and others were hurrying to join them; but the Crown Prince waved his hand dismissively as he got out. "No ceremony, please, Colonel Khan. Your soldiers have more than enough to do."

"Yes, Your Highness. Would you like some coffee?"

"No, thank you. You're the senior officer remaining on Laredo – I mean, Termaz." The renaming of the planet had taken effect as of the previous day. "Have you compiled casualty lists yet? What's the status of our forces?"

The Colonel glanced at the young Lieutenant who got out of the vehicle behind the Prince. Her name and reputation had already spread far and wide. He forced himself to refocus on his Crown Prince.

"Your Highness, it's too early to be sure of our casualties, but they're extraordinarily severe. The arena is the worst concentration. There were at least seven to eight thousand dead there, military and civilian, with as many again wounded, most of them seriously. Many have lost limbs. I'm afraid the arena is now known among my forces as the 'Red Arena', thanks to the amount of blood that was spilled there. Until this rain started the interior surfaces, grass and plascrete alike, were literally blood-red almost from top to bottom. Bodies and body parts were everywhere – one could almost have walked from one end of the arena to the other on them without ever touching the ground."

"I'm aware of that, Colonel. I was there, remember?"

"Yes, Your Highness. Many of the young conscript troops detailed to the cleanup there have had to be relieved. They simply can't take it."

"I don't blame them. About the casualties?"

"I'm sorry, Your Highness." The man visibly made an effort to collect himself. "Many bodies are still buried under rubble, and we can't get into some buildings at all due to nanobugs and flitterbugs still lurking inside, looking for targets. The best I can say right now is that we have at least four thousand military fatalities, including those at the four garrisons the rebels attacked to get their hands on the assault shuttles they used to such terrible effect. We have more than three thousand wounded and over a thousand still missing. The Security Service contingent on the planet has been almost wiped out. Of their thousand-plus personnel, only fifty-five answered muster this morning."

He took a deep breath. "I… I'm very sorry to report that we inflicted several hundred of our own casualties, Your Highness. The rebels were using captured assault shuttles to attack us, and captured vehicles to escape. In their attempts to defend themselves and prevent escapes, I fear our forces often fired on each other in the confusion. We shot down at least five of our own shuttles and destroyed at least forty of our own armored cars, trucks and transporters, to say nothing of soldiers firing at individuals without taking time to identify them."

The Crown Prince nodded. "That was probably unavoidable under the circumstances. What about civilian casualties?"

"They're heavy, Your Highness; certainly in excess of six thousand dead, with a similar number injured or not yet accounted for. Almost all are military and civil administrative employees who were at the arena or on duty in the buildings and installations that were destroyed. The rebels seem to have taken great care to avoid hitting residential areas. Many of the wounded will die, of course, because we have nothing like enough hospital beds or medical personnel to treat them all. Also, most of our medical supplies were destroyed in the depot."

The Prince's face fell. "Yes, I understand. I've turned over the Satrap's Palace to your medical staff for use as an auxiliary hospital, and I've told them to fill *Oxyartes* with amputees who have a reasonable chance of surviving the journey. I'll take them to Bactria with me for further treatment and the fitting of prosthetic limbs until new ones can be cloned."

"That's very good of you, Your Highness."

"No, it's not! It's no more than they deserve. What about rebel casualties?"

"Relatively few in comparison to ours, Your Highness. We're still collecting their dead, but I suspect they had no more than three hundred people in all on this operation. More than half appear to have died, and we're not sure how many managed to escape. We stopped those fleeing the arena, and some in the city, but three shuttles and a few ground convoys made it out through our perimeter. They were helped by the fact that much of it had to be left unguarded, because forces stationed there had to be sent to Tapuria."

"That couldn't be helped. What about prisoners?"

"We took only eighteen rebels alive, Your Highness. All of them were injured and lost consciousness before they could commit suicide. That's the only reason we were able to capture them."

"Let's not deny their courage, Colonel. It's going to force us to re-evaluate our whole approach on this planet. Where are they?"

"We've assembled them under guard in that building, Your Highness."
He pointed to a nearby warehouse. "As you directed, we treated the rebel
doctor's injuries. Fortunately, they were light. When she regained
consciousness we gave her medical supplies and asked her to help look after
the other rebel wounded. She was astonished they hadn't all been executed
out of hand. She took care of their immediate needs, then helped us treat
our own civilian casualties."

"That was good of her. Have we any idea who the prisoners are? Is
there anyone of importance among them?"

"The doctor was the wife of the rebel General, Your Highness. She
was supervising the loading of casualties onto a shuttle at the arena when
our missile destroyed it and killed her husband. The SS claim she's an
influential figure in her own right. We captured only one other officer. His
vehicle was blown up as he tried to escape. The doctor says he's been
blinded by his injuries. She claims not to know his name or rank, but I
suspect she's lying. We'll have to ask him when – if – he regains
consciousness. All the other prisoners are enlisted troops and NCO's."

"You've ordered that they're to be well treated?"

"Yes, Your Highness, but the Security Service is disputing that. In fact,
here they come now." He indicated a black transporter that was slowing
down and turning off the road towards the warehouse.

"We'll see about *that!* Come with me – and you, please, Lieutenant
Yazata."

"Yes, Your Highness," the young officer answered, limping after him,
favoring her bandaged leg. The Colonel noticed that her arm was bandaged
too, and she had a plaster across her forehead.

A Major in the black uniform of the SS was marshalling a squad of
riflemen as they came up. He turned to face them, frowning, then his eyes
widened with astonishment to see the Crown Prince. He snapped to
attention and saluted. "Major Moshira at your service, Your Highness!"

"What are you doing here, Major?"

"Your Highness, I came to execute the rebel prisoners held here, in
accordance with our standard policy."

"I ordered them to be treated well and not harmed. Were you not
informed?"

Moshira drew himself up indignantly. "Your Highness, you are not yet Satrap. Until you are officially installed and gain the authority to change them, the policies approved by your late father are still in force and effect. I am therefore acting in accordance with my lawful orders."

"And I am ordering you now to ignore those policies as far as captured rebels are concerned. They are not to be harmed."

"Your Highness, with respect, you do not yet have the authority to issue that order."

"Oh, *really?* Lieutenant Yazata, would you please demonstrate to this cretin the extent of my authority?"

"With pleasure, Your Highness."

She drew the pulser from her holster in a single smooth motion, aimed it at Major Moshira's face and pulled the trigger. The round struck the bridge of his nose, splattering blood and brains out of the back of his shattered head, and his body collapsed to the soggy ground. The black-clad riflemen behind him gaped in utter astonishment and disbelief.

The Crown Prince transferred his gaze to the equally astounded Colonel. "Do *you* have any questions about my authority, Colonel? The late Major Moshira was correct that I am not yet Satrap, but I'll be installed in that office within days of reaching Bactria. As soon as that happens, I'm going to send a team of my guards back here. They'll have orders to publicly hang – not shoot, *hang* – anyone who's disobeyed my instructions concerning the cessation of reprisals and repression against the citizens of the former Laredo, and good treatment for the prisoners captured here. Do you understand me?"

The Colonel drew himself to attention and saluted stiffly. "I understand, *Your Majesty.*" He emphasized the honorific, reserved for the Satrap and his wife alone.

"Thank you, Colonel. You seem to have the right attitude. If that continues, I assure you it'll do wonders for your military career."

"Yes, Your Majesty. Thank you, Your Majesty."

"Good. By the way, take charge of all surviving Security Service personnel – including these clowns – and put them to work on the cleanup. They're all going to be recalled to Bactria in disgrace for failing to warn us about this catastrophe. They may as well do something useful until we can arrange that. If they argue, tell them it's on my authority. If they still argue, remind them of what happened to the last SS officer who questioned that – and feel free to repeat the lesson as often as required, also on my authority."

"As you command, Your Majesty."

"There's another thing you can do for me. You know of my father's awards to those who helped to save us at the arena?"

"Yes, Your Majesty."

"I'll be announcing the award of the Star of Bactria to them at my installation ceremony, and conferring it on Lieutenant Yazata at the same time – my first official act as Satrap. However, there's something more I want to do. I intend to appoint her in command of a company of the Satrap's Guard – the very company that protects me on my journeys, as a matter of fact. That's at least a Captain's position, if not a Major's. Since I'm not yet Satrap I can't personally promote her right away; but I understand that as Senior Officer of our forces on Laredo – I mean, Termaz – you have planet-wide promotion authority up to your own grade and rank. Is that correct?"

"Yes, Your Majesty, and I agree that she's proved herself worthy of promotion." He turned to face the young woman. "Lieutenant Yazata, in recognition of your selfless valor in defense of the late Satrap and the Crown Prince, you are hereby awarded a battlefield promotion to the rank of Captain, to take effect from March 31st, 2850, Galactic Standard Calendar, the date on which you distinguished yourself."

She came to attention as she listened to him. "Thank you, Sir." She saluted smartly, and he returned it.

"I don't have new insignia of rank to give you, Captain, but – "

"If you'll please allow me, Colonel, Sir?" his adjutant said. He unbuttoned his shoulder straps and removed his epaulettes. "Captain Yazata, I'd be most honored if you'll please use my insignia until you can obtain new ones. No need to return them – I have a spare set in my kit."

"Thank you very much, Captain." She smiled gratefully at him as he removed her old insignia, slid his epaulettes over her shirt's shoulder straps and buttoned them in place.

"I thank you as well, Captain. I'll remember your kind assistance to the future commander of my personal guard company," the Crown Prince assured him.

"It's my pleasure, Your Majesty. Word of Lieutenant – I mean, Captain Yazata's heroism has spread throughout the Army here in Tapuria."

"And deservedly so. I certainly wouldn't have survived without her aid. Thank you, Colonel. Please return to your duties. Captain Yazata and I will depart for Bactria in a few hours. It'll be a longer, slower trip than usual in that converted freighter, but that can't be helped given the destruction of my father's yacht."

The Colonel and his adjutant saluted, then headed back to the command shuttle. As they moved away the Crown Prince smiled at the newly-minted Captain.

"I hadn't mentioned commanding a company in my guard. I hope you don't mind being co-opted like this."

She frowned slightly. "I hate to leave here with so much still to do."

"I know, but... I need you, Zeba." She blinked at his use of her first name. "I haven't forgotten that you came up with the plan that helped me survive at the arena. Major-General Huvishka spoke highly of you, too. I need someone I can trust, someone I can rely on. I'm very young to become Satrap, without the experience most of my predecessors had. That means Palace insiders and the political administration will try to 'manage' me, coach me into letting them do things their way and simply rubber-stamping their decisions. I don't wish to speak ill of my father, but they did that to him. I think it has a lot to do with why things went so badly wrong here, so I'm determined not to allow them to do the same to me; but I'm going to need a lot of help."

"I'll do my best, of course, Your Majesty, but I'm still a junior and relatively inexperienced officer, despite my promotion – for which thank you very much!"

"That's all right. I've seen you at work under the most difficult circumstances imaginable. Believe me, your references are good!" They laughed together, a little shakily.

"To get back to the Palace and Administration, I'm going to take advantage of an old custom. It's traditional for every appointed official and office-holder to submit their resignations to the new Satrap when he ascends the throne. In the past the new ruler has simply issued a decree confirming almost everyone in their posts. That's not going to happen this time. We're going to make a clean sweep and a fresh start, even though it'll take some time to find suitable replacements. I'll probably have to make a lot of temporary reappointments, or shuffle people around to break up their personal fiefdoms within the Administration. Those who've grown used to the trappings of power are going to scream in outrage, of course. They're not going to take it lying down. I expect there'll be more than a few plots to assassinate me or forcibly make me into a figurehead ruler, controlled by the 'old guard'. I'm going to rely on you to help nip such ideas in the bud."

"I'll gladly do that, Your Majesty, as far as I can. I learned a lot from General Huvishka about the damage caused by fossilized thinking. I agree that if you have an opportunity to clean out the Augean stables, you should seize it." She hesitated. "As a matter of fact, I suggest you take a number of combat veterans with you from this planet to join your bodyguard. You're going to need replacements for those who died at the arena. Combat veterans will understand and appreciate what you're trying to do to stabilize the situation here, and they'll be able to tell your other guards about their experiences. That should help to buttress the Satrap's Guard against any attempts by the 'old guard', as you called them, to suborn its loyalty, and also improve relations between it and the regular Army."

"That's a good idea, but where would I find such soldiers at short notice?"

"I'd begin by recruiting the late Major-General Huvishka's bodyguard, Your Majesty. He was wounded at the arena, but not too badly. He can suggest more names. If we can get fifteen to twenty good people, I think that would be enough for a start."

"Where is he?"

"He's helping to sort out the mess at the Military Governor's compound. He refused to stay in hospital, saying there were many who needed his bed more than he did."

"He sounds like just the kind of soldier we need. We'll go there right away." They began to walk back towards his vehicle. "I also want your help in radically reassessing our security organs. I haven't forgotten what my father said at the arena about the Security Service. They failed us abominably. It was their job to predict events such as this massacre, yet they didn't issue a single warning – instead, they kept mouthing pious platitudes about how well things were going for us. If they hadn't already suffered so many casualties during the attack, I can assure you that heads would have rolled among their local command structure. I understand you worked with them for a short time?"

"Yes, Your Majesty. It wasn't a pleasant experience."

"You can give me the benefit of that experience when I restructure them. I think it's long gone time they were made more accountable to the Throne and lost their status as a privileged private fiefdom." He stopped walking, clearly searching for the right words. "More important than any of that, though; I need a personal advisor whose courage and commitment are unquestionable, someone of the same age group as me who can act as a counterweight to older advisors who are more set in their ways. I want someone who can speak from personal experience about what needs to be done here on Laredo – I mean, Termaz. I think you're that person."

"I… I'm very junior, and my experience isn't nearly as extensive as you seem to think, but if that's what Your Majesty wants, I'll do my best."

"It's not just 'His Majesty' that wants it – it's *me*, the person inside the title. I need a confidant. I'm sick of the pettiness of Court politics, nobles trying to influence me on behalf of their sons and their wives scheming to get me into bed with one of their daughters – or all of them! Even if I don't marry one of them, to have a Satrap's by-blow in the family has traditionally been a source of influence and profit. You aren't like them. You're down-to-earth. If I'm to have any woman at all in my life at a time like this, I need someone like you."

She fell back a pace, her face aghast. "Are you asking me to be your…" She couldn't finish the sentence.

"No. No, I'm not. All I'm asking right now is for you to be my friend and confidant."

She looked at him narrowly for a long moment, then sighed. "Very well, Your High – I mean, Your Majesty. I'll do my best."

"Good. In that case, when we're alone my name's Rostam, all right?"

Her eyes widened. "You – you *can't* be serious! How can I, a commoner, be on first name terms with the Satrap?"

"Because the Satrap wants you to be on first name terms with him, at least in private. How about it?"

A slow smile dawned on her face. "I don't know how this is going to work out, but… all right, Rostam. Let's see where this takes us."

PART THREE

May 15th 2850 GSC

NEUE HELVETICA SYSTEM

They assembled in the courier ship's tiny lounge. There wasn't enough space for a standing formation, so they had to abandon the usual military formality. Dave stood in front of them wearing his new insignia of rank as a Major, his promotion having taken effect as *Benbecula* left the Laredo system. He surveyed everyone's brand-new uniforms and medal ribbons. He wore a double row of them on his own chest, and Sergeant-Major Deacon wore three rows.

"Thank you all for voting for officers. I didn't want to randomly select individuals when we've been through so much together. I figured you all deserved a say. You've elected Sergeant-Major Deacon as your new Captain, and Sergeant Gray as your Lieutenant. I hope you didn't vote for her just because she's now my wife!" A chuckle ran through the assembled soldiers. "Be that as it may, I've approved both appointments and used my authority to commission personnel for the first time. They've already signed the necessary documents, so they'll take their oath of office now in the presence of us all."

He led them through the formula, the new officers standing stiffly to attention, then fastened the epaulettes bearing their new insignia of commissioned rank to the shoulder straps of their shirts.

"Right. You've been divided into three groups for duty purposes. Captain Deacon will command one, Lieutenant Gray the second, and I the third. I've no idea what will confront us when we land on Neue Helvetica in a few hours, but this structure will hopefully give us flexibility to adapt to whatever we find. Expect changes in the short term."

Manuel stepped into the lounge. "She's here! She left a message with System Control to forward to us when we made our arrival signal." He passed a sheet of paper to Dave, who read it quickly.

"Vice-President Johns is waiting for us planetside," he announced. "She thanks us for forwarding news of our escape, our plans and our passport details by interplanetary courier when we reached New Brisbane. She's already registered us with the United Planets as staff of our Government-in-Exile, so our diplomatic immunity is now official, and she's notified Neue Helvetica of our status. She'll meet us at the Planetary Elevator terminus planetside tomorrow morning. Journalists will be there, so we're to be on our best behavior."

"As if we'd be anything else," the newly-commissioned Captain Deacon protested, rolling his eyes. Another laugh rippled around the group.

Grinning, Dave went on, "She's set up an appointment at the Handelsbank at sixteen tomorrow afternoon, to claim control of our planetary account. She approves our expenditure in chartering this private communications vessel to make the fastest possible passage to Neue Helvetica from New Brisbane. She says it was a very good idea, because she wants to have all this evidence on hand before the news of the Satrap's death becomes public knowledge – assuming he was killed, of course; we still don't know for sure. She'll use our material to boost the story from Laredo's perspective. She's pleased we hired a publicist to come with us and use the passage time to assemble a montage of vid highlights from the evidence. She says that'll give her a head start on preparing a press release for when the news breaks."

"When do you think we'll hear about the Satrap, Sir?" Deacon asked.

"Only when Bactria decides to announce either his survival or his death. We don't know what they may have released since we left New Brisbane. Anyway, we'll be entering our parking orbit at seventeen, and proceeding to the orbital Planetary Elevator terminal later this evening. Have your gear packed and ready."

~ ~ ~

No sooner had Customs cleared the vessel after they entered their parking orbit than the ship's Captain called Dave to the bridge. "Sir, there's a cutter asking to dock with us," he told him. "Her pilot says she has your Ambassador to the United Planets on board. He needs to see you urgently."

Dave frowned. "As far as I'm aware he has no business with us at all. We're to report to Vice-President Johns tomorrow morning."

"Do you want me to refuse him permission to come aboard, Sir? As the chartering party, you have control over those decisions."

"No, don't do that. I'd better see what he wants. I'll meet him in the docking bay vestibule."

"Very well, Sir. He'll arrive in about ten minutes."

Dave collected Captain Deacon and Tamsin on his way to the docking bay. "I don't know what the Ambassador wants," he explained, "but General Aldred said they weren't too sure about his loyalty. I'd like to have you as witnesses to whatever happens."

They waited in the vestibule, the other two slightly behind and on either side of Dave as the airlock indicator light turned from red to green. There was a subdued click, and it opened to reveal a thin, hawk-faced older individual in a gray pinstriped suit, accompanied by two burly men in plain black suits. Their muscular build was very evident, and they carried themselves warily, as if expecting a fight.

Dave drew himself to attention and saluted the older man. "Ambassador McNairy, I presume?"

"Yes, that's right. I've come to collect the evidence, Major, and also our bank keys."

"I'm sorry, Sir, but I'm under strict orders to deliver them only to Vice-President Johns."

"What do you mean? Your diplomatic passports are registered to Laredo's mission to the United Planets. I'm in charge of that mission, so that makes me your boss. Hand over the evidence and keys at once!"

"Sir, as far as I know we're not registered to our UP Embassy, but to our Government-in-Exile. You aren't in charge of that. Besides, I was ordered very specifically by my military superiors on Laredo to hand over the evidence only to the Vice-President. I take orders from nobody else unless and until she tells me to accept their authority, Sir."

"But this is *preposterous!*" The man was bluffing, Dave was sure. His outward manner was blustering, indignant and offended, but his eyes were cold and calculating. "How dare you dispute the authority of an Ambassador?"

"You have no place in my military chain of command, Sir, and therefore have no authority over me at all and no business giving me orders. I'm sorry, but I won't hand over anything to you."

"We'll see about that! I'm going to lodge an official complaint about you with the Vice-President!"

"That's your privilege, Sir. We'll discuss it with her tomorrow."

"Perhaps we should *persuade* the Major to hand over the evidence and the keys, Sir?" one of the burly men behind him suggested, adopting a menacing tone as he rubbed his right fist in the palm of his left hand.

Dave grinned coldly. "Don't try to bluff combat veterans. It costs a fortune in flowers. Our last fight was about six weeks ago when our team, individually and collectively, killed what must have totaled several hundred enemy personnel. I don't think we'll have any problem adding two muscle-bound idiots to our score, do you, Captain Deacon?"

"I doubt it, Sir. Why don't we leave them to Lieutenant Gray? She was saying she could use some exercise."

"Oh, yes, please!" Tamsin agreed eagerly, taking a step forward.

The Ambassador's face was a picture of indignation. "Stop that!" he spluttered. "How dare you threaten my security guards?"

"That's not a threat, Sir – it's a promise," Tamsin retorted unrepentantly.

"*Oh!* This is *impossible!* You'll hear more about this nonsense tomorrow!"

The Ambassador turned on his heel and re-entered the airlock, followed by his two guards. The three glared at Dave as the door slid shut once more.

"Well, well, well," he mused, looking at the others. "I'd say we made a bad enemy there, wouldn't you?"

Deacon shrugged. "I've never made a good one yet."

"Funny you should say that – neither have I! Let's get everyone together in the lounge."

"Yes, Sir."

As he waited for the others to assemble, Dave blessed Manuel's advice to open a Commonwealth bank account and lay in a supply of ready money as soon as he reached New Brisbane. He'd cashed two of the Neue Helvetica bearer drafts totaling ten million francs. That had netted him nine and a half million francs after bank charges, which had converted to just over eleven million Lancastrian Commonwealth credits. It had been amazing to see the change in vendors' attitudes when they realized that, far from being penniless refugees from a distant war, the Laredo party had money to pay for its needs and wasn't afraid to spend it. It had bought their new uniforms and medals, produced by fabric extruders and fabbers as General Aldred had specified, plus civilian clothing, luggage and everything else they needed. It had also paid for the expensive interplanetary express courier notification to the Vice-President that they'd escaped with the evidence and bank keys, and made chartering this ship possible as soon as the Neue Helvetica embassy had issued visas.

"I'm changing our plans," he told the assembled soldiers. "I'm going to leave Captain Deacon and his team on board this ship for at least one more day. I'll leave the evidence on board as well, and I want them to guard it with their lives." He explained about the attempt by the Ambassador to take custody of it. "He was way out of line. For our Ambassador to behave like that means that something is seriously wrong. I intend to find out what it is before I give anything to anybody."

"Sounds good to me," Deacon agreed as a rumble of approval ran around the group. "What about the bearer bank keys, Sir?"

"I'll take them with me. I'll also take the suitcase currently holding the evidence. We'll re-pack it into some of the luggage we bought at New Brisbane. I'll fill the case with something weighing about the same, just in case the Bactrians have something up their sleeve."

"How about our dirty laundry, Sir?" one of the soldiers quipped, drawing laughter from the others.

"You know, that's not a bad idea, but we've just bought new clothes and had new uniforms tailored. I'd hate to waste them, even if they do need laundering. I'll use bedclothes and towels instead. Those of us going planetside will assemble in the docking bay vestibule in half an hour. The ship's cutter will take us to the orbital Terminal, where we'll go through Customs and Immigration then take the next available passenger pod down the Elevator. Bring some stim-tabs with you in case you aren't able to sleep during the trip. We'll be on the surface by mid-morning."

As he and Captain Deacon walked back to the cabin he shared with Tamsin, they heard footsteps hurrying to catch up. Looking round, they saw Sergeant Higgs with a box in his hands. "Sir, d'you really think the Bactrians will try to steal the evidence?" he asked.

"It wouldn't surprise me at all. They'll be desperate to prevent its release."

"In that case, Sir, you may remember I bought this at New Brisbane to help secure our storage area against thieves. D'you think you might have a use for it?"

Dave lifted the lid, saw what was inside, and smiled evilly. "Oh, yes! That's a very good idea. Come and help us set it up."

May 16th 2850 GSC

NEUE HELVETICA

The personnel pod creaked and groaned as the forces of deceleration acted on its structure. It sounded alarming, and those unused to its vagaries looked concerned, but the majority of those aboard were accustomed to the noises made by Planetary Elevators. They buried their heads in their reading material or watched entertainment vids projected in their headsets. The few lucky enough to have seats with viewports stared through them as the ground approached.

Dave and the others remained alert, looking around the pod, watching their fellow passengers as it slowed to a crawl, then eased into its restraints with a muffled clanging sound. The structure bobbed and jerked slightly, then settled to rest. A mechanical voice advised in Galactic Standard English, "We have arrived at the planetside Terminal of Neue Helvetica's Number Three space elevator. Please remain seated until the air pressure has equalized and the doors are opened." It repeated the announcement in German, Spanish and Mandarin.

"Remember, people, wait for the rush to subside," Dave warned as he kept a wary eye on the big suitcase with a red diplomatic seal over each of its two locks. "We'll exit together, looking as smart as possible even if we are pulling our baggage behind us." A rumble of agreement answered him. "Tamsin, would you please take my case of clothes as well as your own? I'll have the evidence suitcase to deal with."

"Of course."

A terminal agent was waiting outside the pod, holding a sign with his name on it. As he came over, she saw his uniform and her eyes lit up. "Major Carson?"

"That's right."

"This way, please. Vice-President Johns is waiting for you in the main concourse. She's had our Terminal Police clear a space to one side of the entrance doors so that the journalists can get pictures of your arrival."

"Thank you."

They followed her down the corridor to where it opened into a huge marble-floored area, lined with counters, shops and booths. She indicated a small group waiting in a roped-off area next to a serried rank of swinging doors on the far side. "There they are, Sir."

"Thank you," he said again, studying the tall woman standing to one side of a group of half a dozen people with vid cameras and recording gear. He recognized her at once from her photograph. She wore a large light-colored leather attaché case on a strap over her left shoulder, holding it with her left hand. She was accompanied by a younger woman, probably a secretary or aide, he guessed. Laredo's Ambassador to the UP waited behind them, glowering at him as he led his party towards them. Two uniformed Terminal Police stood to one side.

As he drew near the others fell back, allowing him to approach her alone. He settled the big wheeled suitcase upright on its base, came to attention, and saluted formally. "Major Carson reports to Vice-President Johns as ordered, Ma'am!"

She straightened, pulled her shoulders back and half-bowed her head to acknowledge his salute. "You're very welcome here, Major. Congratulations on your spectacularly successful escape from the Bactrian forces illegally occupying Laredo." She spoke loudly, presumably for the benefit of the journalists who were photographing and recording everything.

He smiled inwardly as he raised his voice in response. If public relations sound bites were what she wanted, he could oblige. "They did their best to stop us reaching you, Ma'am, but their best wasn't anywhere near good enough."

He saw approval flicker in her eyes. She opened her mouth to speak just as a high-pitched whine approached rapidly from behind him, growing louder and louder. He saw alarm flicker in her eyes as the Ambassador dived for the floor, then gunshots exploded. He felt three sharp blows across his back as bullets struck him, making him arch from the pain of their impact even though they didn't penetrate his ballistic-fabric uniform. As he fell forward Vice-President Johns doubled over, clutching at her stomach, then her chest as red blood fountained. The younger woman standing beside her crumpled to the floor as a red line appeared on the side of her head. Shouts of alarm erupted from everywhere except directly behind him, where his soldiers were standing.

An electric utility cart squealed to a halt beside him. He rolled over, wincing at the pain as a big burly man wearing a mask grabbed the suitcase. Another masked figure beside him aimed a pulser down at Dave, clearly intending to shoot him again, but he was knocked sideways, shouting in pain, as a carry-on bag flew through the air and smacked into his head. He grabbed wildly at the side of the utility cart to stop himself falling out, dropping his pulser in the process. It skittered across the floor.

The driver stamped on the accelerator and the power pack whined to shrill, screaming life once more as he steered for the exit. A double swinging door was open to allow the passage of an older couple, and he drove right over them as he sped through the opening. As he did so a uniformed figure dived for the pulser, picked it up and rolled onto one knee, lining it at the fleeing cart. Dave yelled, "NO! DON'T SHOOT!"

The figure hesitated, then lowered the weapon as it turned to look at him. It was Tamsin. "Are you all right?" she gasped.

Dave shook his head, watching as a van screeched to a stop outside, tires leaving black marks on the road surface, side door already open. The utility cart couldn't stop in time and bounced off the sidewalk, ramming the van's front tire as the three men threw themselves and the case through its open door. The van accelerated away with a scream of plastic on metal, tossing the utility cart onto its side as the door slid closed.

He looked back at Tamsin. "My back hurts like hell," he gritted through clenched teeth. "Who threw that suitcase?"

"That was me, Sir," Sergeant Higgs said.

"Well done! You saved my ass. I know our uniforms are proof against pulsers, but he was aiming at my head when your case hit him."

"Why wouldn't you let me shoot?" Tamsin demanded.

"Too many civilians. A ricochet might have hit one of them." As he spoke he rose to his hands and knees and crawled painfully over to Vice-President Johns. One of the terminal policemen was already kneeling beside her, cradling her head as she gasped for breath. Tamsin stooped to help him as the rest of his team gathered around. He saw the journalists avidly filming everything and bit back a curse. As far as he was concerned they were a bunch of ghouls and vultures to take such delight in killing, but at least their vid might help to identify those responsible.

Dave glared across the Vice-President at the Ambassador. "You *knew* about this, you bastard! You hit the deck before a single shot was fired!"

The man got to his feet, looking nervous. "I don't know what you're talking about, Major."

"The vid will show it clearly enough. You knew this attack was coming!"

Johns plucked weakly at Dave's sleeve. He looked down as she moved her right hand slowly, laboriously across her body and fumbled with the strap of the attaché case. As he reached down to help her she placed the strap in his hand, took an agonized breath, and gasped, "You – take this – appoint you – my successor – I – " She arched her back in another spasm of excruciating pain, then went limp. Dave had seen too many people die to be in any doubt that she'd taken her last breath.

He looked at Tamsin. "Help me up." As she did, he pulled the strap from around the Vice-President's shoulder and slid it over his own. Her blood was on the strap and case. Some wiped off on his new uniform, staining it, but he neither noticed nor cared.

"I'll take that, Major!" the Ambassador said sharply, striding forward and holding out his hand. "I'm now the most senior representative of Laredo's Government-in-Exile. Hand it over!"

"Like hell!" Dave snapped. He looked down at the Terminal police sergeant still kneeling by the dead Vice-President's side. "Sergeant, will you please state publicly and for the record what you heard the Vice-President say and do before she died?"

"Yes, Sir." He rose to his feet. "She gave you that bag and appointed you her successor, Sir."

"Nonsense!" the Ambassador exploded. "You must have misheard!"

"No, he didn't," one of the journalists corrected him. "I filmed the whole thing. It's all in here." She patted her vid recorder. "She did just what the Sergeant said."

"Thank you," Dave said, nodding to her in acknowledgment. "I'd be grateful if you'd please let me have a copy of that vid for our records. I'll pay for it, of course."

"Sure." The woman's face was white and strained.

"How's the other lady?" he asked the policeman.

"She's out cold. The bullet grazed her head, but didn't penetrate the skull that I can see."

"She should be OK then."

Dave opened the attaché case, already knowing what he'd find inside it. Sure enough, the Great Seal of Laredo nestled in a special container in the front compartment. The metal seal matrix was attached to a low, flat handle carved from stone quarried in the Matopo Hills. Beside it was a flat box holding different-colored sticks of sealing wax. A small leather wallet held a card that Dave recognized as a bearer key for Laredo's account at the Handelsbank, identical to the two already in his possession. The rear compartment held what looked like official documents.

Dave took out the Great Seal and held it up for everyone to see. "As Vice-President Johns' freely chosen successor, I've assumed her office as President Pro Tem of Laredo's Government-in-Exile in accordance with the Declaration of Emergency filed with the United Planets. Ladies and gentlemen of the Press, please witness my first official action in that capacity." He turned to the Ambassador, his voice coldly formal. "Ambassador McNairy, you are dismissed with immediate effect from all your posts and offices. Your diplomatic immunity is also revoked as of this moment. You no longer have the authority to represent the Republic of Laredo in any way, shape or form, or make use of any of her assets or funds. You will hand over all official documents, records, equipment and other paraphernalia to me or to anyone I designate to receive them from you."

"You can't do that! It's preposterous! You're acting illegally!"

Dave lost his temper as he shook the Seal under his nose. *"This* makes it legal, damn you! You *know* that – just as your behavior proves you knew the attack was coming! If this weren't a neutral planet, I'd execute you here and now as a traitor to Laredo. *Get out of my sight before I change my mind!"*

McNairy opened his mouth to reply, then caught sight of the fury blazing in Dave's eyes. He gulped, sidled backwards, then turned and fled into the crowd of onlookers that was picking themselves up from the floor, gathering round, staring, pointing, exclaiming in shock and horror.

"I'll take that, please, Ma'am," he heard the second Terminal policeman say. As he turned to watch Tamsin handed him the pulser she'd picked up, holding it by the frame, barrel pointing downwards. "Thank you for not shooting," the policeman went on. "The risk of hitting innocent bystanders would have been too great." Tamsin rolled her eyes rebelliously, but said nothing.

The police sergeant asked, "What was in that suitcase they took, Sir?"

Dave thought fast and chose his words carefully. He was being recorded, and knew whatever he said would doubtless be on news bulletins within the hour. He didn't want to give anything away. "That suitcase was prepared on Laredo to contain all the evidence we'd accumulated over the past three and a half years of Bactria's atrocities and war crimes, plus our bearer bank account keys and other information and materials that Vice-President Johns would have found useful."

A contingent of police approached on the run, bursting through the crowd with two medical carts hot on their heels. Dave could see more heading for the doors to assist the older couple who'd been bowled over by the escaping attackers. As the medics bent over the Vice-President's body, the police Sergeant asked, "Do you need medical attention, Sir? Even if those bullets didn't penetrate your uniform, they've got to have left a mark."

"They did. I'm going to have some bad bruises there come morning. I'll want to change, and get a doctor to look at them."

"We can do that at our station here, Sir. If you'll all come with me, please?"

"No, Sergeant." Dave spoke as firmly as he could. "I realize you want statements from us, but we have work to do – even more urgently now that Vice-President Johns is dead. We're all traveling on diplomatic passports, so you can't detain us. I'll arrange to give statements tomorrow once we've had time to begin putting the affairs of our Government-in-Exile in order."

"I'll need to confirm your diplomatic credentials, Sir."

"Of course. Passports, everyone, please."

It took less than five minutes for the Sergeant to scan all the passport numbers, compare them to a list of accredited diplomats, and find where Vice-President Johns had registered them in the Neue Helvetica Foreign Ministry database. "You're free to go, Sir," the policeman advised reluctantly. "Please don't forget those statements."

"We won't," Dave promised. "We want Vice-President Johns' killers apprehended far more than you possibly could!" He turned to his team, wincing at the pain in his back. "All right, people. If someone could please deal with my suitcase, I don't feel up to it right now. Let's get a passenger van and head for our hotel, call a doctor, then send a message to the others aboard ship to let them know we're safe. If they hear about this first from news reports, they won't be happy with us. I'll tell them to join us as soon as possible. I think the immediate danger has passed."

~ ~ ~

The tall, graying man rose from behind the ornate wooden desk as his receptionist showed Dave and Tamsin through the door of his office. His face was creased with concern.

"Major Carson, Lieutenant Gray, I was so terribly sorry to hear the news this morning! Vice-President Johns was a remarkable lady. Even though she couldn't access your planetary account, she set up a secondary account for her mission with us, depositing in it the funds she brought from Laredo plus occasional contributions from sympathizers and well-wishers. She was a frequent visitor."

Dave shook his hand. "Thank you, Herr Gottschalk. I'm glad she had the services of the Handelsbank at her disposal during the past few difficult years."

"We tried to ease her way through the jungle of interplanetary finance," the executive agreed as he shook Tamsin's hand, then waved to comfortable seats around a table in the corner. As they sat down, he asked, "How is her assistant?"

"She'll be OK," Dave responded as he lowered himself carefully into the chair. He was unable to suppress a wince as his bruised back touched its softly upholstered surface. He tried to sit in such a way that he hunched forward, away from the pain. "She has a mild concussion, nothing worse."

"Are you all right?" Gottschalk asked in concern.

"Not really, but I'll cope. You said the Vice-President had a secondary account here. I've succeeded to her office, as you'll know if you saw the news reports about this morning's events. How much is in it?"

The man flushed, seeming almost ashamed. "There were two authorized operators of the account, herself and your Ambassador to the United Planets, Mr. McNairy. Within an hour of her assassination he entered our banking hall downstairs and withdrew the entire contents of the account in cash. I'm very sorry to say – particularly in the light of what you said to him this morning, as reported by the news vids – that he left here with all her funds."

Dave tightened his fists in frustration. "How much did he steal?"

"It's not technically theft, Major – he did have authority to use the account, after all. He withdrew the balance of close to half a million Neue Helvetica francs."

"It's theft all right, Herr Gottschalk. He'd already been relieved of his post and his authority to make use of Laredo assets, which would include bank accounts. However, I'm glad to hear it was a relatively small amount compared to Laredo's main planetary account. I'm here to take charge of that and make new arrangements."

"Ah, yes." The executive sat back in his chair, steepling his fingers together, shrewd eyes fixed on him. "Do you have three bearer bank keys?"

"I do; Vice-President Johns' key, plus two that I brought from Laredo." He reached into his jacket pocket and took out the three cards in their protective envelopes.

Gottschalk accepted them from him. "May I please validate these, Major? There are certain security checks, you understand. They won't leave this room."

"In that case, go ahead."

"Thank you."

Gottschalk summoned his secretary, who made a call. Within five minutes two uniformed security officials came through the door, pushing a cart bearing a large, sophisticated card reader on its surface. Gottschalk inserted each card in turn into a slot in the top of the machine. After a few moments, each card elicited a sharp *beep!* as a green light illuminated.

"These are in order," Gottschalk agreed as the men wheeled the card out again. "If you also have the Great Seal of Laredo with you, to authenticate your office as the new President Pro Tem of Laredo's Government-in-Exile, we can proceed."

"I do." Dave produced the Seal from the attaché case he'd brought with him.

"Excellent! What are your instructions concerning your planetary account?"

"I see no reason to transfer the funds anywhere else. The Handelsbank has looked after them safely for several years, which we appreciate. However, we're going to be doing a great deal of space travel over the next few years. I'd appreciate your advice on how best to arrange access to our funds from other planets whilst preserving security. I also want to set up an operating account for everyday expenses, separate from our reserve account. I'll need two certified drafts, the first payable in Lancastrian Commonwealth credits to a Mr. Manuel Espada for five per cent of the current balance of our account, the second payable to the United Planets for twenty-five million Neue Helvetica francs. I need to withdraw more funds in the form of cash and prepaid debit chips. I want to cancel all our existing bearer bank keys and have new ones issued of a different type, so the old cards can't be used by anyone else. Finally, I need your advice on valuing and selling a number of large and very high quality uncut diamonds that I've brought from Laredo. The proceeds will be deposited in our account. I'm told they should fetch several hundred million Neue Helvetica francs."

Gottschalk was smiling. Dave imagined he could hear old-fashioned cash register chimes in his head as he contemplated the fees that the Handelsbank would earn from all those transactions. "I'll introduce you to one of our banking specialists, who'll be delighted to take care of all your needs, and I'll start researching the names of trustworthy diamond brokers. With an account balance currently in excess of six hundred million Neue Helvetica francs, and more to come from the sale of your diamonds, you certainly count among our more valued clients. Where shall we – "

His secretary interrupted, opening the door and looking inside. He frowned angrily at her. "I gave orders that we were not to be disturbed!"

"Yes, Herr Gottschalk, but after the Vice-President of Laredo was shot this morning, journalists besieged the Bactrian Consulate. Something's happening there! It's on Channel 5!"

"What?" The executive clapped his hands sharply. "Open Channel 5!"

A holovid display sprang to life on a cabinet against the far wall. It showed a two-story building on a commercial street, flanked by shops. Thick green smoke was billowing from the open front door, and several figures were coughing and spluttering on the sidewalk outside. As they watched another man stumbled blindly through the door, gray suit stained with green, eyes streaming uncontrollably. Despite his screwed-up face, he was clearly recognizable as Ambassador McNairy. A news reporter was babbling excitedly in German, which neither Dave nor Tamsin understood; but they didn't need to under the circumstances.

"*Got* you, you bastard!" Dave exclaimed in savage glee.

"What do you mean?" the banker demanded.

"I chose my words very carefully this morning when I described the suitcase that was stolen. Everything I said about it was true, but designed to make listeners believe that the evidence we brought from Laredo was still in it. It wasn't. We took it out last night, and substituted a few folded blankets and towels to make it feel heavy. One of my team bought a super-pressurized security cartridge on New Brisbane to help secure our belongings. Do you know them?"

"Of course – we use them as well. They emit a dense impenetrable smoke, enough to fill several rooms very quickly, which carries teargas and pepper spray elements in suspension and will also stain everything it touches. It can't be washed off by conventional means."

"That's right. Ours went even further. It had DNA markers suspended in the smoke, to attach themselves to every surface it touched. We have the invoice for the purchase of the cartridge. It lists its DNA code, so the markers can be identified. We rigged it inside the case, set to go off if the lock was forced without a disarming code being entered on the cartridge's remote. If that's the source of the smoke in the Bactrian Consulate, it'll demonstrate beyond reasonable doubt that they were connected to this morning's tragedy. The fact that our former Ambassador to the UP has been caught on camera coming out of the enemy's consulate also proves I was right to be suspicious of him." Inwardly Dave vowed to arrange a very nasty surprise for McNairy as soon as possible.

"That's outstanding!" The man's pleasure and excitement were clearly unfeigned as he reached for a comm unit. "With your permission, Major, I'd like to tip off an independent journalist, a personal friend of my wife's. Her name's Gretchen Griessel. She's very well-known and highly regarded. I'll advise her to take swabs from the wall of the Consulate, and perhaps from some of the railings and trees outside it. If the swabs match up with the DNA markers your cartridge used, not only will she have a scoop for the morning news, but you'll get all the publicity you could wish to implicate your enemies in the murder of Vice-President Johns."

"Thank you, Herr Gottschalk. Please do that before we continue."

The banker made the call, speaking in rapid German to someone on the other end. He looked at Dave as he said, "Gretchen will have swabs taken at once, and have them analyzed this evening at a laboratory she's used before. They'll do a rush job for her. She asks whether she can get details of the DNA marker code from you."

"Of course. She can contact me at our hotel this evening. I'll set up a press conference tomorrow to discuss this morning's events and anything she learns, and to make certain announcements. If you vouch for her competence and discretion, and if she can guarantee it'll get into major news media, I'm willing to give her an exclusive interview."

"Thank you." Gottschalk began talking in German into the comm unit once more.

"It's a good thing we brought our own publicist with us," Tamsin observed in a low voice. "She can advise us on how to handle all this."

"You're right. The fact that she's Manuel's sister makes me a lot more comfortable working with her. With a brother as competent as he is, I'm hoping it runs in the family."

"You and me both!"

May 17th 2850 GSC

NEUE HELVETICA

The team assembled next morning for a shared breakfast. They didn't dare use the dining-room after the barrage of publicity following the previous day's events, because journalists were waiting in hordes to swamp them with questions. Instead, the hotel offered to cater their meal in a room at its business center. Waiters set up a buffet on side tables, and everyone helped themselves as Manuel scanned the room with an instrument he guaranteed would detect any listening devices. Finding none, he locked the door behind the waiters, took a plate of food for himself, and joined the others at the table. For a few minutes there was silence as everyone ate and drank.

At last Dave came to his feet. "There's a lot to tell you," he began. "Tamsin and I haven't slept all night – we're living on stim-tabs at the moment. Let's start with current developments, then go on to our plans for the foreseeable future.

"Gretchen Griessel spent two hours with us last night. She's a very influential Neue Helvetica journalist – we checked her background – and comes highly recommended. We gave her an exclusive interview on the situation on Laredo, our escape, the death of Vice-President Johns, and a brief glimpse of our plans for the future. She'll be doing a series of articles about all of us, and we're going to give her priority access to our archives. Elisabeta," and he nodded at the publicist, "sat in on the interview, and she'll act as our liaison with Gretchen. In fact, I'm pleased to inform you that she's accepted a permanent position with us as our press secretary." The others grinned. Manuel's sister had become popular among them on the journey here, and she and Captain Deacon had been seen together more and more often.

"Her work is certainly going to kick off with a bang. We have a news conference scheduled at noon. Where only half a dozen journalists were present yesterday, because Laredo was so insignificant no-one bothered about it, Gretchen tells us we can expect several hundred today – so many, in fact, that the Handelsbank has offered us the use of their auditorium. It can seat a thousand, and has all the facilities a major news conference will need. I've accepted their offer on her advice, and Elisabeta is working with their staff to set it up. It'll be good practice for dealing with this sort of thing in future. I'm going to use the conference to blast Bactria, blame them for the murder of Vice-President Johns, and appeal for interplanetary aid and assistance for our mission. I'm going to make hay while the sun shines, in publicity terms.

"You'll notice I'll be wearing a civilian suit at the conference. That's because yesterday I was the Commanding Officer of a detachment of the Laredo Army, arriving here on official business. Today I'm the President Pro Tem of the Government-in-Exile of the Republic of Laredo. That's a totally different job, and I'm going to dress accordingly. Over the next few days we'll all be fitted for suits and transition to civilian clothing while we're on Neue Helvetica. However, don't throw your uniforms away. We'll all need them again."

He began to pace up and down behind the table as he spoke. "Gretchen provided a lot of background information that was new to Tamsin and I, and pointed us to several information resources that we spent all night studying. Briefly, here's what I have in mind. You all remember what General Aldred's wife asked me to do with our archives, right?" Everyone nodded. He'd briefed them about it during their journey from Laredo to New Brisbane. "We're going to honor her request, and make copies of all our data available to Commonwealth University. We probably won't be able to go there, but if they're interested enough – Gretchen says she thinks they'll jump at it – they'll send a team to work with us wherever we are. Some of them can help us get over our own stresses, while others discuss questions arising out of the archive and add our recollections to the record. Gretchen is also very interested in writing the book Gloria Aldred had in mind. She can bring in an award-winning documentary maker to work with her on a movie to go with it, so that both can be released together. If she proves herself on our behalf over the next few weeks, I see no reason not to give her the larger job as well."

"If this story becomes as big as I think it will, it'll make her an even bigger interplanetary news star – not to mention a lot of money," Elisabeta observed. "She's not just offering out of the goodness of her heart."

"That's OK. It'll motivate her to work harder. Our success will mean her success, and vice versa." The others rumbled their agreement. "I'll insist that we share in the royalties, though."

Dave paused to take a mouthful of coffee. "Any team from Commonwealth U. is going to have to work around our other activities, because we're going to be very busy indeed. The murder of Vice-President Johns looks like it'll blow the lid right off our war with Bactria. Gretchen says it's bound to give an almighty great kick in the behind to the United Planets to take seriously Laredo's call for an investigation, particularly since our funds to pay the initial fees have just been unlocked. I drew a bank draft for them yesterday. She says Neue Helvetica will almost certainly support our call, because its government will be furious at having an assassination take place on its soil. It'll be the first major planet to line up with us, which may help to persuade many others to follow its example.

"She told us that in the absence of direct evidence, the authorities would probably have preferred to portray this as a murder committed during the course of an armed robbery, rather than an assassination – criminal rather than political, in other words. However, we've proved conclusively through DNA swabs that our stolen evidence suitcase was opened inside the Bactrian Consulate. Gretchen's special report this morning blows that wide open. It means this incident can't be written off as a simple crime. She says that for a start, the entire Bactrian consulate staff is likely to be declared *persona non grata*. Sergeant Higgs, we owe you *big-time* for your suggestion to use that security cartridge. It's put enormous leverage into our hands, and I intend to make full use of it."

Higgs flushed as others called their approval or reached over to clap him on the shoulder. "Thank you, Sir. What's going to happen to our former Ambassador?"

"I'm going to bring criminal and civil charges against him for the theft of the money from Vice-President Johns' account, because he was fired and lost the right to access it half an hour before he did so. I think we can make that stick, and since he also lost his diplomatic immunity half an hour before the crime, I hope he'll be convicted and jailed under local law. I'm personally sure he knew in advance about a plot to steal the suitcase, if not to murder the Vice-President, but we can't charge him with that without direct evidence. The fact that he ducked early is circumstantial evidence, not enough to convict him."

"Permission to gut him like a fish, please, Sir?" The others growled their angry agreement.

"Yesterday afternoon I'd have said 'Yes' without a second thought, but after thinking about it I'm afraid we have to stay strictly within the law in everything we do on Neue Helvetica. We've gained enormous public sympathy since the murder as the 'good guys' in this fight, but if we break the law ourselves that'll change overnight. We'll be dismissed as nothing more than a gang of thugs who got into a fight with another gang. We daren't take that chance."

Higgs nodded reluctantly. "I guess not, Sir. If he does hard time, maybe we can arrange a really nasty cellmate for him." His comment drew a grim, angry, bitter laugh from around the table.

Captain Deacon remarked, his voice baffled, "What I can't get my head around is why the Bactrian Consulate did something so stupid. *Surely* they could see they'd harm their own cause, rather than help it, by murdering the Vice-President in public like that?"

Corporal Bujold raised his hand. "Sir," he responded thoughtfully, "perhaps they'd just had confirmation of the death of the Satrap. They've said nothing publicly about that yet, but if they'd just received a message from Bactria – couriers arrive at this planet every week from all over, so that's possible – it might have made them lose their tempers. The murder might have been an eye-for-an-eye tit-for-tat response – 'you kill our Satrap, we kill the leader of your Government-in-Exile', that sort of thing. They may not have had enough time to calm down and think about the likely consequences."

"Now *that* is a *very* interesting thought, Corporal!" A buzz of agreement greeted Dave's enthusiastic reaction. "You may have put your finger on it. In fact, the idea may have come from someone at low level in the Consulate. It's even possible the shooting wasn't planned at all – it might have been a spur-of-the-moment knee-jerk reaction to the news. Planned or not, the Consul and his senior staff might have known nothing about it until after the event."

"That makes me wonder about an item on the early news this morning," Elisabeta said in a musing tone. "The Bactrian Consulate announced that one of their drivers was killed in an accident in their parking garage yesterday evening. A vehicle crushed him against a wall."

"A-*ha!*" Dave exclaimed triumphantly. "Ten will get you one he was the shooter yesterday morning, or issued the orders to shoot. Dead men tell no tales. They also make useful scapegoats. You can blame them to your superiors for anything and everything, and they can't argue or object."

"Then we'll still blame Bactria for the murder, Sir?" Sergeant Hein asked.

"Oh, yes! We're going to publicly blame Bactria at every opportunity, because ultimately they're responsible for anything done by their people or in their name. Of course, the only thing we can actually prove for certain is that our stolen suitcase was opened in their consulate. That's not the same as proving they stole it or murdered Vice-President Johns. They'll probably claim the case was delivered to them anonymously without their knowing what it was or how it was obtained."

Deacon frowned incredulously. "Surely they can't expect anyone to believe that?"

"Have you ever heard of the so-called 'Big Lie' theory? It says that if you tell a big enough lie often enough, sooner or later at least some people will start to believe it. I wouldn't be surprised if the Bactrian consulate tries to do that in this case. If they do, we're going to mock the hell out of their claims, of course."

"What role d'you think our former Ambassador played, Sir?" Bujold asked.

"They must have suborned him some time ago – his coming out of their Consulate yesterday certainly suggests that. Vice-President Johns would have told him about our courier message from New Brisbane, and he would have passed on the news to them. They'd have been desperate to stop the evidence reaching her, because if it was released it'd do serious damage to their planet's reputation throughout the settled galaxy. I think they sent McNairy to try to get the evidence from us the night we arrived by running a bluff. When that didn't work, they must have decided to steal it by force before we could hand it over – but they should have drawn the line at theft. To assassinate the Vice-President as well was sheer lunacy. I think Corporal Bujold's theory is the only one that makes sense of that under the circumstances."

Dave drank some more coffee, then looked around the room. "We have a number of tasks ahead of us in the short term. We need to establish contact with Commonwealth University on Lancaster and begin the process of turning over copies of Laredo's archives to them. We'll also need to liaise with their medical personnel concerning the debriefings and counseling Gloria Aldred said we'd all need. I think we've all realized the truth of her words in the six weeks we've been out of a combat zone. Tamsin and I have noticed the amount of sheer stress we're carrying, and I'm pretty sure we're not alone." Nods of understanding and agreement came from all of his colleagues.

"Second, we have to restructure our Embassy to the United Planets, which will incorporate the office of our Government-in-Exile. Everything done before our arrival and its entire present staff must be considered compromised, thanks to McNairy's defection. We'll have to recruit new staff, then the Embassy will have to take part in the UP inquiry and mobilize public opinion on our side. It must also try to obtain assistance from other planets, financial and material. I think the assassination of Vice-President Johns will lend a powerful emotional appeal to those efforts, and I'm going to play that hand for all it's worth. I think she'd understand and approve.

"I'm thinking of asking Captain Deacon to act as our Ambassador for a year or two. He's the most experienced of us, and also the oldest and most decorated. He'll be a good public face for Laredo. We can't afford to leave him in that post, of course, because we'll need him operationally; but in the short term I think he's our best choice." Smiles and nods from most of the others indicated their agreement. "What do you think, Captain? You're free to disagree if you wish."

Deacon grimaced. "I'm no politician, Sir."

"I'm not either, but as a Sergeant-Major you were the main regimental liaison between officers on the one hand, and NCO's and enlisted personnel on the other, weren't you?"

"Yes, Sir, I suppose I was."

"That strikes me as pretty much the work of a diplomat – acting as liaison between different groups of people. The only difference is that if you don't like one group as a diplomat, you can't scream at them while double-timing them around the parade-ground!" A roar of laughter greeted his words.

"I'll try not to give in to that temptation, Sir," Deacon agreed, shaking with amusement.

"As an incentive, Elisabeta will be stationed at our Embassy because most of our relations with the media will flow through it. You'll be working closely together."

"Ah! That's good to know." He winked at Elisabeta, who blushed, eliciting knowing smiles from the rest of the group. "You said you'd need me operationally, Sir. What will that involve?"

"I was coming to that. I'm going to soft-pedal the military aspects for a year or so while we reorganize our Embassy, start the United Planets inquiry, and work with Commonwealth University. Furthermore, as we deal with the stresses and tensions of three and a half years of war, some of us may decide that they'd prefer to make a fresh start in civilian life. That's OK with me – they've absolutely earned the right to do so.

"Oh – speaking of earning, we all have back pay coming. Most of us haven't been paid for at least two years, some for three or more, and General Aldred authorized me to pay everyone what they were owed. I couldn't possibly figure out individual amounts without records, so I asked Mr. Gottschalk to find out the annual salary of a First Lieutenant in Neue Helvetica's armed forces and multiplied it by three. The total came to just under a hundred and fifty thousand Neue Helvetica francs, so I rounded it up to that figure."

He reached into Vice-President Johns' – now his – attaché case and produced a handful of debit chips. "Each of these has been pre-loaded with that amount. It should be more than any of you were owed, and I'm not going to worry about different salary scales or rates of exchange. It's enough to live reasonably comfortably for two to three years in civilian life on Neue Helvetica, or serve as a nest egg for you to start a new life anywhere you please. You're welcome to deposit it in your own bank accounts – I've asked our specialist at the Handelsbank to open personal accounts for everyone who wants one – or you can spend it using these chips. It's your call." He passed the chips around the table, each soldier taking one and pocketing it.

"I'm in the process of discussing our present rank structure with Captain Deacon," he continued. "I think we're going to promote all who aren't yet Staff Sergeants to that rank, because we'll all be working at that level at least, and everyone has more than enough combat experience to justify the rank. I've put us all on Neue Helvetica rates of pay for our rank and grade with effect from this month, since we'll be living here for the foreseeable future. As I said earlier, we'll transition to civilian clothing for the duration of our stay, and I'll probably buy or lease a building – perhaps a small hotel or apartment block – so we can live together. We'll move the Embassy offices to the building, too. That'll make it easier to consolidate security arrangements for all of us and our work, and the entire premises will be covered by diplomatic immunity. That might come in useful."

He looked around the table. "Once we've taken care of the initial tasks I mentioned, we have unfinished business with Bactria." There was a growl of angry agreement. "All of us choosing to continue the fight will train as Spacers, because our fight is likely to continue in space rather than planetside. We'll have to buy spaceships, equip them with weapons, and select targets where we can cause the maximum damage to the Bactrian economy at minimal cost to ourselves. That'll almost certainly mean hiring mercenaries to work with us. That's risky business, because there are an awful lot of shysters and conmen in that field, but I think between our combat experience and the advice of the most trustworthy advisers we can hire, we'll be able to work around those problems.

"Gretchen opened our eyes to a much more important implication of all this. Tamsin and I spent all night discussing and researching it. I'm going to ask her to speak to that."

He sat down as his wife rose from her seat next to him. She smiled at him and squeezed his shoulder before turning to the others.

"Gretchen pointed out that there are well over a hundred planets in the settled galaxy that are plus-or-minus the same size as Laredo in terms of population. All have small economies and relatively ill-equipped military forces. A lot of them live in a permanent state of worry that someone with a stronger military and a bigger economy might decide to take what they've got. Our war with Bactria is by no means the first time something like that has happened.

"Dave and I thought about what she'd said after she left. The Vice-President's murder is bound to get the attention of other small planets, even if the Bactrian invasion didn't. If we approach them, pointing out that they're as vulnerable as Laredo was, we might be able to interest some of them in working with us to not only kick Bactria out of Laredo, but set up a shared security mechanism – a loose defensive alliance – that will be available to all participants to deter aggressors in future."

She began to pace back and forth, her brow furrowing in thought as she continued. "They'd have to contribute money and people to a joint force. It wouldn't be on the size and scale of the battle fleets maintained by the major powers, because small planets don't usually face threats that big. Let's face it, if a big power were to move in on a minor planet, the war would be over before it began! No, small planets need protection against the Bactrias of the settled galaxy. Why shouldn't we provide it, or at least help start it?

"We could build up a squadron or two of warships. Spread over a number of minor worlds, the cost per planet wouldn't be prohibitive, and they'd all benefit from the deterrent effect of a shared force big enough to deal with a typical aggressor. If another Bactria reared its head, the joint force would be big enough to destroy its orbital and space-based economy and blockade it, isolating it from the rest of the settled galaxy. That's a big deterrent, right there; and if it wasn't enough, the blockading force could begin bombarding critical installations with kinetic projectiles from orbit – avoiding population centers, of course, and giving warnings to target areas in time to evacuate everyone. A few flattened dams, roads, airports and harbors should drive home the message."

She stopped walking and looked around. "Clearly, this is a longer-term proposition. Our main focus will be on Bactria in the short term. However, if we can parlay that into something that will help other planets besides Laredo, we'll be helping ourselves as much as we help them – and I'd hate to see another planet suffer the way ours did."

Sergeant Higgs asked, "Ma'am, what if we don't want to make a career in the military? I'm a reservist, even though I've been full-time since the war began. I don't mind fighting Bactria, but I'd like to get back to civilian life sometime. I don't want to spend the next twenty years training others and supporting a deterrent force in which I don't have a personal stake."

"Dave's already said we'll be free to make new lives for ourselves," she pointed out. "We really mean that. This is going to take a lot of commitment, and anyone feeling burned out after Laredo should consider their options very carefully. We won't blame you in the least if you decide to do that. We'll still have work for you in our Embassy as a civilian, or you can do something on your own – even move to another planet and start afresh there. It's up to you."

Dave stood up beside her and took the attaché case from behind his chair. Its leather still bore several dark crusted streaks and stains, standing out starkly against its tan color. He pointed to them as he said, "Let me tell you where Tamsin and I stand. That's Vice-President Johns' blood from yesterday. I'm not going to clean it off; in fact, I'm going to spray sealant over it to preserve it. After this morning's news conference, I'm going to mount this in a glass display case in the foyer of our Embassy. It'll be a permanent reminder to us and everyone who visits us of why we're doing this – as if we needed another one!

"It doesn't matter to me whether a Bactrian thug acted on his own initiative, or whether he was ordered to kill her. We're going to make Bactria pay for her murder as much as for their invasion of Laredo. Both Tamsin and I were slowly coming to the conclusion that we couldn't do much as individuals, or with such a small group of soldiers, and asking ourselves whether we should end hostilities. Not anymore. From now on, whether we stand alone or with others, it's going to be war to the knife."

There was a savage yell of agreement as most of those around the table thrust themselves to their feet. "WAR TO THE KNIFE!"

Manuel bent to whisper in his sister's ear where they sat at the foot of the table. "It may sound stupid when we're talking about so few people, but I think Bactria just made the worst mistake of its life."

"Me too," she murmured. "They won't give up. They're fighting mad now. Bactria has no idea of the passions it's aroused."

"Not yet... but it'll learn. Oh, *how* it'll learn!"

ABOUT THE AUTHOR

Peter Grant was born and raised in Cape Town, South Africa. Between military service, the IT industry and humanitarian involvement, he traveled throughout sub-Saharan Africa before being ordained as a pastor. He later immigrated to the USA, where he worked as a pastor and prison chaplain until an injury forced his retirement. He is now a full-time writer, and married to a pilot from Alaska. They currently live in Tennessee.

See all of Peter's books at his Amazon.com author page, or visit him at his blog, Bayou Renaissance Man, where you can also sign up for his mailing list to receive a monthly newsletter and be kept informed of upcoming books.

Made in the USA
Lexington, KY
09 May 2016